ORDER OF BATTLE

DAVID BRUNS

J.R. OLSON

Severn River
PUBLISHING

To Sydney

A NOTE TO OUR READERS

In the novel which you are about to read, you will notice two different spellings for the capital of Ukraine: Kiev and Kyiv. It's not a typo; there's an important reason for this detail.

When we began work on this manuscript in the summer of 2021, long before the Russian invasion of Ukraine, the first draft used the name "Kiev" to describe the capital of Ukraine.

That was a mistake.

Until the dissolution of the Soviet Union in 1991, "the Ukraine" was part of Russia and her capital was "Kiev." Today, Ukraine is a sovereign country and the name of her capital in her native tongue is Kyiv (rhymes with *Steve*).

Like many Americans of our vintage, we were familiar with the old spelling and didn't really give it much thought. As you might imagine, this story took on renewed importance after the real-life Russian invasion of Ukraine. In subsequent drafts, we educated ourselves. In the following pages, the Russian characters will use the "Kiev" spelling and everybody else will use the correct name "Kyiv" for the capital of Ukraine.

A small detail? Maybe, but we figure if the Ukrainian

people are willing to risk their lives for their freedom, the absolute least we can do is call their capital by the correct name.

We'll end with this thought: the bravery, ingenuity, and resilience of the Ukrainian people is beyond anything we could have imagined—and we write fiction for a living.

David Bruns & J.R. Olson
    March 30, 2022

1

Kiev, Ukraine

The bar of the Ukraine Hotel was from another time, the peak of the Soviet era, and had not been updated since. High ceilings, marble floors, dark wood, dim lighting. A faded royal red carpet with gold trim, worn thin by time and too many feet, covered the steps leading down into the bar proper.

Attaché case in hand, Pavel Kozlov descended into the crowded room and slipped through the clusters of drinkers to the far side of the bar. It was thirty minutes to midnight on a Friday. The space was crowded, the air thick with cigarette smoke and the buzzing of multiple languages as one might expect in a place frequented by foreign correspondents.

He paused when he reached the narrow bar that ran along the length of the windows. The view was really the only thing this place had to offer, and it was spectacular.

Twenty floors below lay the Maidan Nezalezhnosti, the historic Independence Square of Kiev. Even at this hour the Maidan teemed with people, and more were arriving every minute from the metro that ran underneath the square. He could pick out policemen in their neon yellow jackets.

It was perfect.

"First time?" a voice said in Russian.

She was a platinum blonde on the far side of forty but with the physique of someone who spent time outdoors. She wore faded blue jeans and a man's white shirt. The woman put out her hand. "Ekaterina Nillson."

Pavel shook her hand. Solid grip, fingernails of a sensible length and coated with clear polish.

"How did you know I spoke Russian?" Pavel said. He parked the attaché case on the floor and kicked it flat against the radiator. That was as good a place as any for it.

Her eyes—they were wintry blue, he saw—traveled over his upper body. They took in his leather jacket, his pumped-up biceps and chest, his twice-broken nose, and the scar along his jawline that was not quite hidden by the salt-and-pepper of his three-day beard.

She cocked an eyebrow as if to say, *Really*? Then turned back to study the activity in the square. In the soft light, with her blond hair catching illumination from the window, she looked like royalty.

"What are you drinking, Ekaterina?" Pavel said.

"Johnnie Walker Blue," she replied without turning her head. "Make it a double."

An expensive drink, Pavel thought. Too bad he was working tonight.

At the bar, Pavel edged next to a thirty-something guy who seemed intent on impressing a young woman in a too-short, glittery dress who might have been twenty. Pavel caught a snippet of conversation as he ordered the drinks.

"Syria," the guy said, "now that was a shit show if ever I saw one. The fall of Idlib province was a tragedy."

You can say that again, Pavel thought. I lost three guys in that campaign.

"You were there?" the girl asked breathlessly.

The guy shook his head. "Too dangerous. I had to cover it from Turkey."

Another damned reporter trying to get laid. Pavel checked the urge to knock the guy off the bar stool and beat the shit out of him.

No, he thought, that was the old Pavel. The boss had been on him to think more strategically about his actions, so maybe this was a good test.

The drinks arrived, and Pavel paid with cash. He motioned the bartender close and indicated the man next to him with a jerk of his head.

"See this guy?" The bartender nodded, and Pavel placed a wad of cash in his hand. "Buy him whatever he wants. On me, but don't tell him who it's from." He placed more cash on the pile. "If you keep him here for two hours, you get to keep that. If not, I'll be back for my change. Got it?"

The stack of cash disappeared into the bartender's pocket. Pavel carried the drinks back to Ekaterina.

"I thought you got lost," she said, still studying the view out the window.

In the corner of his vision, Pavel saw the bartender place fresh drinks in front of the Richard Engel wannabe and his date. They smiled when they found out the drinks were free, looked around the room, then toasted each other.

Ekaterina followed his gaze to the glittery dress. "You see something more interesting at the bar?" she said. "I'm used to drinking alone if you want to move on."

Strange, Pavel thought. He didn't want to move on. In fact, although definitely not his type, he thought Ekaterina was beautiful. Maybe this was the new Pavel, the *strategic* Pavel that the boss kept bashing on about.

When he gave his full attention to Ekaterina, she finally turned toward him. He felt like her eyes were looking through him.

"Sorry," Pavel said. "I thought I knew that guy at the bar."

"You do know him," she replied. "Do you watch TV?"

"Not much."

Ekaterina moved closer. Pavel caught a whiff of perfume, a hint of musky flowers.

"It's William Sommers," she said.

Pavel shrugged.

Ekaterina deepened her voice and puffed out her chest. "I'm foreign correspondent William Sommers, reporting from Bumfuckistan." She studied his face. "Nothing?"

Pavel shook his head. To his surprise, she leaned over and kissed him on the cheek. "You just made my night." She lowered her voice. "He's an asshole, by the way, but he gets the ratings, so he can do whatever he wants. Including dating girls that are far too young for him."

Pavel sipped his drink. Although he preferred vodka, this scotch seemed to fit the mood.

"You're a reporter, too?" he asked.

"Yes." Ekaterina turned back to the window, her face pensive. "Everyone thinks the story's out there, including my editors. But the real story is in a Russian basement somewhere."

"I don't understand," Pavel replied. The square, full of people, looked like rough water from this height. Flickers of light popped and faded as people took pictures and livestreamed their presence to the world.

The police had converted Khreshchatyk Street, the thoroughfare that ran through the Maidan, to pedestrian traffic only. They'd given up trying to control the crowd.

So far, this demonstration certainly exceeded his expectations. The boss was going to be very happy.

Ekaterina drank deeply. "Those people out there are puppets. Nobody pays for news anymore, they just believe what they're being fed on social media."

Pavel signaled the bartender for two more drinks. "That's a pretty cynical view."

"Thousands of people die every year in Ukraine." Ekaterina accepted the fresh drink. "And no one cares. Hell, the people of Ukraine don't even seem to care anymore. They're numb. The threat of Russian soldiers on their doorstep is so common that they've just given up."

She toasted the window. "And now this. The March for Freedom. What does that even mean?"

Pavel's mobile buzzed with an incoming text. *Alpha – check*, it read.

She pointed to the Independence Monument, a victory column rising two hundred feet above the Maidan, topped by the statue of a woman with flowing robes holding a leafy branch over her head. Spotlights illuminated the female figure, making it look like the golden angel floated over the square.

"I was down there when they dedicated the monument in 2001," she said. "I reported on life in Ukraine ten years after she had gained her independence."

Bravo – check, his phone read. *Charlie – check*. The screen showed it was ten minutes to midnight.

Ekaterina hadn't noticed his divided attention. "In 2008, for the Paul McCartney concert, there were a million people in the square. It was magic."

"Why aren't you out there now?" Pavel asked. "Reporting, I mean."

The woman scowled. "I told you: that's not the story anymore."

In the square below, there was a backup of people trying to exit the doors of the metro. The police directed foot traffic away from the congestion.

"What is the story?" Pavel asked.

Delta – check, his phone read. One more update and he was done with this conversation. He felt the familiar rush of tension that electrified his muscles just before an operation began, like a compressed spring waiting for a release.

"This is the story," Ekaterina said, holding her mobile phone. "How the internet has turned information into weapons of mass destruction."

"That's a little extreme," Pavel said.

"It's that fucking Luchnik," she hissed. "He thrives on chaos. Him and his cronies, Wagner Group, the whole lot of them will burn in hell someday."

True, Pavel thought. President Luchnik knew how to spin shit into gold. He was kind of a genius, actually.

Ekaterina touched the screen of her phone. "Do you have a signal?"

Echo – check, the face of Pavel's phone read.

"No," he lied. "But that reminds me. I need to make a call." He stood. "Will you be here when I get back?"

Ekaterina looked at him. There was no playing coy with this woman. "I'll stay until half past midnight. Will that be enough time?"

"That's perfect." He took her hand and kissed it. "Until we meet again."

Ekaterina kept his hand. "What line of work are you in? I'm curious."

Pavel grinned at her. "Customer service."

The elevators in the Ukraine Hotel looked like the original Soviet model. Pavel thought how ironic it would be if he died in a freak Russian elevator accident on his way to starting a revolution.

The creaky box arrived at the lobby, and the doors wheezed open. As Pavel strode through the lobby, he removed an earpiece from his jacket pocket and inserted it into his left ear. His watch read one minute to midnight.

"All stations, this is team leader. Stand by for go signal on my mark."

"Alpha team has target in sight. Ready to launch," came the crisp reply.

Pavel reached the doors and pushed through onto the steps of the Ukraine Hotel. He stayed on the periphery of the crowd, bulling his way past people until he was away from the hotel.

The late spring night was mild. It had rained earlier in the evening, and the churning feet and body heat of so many people created a mist in the air. The noise of hundreds of thousands of voices sounded like the ocean.

He took a covering position in the lee of a heavy stone column. He looked up at the top of the Independence Monument where the golden statue floated in the dark sky like an angel descending from heaven.

"Alpha team, you are cleared for launch," Pavel said.

A pinpoint of light sparked in the sky, then flared. A streak of fire crossed the heavens, and the golden statue exploded.

For a split second, the world paused in silence. Then chaos erupted in the square. Screams, waves of people trying to get away from the explosion.

On the far side of the Maidan, gunfire broke out and the crowd contracted again like a riptide in this ocean of humanity. Lights began to go out as the power outages struck, provoking more panic.

Pavel flattened against the column, allowing hordes of people to flow past him. He extracted a satellite phone from his pocket and thumbed to a preset number.

Ekaterina, he thought with no small measure of regret, I won't be able to make our date. Something came up.

He depressed the send key. He imagined the phone in the attaché case he'd left in the hotel bar receiving the call.

One ring...two...

The top of the Ukraine Hotel exploded in a ball of fire.

2

The Kremlin
Moscow, Russia

The sun had not yet risen when Russian President Vitaly Luchnik strode into the emergency cabinet meeting. Konstantin Kulukov, head of the Russian National Guard, known as the Rosgvardiya, met him at the door.

"He's here, sir," Kulukov reported in a low voice. Kulukov was a wiry man, slight of frame with a shaved head and a grim set to his lips. Luchnik admired the younger man's intensity. As the man responsible for the President's personal security as well as managing public dissent inside the vast Russian state, intensity was a necessary quality.

"Very well," Luchnik murmured. "I'll tell you when to send him in."

"Of course, sir." Kulukov gave a curt nod and took his place with the other ministers at the long mahogany table.

Luchnik stood by his own seat, studying the twenty men before him. He was of the belief that you could tell a lot about a person by how they presented themselves early in the morning. Many of the men in his cabinet failed that arbitrary test. They were disheveled, the crust of sleep still in the corners of their eyes. A few stank of unprocessed vodka.

It didn't matter. They weren't in his cabinet for their sartorial splendor; they were here for their willingness to wield power on behalf of their leader.

And he was about to test the limits of their willingness.

Despite the fact that he had barely slept the night before, Luchnik felt alive with excitement about the events to come. He'd dressed carefully in a dark blue worsted wool suit from Savile Row, crisp white shirt, and blood-red tie. History would record every detail of this day, no matter how small, and Luchnik wanted every detail to be perfect.

He took his seat at the head of the table and gestured for his cabinet to do the same.

To his right, Foreign Minister Sergey Irimov was one of the men struggling with the early hour. His thin hair had been hastily combed, and his rimless glasses were smudged with fingerprints. He stared at the table, shoulders slumped.

"Cheer up, Sergey," Luchnik said, but even as he spoke, he wondered if his oldest confidant was up to one more campaign, the crowning achievement of a long, hard-fought career in the service of the Rodina.

On his left sat Vladimir Federov, Luchnik's handpicked leader of the FSB. The Federal Security Service of the Russian Federation was roughly equivalent to the FBI in the United States, but larger, and less prone to following strict legal rules. The FSB was an offshoot of the old KGB from Soviet times, where Luchnik had spent his early career.

In modern times, the FSB officially shared security duties with the SVR, or the Foreign Intelligence Service, and the GRU, Russian military intelligence. With Luchnik's tacit consent, Federov had spent years expanding the unofficial reach of the FSB into all areas of the Russian security state—except the National Guard.

Although Federov would never admit it, Luchnik knew it galled him that his reach into the Rosgvardiya was limited by Kulukov. Still, Luchnik thought, it was always good to have his security organizations competing against each other. It tended to keep senior leaders in check.

"Good morning, Vladimir," Luchnik said.

Federov's bald head nodded once in reply, a man of few words. Luchnik knew he had been up all night, but the whites of his eyes were clear and he seemed alert.

The President addressed the group. "In light of the unstable situation in the Ukraine, I'm adding a consultant to our number this morning." He nodded at Kulukov. "Send him in."

The ever-efficient Kulukov was ready. He tapped his mobile phone, and the elaborately carved door, twice the height of a man, swung open to admit Yuri Plotnikov. He was a tall man, thin, with sharp features. His dark, stringy hair was combed straight back from his high, pale forehead. He carried a small cardboard box with two hands.

"What have you brought me this morning, Yuri?" Luchnik called.

Plotnikov strode to the head of the table and placed the box in front of the President. The smell of baked goods leaked out of the gaps in the cardboard, making Luchnik's stomach grumble with hunger.

"Tvorog rings, Mr. President," Plotnikov said with a small bow. "Made with my own hands this very morning."

"You will make me fat, Yuri," Luchnik said with a laugh. He noted the looks snapping between the other men at the table. Why, they wondered, did the President banter with The Chef while a national emergency unfolded on their doorstep?

"Sergey," Luchnik said, placing a firm hand on the Foreign Minister's arm, "perhaps you could move down so Yuri can sit next to me."

The room went still, all eyes on Irimov. Luchnik could almost feel the dots connecting in the minds of every man present.

It was common knowledge that Yuri Plotnikov was a childhood friend of the President and also a trained chef. The President's cabinet also knew of Plotnikov's other duties as Chief Executive Officer of the Wagner Group, a private military contractor often used by the Russian military for off-the-books operations.

The fact that Wagner maintained assets in the Ukraine was news to no one, but the sudden appearance of The Chef at a cabinet meeting could mean only one thing: What had happened in the Ukraine was no accident. It was the work of the Wagner Group.

Irimov stared at his president, blinked, then got to his feet stiffly. He turned to the man on his right. "Move down," he ordered. The process repeated itself until the entire row erupted into a state of shuffling disorganization. The left side of the table watched silently, each understanding the message in the movement: fall in line or your place will be taken by one who has the right attitude.

Luchnik ate one of the pastries Plotnikov had brought him. The delicate crust was filled with silky cream, and the sweet-sour flavor exploded on his tongue. He licked his fingers, nodding at The Chef. "You have outdone yourself, Yuri. A masterpiece."

The room fell silent as Luchnik pushed away the empty container. He crossed his legs, leaned back in his chair. "Shall we begin?" he said to Federov.

The FSB Chief's features might have been made of plaster.

Luchnik admired the man's steel. He had not known about The Chef's arrival, yet he'd not reacted with surprise. That passive display would lead all the others in the room to conclude that Federov had known.

Impressive control, Luchnik concluded. A worthy ally.

"At approximately midnight last night, a so-called March for Freedom in Kiev turned violent. Initial reports are that as many as two hundred and fifty people were killed and thousands more injured." Federov cut a look at The Chef, who listened with interest.

"Both the death toll and the casualty count are expected to rise. Simultaneous with the riot, the power grid in the capital city collapsed. Internet is down in the eastern half of the country, as are all mobile phone towers. There are reports of widespread looting and general lawlessness. The President of the Ukraine has declared a national emergency and mobilized the military. He is appealing to the European Union for aid, but it's only been a few hours and there has been, as of yet, no response.

"In a word," Federov concluded, "chaos."

Luchnik shifted his gaze to Defense Minister Yakov. "Viktor, do you have anything to add?"

Yakov looked much the worse for wear at this hour, and Luchnik was glad the Defense Minister was seated well down the table. He probably smelled like a vodka distillery. The man blinked his red-rimmed eyes and shook his head.

"Minister Federov covers the facts well, Mr. President," Yakov said, his voice like gravel. "I would just add that we have close to one hundred thousand troops on a training exercise within one hundred kilometers of the border with the Ukraine, sir. We could quickly move more units forward if needed."

Luchnik raised his eyebrows, as if this fact was news

to him.

"Foreign Minister." Luchnik was so used to having Irimov at his elbow that he had to force himself to look down the table. "We are faced with a national emergency on our border. We have long expected the collapse of the Ukraine government, but the speed with which it has happened is remarkable. What is the international perspective on this crisis?"

Irimov adjusted his spectacles and cleared his throat. "The international community will blame the Russian Federation—it is a knee-jerk reaction to any crisis in the Ukraine. If we take any action, there will be repercussions."

"And yet, Sergey," Luchnik said, "I fear we must act in our national interest."

"A military intervention in the Ukraine would spark outrage, Mr. President," the Foreign Minister said. "Only a few months ago the world seemed headed for World War Three between United States and China. The world is an unsettled place, sir. Anything could happen."

"Precisely," Luchnik said.

He sat forward suddenly and steepled his fingers. He looked down the table to find the eyes of the one man he had avoided up to this point.

Admiral Nikolay Sokolov was not only Commander of the Pacific Fleet, he was Luchnik's nephew. He wondered what his nephew thought of what had happened in the last twelve hours. He met the younger man's eyes, found no immediate answers, and moved on to the other faces at the table.

"The Foreign Minister is correct," Luchnik said. "The world is an unsettled place. The Ukraine, once a part of Mother Russia, has been unstable for twenty years, the government always on the edge of collapse. If we act now, the world will throw up their hands and decry the state of affairs, but what will they *do*?"

Luchnik crashed his fist on the table. Irimov started in his chair.

"Nothing," Luchnik shouted. "They will do nothing."

He heard the ringing hum of complete silence in his ears.

"I give you my word as your president and your leader that the Russian state had nothing to do with this unfortunate incident, but that does not matter. The West will blame us anyway. Even as they do nothing to help the people of the Ukraine."

He said to Irimov, "We have made it clear to the world that all Russian-speaking peoples of the region are under the protection of Mother Russia, is that not true?"

The Foreign Minister nodded.

"We have a choice to make," Luchnik said. "Right here, right now. We honor that commitment or we are no better than those who oppose us. Russians inside the Ukraine participated in a peaceful demonstration in the Maidan, and they were slaughtered by Ukrainian nationalists. We cannot stand by and let this go on. The government in the Ukraine is a security risk that has festered on our border for too long. The time to act is now."

Luchnik sat back in his chair. Who would speak first, he wondered. They would all come to agree with his position, of course. Most of these men had sold their souls to him long ago. Country dachas, apartments in Miami and the south of France, numbered bank accounts, whatever they wanted he provided—all for moments like this.

But the illusion of free will was an essential element in this game. These men needed to convince themselves that what they were doing was not just a convenient action but the right thing for their country.

All it took was someone to start the process. The rest would follow.

Defense Minister Yakov would speak first, Luchnik

decided. A chance to exercise his military would be too good to pass up.

"This is a moral imperative, Mr. President."

Luchnik looked up sharply. His nephew, Nikolay, was standing, the gold buttons of his admiral's uniform gleaming in the light.

For a moment, Luchnik was lost in thought. The only person he'd ever truly cared about was his sister, Nikolay's mother. He imagined Natasha seeing her son as an admiral in the Russian Navy. The look of delight and wonder on her beautiful face.

Yakov's growl interrupted the image in his mind's eye. "I can have the Western and Southern Military districts fully mobilized within hours, Mr. President."

Luchnik nodded to cover his lapse in attention. He scanned the faces at the table, seeing nods of approval. Resistance to the invasion of the Ukraine melted like snow in the rains of April. He settled his gaze on Irimov.

The Foreign Minister's craggy features were a study in contrast. He followed Luchnik's reasoning, probably even agreed with it. Still, he searched for a way to demonstrate his value in light of the deliberate snub of The Chef taking his seat at his president's right hand.

My oldest friend is an old man, Luchnik thought. What does that make me?

Irimov cleared his throat. "I see this action as an extension of the Crimean campaign, Mr. President. A way for us to stabilize the areas near the border and protect the Russian population. May I represent this as a temporary action to the world community, sir?"

Luchnik returned the Foreign Minister's knowing smile. "Sergey, all actions are temporary."

3

CIA Headquarters
Langley, Virginia

The windows of the CIA Director's office faced west. Afternoon sun flooded the room with light and warmth, an incongruous counterpoint to the bleak Ukraine update Don Riley had just delivered to the Director.

There was a lull in the conversation as Director Samuel Blank flipped through screens on the briefing tablet. The name matched the man. Medium height and thin, the white-haired leader of the Central Intelligence Agency hid a sharp intellect behind an unassuming demeanor.

Don had been up for thirty-six hours, and the warmth of the sun made him want to curl up on the couch and take a nap.

But he'd gotten the job done—that was the important thing. In a crisis situation, the Director often liked to use two teams of analysts to gather and interpret intelligence. The two teams operated independently and presented their results at the same time.

Don's Emerging Threats Group had been one such group. Populated with analysts, case officers, paramilitary experts, and cyber specialists, ETG was tailor-made for quick response duties like this one. His briefing had been crisp, to the point, and packed with details he leveraged from his connections at Sentinel Holdings, a private military contractor where Don served as CIA Liaison Officer.

The other analytical effort was run by Dylan Mattias, the Deputy Director of Operations for the CIA. Dylan was the polar opposite of his unassuming boss. With his compact, muscular build and long dark hair that he wore swept back from his forehead, Dylan looked more like a movie star than a government employee. It wasn't typical for the Ops side of the house to run analysis, but Mattias was bucking for another promotion. Rumor had it the current number two at the CIA was planning to leave for an industry position paying three times as much as she made working for Uncle Sam. Dylan had his eyes on the prize.

Like Don, Dylan wore jeans and a white dress shirt open at the neck. Unlike Don, he looked fresh and full of energy, as if he'd just stepped out of the shower. The rolled-up sleeves of his shirt revealed forearms corded with muscle.

When did he have time to go to the gym? Don thought. I barely have time to sleep and eat, and this guy looks like an advertisement for Charles Atlas.

Although they were the same age and had started at the CIA at about the same time, Dylan had both the political skills required to climb the ladder of bureaucracy and the desire to do so.

Don had neither political skill nor desire. Although he'd never considered himself to be in competition with Dylan Mattias, Don was well aware that others often compared the two men. He imagined those conversations: "Well, you could be a rock star here at the CIA...or you could be Don Riley."

The Director interrupted the downward spiral of Don's self-assessment. "What do you think, Dylan?" he asked.

Dylan gave a self-deprecating chuckle. "I'd like to know Riley's sources, sir."

I bet you would, thought Don. Okay, maybe he was a little competitive.

"Don?" the Director asked. "Can you discuss sources? Dylan's right. You have some very granular intel that I haven't seen anywhere else. For example, you make a pretty bold claim that this attack on the pro-Russian demonstration is linked to the Wagner Group."

"Directly linked, sir," Don replied, dodging the sources question for the moment. "We have intercepts that put Wagner operatives right in Maidan Square. Blowing up the Independence Monument? Bombing the foreign correspondents bar in the Ukraine Hotel? Those are big old 'screw you' messages to the West. There's no way Wagner would be that provocative unless they had Luchnik's backing."

"Those are symbolic actions," Dylan interjected. "They can be interpreted in different ways. What about the attacks on the infrastructure? Can you prove that was Wagner?"

Don's energy was back. He leaned forward. "Can I prove it? No, but we don't have to. The answer is staring us in the face."

"I don't follow," the Director said.

"The cyberattacks in 2015," Don said. "That was a dry run. Russia wrote the playbook and handed it off to Wagner for action. Massive cyberattack on the Ukraine power grid. Take down banks, utilities, anything with an internet connection. They did it once, why not do the same thing again?"

"Because the Ukrainians got smarter about security,"

Dylan countered. "There was nowhere near the level of damage this time."

"Cyber always finds a way," Don said, "but that's not the point. Luchnik is priming the pump for a big move."

"I'll grant you the large military exercises are troubling, but the world situation has changed, Don," the Director said. "There's less appetite for a confrontation in this climate. Luchnik wants attention. He'll step up activity in the Donbas and call it a day."

"I'm sorry, sir," Don said, "but I'm afraid this is just the beginning."

"I disagree," Dylan said. "Luchnik wants to put a buffer on his western flank. He doesn't want to tangle with the EU. At most, he'll make a show in the contested eastern provinces."

"I don't think so," Don replied. "If all he wanted to do was secure a buffer zone, he didn't need to turn the Maidan into a killing field. He's sending a message."

"And what is the message, Don?" the Director asked. "How far will Luchnik go?"

"That's the part we need to figure out," Don replied.

"Where are you getting your information, Riley?" Dylan asked, his voice testy.

"Don?" the Director added.

Don considered the question. It was ironic that the primary source for most of his intel came from Sentinel Holdings, which had been executing military training contracts inside Ukraine for years. Another private military contractor, just like the Wagner Group.

No, not like Wagner, he thought. Wagner was the worst kind of mercenary, the kind that would do anything for money. He'd seen the evidence of their handiwork in Syria, Iraq, Africa.

Sentinel, under the leadership of Abby Cromwell, was different. Not only had she shared her Ukraine assets with Don, she'd given him access to the company's artificial intelligence, known as Mama, for his analysis.

Don looked at Dylan, then at the Director. "I think we're best served right now if our two teams of analysts stay independent, sir. Dylan's team has a very different take on where this is going. I would hate to contaminate his line of reasoning."

Dylan glowered at him but said nothing.

The Director shrugged. "That's fine by me, but if the President asks you a direct question, he will expect a direct answer." He stood and looked at his watch. "The helo leaves from the pad in twenty minutes. We'd best be on our way, Don."

Don looked down at his wrinkled shirt, blue jeans, and running shoes. He'd been told to dress for comfort for this meeting. There had been no indication of a visit to the White House.

"Sir," Don said, "I'm not dressed for the White House."

"Don't sweat it, Don," the Director replied. "We're headed to Camp David. It's casual there. What you're wearing works just fine."

Dylan was on his feet. "Let me grab my overnight bag from my office, Director. I'll meet you at the pad."

"That won't be necessary, Dylan," the Director said. "The President has asked for Mr. Riley by name. Thank you for coming in. I'll see you on Monday."

As a man approaching middle age, Don knew he should be above the pettiness of office politics. The glow he felt about having been chosen over the great Dylan Mattias was beneath him.

Except it wasn't.

As he followed the Director out of his office, Don smiled at his colleague.

"Have a good weekend, Dylan."

4

Kiev, Ukraine

Pavel Kozlov snapped open the top of his silver Zippo lighter and sparked a flame. He touched the flame to the tip of a Prima and drew hard on the cigarette. By force of habit, he held the cigarette between the thumb and forefinger of his non-dominant hand, the glowing tip facing his palm, shielding the light from outside eyes.

The Zippo had ruined his night vision for the moment, but he didn't care. It was past midnight now, and he hadn't eaten anything since breakfast. His ass ached from the hours of sitting in a car across the street from the Ukrainian Ministry of Defense. The radio stations that had come back on the air after the attacks were just delivering public service announcements instead of playing music.

But the boredom, the fatigue, the hunger all paled in comparison to his rage. He sucked the cigarette down to the filter and tossed it out the window.

If The Chef could see him now. He imagined how his boss

would shake his head and say something like: "If you want to be a leader, you need to think strategically, Pavel."

Pavel glared at the guardhouse two blocks away.

Go bake a quiche, boss, he thought. I've got a score to settle.

In contrast to the surrounding neighbors, the Ministry of Defense was brightly lit, undoubtedly operating under power from diesel generators. At night, the city of Kiev turned into a patchwork of light and dark, a visual representation of economic inequality. Those with access to emergency generators lived with light and heat. Those without lived in darkness.

Pavel shifted in his seat. The old shrapnel wound in his lower back was acting up tonight. The lack of power and the state of emergency also meant that some very important people stayed at their offices instead of going home.

People like Brigadier General Ruslan Bizhan.

Pavel snatched the tablet off the seat next to him and opened it with the screen in night mode. The face that stared back at him was late forties—young for general officer rank, even in the Ukraine armed forces—with a full head of dark hair and piercing blue eyes. The half-smile taunted Pavel.

"You should have been on my initial kill list," Pavel said to the screen.

An Air Force officer by trade, Bizhan was only three months into his appointment as Chief of Directorate of Operations to the Ukrainian General Staff. It was rare for a pilot to be placed in such a critical position as J3 to the General Staff. When Wagner planned their attack on the Kiev infrastructure, Bizhan was left off the kill list. He was deemed a nonentity, a nobody who had reached his post by dint of political wrangling.

The Wagner planners were wrong. Pavel smacked the tablet back onto the leather seat next to him.

I was wrong, he thought. And that arrogance cost me two men.

General Bizhan had figured out at least part of Wagner's plan, and he had deployed a team of commandos to a water purification facility on the outskirts of Kiev.

Pavel gripped the steering wheel. The muscles in his forearms corded in pent-up fury. If he had his two men here now, he'd wring their necks himself. They'd been careless, overconfident, probably even annoyed that they were taking down a local waterworks while the rest of their comrades got high-profile assignments like the assault in Independence Square. They'd paid the price for their arrogance.

Pavel shuddered to think what might have happened if the Ukrainian General Staff had actually listened to their new J3. Bizhan might have upended the entire Wagner operation.

And that, Pavel concluded, made the elimination of Brigadier General Ruslan Bizhan a strategic imperative. At least that's what he told The Chef.

Bizhan lived fifteen minutes away from the Ministry building in a high-rise condominium called Green Island. That route home was their window of opportunity. There was no way Wagner would get away with an assault on the Ministry of Defense compound, and The Chef would freak out if they attacked a high-rise condominium filled with civilians just to kill one lowly general.

Pavel had considered going after Bizhan's family. After all, Bizhan had killed members of the Wagner family. Bizhan had two daughters who studied dance at the State Choreographic School a few blocks from their home. His wife was the department head of the School of International Economic Relations at Krok University. On nice days, she walked to work.

Soft targets, Pavel thought. All three of them.

He dismissed the idea. Killing women and children was

not the answer. Bizhan had outsmarted Pavel, and he would do it again.

No, Bizhan had to die. Yawning, Pavel checked his watch and saw it was after two in the morning. But maybe not tonight.

It had cost him twenty-five thousand dollars—in advance —to secure a snitch inside the Ministry of Defense. The man had one job: to warn Pavel when Bizhan left the compound.

Then, as if just thinking about his snitch had summoned him, Pavel's burner mobile phone chimed with an incoming message.

3, it read.

Pavel waited. The phone chimed again.

2, it said.

Pavel keyed his throat microphone. "Bishop is on the move," he said. "Three cars, target is in the second vehicle."

Double-click acknowledgments from the Wagner teams stationed along the three different routes that Bizhan could take home sounded in his ear. He counted six replies. All teams in place.

He flexed his fingers on the steering wheel, anxious to begin. He took in a four-count breath, held it for six counts, then released.

Car headlights rounded the corner of the four-story Ministry of Defense building. The staff who had drivers loaded their vehicles in a secure courtyard in the back of the horseshoe-shaped structure. As three black Mercedes-Benz S-class sedans approached the guardhouse, the front gates opened.

The convoy made a left turn onto Povitroflots'kyi Avenue without stopping and sped away.

Pavel keyed his microphone. "Bishop moving north on Pi." He forced himself to count to ten, then started his own car and turned onto the street in front of the Ministry. He accelerated until he could see the taillights of his quarry, then backed off the gas. He passed over the railyards, which were clogged with stranded boxcars.

From this route, Bizhan had two possible options to get home.

The convoy approached the first turning point and blew past it at over a hundred kilometers per hour.

"Bishop passed P2," Pavel reported and received click acknowledgments.

That left one likely route to their destination—unless the security team decided to take a detour. Pavel tried to put himself in the mind of Bizhan.

Paranoid, yes. But also tired, and anxious to see his family after two days. Pavel's teams were well concealed, so there was little chance the general's security force would spot them.

The convoy slowed as it approached Peremohy Avenue, the main east-west thoroughfare through the heart of Kiev. The vehicles looped right, headed down the cloverleaf, and entered onto Peremohy. Pavel growled into the mic, "Bishop moving west on P2."

One more turn, you bastard, Pavel thought, and your ass is mine.

There were more lights in this section of the city, and more cars. The convoy wove through light traffic at high speed, making it difficult for Pavel to keep up without attracting attention.

He cursed and braked behind a slow driver, then wrenched the wheel and roared around them. Pavel's BMW M550i leaped forward as he punched the accelerator.

He scanned the road in front of him. Where were they? The Shuliavsky Bridge loomed up ahead. If they stayed on the expected route, they'd make the final turn on the other side of the bridge.

Pavel cursed as he swerved around another driver going the speed limit. What the hell were all these people doing on the road at two in the morning? He reached the bridge and still could not see the general's motorcade. The turn lane was full, so he ran a parallel course past the turnoff, ready to continue on if needed.

But the convoy had already turned onto Mykoly Shpaka Street. Now Pavel was out of position.

"Bishop turned right onto final approach," he shouted. "Stand by for authorization."

He accelerated past the turnoff, spun the steering wheel, and took the car into a controlled one-eighty. Pavel punched the gas, then made the left to follow the convoy. A chorus of car horns and curses followed in his wake.

Not too close, he reminded himself. When he reacquired the taillights of the motorcade, he backed off the accelerator.

The street narrowed to two lanes. Civilian traffic thinned until it was only the three-car convoy on the road.

Pavel's tongue felt like sandpaper against the roof of his mouth. "Operation is a go. I say again, go, go, go."

Click-click, click-click. Acknowledgments from the two kill teams snapped in his ears.

The convoy passed the Kyiv School of Economics and came abreast of Voline House traveling at eighty kilometers per hour.

They're moving too fast, Pavel thought. But it was too late to abort.

When the last car crossed the plane of the Voline House entrance, the first car entered the kill zone.

Pavel instinctively ducked his head as the improvised explosive device concealed in the trunk of a parked car detonated. The IED wiped out the lead security vehicle, spinning it lengthwise across the avenue.

A Wagner team unloaded a hail of automatic weapons fire on the trailing security car. From a second-story window, a rocket-propelled grenade lanced down in a flash of white-hot flame. The trail car lifted off the ground in a deafening explosion.

General Bizhan's car, the second vehicle in the motorcade, was trapped.

The plan was for the Wagner team to dispatch the general's security force and take the man alive. After seeing both of his security teams wiped out, Pavel predicted there was no way Bizhan would leave the safety of his vehicle.

Except he did. All four doors of the general's car popped open at the same time, and four men piled out. In the smoke, it was impossible to see which one was the general.

The driver went down immediately, and the other three men made a run for an alley. The Wagner team moved to intercept. Pavel blinked in surprise as he saw one of his men go down. Somehow, one of the security detail in the lead car had survived the IED blast and was laying down covering fire for his boss.

Pavel saw a man duck into the alley next to Voline House, leaving his men behind.

"No, you don't," Pavel whispered. He drove his car onto the sidewalk, bashing through a row of garbage cans. He lost a side mirror on a signpost before he skidded into the alley.

Pinned in the glare of his headlights was the back of a running man, a man wearing the uniform of the Ukrainian Air Force. He pressed the gas pedal to the floor.

The distance to the running man collapsed in a few seconds. Pavel saw a flash of white face as the man looked over his shoulder, and he grinned.

Payback is a bitch.

But General Bizhan was an athletic man—and he had one more trick to play. Just before the car cut him down, he leaped in the air, tucking his knees to his chest. His body impacted the windshield, and he rolled over the roof of the BMW.

Pavel swore and slammed on the brakes. He got out of the car, extracting the SR-1 Vektor from his shoulder holster as he stood.

This guy is a pain in the ass, Pavel thought. This ends now.

Bizhan was on his knees when Pavel reached him. He was gasping for breath but seemed otherwise okay.

A survivor, Pavel thought.

"Stay down," he ordered.

The general ignored him. He got to his feet. The buttons of his uniform tunic had been ripped off by the impact, and the jacket hung open. Pavel raised the weapon, pointing the muzzle at the man's head. The brake lights of the BMW cast the scene in a red glare.

"Do you know who I am?" Pavel hissed.

"You are Wagner," Bizhan said in a voice filled with venom.

If words could kill, Pavel would be dead. But words don't kill; guns do.

"Correct," Pavel said.

He pulled the trigger.

5

Camp David, Maryland

Abby Cromwell relaxed into the overstuffed armchair in the living room of the Aspen Lodge, a snifter of fragrant brandy cupped in her hand. The presidential cabin occupied the high ground overlooking the wooded Catoctin Mountain. Although they were only thirty minutes from Washington, DC, by helicopter, Camp David felt as far away from the pressures of the nation's capital as the moon.

You're drunk, she thought.

After appetizers, with which she'd had two Manhattans, the President ushered his group of special guests into the dining room for a five-course meal, with wine pairings for each course.

And why not? The dialogue continued in her head. You deserve it. You haven't tied one on since... A long time. She took another sip of brandy.

Abby smiled to no one in particular. She was right. She did deserve this.

This was her introduction into President Rick Serrano's

famous "Sitting Room" cabinet. As a bona fide billionaire before reaching the White House, the forty-eighth president's occasional soirees with his cabal of billionaire buddies were like catnip to the press corps. Although no one apart from the members of the select group knew what was discussed in these informal gatherings, news analysts had a field day dissecting the attendees and any subsequent policy moves by the Serrano administration.

The President had been her gracious host for the day. After lunch at the White House and a private tour of the residence, they'd flown to Camp David on Marine One. Along the route, Serrano pointed out historic sites and talked at length about the storied history of the Camp David compound, such as the 1978 peace agreement between Egypt and Israel brokered by President Carter.

From the air, the Aspen Lodge was a sprawling, cedar-shingled, one-story cabin atop a small hill. To Abby's practiced eye, the modest dwelling concealed a number of security measures ranging from bulletproof window glass to state-of-the-art electronic surveillance to armed security. A timely reminder to her that this was no ordinary dinner party.

The President had invited seven guests for the weekend, including Abby, and they all lounged in the Aspen Lodge living room with her. Sumner Vogel, the fire-breathing owner of the largest conservative news network in the world, had sat next to her at dinner. Sumner, who insisted she call him "Summy," was a wonderful and witty dinner companion. Gayle Queensley, sole owner of the Cara beauty empire and a raging liberal, sat across from Abby. She was a sculpted beauty who looked two decades younger than her seventy years. Queenie and Summy were engaged in a private chat on the loveseat opposite Abby right now—a picture any card-carrying member of the paparazzi would trade their firstborn child for.

Abby looked around the room at the smiling faces. A software mogul, a real estate tycoon, a banker, and the owner of the world's largest cryptocurrency trading site rounded out the group. There was enough wealth in this hundred square feet of real estate to buy and sell half of the countries in the world. To a person, they had all been caricatured, praised, and vilified by any number of politicians, news outlets (including their own), and internet conspiracy sites so many times that they did not seem like real people to Abby.

And yet, here they were. Chatting, joking, laughing with hardly a cross word all evening.

And she was here, too, part of the most exclusive club on the planet. Abby wanted to pinch herself. If her late husband could see her now... She took a sip of brandy instead and savored the glow in her belly.

Serrano stood, glass in hand. "Ladies and gentlemen, we've now reached the point in the evening where I seek your wise counsel."

"You mean when you've gotten us drunk enough to speak truth to power," Summy said, elbowing his best friend, Queenie.

"In vino veritas," Serrano said, raising his glass. His gaze found Abby and his smile broadened. "And a warm welcome to the newest member of our circle."

"Here, here," Queenie said, saluting Abby with a tip of her wine glass.

"Friends, I have a problem to put before you." Serrano sat on the edge of an overstuffed armchair and leaned forward.

"I find myself at a crossroads. How to not let the last eighteen months define my presidency. Don't get me wrong. The win over the Chinese in Taiwan polls very well, but that's just political adrenaline. It will wear off in a matter of weeks, and then I'm in the fight of my political life."

Abby found herself nodding. She didn't follow politics closely, but the President was right to be concerned. Already his poll numbers had peaked. Each week he lost a few more points as the public turned away from the high-stakes drama of war to their own lives.

Inflation was up due to supply chain disruptions from the war in Taiwan. The stock market was down as traders tried to find a new global equilibrium. Every day, news outlets from across the political spectrum ran human interest stories about how the last year of unrelenting conflict across the globe impacted soldiers, airmen, sailors, and their families.

To be sure, there were winners among the economic wreckage. Big winners, including Sentinel Holdings, but the general feeling across the country was a sense of loss and unease.

"Rick," said Sumner, his fleshy face serious, "the first thing is you need to change the story. People are tired of war, and dying, and economic back-and-forth. They want to feel secure again, stable."

"Agreed," said Queenie, "this is the perfect time to launch a piece of lasting domestic policy. Something that sets you up as being a man of the people."

"There's only a few months until the midterms," said the banker. "The campaigns are already set in their messages."

"Then put something out there that resets the narrative," Queenie said. "Something everyone can agree on—something with children or seniors."

Abby listened to the back-and-forth without contributing. Although she had heard many of these ideas before, what struck her was that no one in the room spoke about any of the ideas from a partisan point of view. Yes, they all had their ideological foundations, but no one made it personal. It occurred to her that for these people—and for her—none of it really mattered. Nothing Congress passed was going to affect them in any meaningful way. Sure, they might pay more taxes or lose some tax breaks for their companies, but they already had more money than any person could spend in many lifetimes. For these people, the question of how to run the country was an academic exercise.

"What do you think, Abby?" Serrano asked, interrupting her contemplations.

"I was just taking it all in," she stammered in reply.

Summy leaned forward and tapped the coffee table between them. "No bystanders, Abby. Everyone contributes."

Abby sat up straighter and placed her drink on the coffee table. "Well, I'm a soldier turned businesswoman. I don't have strong opinions on domestic policy."

"Come now, dear," Queenie said sternly. "Rickie owes you a great deal. Without your company, and your support, the island of Taiwan would be flying the flag of the People's Republic of China right now. The conversation about domestic policy would not even be on the table were it not for you."

"Well," Abby said, "I can only discuss what I know. My only contribution to this forum is that the United States must not get drawn into another international conflict. I don't think the military can handle any more losses, and I'm sure the public won't stand for it."

Nods circled the room.

"You're talking about Ukraine," Serrano said.

"I am, sir," Abby said. "I've seen the intel. Luchnik is baiting you. He's creating a problem that only he can solve. We need to stay away."

Serrano nodded, then looked up as a man appeared in the doorway of the living room.

"They're ready for you, Mr. President," the man said.

"Duty calls, my friends." Serrano stood. "I'm afraid that Ms. Cromwell and I have another engagement."

Abby wasn't sure she'd heard correctly. "I do?"

Serrano smiled and held out his hand to help her to her feet. "I'd like your expert opinion on something, Abby." He put a hand on the small of her back, pressing her toward the door. "We'll be back soon, everyone. Please, continue the discussion. We'll catch up when we get back."

As they walked through the halls of the Aspen Lodge, Abby really wished she'd paced herself better on the alcohol. While not exactly drunk, she wasn't at the top of her game either.

Their guide reached a set of double doors at the far end of the house and opened it for them.

Inside, there was a rustic wood table with eight chairs. Chief of Staff Irving Wilkerson, wearing a baggy gray cardigan, occupied the chair at the head of the table, facing a large flat-screen monitor showing a map of eastern Europe.

As everyone rose to their feet, Abby ran her gaze around the room. Secretary of State Henry Hahn, Secretary of Defense Kathleen Howard, National Security Advisor Valentina Flores, General Nikolaides, and CIA Director Samuel Blank all looked back at her.

Abby tamped down a surge of annoyance. She'd just stepped into a meeting of the National Security Council and was half-buzzed. Her mind ran through her day with Serrano, and she felt like a wild deer who'd been herded from the safety of the forest into an open field.

Her spirits lifted slightly when Don Riley stepped out from behind the bulk of the Chairman of the Joint Chiefs. Like everyone in the room, Don was dressed casually in jeans and a button-down shirt. He looked surprised to see her. While the room played musical chairs to accommodate the new arrivals, she gave him a quick smile and a slight shrug of her shoulders as if to say, "I don't know any more than you do, buddy."

Serrano took his chair at the head of the table with Wilkerson on his right and Abby on his left.

"Take it from the top, Mr. Riley," Wilkerson said with a side-eyed glance at Abby. Was he annoyed she was here?

Abby had the advantage over most of the people in the room in that she already knew what Don was going to say. He had used Sentinel sources and Mama, the company AI, as the raw material for his briefing.

She half listened as he went through the highlights. The country of Ukraine was on the ropes. Power, water, and communications infrastructure were on life support. Hundreds dead from riots was a low estimate. The Russian military was on the move to "help" their neighbors, and the Ukrainian military was resisting all along the border.

"The prime mover of all this chaos," said Don, "is the Wagner Group, a Russian private military contractor. We also have reports that Wagner operatives assassinated a number of key Ukrainian military leaders and defense ministry officials."

As Don spoke, Abby became aware that Nikolaides watched her with an unwavering glare, clearly unhappy she was in the meeting. She guessed he'd never gotten over the use of the Sentinel Cicada drone weapons in Taiwan.

Sour grapes, she thought. The commander in chief had gone against the recommendations of his top military advisers, but it had worked out. That's all that mattered in the end.

Riley finished the briefing and looked at Wilkerson. The Chief of Staff turned to his boss.

"Mr. President, we have two options here. The preferred

path is to let the European Union handle this. It's in their backyard, so we can say it's their problem. We offer thoughts and prayers, but we stay away."

"And what if Luchnik expands the conflict?" Serrano asked.

"Then we look like we failed to take action when the problem was small and manageable."

Serrano grimaced. "Not ideal. What's the second option?"

"We go in hard right now," Nikolaides said. "The whole nine yards. Spec ops, boots on the ground, NATO air cover, full diplomatic support. We slap that Russian idiot back to the border and go home."

"That has obvious drawbacks, Mr. President," Wilkerson said drily.

"Sounds like a political death wish to me." Serrano looked around the table. "That's all we've got in the idea factory? Go big or go away?"

Abby saw a glance pass between Wilkerson and Flores. The National Security Advisor somehow managed to make an oversized red-and-black-checked lumberjack shirt look like it belonged on a fashion runway. When Flores raised her hand, Abby saw that her fingernails were painted the exact shade of the red squares on her shirt.

"I have a proposal, Mr. President," she said. "A way to keep the damage in Ukraine under control but not involve the United States military. At least not officially."

Serrano held up his hands in a let's-have-it gesture.

Flores's dark gaze latched onto Abby.

"Since Luchnik used his mercenaries to start this war, we fight fire with fire. I propose we contract with Sentinel Holdings to provide security in Ukraine. We can alter their rules of engagement as needed based on the situation, all the while keeping our own hands clean."

Abby felt strangely exposed as all eyes in the room focused on her. She opened her mouth, then closed it again. There was no way she was getting involved in a proxy war.

"Abby?" the President said. "What do you think?"

What do I think? her inner voice shouted. I think this entire day has been a setup. She wondered if Summy and Queenie were in on the scam.

But before she could respond, the Chairman spoke.

"I think it's a fucking terrible idea, Mr. President," he said flatly. "The situation in Ukraine is either a national security risk to the US, or it's not. If it is, we act on it. If not, we don't. We can't buy our way out of this. Paying a bunch of GI Joes to play Rambo-ski is not the answer."

It was a pretty funny comment, Abby thought, but no one laughed. In fact, Serrano got red in the face.

Then Don Riley spoke. "The Chairman's analysis is correct, Mr. President. If we ignore the threat Luchnik will expand—"

"That's enough, Riley," the CIA Director said.

But Riley continued, "We have to meet the Russian threat head on, sir, with our allies—"

"Enough," Wilkerson interrupted in a sharp voice.

There was a long moment of icy silence.

"Thank you for the briefing, Mr. Riley," Wilkerson said stiffly. "You can wait outside."

Kathleen Howard, the Secretary of Defense, said, "Mr. President, may I say something?"

"You may not," Wilkerson snapped. "In fact, let's clear the room and let the President confer with Ms. Cromwell. Alone."

Abby took stock of her situation as the room emptied. There was a warm glow in her belly, but not from the brandy. She took a deep breath in an attempt to control her anger and knotted her fingers together.

The door closed behind Chief of Staff Wilkerson, leaving her alone with the leader of the free world.

"You're angry with me, Abby," Serrano said.

"I am, Mr. President."

"You feel used."

She did not answer. The statement didn't deserve an answer.

"I need your help, Abby," he said finally. "I need to buy time. You heard what they said in the living room. These are the smartest people I know. The smartest people in the world."

"I can't do it, Mr. President," she said. "I don't have the people, the infrastructure."

"Name your price. You'll have money, as much as you need, as much as you want, but I need you to do this for me."

"It's not the money, sir," Abby said.

Serrano reached across the table and put his hand on hers.

"I'm not asking as your president, Abby," he said in a soft voice. "I'm asking as a friend." His eyes locked on hers, the famous Serrano Stare. "A few months, that's all I need to get things back on track. Please."

Abby swallowed. The gentle buzz of alcohol had faded, and she felt washed out.

Slowly, she nodded.

6

Annapolis, Maryland

"What the hell were you thinking?"

CIA Director Samuel Blank was known for his even-keeled demeanor, a man whose personality lived up to his family name.

But on the morning after their trip to Camp David, Director Blank was anything but calm. In fact, Don had never seen him so angry. His face had the hue of a sun-ripened tomato, and when he spoke little flecks of spit showered the breakfast table between them.

It was a real pity, Don reflected. The French toast that the lady of the house had made for them lay untouched, and he was fond of French toast. Outside, the green lawn of the Blank estate sloped down to the banks of the Severn River. It was a glorious summer day. In the distance, across the river, Don could see the dome of the Naval Academy chapel. The sight gave Don a pang of nostalgia.

"Are you listening to me, Riley?" the Director snapped.

Don turned his attention back to spit-flecked French toast and his boss's red, angry face. "Yes, sir."

He and the Director had returned to Langley by helicopter, arriving about midnight. The Director had said nothing to Don since his outburst in, and subsequent ejection from, the NSC meeting at Camp David.

They disembarked from the helo together and stood on the brightly lit landing pad. "I'll send a car for you tomorrow morning," the Director said. "Be ready at seven sharp."

Don's first thought was that he was going to get fired.

His second thought was that he didn't care.

On the drive back to his apartment in Tysons Corner, Don took stock of his life, and what he saw did not please him.

For the last twenty-five years, he had hunted down terrorists, foiled plots against his country, and fought a cyber war that no one knew or cared about. Over the past two years, he'd helped avert World War Three not once, but twice. The President of the United States had personally asked him to speak up when he saw an issue.

He pulled into his parking spot at his apartment and said aloud: "If you see something, say something."

What a crock of shit, he thought.

Although it was nearly two in the morning when he entered his apartment, Don got a beer from the refrigerator and drank it fast. He'd hoped the cold liquid and the alcohol might calm him down, but it had the opposite effect. He got another beer and began to pace.

He was sliding toward fifty and his work was his life. His entire life. He had no girlfriend, no friends apart from work. His hair was thinning, his waistline thickening, and he had a severe case of recurring insomnia.

Don finished the beer and got another. He was too jumpy to sleep, so he cleaned his apartment. When the car arrived at seven o'clock, Don's apartment was spotless and his attitude had not improved. During the forty-five-minute drive to the Director's home in Annapolis, Don brooded.

"Riley!" Director Blank's tone snapped Don back to reality. "What possessed you to speak to the President like that?"

"He asked me to," Don replied.

"What?"

"During the Taiwan crisis, the President told me that he wanted me to speak up if I saw something going on."

Blank's lip curled. "Don't act like you just fell off the turnip truck, Don. We work for politicians. They all say crap like that, but they don't mean it." Blank stabbed a piece of French toast with murderous intent. "Unless it helps them, of course."

Don stayed silent.

Blank slammed down his cutlery with a clatter. "We're analysts, not decision-makers. Even I try to avoid giving the President an opinion about a national security decision."

Even when you should, Don thought.

"The Chairman raised the subject," Don said. "I was trying to add color to his comment. Like a briefer should, sir." Even as the words left his mouth, Don knew how lame he sounded.

To his surprise, Blank's anger seemed to drain away. The Director put both elbows on the table and sighed. His shoulders sagged.

"General Nikolaides resigned last night, Don," the Director said. "It was not unexpected, but it's a huge loss for the country."

Don looked out the window at the sparkling water. A Naval Academy sailboat crossed the bay, her sail bellied out in the freshening breeze. He felt the weight of his sleepless night come crashing down. He wanted to be on that sailboat and go back in time to a place that was much less complicated than where he was right now.

"Eat something, Don," the Director said, not unkindly.

Don moved the top pieces of French toast aside to uncover the ones that had not been spit upon. He smothered them in syrup and stuffed a too-large piece in his mouth. A sugar rush would be most welcome right about now.

"Nikolaides has been on thin ice ever since he went against the President on the use of the Cicada drone weapons in Taiwan," Blank said.

"Yes, sir," Don replied. Without really understanding it, Don felt a sense of disappointment in President Serrano. Up until last night, he'd felt the President had been a strong leader. While he didn't agree with everything the President had done, Don believed that the man had acted on principle.

After last night, he didn't know what to think.

"Why am I here, sir?" Don asked.

Blank pushed his plate back, his French toast untouched. He looked out the window, away from Don's gaze. "I think it's safe to say that your favored status with the President has ended," the Director said quietly.

Don ate more French toast.

"As a matter fact, Chief of Staff Wilkerson has made it clear that he does not want you anywhere near the White House. He does not want the name Don Riley to be spoken of in the presence of the President or even see your name on an analytical report."

"So, you're firing me," Don said.

"Don't be ridiculous," Blank replied with a note of irritation in his tone. "You're PNG'd, for sure, but you're also one of my best people. Politicians come and go, but we stick around."

"Persona non grata," Don said, making no attempt to hide the bitterness in his tone. He stood. "Is that all, sir?"

Blank finally looked him in the eye. "I'm not finished yet, Don. Please. Sit down."

Don sat down on the edge of his chair. He was exhausted, a little hungover, and a lot pissed off. He imagined flipping over the breakfast table and storming out of the room. Instead, he stayed very still.

"You're being pulled off the Sentinel Holdings liaison duties," Blank said. He held up a hand to stop Don from interrupting. "Wilkerson wants a supporter in that role, not someone who doesn't believe in the use of PMCs."

"Who?"

Blank shrugged. "I'll figure it out and let you know." He stood and held out his hand. "I'm sorry, Don. It's out of my control."

Don stepped into the bright spring sunshine a few minutes later. Crushed gravel crunched under his feet as he walked to the waiting black Chevy Suburban.

"Where can I take you, sir?" the driver asked.

I can go anywhere, Don thought. The beach, the Smithsonian, go see a movie...

"Sir?"

Don gave the driver the address for the Emerging Threats Group building in Tysons Corner. Then he relaxed into the soft leather seat and closed his eyes.

The Emerging Threats Group office was mostly empty on a Sunday afternoon, except for Harrison Kohl. Don found the acting Director of ETG in his office hunched behind a computer, reading glasses perched on his nose. While Don had been assigned to Sentinel Holdings as a liaison officer, Harrison had taken over his management duties.

Harrison was a trim man with short gray hair. A twenty-year veteran of the CIA and NSA, he had spent his career avoiding management roles in both organizations. When Don relayed what had happened with the Director, Harrison came around his desk and hugged Don in mock relief.

"I am so glad to hear you shit the bed, boss," he said. "You have the deck and the conn of this fine organization. Just be glad I didn't run her aground while you were out saving the world." He pulled a duffel bag out from under his desk. "I'm going to the gym and I'm coming in late tomorrow."

In spite of his dark mood, Don smiled as he realized how much he missed this place. Maybe being back at ETG would be good for him after all.

Harrison departed, and Don sat back down, too tired to care where he was.

Maybe I'll take a nap right here, he thought.

Harrison reappeared in the doorway. "You've got a visitor, Don. I put him in your office."

"Who?" Don said.

"You're an analyst," Harrison called from the hallway. "Figure it out."

Don pulled himself upright. Despite the nap in the car, he was still tired and the sugar in the syrup had turned sour inside his mouth. He walked to his office on the other side of the building. When he turned the corner, he saw his office door was open and the light on. When Don reached the doorway, he paused.

Somehow, his shitty day had just gotten worse. Dylan Mattias sat behind his desk, using Don's computer.

As usual, Dylan looked like he'd just stepped off the cover of *GQ*. He wore faded blue jeans, loafers without socks, and a dark blue polo shirt that stretched across his bulging pectoral muscles. He looked up and gave Don a smug smile.

"I'm just checking my secure email," he said. "Hope you don't mind."

Looking down, Don noticed a spot of syrup on the front of his own shirt.

"Dylan," Don said in as neutral a tone as he could manage. "You came all this way on a Sunday afternoon just to check your email?"

"I'm the new liaison officer for Sentinel Holdings," Dylan said. "I'd like you to brief me on the operations over there."

Don swallowed. That was fast. He wondered if the Director had already selected Dylan before they'd met over breakfast.

"The President's Chief of Staff called me this morning," Dylan said. "He suggested I volunteer my services to the Director for the position." He got up from Don's desk. "Sorry things didn't work out, Don."

Under normal circumstances, Don would have accepted the comment at face value, but not now. Of course his replacement was Dylan. He should've figured that out on his own. Dylan was a known quantity at the White House, and the President would want the Sentinel operations in Ukraine spooled up as fast as possible. If there was pushback from anyone at CIA, even from the Director, a political operator like Dylan would know how to neutralize it immediately.

"Well?" Dylan dropped into one of Don's office chairs and slouched down with his legs extended in front of him. He looked at the piles of papers and reports heaped on Don's desk and credenza. "This place is a pigsty, man. How do you ever get anything done in here?"

"I manage," Don replied sharply as he took his own seat behind his desk. His emotions were all over the place. He should be relieved that he was not dealing with Sentinel anymore, but instead, he was pissed off.

Don saw his unclassified web browser was in use, and he

clicked on the open tab. Dylan had been shopping for Italian loafers while he waited in Don's office.

"Don," Dylan said from his relaxed pose, "if you just talk to me, we can get this done fast. Then we can go enjoy this beautiful day. You could use some sun, dude."

"What do you want to know, Dylan?"

"Let's start with their people," Dylan replied. "Aberdeen Cromwell. What makes her tick?"

Don sighed.

Now that, he thought, was an excellent question.

7

Sterling, Virginia

Abby Cromwell wasn't sure what to make of the new CIA liaison officer. Although they'd gotten off to a slow start, she'd grown oddly comfortable with Don Riley in the position. He was a steady hand, someone she could rely on as she managed her rapidly growing private military contracting company through a very turbulent time.

Now, with a new mission she wasn't sure her company was ready for, everything felt unstable around her. The last thing she needed was a change in her relationship with the CIA.

In the close confines of the elevator, she studied Dylan Mattias out of the corner of her eye. He was about her age and height, with the body of a man who knew his way around a gym. He moved with athletic surety, controlled, with no wasted movements.

In fact, Abby thought, his entire manner was one of complete self-confidence. Maybe not arrogant, but she guessed that Dylan Mattias never doubted what he wanted and he always got it.

Was that a good quality in a liaison officer? Don's manner had been to question everything, including himself, in every situation. While challenging to get used to, he somehow managed to find the right answer every time. Abby had a sneaking suspicion that Dylan Mattias would have a very different style.

The elevator doors opened onto the Sentinel Holdings underground operations bunker. Abby's heels echoed as she stepped onto the polished floor.

"We call this the Planetarium," she said.

Dylan's dark eyes took in the domed ceiling, the Sentinel teams at work, the raised central command cockpit, and he let out a low whistle.

"Now this is an intelligence operations center," he said in an appreciative tone.

Abby walked slowly as she talked. "Traditional ops centers are set up classroom style, with fixed workstations facing forward to wall screens. We decided to flip the design on its head."

She pointed at a cluster of four workstations. "Work teams are flexible. We place equipment and team members onto the floor and configure them as needed. Shared data gets projected on the ceiling, where it's visible to all. During the privateering operation earlier this year, we had over a hundred people on the floor in configurable teams. We're down to about forty people now, mostly financial types, working on the sale of the seized vessels."

"Brilliant," Dylan said.

Abby glowed with pride. They arrived at the command cockpit.

"Hub and spoke," Dylan said. "Everything is controlled from the central command platform." He gestured at the three steps up to the cockpit. "May I?"

"Of course," Abby replied. She watched him mount the steps lightly. Whatever flaws she might yet learn about the new liaison officer, he was easy on the eyes.

Manson Skelly occupied the command chair. He watched Dylan enter the cockpit and said into a slim headset microphone, "All stations, command will be offline for five."

Without waiting for an acknowledgment, he pushed the attached console aside and stood.

Abby's late husband and Sentinel co-founder, Joe, used to say that his best friend Manson Skelly was "built like a brick shithouse." Abby had never seen a brick shithouse, but Skelly was short and powerfully built, with corded muscles rippling under his tight T-shirt that read: "Guns don't kill people. I do."

Abby cringed, knowing he'd probably worn the inappropriate shirt just to annoy her.

Skelly had thick dark hair cut short and a perpetual five o'clock shadow. His heavy features twisted into a humorless smile as he stuck out his hand.

"Call me Skelly," he said to Dylan. "I hope you're not one of those Washington types who likes to get in the way. We get things done here; no bureaucratic bullshit allowed." His gruff tone was challenging, and Abby guessed he was probably trying to crush Dylan's hand in his meaty grip.

What a child, she thought.

Dylan met the other man's gaze with cool regard. If Skelly's handshake was causing him pain, Dylan's face betrayed no discomfort.

"I don't think you'll have any difficulties with me, Skelly," Dylan said. "For this new mission, we have the same goal. Cause as much damage as possible in the shortest amount of time for the least cost. Economy in action, but lethal in all regards."

Skelly looked at Abby. "We have a new job? Oh my god,

tell me it's fucking Ukraine. Please, tell me it's Ukraine." He released Dylan's hand.

"It's Ukraine," Dylan said.

Skelly pumped a scarred fist. "I can't wait to take it to those Wagner bastards. They got some payback coming."

Dylan studied Skelly, and Abby wondered what he was thinking. "How soon can you get offensive operations started?" Dylan asked.

Skelly looked like he wanted to hug the CIA officer. "Where did you find this guy?" he said to Abby. "I fucking love him. I'll be there by tonight," he said to Dylan. "Weapons free."

"Let's not get ahead of ourselves," Abby said. "I need you running ops from here, Manson, not playing commando in the field."

"No problem," Skelly said, "You're right, boss. I'll ride a desk here in the office and we'll let Landersmann handle the field operations." He turned back to the command chair.

Abby cursed to herself. David Landersmann was not the man she wanted in charge of the mission in Ukraine.

"Wait," she said.

When he turned back around, Skelly's grin was more of a leer. "Yes, ma'am?"

"Maybe it would be better if you went into the field to oversee the start—just the start—of operations, Manson," she said.

Skelly gave her a mock salute. "Yes, ma'am. I'll get on it right away." He consulted his wristwatch. "I can use Mama to pull together an initial logistics package and be wheels up by tonight."

"All right," Abby said. "We'll let you get to it. Keep me—us, I mean—posted on your progress."

Skelly was already back in his command chair issuing

rapid-fire orders over his headset. Abby led Dylan back down to the operations floor where technicians were already rolling new workstations into place.

"We'll have primary ops shifted to the Ukraine theater within the hour," she said. "The team we have in place in eastern Europe is small but competent."

"What's your data stream in theater look like?"

"We have sources in place," Abby replied. "Sentinel-owned aerial surveillance, HUMINT, as well as whatever we can scrape from local channels, like traffic cams and so on."

"Efficient operation," Dylan commented. "You helped Riley with his Ukraine presidential briefing, didn't you?"

"Yes," Abby replied, "we did. Is that a problem?"

Dylan shook his head. "I couldn't figure out how he did the analysis that fast."

Abby laughed. "I gave him access to Mama."

"Skelly said that, too. Who is Mama?"

"Our resident AI," Abby said. "She handles housekeeping, logistics, operational planning, data analysis. You name it, she does it for us."

"You rely on an AI that much?"

"Without Mama, Sentinel would not exist," Abby said. "She's the secret sauce behind this company. She never takes a day off, never asks for a raise, never tells her girlfriend classified information that might compromise a mission. She's the perfect employee."

Dylan studied her as she spoke, and Abby found her cheeks growing warm. "What?" she asked.

"Tell me about Landersmann." Dylan broke eye contact, changed the subject.

"Not much to tell," Abby said. "He's head of eastern Europe operations. Speaks fluent Russian and a bunch of other languages. Can get us access to anyone we want in that part of the world."

And I wouldn't trust him as far as I could throw him, Abby thought.

"He and Skelly have history," she concluded.

"Hmm," Dylan said. "I thought I noticed some tension between you and Skelly back there. Anything I need to worry about?"

"Nothing," Abby replied. "Normal business partner stuff."

Dylan fixed his eyes on hers. His eyes were dark brown, like warm chocolate.

"I might be able to help," Dylan said. "I'm good with people."

I bet you are, Abby thought.

"I'm from the government." Dylan winked. "I'm here to help."

Abby turned away, stabbed at the elevator call button, angry with herself that her cheeks were flushed pink.

Dylan Mattias was an attractive man and he knew it. Still, she thought, he did seem to hit it off with Manson. Maybe he could help repair that relationship.

"I'll think about it," she said.

8

Oleksandriya, Ukraine

The Sentinel Holdings forward operating base occupied an empty warehouse two kilometers south of the E50 highway that ran east-west through the central Ukrainian city of Oleksandriya. Manson Skelly nodded his approval. David Landersmann, his number two in the Ukraine theater of operations, had chosen the site well.

The exterior was red brick, probably pre–World War Two. Judging by the pile of broken toilets they found behind the building, the site was once used as a ceramics factory, a fact that prompted endless potty humor among the Sentinel operators.

The interior of the cavernous building was mostly dry, and a fleet of propane heaters made the space comfortable enough to wear a T-shirt inside. At the far end of the building, next to the double doors, there were five black Land Rovers and four sleek surveillance drones covered in dull radar-absorbent material. Landersmann had cleared a makeshift runway alongside the building that was long enough to launch and recover the drones—at night, of course.

The other end of the warehouse had been turned into an operations center and temporary living quarters for the Sentinel crew. Skelly stood in front of the dozen operators who lounged in a collection of camp chairs or on packing crates. The warm air smelled of gun oil and body odor.

Damn, he thought, it felt good to be back in the field again.

He held up a single sheet of paper and cleared his throat.

"May I have your attention please, gentlemen." He threw an exaggerated glance at the three women seated together. "And ladies." One of the women gave him the finger, and he waited for the obligatory laughter to die down.

The three women on the team were some of his best operators, but that joke never got old.

"I am required by our fearless leader, Ms. Aberdeen Cromwell, to brief you on the rules of engagement for operations in Ukraine." He pretended to move the paper back and forth as if trying to focus. The gesture was only half-joking. Lately he'd noticed his near vision was not as crisp as it once had been. He cleared his throat dramatically.

"The mission of Sentinel Holdings in Ukraine is to harass, degrade, and destroy Wagner Group operations in the region. We are directed to interdict Wagner lines of communications, disrupt operations, and destroy Wagner-owned equipment and bases. Furthermore, any intelligence on Wagner personnel and operations should be reported to the US intelligence community as quicky as possible."

He ran his gaze over the assembled crew. All eyes were on him. The normal joking and easygoing banter were gone.

"Deadly force is authorized against known Wagner personnel. However, Sentinel will avoid direct engagement with Russian regular forces unless fired upon first by said forces."

Skelly looked up and grinned. "So ends the reading of the corporate directive."

He tore the sheet of paper in half, matched the two halves together, then tore it again and again until he had a handful of shredded squares. He threw them in the air like confetti.

"I've done my duty as a corporate officer," he said. "Now it's time for the real briefing. This is a fucking war zone, people. You keep your head on a swivel and your weapons loose. Shoot first, ask questions later. Most of you did time in the Sandbox and you know how Wagner operates. If you give them the drop, you're a dead man." He looked at the women. "Excuse me, dead *person*."

"Bite me, Skelly," one of the women shot back.

Skelly ignored her. "These assholes invaded the wrong country this time. The gloves are off. This time, they get what they deserve—and we're the ones to give it to them."

The room of mercenaries stirred. The ooh-rah had long since left this crowd, but there was an undeniable sense of electricity in the air.

Point the weapon, Skelly thought. These men and women killed for a living, and they were good at their job. All he needed to do was to give them a target. He adopted a businesslike tone.

"Tonight is our coming-out party with Wagner. Landersmann has a Ukrainian intel officer on the take who will provide the exact coordinates of a Wagner FOB on the other side of the river." Skelly shot a look at Landersmann. "This guy is good, Landie? We can rely on him?"

Landersmann was on the shorter side with patchy brown hair and a slight paunch. He had an annoying habit of only smiling on the right side of his face, so Skelly could never tell whether he was smiling for real or ironically.

"He's the best money can buy, boss," Landersmann assured him.

"Whatever," Skelly replied. "This is our first foray into this theater of operations, and I want to put those Wagner assholes on notice that there's a new bully in town. This is a search-and-destroy, deadly-force-authorized mission. Questions." He said the last like a statement, not an inquiry.

Michael "Zap" Zapasso raised his hand. He was a former senior chief Navy SEAL who had only been with Sentinel for three months. With his blond hair, blue eyes, and chiseled features, the guy looked like Captain America. Unfortunately, this Captain America had a gambling problem. Fortunately, Sentinel Holdings paid very well.

"What is it, Zap?" Skelly asked.

"Who do we turn the intel over to? Laptops, mobile phones, stuff like that."

Skelly rolled his eyes. "Listen, Zap, gathering intel is a second priority, and frankly, I don't give a shit. Landie has his people. We pay them and we get information. If the intel weenies back in DC want to know what's going on, they can get their asses on a plane and come visit. You're hired to point and shoot. Any other questions?"

There were none.

"Good, we leave in fifteen."

The Land Rovers were black with tinted windows, the same vehicles used by Wagner, according to Landersmann. Four operators per vehicle, each person outfitted and armed according to their personal tastes. Most wore some combination of top-of-the-line sporting gear and customized body armor. All of them, Skelly included, were tagged with a GPS chip that could be used to locate them and pinged to provide vital signs. The monitoring capability was contained in a protected program, accessible only by Abby and Skelly.

Skelly's brand of choice was an Under Armour shirt and Vuori Ripstop pants. To his Dragon Skin body armor, he'd added front and back titanium trauma plates to cover his vital organs. For weapons, Skelly went with his old favorites, an FN SCAR combat rifle, a Glock 9mm as his side arm, and a combat knife fixed to his body armor.

The sun was setting as they crossed the Dnieper River on the M22 bridge at the city Kremenchuk.

The geography of eastern Ukraine definitely favored Wagner and the Russians. The land was bordered to the north by Belarus, essentially a Russian puppet state, and to the south by Crimea, a recent Russian acquisition. In the contested areas along the eastern border, Russian President Luchnik and his "little green men," a euphemism for plain-clothed Russian soldiers, had been battling with Ukrainians for more than a decade.

And now Luchnik was going to finish the job, Skelly thought sourly as he consulted a paper map of the region.

When they left the city limits, they began to see the human toll of the Russian invasion. Although the highways headed east were clear, the road west was choked with cars, trucks, motorcycles, bicycles, even tractors pulling loaded wagons. On the side of the road, in the freshly plowed fields and grassy embankments, Skelly could see hundreds of camp-fires where people had stopped for the night.

It got worse when they reached the city of Poltava. According to Landersmann, the area had been home to a Soviet military school during the Cold War and remained pro-Russian today. They passed a string of burned out civilian cars, and Skelly could see bodies lined up along the side of the road, as if they'd been executed. Groups of armed civilians manned checkpoints along the route, but they let the black Land Rovers pass without stopping.

"It's good to be the king," Landersmann said.

They left the carnage behind, reentering open farmland. Landersmann left the highway for a small two-lane country road. Using a penlight, Skelly consulted his map. They were headed for the village of Vasylivka.

To call the place a village was being kind. A grouping of six buildings, two of them bombed-out shells, huddled around a crossroads. Landersmann pulled off the road, drove behind a barn, and shut off the car engine.

Skelly rolled down the window. Chill, damp air, smelling of freshly turned soil and cow manure flooded the car. The night was silent save for the ticking of the cooling car engines.

A man stepped around the corner of the barn and walked toward them. Skelly's grip tightened on his combat rifle.

Landersmann opened the car door. "It's him."

Major Oleksiy Melnyk wore a civilian overcoat over his Ukrainian Army uniform. Tall and thin, he acted nervous to Skelly, but Landersmann seemed not to notice. The intel officer unfolded a map on the hood of the Land Rover and spoke in low urgent tones to Landersmann, who tapped on his tablet as they talked.

"You want to fill us in on what's going on, Landie?" Skelly said, tiring of the show.

"Uploading now," Landersmann replied, then tapped his tablet.

The map on Skelly's tablet showed a boxed area next to a small hamlet about three kilometers to the north. He leaned closer and squinted: the town was called Zelenkivka.

"We have a target," Landersmann called out. "Let's get some eyes in the air, Zap."

Skelly heard the sound of a Land Rover tailgate dropping

and crates being moved. "Wagner's there?" Skelly said. "For sure?"

Landersmann nodded. "I told him I'd find him and cut his nuts off if he was lying to me. He says it's a Wagner forward operating base. They're supposed to secure the area and turn it over to the Russians. He says there's about two dozen hostiles and the Russians won't get there until tomorrow morning."

"Perfect," Skelly said. "When the Russkies get there for breakfast, they'll find a ghost town." He felt his pulse tick up at the thought of imminent action.

Landersmann pulled out a wad of cash and made to hand it to the Ukrainian, only to pull it back at the last second. He laughed with his lopsided smile.

"Stop screwing around, Landie," Skelly growled. "We've got work to do."

"Gremlins away," Zap called out, and Skelly heard the soft whir of three aerial reconnaissance drones taking off.

While he waited for a report, Skelly checked his loadout, ensuring his magazines were locked tight into his weapons. Around him, his handpicked crew went through their own pre-combat rituals.

"Jackpot, bossman." Landersmann approached Skelly holding his tablet out. "Eighteen Wagner assholes all snug in their beds while visions of sugarplums danced in their heads."

Skelly studied the image. There were four tents—set up too close together, in his opinion. Typical Wagner arrogance. One looked to be a combination CP and mess tent, the others sleeping quarters. He made out the infrared images of a dozen forms reclining on cots. Four more were posted as guards, and two were in the command post.

He handed the tablet back to Landersmann. "Good. Tell the FOB to get the Raptors in the air. Sync up with whatever other assets we can access and generate a consolidated feed on the battle network for us." He checked his watch. "We'll be in position in an hour. Let us know if anything changes."

"You got it, boss," Landersmann said.

Skelly bit into an energy bar and took a swig of water. "The rest of you mutts, saddle up. We're taking a walk."

The terrain in this part of Ukraine was gently rolling hills, a patchwork of plowed fields separated by trees and shrubbery. As he moved, Skelly's blood sang in his ears. It was an easy march. Just enough to break a sweat, but not enough to tire him out.

From a prone position two hundred meters from their target, Skelly slipped on a pair of Invader glasses. Using the eyescan feature, he navigated to the aerial view.

The Wagner camp was quiet. His team showed up as blue figures. They enveloped the enemy camp in a L-shape. Using only eye movement, he assigned the Wagner guards to his Sentinel snipers, then blinked back to battle view.

"On the net," he said into his throat mic, "this is Papa Bear. How's our ordnance package?"

"Raptors are on station," Landersmann replied.

"Copy that," Skelly said. "All stations, stand by to engage. Landie, jam the space and bring the heat."

He could hear the crooked smile in Landersmann's voice. "Order up in three...two...one."

The Gremlin drones turned on their jammers, just in case someone in the Wagner camp happened to be on the radio or mobile phone.

"Bombs away," Landersmann called on the net.

Skelly closed his eyes and ducked his head as an explosion shattered the spring night. Two StormBreaker precision-guided glide bombs, launched from a pair of stealth Sentinel

Raptor drones orbiting at fifteen thousand feet above them, had found their marks.

Skelly scrambled to his feet and charged toward the target. The Invader glasses separated hostiles and friendlies on the field of battle. From his right, a figure outlined in blue ran on a parallel course. Fifty meters ahead, a form in red raised a weapon. Skelly's SCAR snapped up, and he fired a three-round burst.

The Sentinel team was deadly efficient. By the time they had breached the camp perimeter, the fight was over. Skelly surveyed the bomb-shattered ground where the Wagner tents had stood only a few minutes ago.

He saw one of the bodies twitch. Skelly raised his weapon and put a bullet into the bloody face of the gravely injured man.

"Take no prisoners," he said, pumping a fist in the air. He watched with satisfaction as two of his team fired rounds into the remaining bodies.

He stooped and searched the pockets of the man he'd just shot. He found a worn silver lighter with a hammer-and-sickle engraving. Skelly stripped a watch off the dead man's wrist. He tossed it to Zap.

"Finders keepers," Skelly said.

Zap made no attempt to grab the purloined watch. It bounced off his body armor and fell to the ground. "I'll pass," he said.

Skelly found a packet of Russian cigarettes in the dead man's vest pocket. "Your loss."

Zap walked away.

"Asshole," Skelly said as he lit a cigarette.

9

Zelenkivka, Ukraine

A line of idling tanks blocked the narrow road. Dark green and belching diesel exhaust, the deadly Russian T-14 Armata battle tanks looked brand new to Pavel. Early morning fog softened the geometric lines of the armored vehicles.

His driver lowered his window and shouted a question at the tank commander dangling his feet off the edge of the turret. The enlisted man shrugged back at them.

"Go around them, you idiot," Pavel barked at his driver.

The man wrenched the wheel of the black Land Rover to the right and hit the gas. The bottom of the vehicle scraped as they bumped through the ditch on the side of the road. The adjacent field was plowed, and the tires spun out rich, black dirt.

The Ukraine, Pavel thought, the breadbasket of Europe. He came from a long line of Russian farmers, and he could tell the richness of the soil just by the smell.

They climbed the shallow rise, and Pavel put all thoughts of his agricultural heritage aside.

The Wagner FOB had been set up just to the north of the lane, in a grove of oak trees. What had been an orderly campsite was a pair of bomb craters.

"Stop." Pavel opened his door without waiting for an answer. His boot sank into the loamy soil. Behind him, he heard the three following Land Rovers stop and car doors slam. He kept walking.

A portly man dressed in the forest-green field uniform of a two-star general waited for him.

"Captain Kozlov," he began.

"I haven't been a captain in ten years," Pavel snapped. "Kozlov will do."

He saw the man's eye stray to the line of late-model Land Rovers and the rest of Pavel's crew. There was no love lost between the Wagner Group and the regular Russian Army, but he had no time or patience for dick-measuring contests. Not today.

"Who found them?" Kozlov asked.

"The vanguard unit arrived at zero five hundred," the general replied. "This is what we found." He pointed to a green tarp covering long shapes that could only be corpses. "We gathered your dead—the ones we could find—and covered them."

Pavel felt a strange rush of gratitude toward this priggish little man. "How many?"

"We found eight," the general said, "and some parts..." His voice trailed off.

Eight, Pavel thought. I had eighteen people here. He turned to the officer.

"Thank you, General," Pavel said. "I'll take it from here. You can detour around the site and continue on to your next objective."

"But we were supposed to get a briefing," the general

protested. "All of our intel is being supplied by Wagner. Our movements controlled by you. I need to report this to—"

"You will not report this incident to anyone," Pavel said. "I will report this to Moscow." He called to his men. "Anton, set up a satellite link with headquarters for the general and get him whatever intel he needs. The rest of you, with me."

Pavel stalked off without acknowledging the general. He paused at the edge of the first bomb crater, waited for his team to gather around him.

"Assign two men to dig a grave," he said to his driver. "Have the rest search the area for any remains."

His men knew to leave him alone. Pavel walked the perimeter of the bomb crater. The smell was a mixture of ruptured earth and burnt cloth. A scrap of shattered electronics crunched under his boot.

Artillery? He dismissed the idea. It was preposterous that a Ukrainian artillery unit could get into range, launch two rounds with pinpoint accuracy, and get away without being detected.

A precision aerial strike, then. He considered the size of the crater. Whatever had done this was on the smaller side. A fifty-kilogram warhead, maybe less. Ukrainian aircraft would be carrying much larger ordnance. Anyway, there had been no sign of enemy air activity in the region overnight.

Process of elimination left a UAV attack as the most likely option. Was it possible the Ukrainians had access to high-end armed drones?

He glared at the hole in the ground. Something still didn't add up. The most common armament for a military drone was a Hellfire missile, and this crater was too small for a nine-kilogram warhead. Besides, Hellfire missiles made a spectacular light show when launched. Someone would have seen something. The more likely scenario was a standoff weapon, something with a long glide path.

"Boss," his driver called from the other side of the crater. "You need to see this."

Still lost in thought, Pavel made his way to the green tarp covering the bodies of his Wagner team. "What is it?" he asked in a sharper tone than he intended.

The man did not answer, he just pointed. The tarp had been thrown back, uncovering the faces of the dead men. It took Pavel a second to realize what he was supposed to see.

There was a bullet hole in the forehead of each man. Kill shots, Pavel thought. Some inflicted post-mortem.

"They're all like that," the driver said.

The Ukrainians hated the Russians, maybe even enough to mutilate the bodies of their enemies after death. But the Wagner team was not Russian military. He found it hard to believe a military unit would do something like this to a civilian outfit.

The pieces started to fit together in his mind. A drone attack on a Wagner camp. His team had probably been jammed before the attack so there was no way to get out a distress call. The survivors of the bombing executed with extreme prejudice.

CIA, Pavel thought. It had to be a covert CIA operation. The Chef needed to hear about this immediately. This changed everything.

"Split up," Pavel ordered. "First two cars head back to base. The rest finish the burial and join us ASAP."

"Do you want to say something over the bodies?" one of the crew asked.

"No," Pavel said, "I don't. You get a paycheck from me, not a prayer."

Pavel stalked back to the lead Land Rover and slid into the

passenger seat. In truth, he felt a twinge of regret about leaving his people like that, but if he was right, they had bigger problems than a shitty burial service.

The driver started the vehicle and spun the car in a one-eighty. They passed the column of tanks with their crews lounging topside in the thin morning sun. The traffic backup had been extended with a dozen armored personnel carriers. His driver got them back on the road and hit the gas, heading south to the Wagner base outside of Krasnohrad.

Although it was just him and the driver in the car, Pavel wanted to wait until they got back to base before he called The Chef. He needed time to think.

His mobile phone rang with an incoming video call.

Or maybe not, Pavel thought. The general had probably already called back to Moscow by the time Pavel had arrived. He cut a glance at his driver. "You hear nothing."

The man stuck an index finger in his ear as if he was rooting for earwax. "What?" he replied.

Pavel took a deep breath and answered the call.

The Chef's thin face filled the screen. He had a prominent nose, like an axe blade projecting out of his long face. His thin dark hair was normally gelled back gangster-style, but at this early hour it was messy and a thick strand of hair crossed his line of vision.

"What the fuck, Pavel?" The Chef snarled.

"Good morning to you, boss," Pavel replied. No one who worked for The Chef ever dared to call him that to his face. The man might look and even act effeminate, but Pavel had never seen a more cold-blooded killer than Yuri Plotnikov. There were rumors that as a KGB agent he would carve up interrogation subjects like cuts of meat—while the subject was still alive. Pavel believed those stories.

As a boss, The Chef was generous with the finances and

kept his hands off the field operations. Everything Pavel wanted—except when things didn't go as planned.

"How bad is it?" The Chef demanded.

"Bad," Pavel admitted. He laid out the facts of the case. The surprise aerial bombardment, probably by a drone, the brutality of the ground assault. The Chef's nostrils flared when Pavel told him he suspected CIA involvement.

"Serrano doesn't have the balls," The Chef declared. "If word leaked to the press that the CIA was operating in the Ukraine, they'd skin him alive. No, this is Ukrainian commandos."

Pavel opened his mouth to say that explanation did not account for the drone attack, but The Chef wasn't done yet.

"This is on you," the boss continued. "They know Wagner's involved because you got sloppy, Pavel, and we're all paying the price. I told you, you need to think more strategically."

So that's how he was going to spin this thing for Luchnik, Pavel thought. Blame the guy on the front line. Typical asshole move by an armchair general.

As they approached the outer perimeter of the Wagner HQ, the driver gave a mock salute to one of his buddies on guard duty. Pavel decided to try again.

"Boss, that doesn't add up..." Pavel paused as the connection glitched. "Piece of shit," he muttered as he lost all signal on his phone.

"My phone's out, too," his driver said.

Pavel glared out the window, still steaming mad that the boss was going to blame this whole thing on him. Getting on The Chef's bad side was bad enough, but Luchnik...

Pavel paused. He'd been using the same phone in the Ukraine for the last month, a secure satellite phone. He'd never lost a call before, not even once.

The driver slowed as they approached the makeshift guardhouse.

There was no reason for him to lose a signal...unless he was being jammed.

"Turn around!" Pavel shouted.

To his credit, the driver did not hesitate. He whipped the wheel around and hit the accelerator. Dirt spun out from the tires, spraying the guard.

Pavel saw the first missile strike the compound just as their vehicle was broadside to the gate.

The shock wave picked up the Land Rover and flung it back the way they had come.

10

Black Sea, Russia

The bar at the large outdoor pool was modelled after a Spanish villa: red tile roof, heavy stucco base, marble countertops, heavy wooden stools. On paper, the magnificent estate was owned by a prominent Russian businessman, but he never visited and frequently offered the property to his close friend, Vitaly Luchnik. So often, in fact, that Luchnik's detractors derisively referred to the property as the "Presidential Palace."

The weather on the Black Sea this afternoon was unseasonably warm, almost 32 degrees Celsius, forcing Vladimir Federov to take shade in the corner of the bar as far away from the poolside revelry as possible. He sipped a seltzer water on ice with a twist of lime, not because he was thirsty, but because he wanted those around him to assume his drink was a gin and tonic. In a further attempt to blend in, he wore a pair of black swim trunks and dark sunglasses. His bare chest was sleek and hairless, not fat, but also lacking in muscle definition. When he viewed himself in the bar mirror, it reminded him of an albino sausage.

From this vantage point at the corner of the bar, behind his dark glasses, he had two viewing choices. He could look beyond the edge of the infinity pool to the Black Sea and the lowering sun. The scene was utterly peaceful, largely because the water and airspace around the palace were designated as secure areas when the President was in residence.

He lowered his gaze to the poolside. Or he could watch the elite of Russia's political machine act like children on amphetamines. Minister of Defense Yakov, clad only in a neon-green Speedo that was mostly obscured by the overhang of his hairy belly, had a woman on either arm.

Girls, more accurately, Federov noted. They were both blond, with identical hairstyles and matching boob jobs. They both had wintry blue eyes, perfect teeth, and cheekbones that could cut glass. They even held their champagne glasses the same way.

A matching set, that was Yakov's fantasy, Federov knew. He knew the desires of most of the men around him—that was his job, after all.

Yakov buried his face in the bosom of one of the women, and she laughed uproariously, as if on cue. Her twin slapped Yakov playfully on the arm and thrust her chest out. "Now do me," she cried.

Yakov obliged. Federov looked away.

Prime Minister Mishinov, derisively called "Little Mishi" for his unstinting support of President Luchnik, was dressed in board shorts and a white linen shirt. He sat on a lounge chair engaged in deep conversation with a raven-haired beauty whose impossibly long legs stretched across the gap between the two chaise lounges. She had a glass of white wine and nodded intently as Mishinov spoke. Little Mishi, Federov knew, enjoyed intellectual foreplay.

The poolside venue served as the holding area for those members of Luchnik's cabinet who had finished their interview with the boss. Luchnik's annual "Board Meeting," as he liked to call it, was when he dispensed the spoils of the prior year's illicit business dealings. One by one, each member of the cabinet was summoned to Luchnik's office and asked to justify his continued service to the most powerful man in the Russian Federation. Although it had been scheduled for months, this year the Board Meeting was taking place only a few weeks after the still-unfolding Ukraine incident. In the world of Vitaly Luchnik, there were no coincidences.

Contrary to the updates Federov delivered daily to the state-controlled news outlets, the war in the Ukraine was not going well. What had been envisioned as a simple takedown of a weakened neighbor had turned into a hard slog. The Russian forces had made some gains in the south, but in the east, they had gained no more than a few kilometers out of the contested Donbas region. The news around Kiev was even worse. The Russian advance on the city had ground to a halt. Instead of pictures of Russian tanks riding through the Maidan in victory, those tanks were arranged in a semicircular perimeter around the capital city of Ukraine.

The Ukrainian military, reinforced by weapons and intelligence from NATO countries, were fierce fighters, but the cause of the delay ran deeper than that. In Federov's analysis, the Wagner Group had not lived up to their reputation for results on the battlefield. His suspicions were only deepened by the fact that Yuri Plotnikov, The Chef, was not in attendance at the Black Sea extravaganza.

During Federov's own meeting with Luchnik, the leader

that he had served for a quarter century seemed preoccupied. That unsettled Federov. Vitaly Luchnik was a great man, a man who had faced adversity throughout his career. The Ukraine situation was a major event, but not unprecedented for the Russian President by any means.

It was not what was said or done in the meeting that bothered him. In fact, Luchnik had been fulsome in his praise of Federov's support and generous to a fault. Judging by the rapidly escalating antics poolside, he had treated others in his cabinet the same way.

Undoubtedly, they had all received another luxury property in Miami Beach or London or Madrid, or perhaps an oil field. The latest money-laundering gambit was art. Paintings or sculptures were purchased and stored in climate-controlled, tax-free warehouses adjacent to a major airport. Federov himself had three masterpieces in storage outside Singapore's Changi Airport. They would never be enjoyed by art afficionados; they were just a holding place for money. He had never seen the paintings, only the statement that showed their increasing value, which he used to secure loans of clean money in whatever currency he needed.

Federov swirled the ice in his glass. Long ago, he'd resigned himself to the fact that he was different than the rest of the men in Luchnik's orbit. Not better, not worse, but different.

He cared not for things. He'd lived in the same apartment in Moscow for the last twenty years. Two bedrooms, a sitting room, and a nice kitchen was all he needed. He'd had the same cleaning woman for the entire period, and she was perfectly adequate. His home was close enough to the Kremlin that he could walk to work if he wanted to, although he rarely did.

He'd realized in his teens that he was a man with no sexual

appetite. It wasn't that he had unfulfilled desires of a perverse nature; he simply did not want or need sexual intimacy. He had occasionally taken women to bed because it was expected of him, but it was a business necessity, not a primal urge. In those rare times when he was able to access unmonitored internet connections, he had discovered that asexuality was not uncommon.

A shout drew Federov's attention. The blond twins had pushed a drunken Yakov into the pool, and he was vowing revenge. The girls shrieked in unison, dancing away from his grasping paws.

The sight made him smile grimly. The level of debauchery was increasing by the minute, and it was only late afternoon. There would be a lavish feast later, then some sort of game. Luchnik loved his games, and he always won.

That was what drove Federov's boss. Winning.

Luchnik had come of age during the zenith of the Soviet Union. He lived and breathed the glory of being respected as a world superpower. He had joined the KGB to further that dream—and then had seen his country fall into chaos.

Lesser men faded into obscurity. Luchnik fought back using the tools of his enemies—money and influence—to rebuild his beloved country. The fact that he became a billionaire robber baron along the way was just a side benefit.

Back at the pool, Yakov managed to snag one of the twins and drag her into the water. Federov made a signal to the bartender to cut off Yakov. At this rate, the Defense Minister would be passed out by dinnertime.

As Luchnik's primary confidant on his rise to power, Federov had more than enough dirt on every man here to twist his life inside out. All ready and waiting for when he needed it.

Now, as a man who studied the inner desires of the men around him, Federov turned that same analysis on himself.

Power, Federov knew, was his motivation, his secret need. He wanted to own people, but not in the same way as Luchnik. He was the id to the President's ego.

Luchnik wanted puppets to do his bidding. Federov wanted to guide his country to a better future. Of course, under Luchnik, the looting of Russia by oligarchs was bad for his country, but in Federov's view, the alternative was worse.

On balance, Luchnik's intentions were good. After decades of economic struggle and international obscurity, he was restoring Russia to its former glory and, in doing so, honoring the Russian people. Through shrewdness, skill, and nerves of titanium, he had dragged his country into the twenty-first century as a world power, a force to be reckoned with. Luchnik played a very weak hand, but he played with the skill of the best poker player in the world, and he'd succeeded beyond what should have been possible.

No other man could have done that, Federov believed that with all his heart. For twenty-five years, he had supported his president without question and been treated as his closest ally. But now...

Federov did his best to examine his feelings objectively. Like all relationships, his time with the President had not been without incident. They had disagreed but always managed to come back together. But the addition of The Chef to Luchnik's orbit felt different. The paramilitary organization had been called into action before, but always at arm's length. More importantly, even Federov's considerable intelligence resources had been unable to plumb the depths of the Wagner Group's involvement in the Ukraine.

"Drinking alone again, Vladimir?" a voice said over his shoulder.

Federov startled, rattled that he had been so lost in thought he had not seen Nikolay Sokolov approach from an oblique angle. When he turned, he noticed Kulukov walking away. Unlike the rest of the ministers, Kulukov was clad in a business suit. Although Federov had his own people on the staff of the seaside villa, the Rosgvardiya had responsibility for overall security and Luchnik's personal safety. The lack of control annoyed Federov more than it should have.

"They say drinking alone is a warning sign." Nikolay took the adjacent bar stool. "I will save you from that fate." He pointed to a bottle of Beluga Gold vodka and held up two fingers. The bartender brought two glasses and the bottle.

Federov nodded at Kulukov's back. "Watch the company you keep, Nikolay. You don't want to be associated with the cult."

"You're just jealous, Vladimir." The younger man laughed as he poured two drinks. "Kulukov and I went to school together. You should get to know him. He's not a bad sort."

Federov turned his dark glasses on the President's nephew. Was that an offer? he wondered.

"I'd appreciate that," Federov said.

Luchnik's nephew was at least a decade younger than most of the men surrounding the pool. He wore khaki trousers, which barely clung to his slim hips, no shoes, and no shirt. He leaned back against the bar, his well-muscled upper body on full display, his eyes masked by sunglasses.

"Disgusting," Nikolay said.

Federov did not reply.

"How was your meeting with the boss?" Nikolay asked. "What did you get this time, another apartment in Miami Beach or a small Caribbean island?" His tone was playful, but Federov detected a bite under the light words.

"To another condo I will never set foot in." Federov tossed back the drink with a snap of his wrist.

"To another painting that will never be seen," Nikolay responded and downed his own shot.

Federov refilled their glasses. "It's just money, Nikolay."

"Exactly." The response was heated. "It's just money. It's just things."

Nikolay picked up his shot. "Drink with me."

Federov clocked a glance at the bartender, and the man moved a few paces further away. The two men clinked glasses and drank again.

"What do you make of this Ukraine business?" Nikolay asked as Federov refilled the glasses.

"An opportunity," Federov deflected.

"And what do you make of Yuri's involvement?" Nikolay asked.

Federov downed his drink. The liquid burned his throat, and he felt the warm glow spread in his empty belly. But the sense of unease that had dogged him for weeks would not go away.

"The Chef troubles me," Federov said. He removed his sunglasses and looked at Nikolay. "And what do you think of the Ukraine?"

Nikolay traced a wet circle on the marble bar with his glass. "It troubles me as well, my friend." He removed his glasses and met Federov's gaze.

"I think I should be back in Moscow, close to my uncle," Nikolay continued, "I believe I could be useful to him in these uncertain times."

So that was his angle, Federov thought. The young lion is renewing his push to come back to Moscow. Federov felt himself relax.

"You must trust your uncle." He placed his hand on Nikolay's shoulder and felt the solid toned muscle beneath his palm. "His only wish is for a strong Russia."

They clinked glasses and drank again.

But the vodka that landed in Federov's stomach had gone sour. For a man who dealt in lies for a living, he wondered if he'd just dealt one too many.

11

Russian Forces Headquarters
Valky, Ukraine

The last time Pavel had seen Maxim Khordovsky was in Syria, more than ten years ago. Pavel remembered the furnace that was Damascus in summer, where the streets smelled of hot asphalt and dust clung to the back of his throat.

The military police escort had told Pavel that while he was not under arrest, Colonel Khordovsky had made it very clear that Captain Kozlov's expeditious presence at the presidential palace was not optional. Apart from the fact that the building was faced with white marble and there was a huge gushing fountain in the center of the circular driveway, Pavel remembered little of the palace itself. He recalled that it felt more like a mausoleum than a place where people lived, but he chalked that feeling up to his nerves at the time.

Pavel had been relieved of his duties as commander of a Russian infantry company while the "incident" was investigated. The battalion commander assured Pavel that he would be cleared in short order, but that was before the armed escort arrived to bring him to the palace.

Pavel's company had wiped out a platoon of Syrian recruits. An accident, an unfortunate friendly fire incident, his report had read. As they marched through the cavernous Syrian presidential palace, Pavel's mouth was so dry he couldn't swallow.

The escorts left him in front of a set of three-meter-high carved wooden doors. Pulse racing like a bunny on the butcher's block, Pavel stepped inside.

It was a large office. At one end a heavy wooden desk, scattered with papers and an open laptop computer. A muted flat-screen television hung on the wall. At the other end of the room was a sitting area and fireplace where two men were taking coffee.

They rose when Pavel entered. Pavel marched to Colonel Khordovsky, saluted, and announced himself. The colonel returned the salute but let Pavel remain at attention.

"This is him?" the other man said. Bashar al-Assad was tall and thin, with a dark toothbrush mustache. His skin was sallow.

"Yes, Your Excellency," replied the colonel.

Khordovsky was a head shorter than Assad. He had skin like saddle leather and a jutting jaw. His quick gaze followed the leader of Syria as the man stalked around Pavel.

"This man is a killer," Assad said in very good Russian. "He is a murderer."

Pavel thought that label was a little rich coming from the guy that Western newspapers called "The Butcher," but he was so terrified that he probably couldn't have formed words even if he'd wanted to.

"It was a strategic error, Your Excellency," Khordovsky

replied smoothly. "A miscommunication in the field that led to a tragic mistake."

Assad approached Pavel from behind and whispered in his ear. "I will have you shot. I will broadcast the whole thing on television."

Khordovsky cleared his throat. "Your Excellency, I cannot support that course of action. Captain Kozlov is an exemplary officer. Indispensable. If I were to lose him, the entire campaign in the Idlib region would be compromised."

"I find it hard to believe that the Russian Army depends on one lowly captain," Assad replied.

"I assure you that even a lowly captain in the Russian Army has a vital role in our support of your civil war, sir," Khordovsky said.

The room sang with tension. Pavel's asshole clenched, and he thought he might piss himself. He'd seen firsthand what Assad's men did to their prisoners—before they killed them.

"No matter what this man has or has not done," Khordovsky said, "if you were to execute him, it would not be viewed favorably in Moscow. It is possible that you might lose your military advisers. Ever since Douma, I have had my doubts, Your Excellency."

Douma, Pavel thought, the chemical weapons attack. The colonel is blackmailing Bashar al-Assad—to save my ass.

Assad turned his back, waving his hand in a dismissive gesture as he stalked away.

Khordovsky wheeled on Pavel. "Get the fuck out of here, you stupid piece of shit," he said through clenched teeth. "Now."

Six hours later, Pavel was on a military transport back to Russia. Less than a year later, thrown out of the Russian Army, he was working for the Wagner Group back in Syria.

Now, as his Land Rover approached the town of Valky,

Pavel wondered if Khordovsky would remember him. He touched the fresh cut on his forehead, a reminder of the attack on the Wagner base at Krasnohrad.

The Chef was in a rage. The progress of the Russian military invasion of the Ukraine depended on Wagner, and Wagner was under attack by an unknown enemy.

Pavel stared out at the darkened countryside as he replayed the call in his head.

"You are making me look bad in front of the boss," The Chef screamed. He tended to shriek when he yelled.

"We've lost thirty-eight men in two days," Pavel said. "It's the CIA. I know it."

"No, *you* lost thirty-eight men, Pavel," The Chef said. "And I don't care who's behind it. Pull your head out of your ass, hire more, and get the job done."

He hung up.

It was after that phone call that Pavel decided to visit the Commander of the Western Military District.

The trip was a drive of more than fifty kilometers away from the Wagner FOBs. Valky was located barely thirty miles from the Russian border, on the edge of the still-contested Donbas region of the Ukraine. Colonel General Khordovsky had chosen to set up his command post in close proximity to the largest Russian military fuel depot inside the Ukraine.

The transition from farmland to town was swift. The settlement was under a curfew, so the Land Rover didn't even need to slow down. Headlights passed over a row of shabby, one-story brick houses, then a grocery store, and a post office.

"The CP is on the other side of the bridge." Even as the driver spoke, the car was already climbing up the steel structure. The only lights visible on the horizon were a glow about a kilometer to the east. The fuel depot, he thought.

The command post for Colonel General Khordovsky was

set up on the cracked, potholed parking lot of the local movie theater. The Land Rover bounced to a halt next to a long trailer painted in green camouflage.

As Pavel opened his door, a uniformed MP trotted up. "You can't park here, sir."

Pavel ignored him. "Wait here," he said to his driver. "I don't know how long this will take."

"Sir—" the MP began.

"I'm here to see General Khordovsky," Pavel interrupted him. "Tell him Pavel Kozlov is here." He followed the MP to the rear of the trailer and up the stairs. The anteroom of the trailer was bathed in red light. A team of four technicians, hunched over computer screens, muttered into headsets. The interior of the command post was unexpectedly dry after the damp night air.

"This way, sir," the MP said.

Pavel followed him through two sets of blackout curtains into a brightly lit meeting room. He squinted in the glare, just able to make out five men standing around a table.

"Captain Kozlov," said a gravelly voice. "Of all the Pavel Kozlovs in Russia, I sincerely hoped that it was not you."

"It's good to see you again, Colonel General," Pavel replied. "Congratulations on your promotion."

Pavel's eyes adjusted to the light, and he studied the man who approached him. Maxim Khordovsky seemed not to have aged a day since his time in Syria. The same leathery hide, the granite chin, the darting eyes.

Neither man offered to shake hands.

"You were a disgrace to the uniform, Kozlov," Khordovsky said, "but somehow now you've made it worse. Fucking Wagner." He looked like he wanted to spit.

"It's a living," Pavel said, then paused. "I need to brief you on an issue, General. It's urgent."

Khordovsky turned to his staff and waved his hand for them to clear the room. Pavel noticed he favored his right leg as he made his way back to the table. Maybe the invincible general was human after all.

"You've put me behind schedule," Khordovsky said. "I've requested that Moscow allow me to advance without the help of the Wagner Group. We are perfectly capable of conducting our own reconnaissance."

No wonder The Chef was so angry, Pavel thought.

"I don't think that's a good idea, sir," Pavel said.

"Of course you don't. You're getting paid by the hour."

"I think we're dealing with more than one enemy," Pavel pressed.

Khordovsky leaned over the detailed map of the Ukraine projected on the horizontal computer screen. Pavel saw the ragged red line representing the front between the Ukrainian and Russian militaries. A fainter yellow line, located much closer to the Dnieper River, marked where the front should have been.

"Excuses," Khordovsky snarled.

"We have a problem, General," Pavel said. Without waiting for permission, he launched into his theory about a group of CIA operatives attacking Wagner forces in the vanguard.

"I'm supposed to be in Kiev by Friday," Khordovsky said, a flush of red creeping up his neck, "and you come in here with this bullshit about the CIA? A more likely explanation is that Ukrainian commandos are kicking the shit out of your undisciplined mercenaries."

Pavel's own anger rode just under the surface. The cut on his forehead throbbed. What had happened between them in the past was history. He was in charge now, not Khordovsky, and this bastard was going to listen if it was the last thing Pavel did.

But the general wasn't done. "You get paid big money for a few days of work in the field, but we both know we only hold this land if we occupy it, put troops in place. That's called strategy, Pavel. If I recall, not your strong suit."

Pavel's anger erupted. He slammed his fist on the table, but before he could speak, there was a noise outside. A dull thump, like someone had tipped over an oil drum in the parking lot. Or the sound of distant artillery fire.

Khordovsky raised his voice. "What was that?"

One of the staff officers came through the blackout curtain. "We're investigating, General. It might be—"

A tremendous explosion sounded in the distance. Pavel felt the trailer tip up on one set of tires, then drop again. The heavy vehicle rocked on the suspension.

A shock wave, thought Pavel. He followed Khordovsky out of the trailer into the damp night.

In the east, an orange fireball erupted over the treetops.

"It's the fuel depot," the general shouted. "Get my car."

Pavel's Land Rover was parked two meters away, still running.

"With me, General," he said, seizing Khordovsky's beefy arm.

They piled into the back seat. Gravel pinged against the underside of the car as the driver accelerated into a turn. They were going seventy kilometers per hour by the time they reached the road, and the driver floored it on the straightaway.

Through the tree line, the sky was bright as day, dancing with light from the burning fuel.

"The fuel depot is in a construction yard," Khordovsky was saying. "Fenced, guarded, anti-aircraft defenses...there's no way."

Out of the corner of his eye, Pavel thought he saw a

pinpoint of light over the trees. Then he saw two, both moving fast. He spun in his seat to keep them in sight.

"Drones!" he yelled. "Stop the car!"

The driver slammed on the brakes, and Pavel's face smashed against the seat in front of him. The cut above his eye reopened, warm blood ran down his face. He wrenched open the door and rolled into the ditch next to the road.

A streak of light lanced down from somewhere above them, and the Land Rover exploded. Pavel buried his face in the mud of the ditch, arms over the back of his head. The blast swept over his prone form, pounding him deeper into the dirt.

He forced himself to his hands and knees, ears ringing, limbs trembling.

The Land Rover was a burning chassis. Pieces of flaming shrapnel littered the road. Pavel took a step forward, his knees buckling. He tried to call out the driver's name, but his voice didn't seem to be working.

He made his way around the wreckage to the other side of the road. There was a ditch on that side as well, but it was empty. Where was the general?

Pavel scanned up and down the road, then into the trees. He raised his gaze, and then he saw Khordovsky. The general's body was not really in the tree, Pavel thought. He was now part of the tree. The force of the blast had stripped the uniform jacket from the body, and a shattered tree branch projected from his torso. He was spread-eagled, like a butterfly pinned in an exhibition.

A flash of movement down the road caught Pavel's attention. It was beyond the reach of the light from the burning Land Rover. Had his driver somehow survived? Pavel took a step in that direction, then froze.

A roaring noise like a jet engine reached his injured ears.

A drone, he thought. Back to finish the job.

He wheeled like a drunken man and threw himself back into the ditch just as the speeding object passed over the remains of the Land Rover.

Pavel stared up, mouth agape. His mind refused to process what he was seeing.

The object was moving fast, at least a hundred kilometers an hour, barely thirty feet above the road.

A man in a jet pack. He wore goggles, a jumpsuit, helmet, and a broad smile.

12

Oleksandriya, Ukraine

Manson Skelly stepped out of the shower and ran a towel across his back. There was no vent fan in the tiny bathroom, so he pushed open the door to let some air in. He wadded up the towel, wiped off the mirror over the sink, and tossed the used towel into the sickly yellow bathtub-shower combo.

His beard was thick, and he needed a haircut. He touched the bolts of silver that had grown in on either side of his chin. He was sure that the last time he'd grown out his beard, that gray wasn't there.

He ran his fingers over the quarter-sized, puckered scar on his left shoulder. That had happened the same day that Joe Cromwell had been killed.

What would Joe think of Sentinel today? Skelly wondered. Would he side with his wife or his best friend? Among the three of them, Joe was always the peacemaker, the one who found the middle road.

Skelly turned in three-quarter profile to the mirror to assess the diagonal bruise that striped his right side. He reached for a tube of Tiger Balm and gingerly spread the anal-gesic ointment on the wound.

I'm lucky the straps on the jet pack didn't crack a rib, he thought, then smiled. But, damn, that was fun.

Still grinning, he washed his hands carefully to make sure the heating balm didn't end up somewhere he didn't mean for it to go.

Strictly speaking, the jet pack had been an operational flourish that was maybe a little over the top, but he justified it to himself as a way to test a piece of Sentinel high-end hard-ware in actual combat conditions.

And it had worked like a charm. Manson winced as he felt the burn of the Tiger Balm on his bruised body. Okay, maybe not perfect, but much better than the prototype version they had bought from the Royal Navy.

He slung his shaving kit over his shoulder and strode naked into the tiny apartment. His skin rippled with goose-flesh in the chill air.

This was a fucking depressing country, Skelly decided. The flat could be generously described as a studio. Kitch-enette, bedroom, and bathroom. Painted cinder block walls and single-pane windows. But it had hot water and a lumpy mattress. He'd slept in worse places in his career.

Besides, he wasn't here for the accommodations. He was here to kick some ass and make some money. So far, he was accomplishing that in spades.

Skelly's phone pulsed with an incoming text.

Call me ASAP, Abby wrote.

Fat chance, he thought. If he ran every operational deci-sion by Abby, the fuel depot job never would have happened. Too risky, she would say. Not within operational parameters.

Screw that, Skelly thought. She might rule the roost at headquarters, but the field was his domain.

Taking out the Russian fuel depot was a masterpiece of operational theater. Skelly and four men conducted a HAHO drop thirty kilometers away and just drifted to their target. Located fifty kilometers behind the front lines of the conflict, the construction yard that housed the fuel depot had piss-poor perimeter security. It was a simple task for his team to infiltrate the field full of fuel tankers and set charges.

But the coup de grace, the crowning moment of the night, was the getaway by jet pack. The team flew to an extraction point five kilometers away from the scene of the crime where a Sentinel stealth helo waited for them.

He looked at his phone again. Abby should be thanking him for his initiative.

Thank you, Skelly, for all your brilliant efforts to make the world safe for democracy. High impact, zero casualties. A magnificent operation. Skelly winced as he pulled his shirt over his head. Okay, maybe a few bruises.

He finished dressing in jeans and a fleece pullover. Then he crammed a ball cap on his still-wet hair and left the room. He took the stairs down to the lobby because he wasn't sure the Soviet-era elevator would make the three flights.

Three women waited in the tired foyer. One of them got up from the tattered sofa and approached. Despite the coolness in the unheated lobby, she wore short-shorts and a crop top. Her bleach-blond hair was pulled into pigtails. She might have been sixteen, Skelly figured.

She took his arm possessively and said something in Russian.

"No sprecken the frances," Skelly replied, brushing her hand from his arm. "Maybe later, after I get a tetanus shot."

He touched the brim of his cap and gave her a winning smile. She pouted at him as he pushed through the glass door into weak sunlight.

Yikes, Skelly thought. He knew Landersmann was doing his best with logistics, but he really needed to up his game on the ancillary services for the Sentinel troops.

It was early morning, and like most days since Skelly had been in this godforsaken country, the weather alternated between overcast and partly cloudy. The sun was a pale disk of silver behind a mask of thin clouds, offering light but no heat to the land. He got behind the wheel of a Land Rover and turned the heater on high for the ten-minute drive to the Sentinel command post.

In the weeks since Sentinel had begun operations in Ukraine, the warehouse had grown from shoestring outpost to a full-fledged command post. The ops center was staffed around the clock with a team of six techs who monitored every possible intel source and fed everything back to Mama in Sterling. Oleksandriya was located west of the Dnieper, so Skelly had ordered three forward operating bases be set up inside the combat zone so they could act quickly on emerging intelligence.

Back in Virginia, Mama was eating up every bit of intelligence available on the internet. Every tweet, social media post, or video about the situation in Ukraine was crunched through her algorithms to look for vulnerabilities in the Russian invasion forces, with a special eye for Wagner Group operations. It was stunning how much open source data was available if you just had the computing power to process it.

Mama regularly passed to Skelly a list of potential operations, always within the strict boundaries of the rules of engagement.

Mama was useful for logistical details and damage estimates, but Skelly liked to pick his own targets. He knew how to hurt the enemy.

One of the techs looked up from his workstation long

enough to toss Skelly a secure tablet. He opened it with facial recognition and scanned the message traffic.

"Abby called for you twice already," the tech reported.

Skelly ignored the information. "What about the three guys who went missing on the mission to Derzhanivka yesterday?" he asked instead.

"Confirmed dead," came the reply.

Skelly cursed to himself. Abby would put that on him, he was sure. Sentinel had almost four hundred staff in country now, so losing a few people was going to happen eventually. They all knew what they'd signed up for, Skelly thought, and no one hesitated to cash their checks.

"Any reaction from Wagner?" he asked.

"Nothing unusual so far," the tech replied. "If Mama picks up on something, I'll let you know."

"Where's Landie?" Skelly asked.

"Mission planning."

Skelly headed for the coffeepot, musing as he fixed himself a blond and sweet. Sentinel had run fifteen missions inside Ukraine, including the fuel depot bombing. Was it possible that Wagner hadn't figured out who they were dealing with yet?

While Sentinel had the element of surprise and superior technology on their side, the Wagner Group mercenaries had good old-fashioned brutality and numbers on theirs. Skelly had seen their handiwork in Syria firsthand, and it was impressive in its thoroughness. Wagner did not simply kill people, they destroyed their target—buildings, people, animals...everything. He doubted if they even knew what the words *collateral damage* meant. Entire villages wiped off the map because Wagner suspected they *might* be hiding terrorists.

Wagner didn't come by their tactics by accident. He'd read

a translated Russian Army field manual covering the topic of "counter-irregular warfare," which put into words just how far the Russian military was willing to go to put down resistance. Wagner had built on that brutal foundation.

He had no doubt the Russians were punishing the locals for actions Sentinel had carried out against Wagner.

Oh, well, he thought. Wrong place, wrong time.

Skelly knew their holiday wouldn't last long. Once Wagner woke up to the fact that they were dealing with another PMC, then his team would have a real fight on their hands. A bare-knuckles, no-rules, street-brawl throwdown.

He sipped the sweet hot coffee. Truth be told, he was kinda looking forward to that.

Skelly pushed through the door marked Mission Planning and found the usual chaos. Landersmann had an interactive display projected on the table and all four mission planners huddled around him.

"Morning, Landie," Skelly announced in a mock cheerful voice. "Whose world are we gonna fuck up today?"

Landersmann looked up, scowling. "New directions from Sterling, boss," he said. "They want us to rework everything. I just sent you an approved mission list."

Skelly reopened the tablet. "Approved mission list? Since when does Sterling tell me what operations we can run in the field? I choose my own jobs."

"Not according to Abby, you don't," Landersmann said. "She left me a voicemail an hour ago and said if I ran anything that was not preapproved by her, she was going to fire me. She can't do that, right?"

Skelly's jaw cracked with tension. "You work for me, Landie. Get Abby on the VTC and pipe it into the conference room. I'll deal with this."

He strode into the adjoining conference room and took a

seat at the end of the table facing the secure videoconference setup. He performed a series of four-count breaths to calm himself. This tension between him and Abby had been building for months, and the stress of operations only made it worse. He needed to handle this correctly, professionally. But most of all, he needed to put Aberdeen Cromwell in her place.

She could charm the pants off bankers and do all the mergers and acquisitions she wanted, but field operations, the tip of the spear, that was his territory, and he would brook no oversight from the likes of Abby.

If Joe were alive, this would not be happening, Skelly thought. Joe would be in the chair a few feet away, and he would be nodding along with everything Skelly was doing.

The VTC blinked on, and Abby's face filled the screen. Judging by the background, she was calling him from a secure tablet at home. He recognized the black leather sofa set from her living room, and there was a fire burning in the fireplace.

"Well, well, well," Abby said, her voice dripping with sarcasm. "Look what the cat dragged in."

"Don't bust my balls, Abby," Skelly snapped, his composure already gone. "I'm doing God's work over here and you're trying to armchair quarterback me, what the fuck?"

When Abby Cromwell got angry, her eyebrows pinched together. Right now, a hideous unibrow hooded her eyes. "I've been calling you for a week, Manson," she said in a dark tone. "A week! And it's been nothing but radio silence."

"I've been busy."

"We lost three people yesterday," she shot back.

"Shit happens."

"I guess it does." Abby was not backing down. In fact, Skelly wasn't sure he'd ever seen her this angry. "Does that shit include going after a Russian military fuel depot?"

"Target of opportunity, with low risk of regular military

fatalities," Skelly said. "The ROE says I can pursue logistics targets, right?"

"You ran that operation through Mama." Abby's voice was laced with heat. "She recommended against it because it was a low-priority target, and you did it anyway. What's the point of having a billion-dollar artificial intelligence if you're not going to use her?"

"I don't need a machine to tell me a good target when I see it. Low cost, high value, low risk. I made the call and I was right."

"Low risk?" Abby threw up her hands. "Low risk? You went thirty kilometers behind enemy lines and used a jet pack to get to the exfil point. That's a prototype piece of equipment. What if one of them didn't work? What if you drove yourself into a fucking tree? That is not low risk, Manson, and I've had it with your bullshit. You can play ball or you can come home."

"May I say something?" a new voice said.

Abby's gaze snapped off screen, and she gave her head a little shake.

"Who else is on this call?" Skelly demanded.

Dylan Mattias crowded into the frame next to Abby.

"I can't help overhearing," Dylan said.

Abby tried to whisper something to the CIA officer, but he ignored her.

"I'd like to congratulate you on the fuel depot operation, Manson," Dylan continued. "I think it was inspired."

Skelly grinned at the screen. "Well, you are very welcome, CIA man. I am glad to see someone back in Sterling still has a backbone."

"That said," Dylan continued, "Abby has a point. High-risk operations are going to get men killed. I assume your field operatives are clean?"

"Absolutely," Skelly said. "No IDs, all fingerprints and DNA have been scrubbed from public databases, even the serial numbers on the weapons are untraceable. These people are ghosts."

Dylan nodded. "Good, I like it. Now let's get to mission parameters, Manson. That comes directly from the White House, by the way." He looked at Abby, who still looked a little shell-shocked that Dylan had taken over her meeting. "Can we agree that any future missions will have at least a sixty percent probability of success from Mama before they get approved?"

"I can live with that," Skelly said quickly. Mama had assigned a forty-two percent probability to the fuel depot operation.

"That sounds reasonable," Abby agreed cautiously.

"Good," Dylan concluded, "then we're agreed. Mission planning stays in the field but must be approved by Mama. We're all on the same team here."

That's something Joe might have said, Skelly thought. When he met Abby's eyes on the screen, he could tell she had the same thought.

Skelly was so involved in the idea that he ended the conference call with a smile. He even forgot to ask what Dylan Mattias was doing in Abby's home at eleven o'clock at night.

13

Don Riley scrolled through the morning intel briefing on his computer screen, paying careful attention to the section on Ukraine. On the opposite screen he'd pulled up a detailed map of the country, and he carefully matched place names in the briefing to points on the map.

A Russian fuel depot destroyed in Valky... A Russian Army convoy hit by small-diameter missiles... Two Wagner command posts completely wiped out by direct action missions... A Russian colonel general killed.

Everything was attributed to the Ukrainian military, of course, but how much of it was Sentinel? Don wondered.

He sighed at the screen in frustration. This was about the level of detail he'd get from a report on CNN, a sure sign that Dylan Mattias was keeping a close hold on any intel coming from Sentinel.

The country of Ukraine was like a peninsula poking into Russian-held territory. Belarus, a Luchnik puppet state, bordered the north of Ukraine. The Russian Federation enveloped the entire eastern border and most of the south, including occupied Crimea. The Dnieper River made a long shallow S-curve through the country, dividing Ukraine east and west. Russian troops had surged into eastern Ukraine from the south, east, and north. Don studied the ragged line that represented the front in this conflict.

The Ukrainian military and civilian militia had done an admirable job of defending their country, aided by Sentinel and logistics support from EU nations, but each day Russian forces chipped away at the territory. Another two weeks, maybe three, and the Russians would probably hold all of eastern Ukraine.

And then what? Don thought. The latest line of thinking, as reflected in the intel brief, suggested that President Luchnik would hold at the Dnieper River. Luchnik's lust to regain control of the once Soviet state would be satisfied—at least for now.

To Don, that analysis smelled like something people told themselves to make the best of a terrible situation. Something they told themselves when the alternative was too ugly to consider.

Luchnik was not going to stop, Don thought. He'd dreamed of this moment and planned for it for too long to stop at the Dnieper River, with the job only half done.

But to make a case against the prevailing wisdom required data. Data which Don did not possess and had no way of getting. If he and Dylan were on the same team, it sure didn't feel that way.

The secure video teleconference program on his computer bleated with an incoming call. The caller ID read: Joint Base Pearl Harbor-Hickam. In spite of his gloomy mood, Don smiled as he accepted the call. There was only one person from Hawaii who would be calling him at this hour.

"Don, it's good to see you." Janet Everett's tanned face wore a bright smile, and her sandy-blond hair had highlights from time spent in the sun. She wore summer whites, and Don immediately noted her black-and-gold shoulder boards. Two thick gold stripes with a narrow gold band between them.

"Well, congratulations, Lieutenant Commander Everett," Don said.

Janet's grin deepened, and she flushed pink under her tan. "Thank you, Don."

Don did a quick mental calculation. She'd been selected for promotion ahead of her year group, a process called deep selection which was used to advance especially gifted officers. Don stroked his chin in mock concentration.

"Based on my excellent powers of observation—your winning smile and the unexpected promotion—am I to assume that you've heard back from the board of inquiry?"

Janet's face grew somber, and she nodded. "Completely cleared. They determined that my actions on the *Manta* were appropriate and reasonable given the circumstances."

Don narrowed his eyes. Typical Janet understatement. From his own conversations with her former commanding officer, Janet's quick thinking during the Battle of Taiwan had saved the life of every man and woman aboard the USS *Idaho*.

"And that's not all," Janet continued, her dark mood gone. "There's more good news."

"Do tell," Don said.

"I've been screened for executive officer," Janet said. "I start training next week. I hope to have an assignment by the fall."

"That's...that's great, Janet." Don forced a smile and kept his tone light. As happy as he was for his friend and colleague,

Don had secretly hoped—okay, not so secretly—that Janet would come back to ETG.

"I wanted you to be the first to know," Janet said with a catch in her voice. "I'm not coming back to ETG, Don. I'm sorry."

"I never expected you would," he lied. "I know Dre and Michael will be disappointed, but I'm glad you're happy."

"I'll call them," Janet said. "They'll understand." She hesitated. "Have you heard from Mark?"

Air Force Captain Mark Westlund had been with Janet on the *Manta*, where he'd suffered a grievous leg injury, resulting in an amputation.

"I saw him about a month ago," Don said. "He's at Walter Reed for physical therapy. He's part of a new program for advanced prosthetics."

"He'll come back to ETG, Don," Janet said. "He has the bug. I can feel it."

Don's visit to Walter Reed had been brief, and he'd not spoken with Mark since. The young officer expected to be discharged from the Air Force with a high disability rating. Don wondered if he'd see Mark Westlund again. He put the thoughts aside.

"Well," Don said, "congratulations on the board of inquiry. I'm not sure what took them so long. I knew you made the right call the day it happened, so did Captain Lannier, by the way."

"If what I'm seeing on the news is any indication, you guys must be really busy these days," Janet said.

Don's gaze strayed to the map of Ukraine, and his frustration with Dylan and Sentinel threatened to bubble up again.

"Busy, busy," he said in as positive a tone as he could manage. "In fact, I need to get going."

"Don." Janet's tone was serious. "You've been good to me. I

hope you don't see this as a brushoff after everything we've been through—"

"Let's not get all mushy now," Don interrupted. "You promised me one tour at ETG, and you did a great job. You don't owe me a thing, Janet, and I'm happy it all worked out."

After he ended the call, Don sank back in his chair. Janet's unexpected good news reminded Don that he'd recently managed to screw up his own career. He'd never had a right to expect Janet to come back to ETG, but he'd hoped for it.

Don imagined that bringing Janet back might help him regain some of the old spark he'd felt when they'd built ETG from nothing. Even then, Dylan Mattias had been a pain in the ass, but somehow it seemed less so. Or maybe that was Don remembering the old days fondly.

A knock at the door interrupted his reverie. Harrison Kohl poked his head in.

"I thought I heard Janet Everett's voice," Harrison said. "How's she doing?"

"Well, she's not coming back to DC anytime soon," Don replied. "She's been picked up for executive officer. I expect our girl will have her own submarine command in the next few years. Heck, she'll probably be CNO someday."

Harrison dropped into a seat across from Don. "Good for her," he said.

Don nodded but said nothing. He stared at the map of Ukraine.

"Tough break for you, though," Harrison continued, "since there's no way in hell I'm going to be your number two. I've had enough management in the last few months to last me the rest of my natural-born life."

Don chuckled. Even by the standards of their business, Harrison's past was murky. Portions of his service jacket were heavily redacted, but based on the man's skill set, Don had assumed those missing pieces dealt with the Russian Federation.

"What can I do for you, Harrison?" Don said, finally giving his visitor his full attention.

"I wanted to get your read on the latest intel coming out of Ukraine." Normally, Harrison slouched in his chair, but today Don noticed he was not only sitting up but leaning forward.

Don decided to play along. "I think this is the part where I say something like: Gee, Harrison, the intel is shit. I wish there was something we could do."

"Indeed." Harrison's gaze was bright and sharp.

"But you have an idea to solve all of that," Don said.

"As a matter of fact, I do, boss." Harrison steepled his fingers. "We find ourselves in a bit of a predicament, I think. The United States is assuming that the Russians will stop at the Dnieper River. We assume this whole mess will become a sanctions and diplomacy play—similar to Crimea. Luchnik gets his piece of candy, and the world moves on."

Harrison's voice took on a new intensity. "I think that's wrong, Don. Dead wrong. I think we're seeing the first step in a much larger campaign involving the whole of eastern Europe. Unfortunately, I can't prove that because you are in a blood feud with the Deputy Director of Operations for the CIA, who has put all intel from Sentinel on close hold."

"That's not fair," Don said. "I'm not in a blood feud with Dylan Mattias. I just think he's a pompous asshole."

"Same difference," Harrison shot back. "We need intel to prove our theory, and every day that goes by, the wait-and-see argument gets stronger. The longer we wait, the more runway we give Luchnik."

"You're saying I should beg Dylan for access?" Don asked.

"Nope," Harrison said. "I'm saying we develop our own sources."

"That'll take months," Don said.

Harrison grinned. "I know a guy."

Don shook his head. "We go poking around in Ukraine and Dylan will have my balls in a cigar box on his desk by dinnertime. I am PNG right now, buddy."

"Who said anything about Ukraine?" Harrison threw up his hands. "We're emerging threats, and I think it would be in everyone's best interest if you sent me to liaise with our NATO allies in the region. Who do you think is the most paranoid about the Russian Federation?"

Don's eyes went back to the map of Ukraine on his computer screen. He traced the western border of the country with his gaze.

"Poland," he said.

"Give that man a gold star." Harrison came around Don's desk and pointed at the screen. "I have a longtime friend in the Agencja Wywiadu, the Polish foreign intelligence service. The Poles are beside themselves over what's happening in Ukraine. They're begging NATO to get involved. I think I need to take a trip, Don, and see for myself what the Russkies are up to. Low profile, of course."

Don scowled at the screen. "Permission denied."

"What?" Harrison said. "Why? I'll be discreet. Dylan will never know I'm in the region."

Don shook his head, hiding his smile. "You're not going to Poland—unless you take me with you."

14

Abby Cromwell balanced the cup and saucer on the knee of her crossed leg. Both pieces of china were emblazoned with the seal of the President of the United States.

She recalled the last time she'd been in this office. President "Please call me Rick" Serrano had been beyond charming as he buttered her up for the trip to Camp David.

"More coffee, Ms. Cromwell?" Dylan's voice. He occupied the seat next to her on the sofa, looking handsome in a charcoal-gray Armani suit. He held up the silver coffeepot, smiling, but his eyes held a message for her:

Pay attention.

But Abby was well aware of the danger in the room. They sat on the opposite side of the coffee table on a matching pale yellow sofa.

National Security Advisor Valentina Flores looked absolutely stunning in a deep crimson pantsuit, black silk blouse, and glossy black Jimmy Choo heels. Her dark hair spilled in silky waves over her shoulders. But Flores's red lips were pursed in a pout that spoiled the effect of her killer outfit. One lacquered fingernail, the exact shade of her jacket, tapped the saucer of her White House coffee cup.

Ting, ting, ting.

Seated next to her, Chief of Staff Irving Wilkerson's grandfatherly face was equally sour. He scowled at Abby.

Screw him, Abby thought. To Dylan she said, "I could use a warm-up, thank you, Mr. Mattias."

Dylan topped off her coffee and held up the pot. "Anyone else?"

Silence.

President Serrano stood at the Resolute desk, his back to them, a telephone receiver tucked between his ear and his shoulder. Beyond his silhouette, Abby could see a bank of brilliant yellow daffodils on the lawn outside.

Another excruciating minute of icy silence passed before Serrano hung up the phone, clapped his hands together, and came around the desk with a spring in his step. He held out his hands, palms forward. "Stay seated," he said, "but I'll take a coffee, Irv. Lots of cream and two sugars, please. You know how I like it.

"The latest numbers are in," Serrano continued, "and they're good. Really good. Strong in the south and in California. The infrastructure bill is just what the doctor ordered, Irv."

"All we have to do is get it through Congress before the August recess, sir," Wilkerson said as he passed the President a cup and saucer.

"Nothing a little horse trading can't solve," Serrano said. "Everybody loves infrastructure." He sipped his coffee, nodding approvingly. "Perfect, Irv. Thanks."

"My pleasure, sir," Wilkerson growled.

With a sigh, Serrano placed the saucer on the coffee table.

"I'm feeling like I've walked into a war council between the Sharks and the Jets here." Serrano settled back into his chair and crossed his legs. "Abby, you asked to see me today. Why don't you start?"

Abby drew in a deep, steady breath. She'd practiced this in the shower, in the mirror, hell, she'd practiced it in her sleep.

Keep it simple and direct, she told herself. You need to get Sentinel out of Ukraine as quickly as possible. She had run multiple scenarios with Mama, and Sentinel Holdings had a less than 50 percent chance of surviving the engagement in Ukraine intact as a company. With each passing day, the company she had founded with her late husband—really, the only thing of him she had left—was slipping away from her.

"I believe we have reached a turning point in the Ukraine situation, Mr. President," Abby began. "In a matter of weeks, the Russian military will occupy the entirety of eastern Ukraine. We can slow them down, make it harder for them, bleed their resources, but if Luchnik fully commits to this operation, we can't stop them."

The bemused half-smile that had graced Serrano's lips faded into a tight line of compressed flesh. "Go on," he said.

His reaction made Abby pause. Did he really not know this? she wondered. She wanted to look at Dylan and gauge his reaction, but that would only make her look like she didn't know what she was doing.

"Up until now, we've run a successful counterinsurgency operation in eastern Ukraine. We've managed to stay off the Wagner Group's radar, so the response has been contained. But when Wagner determines who they're dealing with, we can expect a major change in tactics."

"And that's a problem?" Wilkerson asked, his voice rough, clipped with irritation. "You were given a job to interdict

Wagner, to slow them down. From where I'm sitting, you've done it. Excellent job, Abby. I'm struggling to understand why we're having this conversation."

"I agree," Flores added. "I thought the attack on the Russian fuel depot behind the front lines was genius. The kind of boldness we had hoped to get from Sentinel. You're winning. Keep going."

Abby shared a nervous glance with Dylan. This was not going the way she'd hoped.

Dylan cleared his throat. "I think what Ms. Cromwell is asking," he said, "is what is the endgame for Sentinel Holdings?"

Wilkerson stared at Dylan as if he'd just dropped an f-bomb in the Oval Office.

"Endgame?" Wilkerson said. "Why are we talking about an endgame now? We have four months of campaigning before the midterm elections. You were hired to keep Ukraine contained and off the front page of the news. We can talk endgame in November, after the election."

Dylan tried again. "Sentinel is incurring considerable risk, sir. If the operation in Ukraine gets dirty, it may not be something they can recover from as an organization. More importantly, the potential blowback could implicate the United States government. Our operation inside Ukraine is something even our NATO allies don't know about."

"I think that's the point of a covert operation and is precisely the reason why we hired Sentinel in the first place, Mr. Mattias," Serrano said. "To protect the United States government from being implicated in the Ukraine mess. I agree with Irv: it's way too soon to be talking about an exit strategy. Sentinel has done excellent work thus far. Keep going. Push the envelope. As long as you keep it off the front page, I don't give a hot damn what you do."

"Sir," Abby said. "Wagner is not a company to be trifled with. When they realize that they're not dealing with the Ukrainian military, we will see a whole new level of violence. In Syria, I saw firsthand what they are capable of, and the collateral damage is not something I want to be associated with. The Russians will be willing to level entire towns to destroy insurgent forces."

Abby looked at Flores. "You see the attack on the Russian fuel depot as a good thing. I disagree. Our intel suggests that the Russian military is getting more aggressive. Mr. President, I would like to withdraw my company from Ukraine."

Serrano's face grew scarlet. He leaned forward in his chair, elbows on knees, shoulders rigid with anger.

"This is about money," he snapped. "This is a shakedown, isn't it? You know how much this means to me, Abby, and you're trying to stick it to me when I'm down, right?"

Abby felt her cheeks prickle with heat. "This is about doing the right thing, Mr. President."

She immediately regretted her tone of voice. Serrano sat back in his chair as if he'd been slapped. Wilkerson got to his feet, but Serrano stayed him with an outstretched palm.

Abby held her breath, her eyes locked with Serrano's. The moment lengthened into an uncomfortable, tense silence. She heard Wilkerson's labored breathing in the background, but she dared not look away.

Serrano lowered his arm.

"Give us the room, ladies and gentlemen," he said quietly. "I think Ms. Cromwell and I need to talk privately."

Flores and Wilkerson glared daggers at Abby as they got up.

"Sir, I think—" Dylan began.

"You too, Mr. Mattias."

She felt the sofa shift as Dylan stood. The heavy door to the Oval Office clicked closed.

Serrano reached for the coffeepot and refreshed his drink.

Abby looked out the window at the bright yellow daffodils, waving in the gentle breeze. Outside, it was a warm summer day in DC, but here, in this office, her skin felt cold and clammy.

Serrano tapped his spoon against the rim of the cup, a tinny sound in the silent room.

"I'm sorry I lost my temper, Abby," he said.

"I was angry," Abby replied. "I should have been more respectful, Mr. President."

"Let's start over." Serrano's face was composed. "What is the mission of your company?"

Abby stared at him as if she did not understand the question. "The mission of Sentinel Holdings?"

"You started this company with your husband and his best friend, right?" Serrano said.

Abby nodded.

"I know you come from money," Serrano continued. "You certainly didn't need to start a company, but you did. And after your husband—Joe—passed away, you kept it going. I wonder why. I assume you have a higher purpose than simply making money, and I want to know what that is. So, I'm asking, what is the mission of Sentinel Holdings?"

Her mouth felt dry. She reached for her coffee as much to wet her throat as to gain a few seconds to think. Where is this going? she wondered.

"We have a mission statement—" she began.

Serrano waved his hand, still smiling. "I don't mean the corporate bullshit that's put together by marketing hacks. I mean you, what does Sentinel mean to you?"

"We wanted to make the world a safer place," Abby

blurted out. "That's what Joe and I talked about when we started it."

She thought about her latest conversation with Manson and where they had left things between them. A lot of things had changed since Joe's death. "We both served, and we knew the world is a dangerous place. We've seen it, lived it. The military is a blunt instrument. We thought there was a need for a more flexible solution."

"You want to be the good guys," Serrano replied. "Isn't that what you're saying? You want to defeat evil in the world. You wear the white hats, and Wagner's wearing black. Do I understand that correctly, Abby?"

"That's a little basic, sir," Abby admitted, "but at a high level, I agree."

Serrano toyed with his coffee. "Do you know how to outrun a bear, Abby?"

Abby blinked. "I don't understand the question, Mr. President."

"Humor me," he said. "How do you outrun a bear?"

Abby shrugged. "I don't know, sir. How do you outrun a bear?"

Serrano grinned. "You don't. You outrun the other guy. That gives the bear something to do while you beat feet to safety."

"Okay." In the category of strange Oval Office conversations, this one definitely ranked.

"If your goal is to do good in this world, Abby," Serrano said, "then you need to stay in Ukraine. Not only do you need to stay in Ukraine, but you need to up your game. Whatever you're doing over there, double it, then double it again. Take risks, make them pay, bleed them dry."

"Sir, I don't think you understand what—"

"I understand very well, Abby," Serrano said with an edge

of steely conviction in his tone. "I'm trying to make you see the big picture. There is no good and evil in this world, Abby. There are only shades of gray. We select the best of the bad choices and we move forward. We do it every day, then we get up and do it all over again."

Serrano leaned forward, a fierce intensity in his eyes.

"I'm asking you to make the choice to stand with me. There's nothing you can do for the people of Ukraine, but you can help the people of our country. The American people will vote in a few months. If Ukraine becomes a campaign issue, I will lose my majorities in Congress. I will lose the ability to govern effectively. For the last two years you have helped me fight back against the bad guys all over the world. Wouldn't it be a shame to give up now?"

Abby's laced fingers were clamped around her knee. Serrano reached over and put his hand on hers.

"I need your help, Abby, but I need to know: Are you with me?"

Abby wanted to close her eyes. She wanted to sink back in the chair, tell him she needed some time to think about it. Most of all, she wanted to look away from that magnetic gaze. The Serrano Stare.

Instead, Abby nodded her head.

"I'm with you, Mr. President."

15

---

100 kilometers west of Warsaw, Poland

Don Riley leaned his head against the backseat window of the passenger sedan and watched the Polish countryside fly by. To his jet-lagged brain, the flat, plowed fields on either side of the two-lane divided highway might as well have been in Kansas.

What am I doing here? he thought.

The leaden sky matched his mood. Don pulled his over-coat tighter across his chest and tried to shut his eyes. He hadn't slept a wink on the overnight flight from Dulles to Warsaw, and he felt a headache coming on. Not that he hadn't tried, but his brain would not shut off, even for a second. He went from chastising himself for dumping his career into the shitter to trying to push away the uneasy feeling that nagged at the back of his tired brain.

There were larger forces at play, he could feel it, but the shape of the problem eluded his grasp. Don tried to think through all the permutations, fit the few pieces he knew into some semblance of a narrative, but he gave up. He needed more information. Most of all, he needed to stop obsessing about something he could not control.

In front of him, in the passenger seat of the Skoda sedan, Harrison Kohl chatted with their young driver in Polish. Unlike Don, Harrison seemed none the worse for wear from the overnight flight. Because they had made last-minute flight reservations, Don and Harrison had not been seated together. When he made a circuit of the economy cabin during his sleepless night, Don had passed Harrison's seat. The man was out cold. Apparently, the troubling thoughts that dogged Don's conscience did not bother Harrison in the least.

"Don." Harrison twisted in his seat. "Check it out." He pointed out the window.

In the middle distance, Don spotted a train.

"Are those tanks?" he asked.

"Yup," Harrison replied. "Vanya here says they're headed south to the border with Ukraine. The whole military's on alert. All leave has been cancelled, and their national guard's been called up."

Don squinted at the boxy green shapes and long-barreled guns, trying to recall his training on armor. The profiles looked familiar.

"Are those M1A1 Abrams?" he asked.

"Good eye, bossman," Harrison said, facing forward. "Vanya was just telling me that the Poles bought the M1A2 Abrams SEPv3 tanks. Damn fine platforms. Real kill machines. They purchased two hundred and fifty of those things, and they've been training like their lives depended on it for the last few years."

Harrison and Vanya exchanged a few more sentences in Polish, which, to Don's unpracticed ear, sounded a lot like Russian.

"Vanya says the US Army has been here on the regular for

training." Harrison grinned back at Don. "The Poles are ready."

Out of sheer boredom, Don counted tanks. Four tanks to a platoon...fourteen tanks to a company...fifty-eight tanks to a battalion. He was looking at a brigade-sized movement.

What was Luchnik's endgame? he wondered. Would he stop at the Dnieper River or push on to the border with Poland? Obviously, the Poles had already taken the measure of their enemy and were taking no chances.

Thirty minutes later, the car exited the highway, headed southeast. The driver navigated onto smaller roads until they were driving along what looked like a country lane. They left the plowed fields behind, entering dense hardwood forest. The elevation was lower. In the low light, Don spotted swampy areas among the trees.

He was just about to ask where they were going when the vehicle rounded a bend and a military checkpoint came into view. An armed soldier, dressed in full combat gear, left the shelter of a tarped enclosure strung between two trees. Don noted he wore a surgical mask.

The driver rolled down the window and engaged in a short conversation. Just as the guard was about to wave them through, Harrison leaned over and asked a question in Polish. Don could tell from the accompanying actions that he was asking about the mask. Harrison frowned at the response.

"What was that about?" Don asked as they pulled away.

"I asked about his mask, and he said he didn't want to get the refugee virus," Harrison replied. "Vanya tells me that the news is full of crap about refugees bringing disease into their country."

Don nodded. Like many countries around the world, Poland had flirted with autocracy in recent years. Misinformation to stoke popular fear was a common tactic used to maintain power.

The road ahead split, and Don caught a glimpse of the road sign: Nezyvna – 5 KM. They took the opposite fork and emerged from the woods into weak sunshine. A temporary fence, topped with razor wire and manned by armed and masked soldiers, ran north and south. They were waved through. The car climbed a small rise and paused as the driver spoke to Harrison.

Through the windshield, Don saw a shallow valley brimming with a haphazard collection of tents, tarp shelters, and people huddled around campfires. The air was hazy with smoke. A ruler-straight row of green military tents stood between the chaos of the camp and the fence.

The driver pulled into a parking lot and spoke to Harrison in Polish.

"He says Jakub will be in the CP," Harrison reported.

Don opened his door, and the smell of the refugee camp struck his senses like a slap in the face. Sewage, campfire smoke, refuse, and unwashed bodies merged into a fetid brew. Don felt the churned mud of the parking lot seep into his shoes. He hadn't expected a field visit when he packed. He picked his way to where Harrison waited.

The door of the CP pushed open and a short, stout man with thin spiky hair stepped into the mud. Although he was dressed in combat camouflage, his uniform was new, with creased folds from the original packaging. He greeted Harrison in Polish, threw his arms around him, and planted a kiss on both cheeks. After a lengthy exchange, they turned to Don.

"Welcome to hell on earth," Jakub said in perfect English. Don took the offered hand. The man's grip was thick and fleshy. "Brought to you courtesy of Vitaly Luchnik. May he rot in a hell of his own making."

The interior of the command post was a whirl of controlled activity. They passed through a comms center where an enlisted woman was updating a laminated map of Poland with a grease pencil. The next room was dedicated to the refugee crisis. Whiteboards lined the walls, and although Don could not read Polish, he understood numbers. He spotted the number 311,356 at the bottom of one board and worked out that the Poles were dealing with four different refugee entry points along the four-hundred-kilometer border between Belarus and Poland.

"Nezyvna is the largest refugee camp in Poland," Jakub said in a quiet voice. "The damned Belarus Army directs them here because of the terrain. They tell the refugees that if they go through the swamp, they can bypass the checkpoint and make it into the EU." He shook his head. "We pulled five bodies out this morning. Hypothermia got them."

"Where are they coming from?" Don asked.

Jakub shrugged his broad shoulders. "Everywhere. Iraq, Syria, Lebanon, Afghanistan, Ukraine."

"Ukraine?" Don asked.

"Ukrainians started showing up a few days after the riot in Kyiv," Jakub replied. "We get more each day. A few hundred, maybe a thousand, are in the camp already. Many more are coming. Many more."

Someone handed Don a cup of coffee, and he drank it without thinking.

If he could talk to someone from Ukraine, maybe there would be a clue into what was happening behind the front lines. Don tried to estimate how far it was to the Ukraine border from here. Too far to walk, he guessed.

"How are they getting here?" Don asked.

Jakub gave him a tired smile. "We can find out together," he said. "I was just about to interview one of them."

Outside the CP, they waded through the smell of the camp. People watched them from open tents. Some lay on the damp ground, huddled in blankets. Don doggedly followed Jakub's broad back. The Polish man hawked and spat into the mud.

"It's called a temperature inversion," he said, huffing at his brisk pace. "A layer of colder air gets on top of the valley and seals in this stench. You'll see some of the men wearing masks. They think the smell will get them sick." He shook his head. "We have a lot of great things in Poland, but these days, humanity is in short supply."

Don's eyes strayed from the muddy lane to a little girl with dark hair who huddled next to an unlit campfire. She wore a bright pink winter coat that was spotted with mud. Jakub followed his gaze, then he looked away.

"Luchnik is a pig," he said. "These people are desperate, starving. They have nowhere to go. The Belarus Army dumps them here. It's all part of Luchnik's plan to destabilize my country."

They arrived at a large tent labeled in multiple languages, including English. INTAKE CENTER, the sign read.

Don could almost smell the desperation inside. Rows of benches filled the anteroom, where men, women, and children sat cheek by jowl in silence. The sharp smell of body odor made his eyes water.

Jakub marched forward as if he didn't see the waiting people. "All refugees are required to register here. We select a few for debriefing." They passed a row of soldiers working on laptops, sitting across from a row of people on folding chairs. The refugees clutched papers in their dirty hands. Birth certificates, IDs, passports, family photos, addresses scrawled on papers creased with many folds.

Don cut a look at Harrison. His colleague's face was gray, and a scowl replaced his usual wry smile.

Behind the registration tables was a narrow hallway lined with doors on either side. The three of them entered the fourth door, where Don found a middle-aged man sitting behind a plastic folding table. He stood when they entered, asking a question in Ukrainian. He was mid-fifties, spare of frame, with wire-rimmed glasses and a walrus mustache. Jakub responded in the same language while Harrison unfolded chairs for all three of them.

There was some desultory conversation as Jakub tried to put his subject at ease. A packet of cigarettes appeared and was passed around. A haze of cigarette smoke filled the tiny room.

As Don admired Jakub's easy interview style, Harrison leaned close to Don. "My Ukrainian is pretty rusty, but this guy's name is Fedir Bondarenko. He was mayor of a small town in eastern Ukraine, really small from the sound of it. A few days after the Kyiv riots, a bunch of guys showed up in town and separated the Russians and the non-Russians."

Fedir teared up as he spoke. Jakub talked softly to him and tapped out another cigarette for the man.

"Russian soldiers?" Don asked.

Harrison shook his head. "He's clear about that. These were civilians, but armed. He says he thinks they were ex-military."

"Wagner Group," Don said.

Harrison nodded his agreement, still listening. "The men gave them fifteen minutes to pack one suitcase, then loaded them in trucks. They took them north to the Belarus border." He paused and cursed under his breath.

"His wife died a few years ago," he said. "Fedir lives with his daughter, seventeen years old. They got separated at the border. The Belarus military put them in separate trucks. When they got to where they were going, the other truck never showed up." Harrison's voice dropped even lower. "The other truck was full of women. *Young* women."

Fedir started to sob, and he lowered his head onto clenched fists. Jakub lit another cigarette and looked up at the ceiling. Don tried to swallow the sour taste in his mouth, but it stuck to his tongue like rancid peanut butter.

"Jakub told him he'd get him approved for asylum since he's Ukrainian, but the guy refused. He said he's not leaving without his daughter."

Jakub pushed the half-full pack of cigarettes across the table to Fedir, who accepted them. They all rose. Jakub shook hands with the man and gave him a card. Then the Ukrainian refugee left.

"You see what we're dealing with here," Jakub said, his voice crackling with frustration. "This is the Russian playbook: flood the border with refugees to distract the Polish people from what is going on in Ukraine. If the Russians cross the Dnieper River, they will not stop."

"We saw armor being moved to the south," Harrison said.

Jakub nodded. "We will be ready for the Russians, but this"—he waved his hand around the room—"this human suffering will go on as long as Luchnik remains in power."

"You believe the Russians will invade all of Ukraine?" Don asked. "You think they'll invade Poland?"

Jakub reached for his cigarettes, then realizing he had given them away, he scowled.

"Mr. Riley, I have studied this enemy for my entire life. Trust me, the Russians are coming."

16

Zaslawye, 12 kilometers north of Minsk, Belarus

The clock over the doorway to the kitchen read twenty-five minutes past four in the morning. Stanislau Kulik, dressed only in his boxer shorts, focused on the clock with all his might.

On a normal day, he would automatically wake in twenty minutes—he never used an alarm clock, never had—and get ready for another day as the personal bodyguard of the president of Belarus.

But this was not a normal day.

His hands, bound behind him, had gone numb an hour ago. His ankles were tied to the legs of a sturdy wooden chair. His mind flashed to when they'd bought these kitchen chairs, he and Anya. His wife had been pregnant with their youngest, Polina, and eight-year-old Marta had been with them.

Now, seven years later, he wished maybe he had settled for a cheaper model, something he could break apart and use to beat to death the man who sat opposite him.

"Are you listening to me, Stanislau?" the man asked.

He was a big bastard, obviously Russian, with a crooked nose and a scar on his chin. He was also calm, like he had done this before.

Stanislau was good at reading people. It was part of his job, and he was very good at his job. He knew this man was a hired gun, a mercenary, but what he could not figure out was what these men were doing here, in his home.

They'd arrived sometime around three in the morning, four of them. They'd bypassed his security system, but even in sleep, Stanislau had recognized the threat. He snapped out of a dream, reaching for the handgun on his bedside table, but it was too late. Hands clamped on his arms, a sharp sting in the neck, and he'd woken up in his kitchen, bound like a lamb for slaughter.

Two of them worked him over for a few minutes—body shots only, nothing on the face and nothing broken—then the boss came in. They didn't bother to gag him, and he didn't bother to yell. There was no one to hear him. One of the perks of being part of the President's inner circle was a very big, very private house in an exclusive neighborhood.

"What do you want?" Stanislau hissed. If they wanted to kill him, he'd already be dead. The fact that they'd stayed away from his face told him they needed him to be presentable.

"I have a job for you, Stanislau," the man said. "A simple job. A few moments of looking the other way and a forgetful memory. Then you can go on with your life."

It had something to do with the President, he knew that. It didn't matter what they wanted, the answer was no.

Stanislau had trained for this moment his entire career. When it came to the President, his life was forfeit.

He shook his head.

"Don't be like that, Stanislau," the man said in a tone like he was talking to a recalcitrant child. "It's a simple job. You let someone place a listening device in a cabinet meeting. After the meeting, the device disappears and you never see us again."

He cut a look at the clock. Four thirty. If he could stall them for an hour, maybe less, someone might realize something was wrong. It wasn't much of a plan, but it was better than nothing.

"Tell me more," he said.

"Finally." The man leaned forward, elbows on knees as if he might tell a joke. "There is a cabinet meeting today, no?"

"If you say so."

"There is. I say so." The man took out a package of Prima cigarettes and lit one. He blew a smoke ring at the ceiling.

Stanislau scowled. Anya hated cigarette smoke in her home. She made him quit when she was pregnant with Marta, and he'd never smoked since.

"In this meeting, there will be two Russians briefing the cabinet on a new top-secret operation. I need to know what they say."

"Why?" Stanislau asked the question without thinking.

Slow down, he thought. You need to play for time.

"These men are traitors, and I want to catch them in the act," the man said, "so I need your help."

Stanislau pretended to think about it this time. "Why do you need my help?"

The man spread his hands. "Because you are the President's top security man. You ensure that the cabinet room is swept for listening devices *before* the meeting, therefore we need to get the bug in the room *after* the meeting starts."

"I can listen to what they say," Stanislau countered. "I can report back to you."

From his seated position, the man flicked his cigarette into the sink, a long arc of sparks over Anya's spotless floor. "A generous offer, but it's all arranged, Stanislau. All we need is your cooperation."

"How?" Stanislau asked. Too fast! he thought.

"Since I know you are going to help us, I will tell you," the man said. "When the meeting starts, the tea service will be brought in."

"How do you know?"

"The President loves his tea, and he loves it hot and sweet," the man said. "There is always tea in these meetings."

Stanislau nodded. It was true. The President loved his tea.

"The President has a special sugar bowl, just for him," the man continued. "He likes to keep it next to him so he can drop in a sugar cube whenever he wants. True?"

Stanislau nodded again.

"Today, on the bottom of the sugar bowl, we have placed a tiny listening device. We will listen to the meeting. Afterward, the device will disappear and you will never see me again."

"That's it?"

The man shrugged. "That's it. All you have to do is make sure the tea cart gets in the room without a problem and place the sugar bowl next to the President. Simple."

"What happens if I say no?"

The man sighed. "Nothing."

"Nothing?"

The man stood. "To you? Nothing."

There was a scuffle outside the kitchen, and Anya appeared in the doorway, pinioned between two of the captors. The man took a step forward and backhanded Stanislau's wife across the face.

Although the movement looked casual, Stanislau saw Anya's head snap back, and the crack of flesh on flesh sounded like a rifle shot in the quiet kitchen. As her body arched forward, the man buried a meaty fist into her midsection. Anya's frame folded in two over his forearm.

When the man turned back to face Stanislau, he grinned. "To her? I'm just getting started."

Fifteen minutes later, the same time that Stanislau would wake on a normal day, the face of his beautiful wife was an unrecognizable mess. Her right eye was swollen closed in a bubble of deep purple flesh. She was missing a tooth, and a rope of bloody liquid dripped from her open mouth. In the struggle, the front of her nightgown had torn open, and a slack breast hid among the folds of bloody cloth.

"How about now, Stanislau?" the man asked. "It's a simple task."

He strained at the bonds that held him, his cheeks slick with his own tears.

"Don't do it, my love," Anya said, her speech slurred through smashed lips. "Fuck them."

Without even turning, the man whipped another back-handed blow at Anya. Her head careened to the side like it was attached to a rubber band, then lolled forward.

Stanislau Kulik was not a saint. He had done awful things in the service of his country. He had delivered beatings like this one. Killed people, or worse yet, made them wish they were dead.

He knew with certainty that this could get much worse. But the clock now read five minutes to five. He also knew that these men were almost out of time.

He sensed the tension in the room shift, as if someone had injected an electric charge in the air.

One of the captors appeared, carrying his daughter Marta. She was still drugged, her dark curls masking her face, as he laid her on the kitchen table. It was a sturdy piece of furniture. Oak, the color of dark honey, and Stanislau's mind flashed to the hundreds of family dinners that had happened around that table. Peals of laughter, shouts of childish anger, homework, birthday parties... His mind pinwheeled.

Without ceremony, the man plunged a needle into the girl's neck. She stirred, sat up. She saw his face, and her eyes grew wide. Stanislau winced.

"Papa? What is going on?" Then she saw her mother, and she screamed. Rather, she tried to scream. Her handler anticipated it and clamped a hand over her mouth so it came out as a muffled whine.

The man bent down to her level.

"Stop struggling, girl," he said in a flat voice. "I will let you talk to your Papa if you promise not to scream. Do you promise?"

Marta, dear Marta. She was a good girl, top of her class in school. She knew how to follow directions. Her eyes were white with fear, but she nodded. The handler removed his right hand from her mouth, but his left still held her bicep in a viselike grip.

The girl tried not to cry. "Papa, what is going on?"

Stanislau opened his mouth to speak, then he closed it again. His gaze cut to his wife, who was still unconscious, then back to Marta.

How long would a young girl last in the hands of a man like that? he thought.

Marta saw the fear in his eyes, and she started to cry again. She put her free hand over her mouth to stop herself, but tears streamed down her face.

Stanislau looked at the man in charge, who grinned back at him.

There was only one way this ended. If Stanislau let that happen, he would never forgive himself. He dropped his eyes to the floor. "I'll do it."

He arrived at work only five minutes late. This was unheard of for Stanislau. The night duty officer raised an eyebrow but did not comment. Instead, he said, "He's in a good mood this morning." He jerked a thumb at the silver samovar next to the bank of handheld radios. "The tea is fresh, if you want a cup."

Stanislau did not want a cup of tea. He buried himself in the details of work, checking the duty roster and the schedule for the day. There was a cabinet meeting planned for ten a.m., and there were two visitors expected.

Stanislau reviewed their files. Russians, probably GRU, although their identifications claimed they were from the Ministry of Agriculture. Both on the young side, mid-thirties, and clean-cut. He studied their mug shots as if it would give him the answer he sought.

Are you worth the lives of my wife and children?

No, he decided, they were not. The man with the scarred chin had broken him, Stanislau realized. Just as he had done to so many people, they had turned him into something he never expected to be: a traitor.

The doubts were behind him now. He would do what they told him to and pray that no one ever found out.

Stanislau's thoughts were interrupted by the arrival of the presidential motorcade, an armored Mercedes sedan and two black SUVs for security personnel. He stepped outside and automatically checked his appearance as he waited for his boss to appear.

The president of Belarus descended the steps of the residence like royalty, which he was, of course. He had ruled Belarus with an iron grip for over three decades and showed no sign of giving up power.

The warm summer sun shone on his silver comb-over as he clapped his personal bodyguard on the shoulder before climbing into the waiting vehicle. "It is a beautiful day, Stanislau!" he declared.

"It is, sir." Somehow the words came out.

Stanislau shut the car door and got into the front passenger seat. As he sat, his phone pulsed with a message. The kidnappers had installed a new program on his smart phone, an encrypted application. He opened the app to find a picture of his daughter. Not Marta, but Polina. The six-year-old's blond hair was mussed with sleep, but her blue eyes were round with fear. A man's hand engulfed her throat, and Stanislau could see a man's thick beard and a pink tongue lapping his daughter's ear.

Underneath the photo, it read: *Don't do anything stupid, Papa.* Smiley face emoji. Eggplant emoji.

Stanislau felt his stomach heave, and he swallowed back a wave of bile.

The picture disappeared as the encrypted app destroyed any record of the message.

The car stopped outside the Palace of the Republic, and Stanislau dismounted. He visually cleared the area, then opened the President's door. He followed his leader up the wide stone steps, through the ornate lobby reeking of their Soviet past, and into the cabinet room.

Stanislau paused at the door to consult with his security team. Yes, the room had been swept for listening devices. All cabinet members were present, and the Russian visitors had been screened. The only screw-up in an otherwise flawless start was the delayed tea service. Behind Stanislau came the ping of an elevator and the rattle of a cart.

"Here he is now," the security man said. "Hurry up, Valery. They're about to start."

Stanislau put a hand on his arm. "I've got this," he said.

Valery had been delivering the tea service for the President for more than five years. He halted the cart in front of Stanislau. "Sorry I'm late."

The centerpiece of the cart was a meter-high solid silver tea samovar with an ornate handle shaped like a dragon's head. A blue flame burned underneath. On either side, the samovar was flanked by a few dozen tea glasses, milk, and sugar servers. On the front edge was a separate smaller tray with a covered silver bowl and a pair of tongs arranged on white linen. The President's sugar bowl.

Stanislau removed the lid from the bowl. Where was the device? He wanted to pick it up and inspect the four clawed legs, but he heard Valery draw a quick breath. He looked up sharply. "Problem, Valery?"

"No, sir, but I'm late..." There was a wheedling tone in his voice.

It took ten minutes to serve all the meeting attendees around the table while the Minister of Defense gave an update on the refugee crisis at the border. Stanislau closed the door behind Valery and returned to his post a few paces behind the President.

The silver sugar bowl was at the President's elbow, uncovered. The President reached in, plucked out a sugar cube, and tossed it into his mouth.

Stanislau slipped his mobile phone from his pocket and opened the encrypted app. *Done*, he typed.

Good, came the reply. *They are free.*

Stanislau's hand shook. It was over. His family was safe. He wanted to run from the room and call them.

His phone pulsed again. He opened the app to find a picture.

Anya, Marta, and Polina arranged on their bed. All three with a bullet hole in their forehead.

"No!" Stanislau dropped the phone. When he picked it up again, the picture was gone. Maybe he had imagined it?

He looked up. All the men at the table were staring at him. Even the President had turned around.

There was a loud pop at the tea cart, followed by a hiss. Stanislau smelled smoke, as if the big silver container had run dry. But that was impossible, it held enough tea to serve each man in the room ten times over.

Then the tea samovar exploded.

17

The Kremlin
Moscow, Russia

Vitaly Luchnik was not a superstitious man. Even as a boy he secretly scorned his schoolmates who wished one another "good luck" before a competition. Luck was a crutch for people who lacked the skill to take advantage of the opportunities life presented to them.

His opinion refined as he grew older. Experience taught him that the only tools needed to succeed in this world were two eyes and two fists. The ability to see an opportunity and the ability to seize it, by force if necessary.

He sipped his tea, savoring the sweetness on his tongue. It was late in the evening, nearly midnight in Moscow, as he studied the security monitor of the cabinet room. His ministers milled about the conference table like actors in a silent movie. There were microphones in the room, but Luchnik never turned the sound on. These men all knew their every word was recorded, so none of them, no matter how stupid, would say anything worth hearing.

But even these skilled liars could not disguise their body language, at least not for long. They all had their tells. Under stress, Defense Minister Yakov was a covert nose-picker. Luchnik watched him turn away from a cluster of his colleagues and dig for gold as if his life depended on it.

Luchnik smiled thinly. Maybe it did. Yakov's compliance was a key part of his plan.

Foreign Minister Irimov was a skilled politician and more adept at hiding his feelings, but his shoulders slumped a little lower. Little Mishi, the prime minister, was a leg jiggler, and right now his left pant leg shivered with activity. Even Federov, head of the internal security service and Luchnik's own protégé, scowled at his reflection in the polished table.

But Admiral Nikolay Sokolov was a credit to his breeding. Luchnik watched his nephew with something akin to fatherly pride. On the screen, the younger man smiled and laughed quietly at something a colleague said, completely at ease in a room boiling with chaotic emotions.

There are only two kinds of men, Luchnik thought. Sheep and wolves. He was the latter, of course, but few of the men on the monitor had earned that title. That was by design. If you fed a sheep, it stayed in one place and did what you told it to do. For decades, he had groomed this flock, making them fat with money and power, feeding their vices.

All for this moment when they would fall in line as Luchnik marched his country into the future, a new day where Russia reclaimed her role as a world power to be reckoned with.

One step at a time, he told himself. First Ukraine, then Belarus. A feint within a feint. Keep the world guessing: What would Russia do next?

The thoughts of what was still to come produced a rush of

energy so strong that it forced Luchnik to his feet. He had waited so long, fought so hard for his place in history. He closed his eyes. The power he wielded was like a drug. He felt unstoppable. Invincible.

His valet came forward, and Luchnik allowed the young man to slide the jacket along his arms. He settled the bespoke suit over his shoulders and tugged at the lapels as if he were fitting armor to his frame.

Luchnik's arrival in the cabinet room stilled the desultory conversation. He strode to his place at the head of the table. "Seats," he said curtly.

He peered down the two rows of faces. Whereas he was shaved and showered and dressed in a freshly pressed suit, they were clad in rumpled garments and tired from a long day. Most had probably been drinking with their dinner. They were, in a word, vulnerable.

"You've all seen the news about the terrorist attack in Minsk," Luchnik began. "I've received confirmation that the President and his entire cabinet are dead."

Glances shifted around the table. All day, the news coming from their neighbor to the west was a tornado of conflicting information. One hour the President was dead, the next he was on holiday at a resort in the Black Sea. A cabinet minister had been injured, then he was spotted at a shopping mall. The chaos was carefully curated and nurtured by a group of disinformation specialists hired by the Wagner Group.

Luchnik met Federov's eye. The head of the FSB did not look away, and Luchnik discerned that Federov's own sources had figured all this out hours ago. What he did not know was his president's next move.

It was all Luchnik could do not to smile.

"The country of Belarus is leaderless," he said. "The buffer between the Russian Federation and NATO is gone. Unless"—he let the word hang in the air—"we seize this opportunity.

"In the morning, I will comment on the tragic news about Belarus. At the same time, I will tell the world that Russian forces are on the ground to maintain the peace and stability of this important Russian ally. Defense Minister?"

"Sir!" Yakov's gray brush-cut hair was mussed and his cheeks ruddy, a sure sign that he'd enjoyed vodka with his evening meal.

"I believe the 1st Guards Tank Army from the Western Military District are on maneuvers near the border with Belarus. Is that correct?"

"It is, Mr. President."

"Order the 1st Guards to Minsk immediately. Place the capital under martial law. In addition, put the 6th Army on alert. We don't know what else might happen, and I want that army ready for action."

Yakov stood. "Of course, sir. I will see to it immediately."

Luchnik held up a hand. "I'm not finished yet."

Yakov sat. A stir worked its way around the table like a breeze through an aspen grove.

The sheep are restless, Luchnik thought. The warm thrill of anticipation squirmed in his belly.

"My intention is to reabsorb the country of Belarus into the Russian Federation." Luchnik spread his hands. "I see no other option. A terrorist organization has put the stability of the entire region at risk. We cannot allow this cancer to spread across our borders."

To Luchnik's right, Foreign Minister Irimov stirred, cleared his throat. "Mr. President, given the international pressure from the Ukraine situation, do you think that's wise?"

Luchnik nodded. "You're quite right, Sergey." He looked to

Yakov. "Defense Minister, it's time we put an end to the campaign in the Ukraine. I want you to deploy the 98th and 106th Guards Airborne Divisions into the Ukraine to quell the remaining separatists. I want your word, right now, that you will capture Kiev within the week."

Yakov licked his lips. "Yes, Mr. President."

"Mr. President," Irimov said, "I'm afraid I must renew my concerns, sir. NATO will protest our actions in Belarus."

"Not if you do your job, Sergey," Luchnik shot back. "Our mission in Belarus is humanitarian in nature. We are there to provide stability to a country that has been brutally attacked by terrorists. I suspect in the next few hours we will start to see videos of Russian soldiers giving toys to poor Belarusian children, army units stopping the looting in the capital, ordinary people being fed by soldiers. We are the good guys, Sergey."

A new voice joined the conversation. "Mr. President," said Prime Minister Mishinov. Despite his title, his seat halfway down the table gave away his true value to Luchnik. "I'm concerned about the economy, sir. The ruble continues to fall to the lowest point in fifty years. This is taking a toll in public opinion."

Kulukov, head of the Rosgvardiya, started to speak, but Luchnik held up a hand. "Public opinion is not my concern, Prime Minister," he said. "The national guard can handle any demonstrations."

Inside, he thought: Damn you, Little Mishi.

Irimov twisted the knife. "There will be additional sanctions, sir. It's inevitable."

The word *sanctions* settled over the room like a winter frost.

Sanctions were the one thing the sheep in his flock feared the most. Their real wealth was not in Russian rubles; it was in numbered bank accounts of dollars and euros. In real estate in Miami and New York and London. In wineries in Spain and resorts in Mexico. All hidden behind a thicket of shell companies set up by their president.

The thing these men feared the most was being cut off from their foreign money. They all probably had nightmares about being placed on a travel watchlist, or the United States Treasury finding out about a secret bank account and freezing their assets.

"We can control internal news sources, Mr. President," Federov said. "For now," he added in a lower tone.

Public opinion was a tricky mistress, but Federov's steady hand on the domestic news sources made the job easier. Still, one story coming out at the wrong time could lead to riots in the streets. He was now fighting a war on two fronts. He did not need trouble at home.

Timing was always the wild card in this grand plan, but the path before him was clear. The people of Russia would thank him for generations. Once they tasted his success, they would forget about the short-term pain of sanctions.

"Mr. President," Irimov said, "the Western alliance has shown considerable strength in their last round of sanctions. What comes next could be much worse."

Yakov started to open his mouth to speak again, but Luchnik stilled him with a glare of disgust. This is what money buys in today's world, he thought.

"Listen to all of you." From his position at the junior end of the table, Nikolay stood, his voice dripping with scorn. "You sound like a bunch of old women. You piss and moan about what the West will do to us. Why not the opposite? What will we do to the West?

"This is more than a matter of national security. This is a matter of national pride. Can't you see that my uncle is acting in the best interest of our country? Instead of bringing him your problems, pledge him your loyalty."

Luchnik's face softened with pride. From his peripheral vision, he noted that Federov was eyeing Nikolay with renewed interest as well.

Maybe there was another wolf in this flock after all.

18

---

65 kilometers north of Moscow

The woman lounging in the leather armchair across from Federov had the body of a dancer or an elite athlete, but Iliyana Semenov was neither of those things. She was a prostitute and part owner of a private club at an exclusive address only a few minutes' drive from the Kremlin.

The other owner of the club, the silent partner, was Vladimir Federov.

Even Federov had a hard time believing this Russian beauty was the same girl he had plucked from a seedy Moscow strip club at the tender age of sixteen. Even then, he had seen something in that stripling of a girl. She offered him a lap dance; he offered her a job.

Iliyana unfolded her long frame and sauntered to the bar. The crimson silk robe, loosely knotted at the waist, slipped over the curve of her hips. Straight blond hair spilled down her back like a waterfall.

"Can I get you anything?" Her eyes were the pale blue of a Siberian winter sky.

"I'm working tonight." He sipped his tea.

"You're always working, Vladimir." Her words had the tone of a pouty child, but her smile was as warm and deep as the midnight sun.

Yes, Iliyana Semenov had been an excellent investment.

"Was he difficult?" Federov asked.

Iliyana chuckled as she melted back into her chair. "I drained his balls and he spilled his guts. I've had virgins tell me fewer secrets than him." She rolled a sip of brandy across her palate. "Then again, I'm good at what I do."

"Your modesty is your greatest virtue," Federov replied. "Tell me what Yakov had to say."

He closed his eyes to better concentrate on her narrative. He would listen to the tapes later, but a decade of experience with Iliyana assured him that she would give him what he needed. Plus, then he wouldn't have to listen to Yakov grunting and groaning in her bed like a herniated bear.

Her retelling was concise and direct, just as he'd taught her.

"He's worried," she concluded. "Afraid. Only a few months ago, the country was on the brink of World War Three, and he can't understand why the President is trying to do it again. He thinks Luchnik has gone too far."

Federov opened his eyes to find her studying him.

"What do you think?" she asked.

He ignored the question. "Send me the bill."

"Whores work for money, Vladimir," she said. "I work for you." She made her way to his side of the desk, the robe parting to reveal a tantalizing glimpse of porcelain skin and black lace. "Will I see you later?"

"Doubtful," he said. "I have a long night ahead of me. Right now, I need to think."

Iliyana ran a finger across a red slash on Federov's cheek. "What happened?"

"A branch. Hunting."

"I thought you hated hunting."

"I was working," he snapped.

Iliyana sighed. "I'll go check on the other girls. When do you want him in the sauna?"

Federov checked his watch. Quarter to one. "An hour from now. Make sure he's good and drunk but still sober enough to have a conversation."

"Do you want me to use the drugs on him?"

Federov shook his head. "Absolutely not. Yuri is too smart for that. If he found out, it would be..." He searched for the right word: disaster, treason, fatal. "It would be bad," he said.

Iliyana planted a tender kiss on the crown of his bald head. "I'll leave you to your thinking. Come to me later. I'll make it worth your while."

Federov watched her leave. Every movement of the woman was enticing, and at the same time, calculating. She was magnificent, intelligent, a natural agent. But for the lottery of their births, their roles could easily be reversed.

He supposed she was the closest thing to an actual intimate human relationship he'd ever had. Despite their more than two-decade gap in age and his typical lack of sexual desire, his time with Iliyana was always pleasant, satisfying on a personal level.

Enough woolgathering, he told himself. Time to work.

He had three weekend guests at his dacha in the country: Defense Minister Yakov, Foreign Minister Sergey Irimov, and Yuri "The Chef" Plotnikov. With Iliyana's help, he'd plotted the weekend's activities with precise care, each activity designed to place his guests in a relaxed posture.

Viktor Yakov was a simple man with simple tastes. He

wanted only to get as drunk as possible for as long as possible and get laid repeatedly in the process. Ironically, he seemed indifferent as to whether or not he remembered the sexual encounters.

The Foreign Minister was a little more challenging. Federov winced as he touched the slash on his cheek. Irimov was a sportsman and closet Anglophile. A gift of a bespoke Scottish shooting outfit, a Holland & Holland over-and-under 20-gauge shotgun, and an afternoon traipsing through the forest trying to kill a bird called a western capercaillie was all it took to loosen the man's tongue.

Federov had waited until Irimov had bagged his sixth kill before he suggested a rest. They passed a flask of brandy between them as Irimov waxed poetic about his Scottish estate—an actual castle, so he said—gifted to him by none other than President Vitaly Luchnik.

Federov knew all of this. He had suggested the castle to Luchnik and made all the financial arrangements for the purchase.

The dead birds, appearing to Federov's untrained eye like a cross between a raven and a turkey, stared up at the two men as Irimov confided that he wanted to retire to his Scottish estate and live out his days next to a peat fire.

The smell of the bird carcasses made Federov want to throw up. Killing people was one thing, but shooting innocent birds out of the sky seemed unnecessary to him. Also, Irimov's fantasy was a snooze fest. Still, the afternoon's effort paid off. The man's frame of mind was exactly where Federov wanted him.

He had pretended to drink more brandy when he broached the subject of Belarus.

Irimov, who was drinking for real, stared at his feathered slaughter. "I don't understand it," he said finally.

Federov let the silence between them lengthen. The other man would fill it when he was ready.

"The strategy, I mean," Irimov continued. "Not long ago, he would invite us into the process. We were partners. But now I'm shut out." He looked searchingly at Federov, seeking reassurance.

Federov offered a sympathetic nod.

"It's the damned Chef," Irimov said with sudden anger, his voice rising in the quiet forest. "I don't know where this is going, Vladimir. But unless something changes, I don't think it ends well for either of us. Or for the country," he added.

Federov hefted his shotgun. "Let's go kill some birds, my friend."

The *thunk* of his tea glass touching the desk brought Federov back to the moment. He checked his watch and sighed. Time to get ready to meet The Chef.

Even as he undressed and pulled on a fluffy white bathrobe—supplied by Iliyana, of course—his mind puzzled over what he had learned.

The President of Russia was not acting like himself. He had cut out his closest advisers, including Federov, in favor of The Chef. Luchnik and Plotnikov were childhood friends. Their bond was deep, but why was the President acting this way?

The President and those around him were all rich beyond their wildest dreams. They controlled the levers of power in Russia more completely than at any time since Catherine the Great. Political opposition was a joke. Federov even had his thumb on the few so-called independent news outlets. He let them live as long as they didn't stray too far in their reporting. An uneasy alliance, but necessary to provide the veneer of popular accountability. The country had gone to the brink of World War Three and survived.

Then why, he wondered, was Luchnik risking another confrontation with the United States over the Ukraine? And why was he expanding into Belarus?

He poked his feet into a pair of slippers and padded through the halls of the dacha. The sauna was at the rear of the house, outside.

If anyone knew the mind of Vitaly Luchnik, it would be The Chef.

Yuri Plotnikov became the sole owner of the Wagner Group the Russian way: as a gift from President Luchnik. At the time, it was seen as a way to put some distance between the Ministry of Defense and the private military contractor. The new company was registered in Argentina, with offices in Saint Petersburg and Hong Kong.

Then a strange thing happened. The Chef, who was expected to be a figurehead, turned out to be a very shrewd businessman. He expanded the services of Wagner far beyond its Russian roots to include any despot with money to spare. Wagner operatives began to appear all over the world: Sudan, Libya, Mozambique, Bosnia, the list went on. As the money flowed, the ranks expanded. Federov's sources showed the PMC grew from three thousand paid soldiers to thirty thousand in the space of less than five years.

The Chef did not forget his roots. When President Luchnik needed his assistance in Crimea in 2014, Yuri was only too happy to offer a discount to his childhood friend.

And now? Federov wondered. How deeply was The Chef involved in the President's latest adventure?

Time to find out.

Federov opened the French doors and stepped into the night air. The surrounding forest pressed close to the house. Above him, stars speckled the sliver of dark sky.

His slippers made a shuffling sound on the stone path to

the sauna. A square window in the door glowed with soft light. On the porch of the sauna, he discarded his slippers and robe and donned a wool banya cap that was hanging on a peg.

As he opened the door, a wave of heat made the scratch on his cheek burn. The Chef was already inside, wearing nothing but his own off-white banya cap, which looked comical on his long, thin face.

"Vladimir," he greeted Federov, "I was beginning to think I sent the girl away too soon. Join me."

Federov took the opposite wooden bench, already feeling sweat springing from the pores of his naked flesh.

"What happened to your face?" Plotnikov asked.

"I was hunting. A branch scratched me."

The other man laughed. "You work too hard, Vladimir. You are what they call a 'people-pleaser.' You try too hard, I think."

"I hope you enjoyed the weekend."

"Immensely," Plotnikov said. "Your own chef is very gifted. We had a great afternoon together."

"The dinner you prepared for us was excellent, Yuri. The *korolevskiy* cake you made for dessert was outstanding."

"You flatter me, my friend."

Actually, Federov was being truthful. The royal cake, a towering masterpiece, four layers of sponge cake separated by buttercream and frosted with chocolate, had been one of the best desserts Federov had ever eaten.

"It was delicious, Yuri. I mean that."

Plotnikov nodded. "It was a cake to be proud of, I agree." He motioned to a wooden bucket near the door. "May I?"

Federov nodded and wiped a slick of sweat from his face. This was not going the way he had planned. Plotnikov lifted a *venik*, a bundle of oak leaves, from the water. Federov turned his back, and the other man slapped the cold branches against his hot skin.

"Did you get what you needed from the others?" Plotnikov asked.

"This is just a weekend away from work, Yuri," Federov said. "Sergey and Viktor are old friends."

"And I'm a new friend."

"Exactly." Federov flinched as the branches stung his skin.

"What is the price of your friendship, Vladimir?" Another slash of the branches. Harder this time. "Does the head of the FSB want to know what I think of my oldest friend in the world?"

Federov stood, turned, grabbed the other man's hand before he could strike again. The lashes on his back stung with sweat.

"Was Wagner behind the bombing in Belarus?" he asked.

In the dim light of the sauna, Plotnikov met his gaze, and Federov had his answer.

"Why?" he hissed.

Plotnikov dropped the *venik* into the bucket. He pulled open the door, letting in a knife of cold air.

"Thank you for a wonderful weekend, Vladimir. You are a gifted host."

At four o'clock the following afternoon, Federov rang the doorbell on the President of Russia's personal residence. He ignored the two plain-clothed Rosgvardiya agents on the sidewalk. It was the close of a beautiful day, warm with the promise of a long summer night. Federov wore only a light sweater and blue jeans for his visit with the most powerful man in Russia.

Luchnik himself answered the door. His face creased into a grin when he saw his old friend.

"Come in, Vladimir," he said, swinging the door wide.

Luchnik, dressed in a tight T-shirt, faded blue jeans, and barefoot, led him through the house to his personal office. The President did not allow security inside his personal residence and never in his private office.

The study was small but comfortable, with only a desk, two armchairs, and a well-stocked bar. Upon entering, Federov's eye was drawn to the map hand-painted on the wall. The Russian Federation was laid out in intricate detail from Komsomolets Island in the north, Kazakhstan and Mongolia in the south, the Bering Sea in the east, and the Ukraine, Belarus, and Finland in the west. The tiny oblast of Kaliningrad was a spot of Russian red sandwiched between Lithuania and Poland on the Baltic Sea.

The disputed Donbas region of eastern Ukraine was cross-hatched with red and white. It seemed to Federov that the paint along the western borders looked worn, as if maybe Luchnik had traced the lines with his fingers.

The President followed his gaze. "We're making good progress in the west, Vladimir. Your efforts are appreciated."

He was right, Federov reflected. Just as Luchnik had predicted, the increased activity in eastern Ukraine occupied the Western news attention while Russian forces worked to secure Belarus. Federov directed their patriotic hacker cohorts to amplify the chaos in the Ukraine. A series of deepfake videos showing Ukrainian soldiers slaughtering civilians had done especially well on social media.

At the same time, a separate team pushed a different message in Belarus. There, the Russian military were saviors. Toys for orphanages, state funerals for the late president and his cabinet, terrorist cells being rounded up.

It was all going according to plan, Federov thought, but where did the plan lead?

"What can I do for you on this fine afternoon, Vladimir?" Luchnik put his feet up on the desk, completely at ease.

Federov was tempted just to ask the question, but he hesitated. It was Luchnik himself who had taught him to never ask a question unless you already knew the answer.

"I've been probing at the cabinet level, Mr. President," Federov began. "Some of them are worried."

Luchnik waved his hand. "They're always worried, Vladimir. The sanctions can't touch us. Their money is safe."

"I think it's more than that, Mr. President," Federov said. "There's a concern about your appetite for risk."

To Federov's surprise, Luchnik threw back his head and laughed, a deep belly laugh. When he lowered his head again, Federov could see tears in his eyes.

"My appetite for risk, Vladimir?" he said, still chuckling. "Since when do you play the diplomat with me?"

Federov flushed.

"I have a suggestion, sir," he said. "A suggestion to improve your safety."

Luchnik put his feet down and leaned onto his desk. "Enlighten me. Who do I need protection from? I own these men, every one of them. They all sold me their balls for a few rubles."

Federov chose to ignore the obvious slight.

"Bring Nikolay back to Moscow, sir," Federov said. "It's time. None of us are getting any younger, and he's shown himself to be dedicated and loyal. His presence could be a stabilizing influence among the other cabinet members."

Luchnik went to the sidebar and poured himself a drink. He held the bottle up to Federov, who declined. Another data point, Federov thought. Luchnik rarely drank and never in the afternoon.

Luchnik settled against the edge of the desk, studying the amber liquid in his glass.

"You think it's time for me to bring Nikolay into the family business." It was a statement, not a question.

"I do, sir."

"And what would his new job be, Vladimir?"

"Deputy Minister of Defense."

Luchnik looked up in surprise. "I like it."

"Thank you, sir."

"There's only one problem," Luchnik said. "He's not ready. But he could be—with your help, Vladimir."

Federov smiled. "It would be my honor, Mr. President."

19

Dubai, United Arab Emirates

In addition to his native German, Tomas Horst spoke two languages, neither of which were Arabic. That something so easily accounted for was proving to be a problem this early in his mission did not bode well for success.

And yet, I will succeed, Tomas thought. Herr Mueller picked me out of all the legal apprentices at the firm for this job. I *will* be successful.

He pushed away the tiny voice in his head that reminded him, "Of course you will succeed. You don't have a choice, Tomas."

The man opposite him wore a white *kaffiyeh* with a black-and-gold headband and a dark blue business suit with matching tie. Based on his age, about the same as Tomas, and the cut of his suit, Tomas guessed his contact was also a newer associate in the Al Sharifa law firm of Dubai.

The other lawyer's experience was fine with Tomas. None of the business they needed to transact was technically challenging. It simply required a willful ignorance about certain details of the transaction.

By the way the man searched the drawers for a pen, Tomas guessed this was not his office. And no wonder. Outside the floor-to-ceiling windows was a stunning view of the tallest building in the world. The city of Dubai was a forest of skyscrapers, but the Burj Khalifa knifed far above them all into a clear blue sky.

After a series of false starts in German and French, they settled on English as their common language. Tomas introduced himself, and his counterpart said his name was Mr. Abadi.

"How can I help you today, Mr. Horst?" Abadi said. Although the office was air-conditioned, the man's forehead gleamed with a sheen of sweat. Tomas wondered if they were being recorded, and he decided they probably were.

"I need to form an international business corporation today and assign it as a subsidiary to a series of existing corporations," Tomas replied. An international business corporation was the legal term used for a shell company.

Abadi smiled. "Of course, sir. Simple enough."

Tomas noticed that even though there was a computer on the credenza on the right side of the desk, Abadi placed a laptop on the leather desk blotter and opened it. He tapped at the keys. "It will just take me a moment to log on to our secure network."

Tomas stared at the spire of glass and steel outside the window, gleaming in the late morning sun. Although beautiful, the dry air outside was like breathing inside a furnace. On the TV in his air-conditioned taxi, he'd seen that the temperature in Dubai was supposed to reach 40 degrees Celsius today.

Mr. Abadi seemed to be having trouble logging on to the

network, and Tomas's mind wandered as the minutes dragged on.

He'd promised his wife they would take a trip in the fall, and the money that Herr Mueller had offered him for this assignment would allow him to take Liesl wherever she wanted to go.

"I'm ready now, sir," Abadi said. "What is the name of your new corporation?"

"Paris," Tomas replied. "Paris Corporation." Mueller had said he could name the new shell company anything he liked as long as it was a common name and had nothing to do with either Germany or Russia. He was very specific on the last point.

I will take Liesl to Paris in the fall, Tomas decided.

"Yes, sir." Abadi went back to his laptop. "Will you be needing a business address here in Dubai? The firm can arrange that."

"Yes, please," Tomas replied. A Dubai corporation needed a Dubai business address.

"You mentioned subsidiaries, sir?" Abadi asked.

Tomas reached into his breast pocket and extracted a slim thumb drive, which he passed to Abadi. It contained a list of twenty-five shell companies and their registration details. He'd scanned the list on the plane. Although Herr Mueller had not specifically forbidden him from doing so, Tomas doubted the man would approve, either.

It was a risk, he knew, but Tomas felt he was entitled to know what he was carrying across international borders. Of course, he had a pretty good idea what he would find. Herr Mueller ran the Basement, the name given to the operation located on the subterranean floor in the firm's Zurich office. Among the apprentices, the rumor was that Mueller ran a money-laundering operation. Among the partners, Mueller's name and his Zurich operation were never mentioned. On the organization chart, Mueller appeared as an account consultant based in Vienna.

The thumb drive contained the names and registration information for twenty-five shell companies, all of which were unremarkable. Innocuous names like Beachfront Corporation and Timberdown, registered all over the world. Cayman Islands, Bermuda, Cyprus, Luxembourg, Switzerland.

Abadi loaded the information and tapped away for another ten minutes. He seemed calmer when he worked, and when he looked up again, he smiled at Tomas.

"And who will sign as director for the Paris Corporation?" he asked.

"Me," Tomas said, handing his passport across the desk.

"Very good, sir." After another minute of keyboard work, he placed an electronic signature pad in front of his client and handed him the pen.

Tomas hesitated. This was the moment of truth. There was a reason why Herr Mueller had sought out a mediocre student who'd barely passed his bar exam on the second try and struggled in his two-year apprenticeship. He suspected that Herr Mueller also knew that Tomas had used their apartment—a gift from Liesl's father—as collateral for a loan. Liesl didn't know about the transaction. He had tricked her into signing the paperwork. When Herr Mueller paid him, she never would never find out.

These thoughts crashed through his head as he gripped the fat electronic pen.

None of this is illegal, Tomas told himself.

He smiled at the sweaty Mr. Abadi, who smiled back. Two young legal professionals executing a perfectly legal business transaction.

Then he signed his name on the pad.

Tomas Horst.

20

35,000 feet over western Ukraine

A buzzing sound in the darkness. Invasive, insistent, like a mosquito whining right next to her ear. Without opening her eyes, Abby reached for the bedside table where she left her mobile phone. Her hand closed on the device, thumbed it on. She squinted in the glare of the screen.

No incoming call. Not even a signal.

Her foggy brain searched for an answer.

Bzzt.

This time there was a red flashing light, and the pieces fell into place.

Abby sat up in bed and snatched the receiver from the wall.

"We'll be on the ground in thirty minutes, ma'am," the pilot said.

"Thank you, Mike." She locked the phone in the secure cradle and rolled onto her back. Light leaked around the edges of the shuttered windows of the Bombardier Global 7000 jet. Finally, she turned her gaze to her left. Dylan was still asleep. He had a two-day beard, and his long hair had fallen into his eyes.

Her first thought was: God, he's even gorgeous in the morning. It was followed closely by: What the hell were you thinking?

Abby had not planned on sleeping with her CIA liaison officer. In fact, she made a point of never, ever mixing business and pleasure. But, it just sort of...happened.

Blame it on the crazy hours, lack of sleep, close quarters, pressure from the President, the fact that she was lonely...the champagne.

"Was this a mistake?" she said out loud.

Dylan propped himself up on one elbow. His eyes gleamed in the dimness, and she could see the glint of his smile.

"Let me see," Dylan began in a slightly mocking tone. "I just made love to a confident, beautiful, incredibly fit, not to mention very wealthy, woman. Now, in the cold light of day, she's asking me if it was a mistake. Should I assume I did not measure up to your high standards in the sack?"

Abby giggled. "I meant that we work together. This was a bad idea."

"It *was* a bad idea," Dylan said, planting a kiss on her cheek. "Past tense. We can either regret it or live with the undying shame of being human." He rolled out of bed in one fluid motion. "For the record, I don't think it's a mistake."

He dressed quickly, used the bathroom, and left the room.

Abby got up more slowly. In the bathroom, she splashed water on her face, pulled her blond hair into a ponytail, and applied light makeup, all the while avoiding her own gaze in the mirror.

In the two years since Joe's death, she'd slept with exactly two men, including Dylan. Her emotions were off-balance, and she had a headache from the champagne.

Get your head in the game, she said to her reflection. Dylan was right: mistake or not, what's done is done.

She dressed quickly in blue jeans, a blue oxford button-down, and hiking boots and zipped her duffel bag closed.

Dylan had coffee waiting for her. The private jet usually flew with at least one flight attendant, but she had requested only a pilot and copilot for this flight to Ukraine.

Face it, she thought. You knew this was going to happen. You planned it. You *wanted* it to happen.

"Still asking yourself that question?" Dylan poured her a cup of coffee.

"No comment," she muttered. She took a sip and sat up in her chair. "Whoa! Feed me two of these and you'll be peeling me off the ceiling."

Dylan winked. "Since you kept me awake most of the night, I figured I deserved an extra jolt this morning." He opened his tablet and scrolled through the screen. A scowl came over his face.

"What is it?" she asked.

Instead of answering, he flipped the screen around. It showed a *New York Times* article with the headline: *Russians claim American covert action in Ukraine.*

She skimmed the article. It was short and thin on details. RT, the Russian state-controlled television network, was reporting that two US covert operatives had been captured in Russian-controlled areas of eastern Ukraine. There was no mention of Sentinel Holdings, but it was tagged as a developing story.

"This was bound to happen at some point," Dylan said.

Abby glared at the screen. "Maybe, but Skelly made it so much worse."

The operation had been pretty tame by Skelly's standards. A four-person team was tasked to raid a Wagner forward listening post in the western outskirts of the tiny Ukrainian town of Holenka. It was a solid target, lightly defended—and it was a trap.

The Sentinel team came under fire as soon as they entered the town. Open fields ringed the area, and the town backed up onto the Sula River. A Wagner team, hidden only two kilometers away, moved in by chopper and swarmed the area.

Two of the Sentinel team members died almost immediately in a rocket attack. The remaining two, injured, fought on. Skelly claimed that they'd taken out six Wagner people, but Abby had seen the overwatch video, and that was probably wishful thinking.

Later that day, things went from bad to worse. If there had been any doubt in the minds of the Wagner leadership about who was behind the guerilla attacks in Ukraine, those doubts were put to rest when Sentinel received a ransom request.

Abby blew out a breath and looked out the window. The Ukraine countryside was a patchwork of rectangles; fields in different stages of cultivation were different colors. The deep brown of freshly plowed fields, the green of winter grains, the pale yellow of harvested areas, irregular clumps of trees along the borders.

The Wagner ransom was most likely a way to poke at Sentinel, to let them know that Wagner knew who their real enemies were now. The equivalent of a schoolyard taunt.

Still, they were her people. She had to try to get them back. The company had billions of dollars at their disposal. So what if she spent a few million to save the life of an employee? This was her call.

Until it wasn't. Without consulting her, Skelly responded to his counterpart at Wagner, a man named Pavel Kozlov, that Sentinel was not interested in a ransom arrangement. Except that Skelly said it in his own special Skelly way, laden with expletives and anatomical descriptors.

She opened her own tablet and checked on the hostages. Each Sentinel field operator had a SentiMonitor chip implanted underneath their right scapula. Once an hour, an overflight drone queried the device to receive an exact GPS location and basic vital functions.

The SentiMonitor indicated both men were alive. Michael "Zap" Zapasso was in much better shape than his companion, Art "Shipwreck" Stokes. Zap was new to Sentinel, but she knew Shipwreck well. He was one of Joe's first hires in Sentinel, a former US Navy SEAL and top-notch operator. Heart rates were elevated in both men, but that was to be expected. They were being held by an organization that had a reputation for brutal treatment of prisoners.

"How are they doing this morning?" Dylan asked. Access to the SentiMonitor data was restricted to Abby, Skelly, and Mama.

"They're alive," she replied. "That's more than you'll be able to say for Manson when I get done with him."

For months, she and Skelly had been at odds. She put up with his outbursts and his insubordination, but this time he had crossed a line. Not only had he undercut her with her employees, now he'd placed the entire Ukraine mission in jeopardy. Sentinel's participation was supposed to be covert. Skelly's remarkable luck with bold operations backfired this time, putting personnel at risk and exposing Sentinel's involvement in a foreign conflict.

From there, it was a short hop to linking Sentinel to the White House. This would make the pages of the *Washington Post*, and the pressure would fall on President Serrano—exactly the opposite of what they were trying to achieve.

As soon as she found out about his response to Wagner,

Abby ordered Skelly to stand down. She was personally going to handle the negotiation with the Russian PMC.

Rather than fight her, Skelly went radio silent. He stopped answering his phone, and when she called the ops center, she was told he was "out in the field." The tone of Skelly's man Landersmann told her that she wasn't going to get anything from him or any of his team no matter how many threats she made.

In a rage, she took the company jet to Ukraine, taking care to keep her travel plans closely held.

Two can play this game of hide-and-seek, she thought. She planned to make a surprise visit to the Sentinel command post in Ukraine and rain hellfire down on one Manson Skelly.

She wrestled with whether or not to include Dylan on the trip. The situation with Skelly was an internal company matter and technically none of the CIA's business. But Dylan figured it out and insisted on coming along.

She protested, but not really. She'd grown to trust him, and she welcomed his company—maybe a little too much.

"Penny for your thoughts," Dylan said.

"You'd be overpaying," she replied.

She sipped her coffee, sitting across from the man she'd just slept with, and wondered how her late husband would handle this situation with Skelly.

WWJD, she thought. What would Joe do?

He always found a way to keep the peace. But that was then; things were different now. A lot more people in a lot more places with lots and lots more money in play.

Everything had changed. Abby didn't see a way forward with Skelly. This time he had gone too far.

"It helps if you talk about it," Dylan said quietly.

"It's Skelly," she said. "Obviously. I think we need to part company."

"That's a big step."

Abby nodded, didn't say anything.

"Are you sure this is the right time for that?" Dylan asked.

"Is there ever a good time to end a business partnership?" Abby countered.

"Well, the middle of a war probably ranks among the worst, in my opinion," Dylan said. "Look, I respect you both as a businesswoman and a leader—other stuff, too." He flashed a wicked grin. "For all his faults, Skelly is getting results on the ground in Ukraine. Serrano, your client, is happy with those results. We can handle the media, but if you cut Skelly loose now..." Dylan let the sentence trail off.

Over Dylan's head, the fasten seat belts sign came on.

"On final approach," the pilot said over the intercom. "Touchdown in five minutes."

Abby tugged at the belt across her waist.

"I'll support whatever you do," Dylan said. He reached across the table and put his hand over hers. She squeezed his fingers.

Her phone buzzed. The caller ID said The White House.

Abby sighed and answered the phone.

21

Oleksandriya, Ukraine

Manson Skelly's boots thumped the concrete floor of the command post as he paced with the intensity of a caged animal.

"Manson, can you stop that, please?" Peter, the head computer geek, said without looking up from his laptop.

Skelly glared at the back of Peter's head, but he stopped pacing.

What he wouldn't give to be back in the Planetarium ops center in Sterling, Virginia, right now. There, he had all the resources a man could dream of to deal with this problem.

Instead, he was hiding away in a closet in the godforsaken country of Ukraine with Peter Ponytail, his laptop, and a thirty-two-inch desk monitor, trying to pull off a secret rescue operation.

He leaned over Peter. This was what Abby hired for Sentinel's field team: a pencil-neck twenty-something with a pint-sized ponytail and a giant-sized ego. He looked with disdain at the dandruff littering the young man's thin shoulders.

"Peter," he said, "get me a goddamned picture. Now."

"I'm trying, Skelly," Peter replied. "I don't control the weather. If you'd let me use Mama, I could bring in other assets and we could use the synthetic aperture radar system."

"Try harder, Peter. We're running out of time."

We're out of time, Skelly thought. The plan had been to attack the Wagner base at dawn, and dawn was an hour ago.

He could feel the walls closing in on him. Zap and Shipwreck were idiots for getting captured. Abby had been calling him nonstop since he'd called that Wagner asshole Kozlov back and set him straight on the situation.

A ransom demand, Skelly thought. Those dirty Russians would do anything for a buck.

Abby stopped calling—finally—and Skelly thought maybe this thing would just blow over.

That happy thought went out the window a few hours ago when Landersmann showed him the placeholder piece in the *New York Times*. Somebody was talking, and that was not good for him—or for Sentinel.

Skelly figured that Kozlov's next move would be to turn the Sentinel captives over to the Russians. He closed his eyes. Once the Russians had his boys, Skelly's ass was going to be hanging so far out in the wind, he'd be suffering from an acute case of hypothermia of the rectum.

No, there was no other way. He needed this plan to work, and he needed it to work right freaking now.

Skelly drew his tablet from the pocket on his cargo pants. He logged in to the screen that showed the life signs of his two captured men.

Zap looked okay. Clearly under stress, but his vitals were solid. The same could not be said for Shipwreck. His pulse was erratic, and he was running a fever. Skelly cursed and wheeled back on Peter. "Show me the pictures from last night," he said.

Peter threw the data to the monitor, and Skelly pulled up a chair so he could study the images.

Wagner's mobile CP was set up around a farmstead on the bank of a river. There was a big stone house that looked like it had started out as a small castle and been modified over the course of the last two centuries. A hundred meters from the house was a large wooden barn, painted red and surrounded by pastures dotted with the shapes of cows.

Next to the barn stood a defunct, ancient grain silo made of mortar and stone. The roofless structure was about eight meters high, with thick walls and one entrance.

That's where the Sentinel captives were being held.

Between the house and the barn, the Wagner vehicles clustered together. There were a half-dozen Land Rovers, a fuel truck, three heavy supply trucks, and a mobile armory.

Skelly grimaced. A full-on assault of the Wagner camp was a nonstarter. It would be a bloodbath. If he wanted to get his people out, he needed to be smart, surgical, and fast. A small team, a quick in-and-out operation. Infiltrate via the river, get the guys, and beat feet to a chopper exfil point.

Easy-peasy. All they needed was a big fucking distraction to occupy their Wagner hosts for about ten minutes.

On further consideration, the presence of the mobile armory was the answer to his prayers. One StormBreaker glide bomb on target and Wagner would be dealing with secondary explosions out the wazoo.

All they had to do was find the armory truck in the thick morning fog that blanketed the entire farm.

He stared at the ancient silo, now a prison for his two men.

You two are morons, he thought. How did you let yourself get captured?

He knew his anger was misplaced. He'd signed off on the mission. He was the one who sent his team straight into a Wagner trap.

"The extraction team is asking for an update," Peter announced.

The technician changed the monitor back to the over-watch video. Four blue dots showed next to the river, about a kilometer downstream from the Wagner camp.

Skelly wondered if they could use the jet packs for the rescue. They were noisy as hell, but maybe they could fly in using the fog as cover and drop right down the open roof of the silo. Could a jet pack get liftoff with two men?

Mama would know that answer, but if he asked the question, Abby would find out.

Skelly threw himself upright and began to pace again. Peter started to protest, but when he saw the look on Skelly's face, he turned back to his laptop without a word.

"I think the fog is starting to clear," Peter said, his voice hesitant.

Skelly turned back to the drone video. Peter was right. Shapes formed and dissolved. "Show me a thermal image," he said.

Skelly frowned in concentration. A few car engines glowed red and two campfires. Peter focused the image on the barn.

"Crap," he said.

"What?"

"The mobile armory is gone. They must have moved it."

"Then find it," Skelly said.

A fresh wave of fog obscured the image. Peter cursed and went to work on his laptop.

Landersmann entered the room and sidled up to Skelly. "I

just thought you'd want to know, boss," he said in a low voice. "She's here."

"Who?" Skelly snapped, still staring at the screen trying to will the fog away.

"The Queen B," Landersmann replied. "Abby. She's on the ground. She's *here*."

Skelly wheeled on him. "What? Abby's in the country?"

"My guy at the airstrip just called. He said the plane with Sentinel's tail number landed ten minutes ago, not on the schedule. Blond lady and a dark-haired guy got off. It's gotta be her, right?"

Skelly pinched the bridge of his nose so tightly he saw stars. If she found him running an off-the-books operation, he was a dead man. Unless he was able to bring his people home.

"How much time do I have?" he asked in a tight voice.

Landersmann shrugged. "Maybe twenty minutes? Half hour at the outside."

Skelly placed both hands on Peter's dandruff-laden shoulders. "Find that ammo truck and you'll be a very rich man, Peter."

"I'm on it, boss."

Skelly turned to Landersmann. "When she gets here, Landie, stall her. Do not tell her where I am. I can do this, I just need time."

"You got it, Manse." Landersmann left the room.

Skelly forced himself to focus on the problem, not the clock, but there was no getting away from the time stamp on the monitor. Seconds raced away, then minutes.

"Tell the extraction team to advance," he said to Peter.

"But we don't—"

"Do it, Peter."

"Yes, sir."

In a chat box on his laptop, he typed: *Team alpha, cleared to advance.*

Roger, came the secure text reply.

"It's clearing," Peter said, excitement lacing his tone. "I've got visual. There's the silo, the farmhouse... There's the armory truck. Acquiring target."

The blue dots representing the extraction team moved to the center of the river, inching their way toward the Wagner camp.

Relief flooded through Skelly. This is going to work, he thought.

Beyond the closed door of the office, Skelly heard raised voices, then Abby's voice rang out.

"Where is he?" she demanded. "Don't give me any of your shit, Landersmann, or I will fire you right here and now."

Skelly crossed to the door and turned the lock.

"Target acquired," Peter reported. "Target—no!"

"What's going on?" Skelly asked.

"The truck is moving," Peter said.

"Do you have a target lock?" Skelly asked. "Yes or no?"

A sharp knock at the door.

"Manson?" Abby's voice. "Manson, I need to speak with you immediately."

Skelly said nothing. When Peter looked up, Skelly shook his head and held his finger to his lips.

"Get me the key, Landersmann," Abby said. "Now."

Skelly looked over Peter's shoulder at the laptop screen. A target reticle tracked the blocky image of a moving truck. On the right side of the screen, a block indicating accuracy read 60 percent.

Fog washed over the image. Accuracy dropped to 47 percent.

"Take the shot," Skelly ordered.

"Skelly, it's a poor confidence solution on a moving target," Peter said. "I can't guarantee that we'll even hit the truck."

Behind them, someone kicked the door. Skelly heard the crackle of splintering wood.

"Take. The. Shot," Skelly ordered.

Peter sat back and folded his arms. "No."

Another kick, the screech of tearing wood fibers.

Skelly reached over Peter's shoulder, toggled the screen to the red FIRE button, and touched the keypad.

Fog rolled across the target image, obscuring the moving truck.

"Tell the extraction team," Skelly said. "Bombs away."

He turned to face the door. On the third kick, the lock buckled and the door burst open.

"Abby," Skelly said, with a smile. "If I knew you were coming, I'da baked a cake."

22

_____

Just outside Sencha, Ukraine

Pavel Kozlov stood at the French doors, sipping his coffee. He squinted at the fog outside the windows. The Sula River was somewhere out there, but right now he could barely see the edge of the flagstone veranda.

He stretched his shoulders. Pavel had claimed the featherbed in the master suite, and last night was the best sleep he'd had in weeks.

He ran his gaze over the exposed stone walls of the room. This place must be owned by an artist, he mused, a rich artist. The rustic kitchen was on the ground floor of the old part of the house. From the outside, the stone building looked like a castle, and he wondered how old it was.

The room was a sleek blend of modern and antique. Bare stone walls merged with high-end stainless steel appliances and granite countertops. A dozen of his men were seated around a long oak table that ran the length of the room and probably weighed as much as a small car. They ate in silence, most of them hungover. In addition to the former owner's exquisite taste in decorating, they also had an extensive wine cellar. The Wagner team had put a sizeable dent in the collection last night.

Maybe I'll own a place like this someday, Pavel thought. Maybe I'll just keep this place. Once the Russians move in, I don't think the owners will want to come back.

Not that they had left willingly, of course. By now, his men were skilled at convincing people that moving on was in their best interest. By the time he'd arrived with the hostages, the job was done. He'd settled the two Sentinel captives into their rustic accommodations in the old grain silo and claimed the master suite for himself.

Hell, he thought, this place even comes with its own prison. It really does have everything.

"More coffee, boss?" Sander De Vries was acting as chef this morning and doing a very passable job. The kitchen was aromatic with the smell of *pannenkoeken* and filled with the sound of men eating.

"Hmm." Pavel held out his cup for a refill. "Ivan," he said without turning around.

"Boss," the man replied, his mouth full of food.

"Get on the radio and find out when the military will be here," Pavel said. "I want to turn over our prisoners and be on our way." He heard Ivan's boots tromp out of the kitchen.

Outside, the fog thinned enough to allow Pavel to see the sun, a pale light in the milky sky. He could see the neatly mown lawn that he knew ran down to the water, but he still couldn't see the river.

He'd spent plenty of time fighting in the Donbas region of eastern Ukraine. Contested for the last decade, it was now a hellscape of shattered buildings, burned-out cars, trenches, and bomb craters.

And yet, people still lived there. Afraid, hunkered down,

resigned to their geographical fate. Many were older, people who had lived in the same house all their lives. Afraid to stay, but more afraid to leave.

Barely thirty kilometers away from the fighting in the Donbas were places like this one. True, an estate like this was rare, but most people in this part of the country had decent homes, cars, good internet, nice clothes.

Wagner's mission was to disrupt all that prosperity as a precursor to the westward Russian advance. Rile up the local population, fill the highways with refugees, making the Ukrainian military choose between family and fighting.

Unfortunately, the strategy was not working. The Ukrainian military was better armed and more tenacious than the Russian generals expected. Although NATO soldiers weren't in the Ukraine, plenty of NATO hardware was. It was clear to anyone paying attention that Russia was paying dearly for every centimeter of their advance.

And it wasn't just the military. The Ukrainian government had passed a new law some years before creating civilian militia forces. Those folks weren't professional military, but they'd proven hard to kill, even for some of his well-trained mercenaries.

Pavel turned around when he heard the sound of Ivan's boots returning to the kitchen.

"They're a half hour away," he said, retaking his seat at the table and spearing another *pannenkoeken*.

Pavel grunted acknowledgment. He'd be glad to be rid of those two. He was a soldier, not a babysitter.

If it had been up to him, he'd have wasted both of them on sight. After all, that was the point of his trap: to lure his enemy in and destroy them. And it had worked. The Sentinel assault team had sought out the poorly defended listening post like a bee searched for wildflowers. His only disappointment was that there had only been four of them.

But The Chef wanted prisoners that he could offer up to the GRU, so Pavel had spared the lives of the two injured men. He patched them up, tied them up, and conducted a short interrogation. It was short not because he was that effective, but because they told him whatever he wanted to know.

That's the good thing about contractors, he thought. They don't mess around with all that patriotism bullshit. They're in it for the paycheck, not to get their fingers broken.

Their story was worth their lives. Pavel had called The Chef as soon as he'd finished talking to the captured mercenaries.

"Sentinel Holdings is behind all the attacks," he told his boss. "They have five hundred people in country and more on the way. Plenty of hardware, too. Armed drones, jet packs—"

"You mean like Iron Man?" The Chef interrupted.

"Yeah, I guess." Pavel recalled the night of the fuel depot bombing. "More like a backpack. It's pretty cool."

"It's bullshit," The Chef snapped. "This changes nothing. They have jet packs, but you have ten times the number of men, Pavel."

Pavel didn't say anything. In truth, he admired what Sentinel had been able to accomplish in such a short time in the Ukraine. They were bold on the attack and carried a light footprint. Like the fuel depot bombing. A small team, they hit hard and got the hell out. In contrast, Wagner's operation felt sluggish, bureaucratic.

"Are you listening, Pavel?" The Chef asked.

"Sure."

"What did I just say?"

Silence.

The Chef sighed like he was lecturing a schoolboy who'd nodded off in class.

"I want you to call Sentinel and tell them we have their men," The Chef said. "Tell them we want ten million dollars ransom. Each. Cash."

"Why?" Pavel asked.

"Strategy," came the reply.

"Okay..."

Another sigh. "Pavel, if you ask for ransom, then they know that we know about them. They'll panic when they know we have proof that the US has hired mercenaries to do their dirty work in the Ukraine. The Western press will eat this up. Vitaly will love it."

Pavel frowned at the phone. The Chef was always name-dropping the Russian President.

"How do I get their number?" he asked.

"Look them up on the fucking internet, you idiot!" The Chef hung up.

That's what Pavel did. He called the Sentinel Holdings headquarters number and asked to speak to the CEO. He got an assistant, a guy named Josh, and told him: "I have two of your men, Stokes and Zapasso. If you want them back, I want ten million dollars each. In cash. In twenty-four hours, I turn them over to the GRU. Call me back."

He felt like a gangster when he hung up the phone. He'd made up the part about the GRU, but when he replayed the conversation in his head, it sounded like something a gangster would say.

He got a response two hours later. The man on the other end started talking as soon as Pavel answered the phone.

"Who the fuck is this?" The voice was pitched just short of shouting and white-hot with anger.

"Pavel Kozlov, who the fuck are you?"

"Okay, Pavel, this is Manson Skelly, and you have two of my men." What followed was a truly impressive tirade of profanity. Pavel's command of the English language wasn't good enough to follow all the nuanced descriptors, but Manson Skelly was clearly an artist in the use of profanity.

"Are you going to give me my money?" he asked when Skelly paused for breath.

"Fuck no," Skelly said, and hung up.

Pavel smiled at the memory. Despite being on different sides of the conflict, he liked Manson Skelly. Given the chance, he'd shoot him on sight, but under different circumstances, they might also be friends.

Pavel glanced out the window. Through a tear in the fog bank, he could see the river. It was calm, like a sheet of dark glass. He finished his coffee and turned to leave his mug on the heavy kitchen table.

The instant his cup touched the scarred oaken surface, the explosion happened. The windows blew in from the shock wave, sending a spray of glass across the crowded kitchen.

His body, schooled by years in a combat zone, reacted on instinct. His knees softened and he hit the polished flagstone floor, rolled underneath the heavy table. In the moment of shocked silence that followed the blast, a picture teetered on its wall hook, then fell. More glass shattered.

The sound brought Pavel to his senses. He rolled out from under the table and ran for the door.

The scene in the courtyard was chaos. A Land Rover flipped on its roof. There was a man behind the wheel and the engine was running. The windshield on a supply truck was blown in, and the tarp covering the cargo was in tatters. One of his men had been thrown against the truck. Pavel knelt next to him and felt for a pulse.

Nothing.

He cursed, then moved deeper into the carnage. He found another man, this one alive, and he called for a medic. Nearly all his men had been inside eating breakfast. This could have been much, much worse, he realized.

A heavy truck lay in his path. It had been flipped end over end and now rested on the roof. He took a shallow breath. It was the mobile armory. If the missile had hit that truck, this entire farmstead would have been leveled. They would all be dead now.

He skirted the capsized vehicle. The bomb crater before him was ten meters across, a pit of chewed-up earth and stone. The blast had dissipated the fog, but the thick gray mist seeped back into the hole.

Pavel looked up, suddenly thankful for the foggy morning. The bomb had missed the mobile armory by only a few meters, impacting in front of the truck, flipping it over.

His gaze moved to the other side of the bomb crater. A few moments ago, there had been another building there, a grain silo.

It was nothing but a pile of ancient stone.

23

Oleksandriya, Ukraine

"Manson, what have you done?"

Abby's teeth were clenched so tightly it was a wonder she could get the words out of her mouth at all. She felt the muscles in her jaw pop under the strain.

Skelly, who had been hunched over the back of the technician, stood up. His face twisted into a sneer.

"I'm doing what it takes, Abby." Skelly put his hand on the tech's shoulder. "Peter, tell the extraction team to move in."

"Put the overwatch video feed on the monitor," Abby said.

The technician looked at Skelly, who nodded.

She studied the screen. The image was a swirling mess of fire, smoke, and fog.

"Have Mama do a BDA," Abby ordered.

"We don't need a bomb damage—" Skelly began.

Abby cut him off. "Do it. That's an order."

Out of the corner of her eye, she saw Skelly nod at Peter.

The video image started to refine. She saw a shadowy bomb crater, then a boxy shape. It took her a second to realize that she was seeing a heavy cargo truck, but it was flipped on its back.

"Oh, my God," Peter said. "It's gone."

"What's gone?" Abby asked. Peter and Skelly both leaned over the screen, squinting.

"What is gone?" she asked again.

Skelly ignored her. "High mag." His voice sounded...hurt. She couldn't think of any other way to describe it.

The image on the screen shifted from the bomb crater and zoomed into focus. She saw a jumble of irregular shapes, like dirty Lego bricks. Fog swirled over the pile.

"What am I looking at?" she said. "Manson?"

Skelly looked like he'd been punched. He said nothing.

"Peter? What am I looking at?"

"The old castle thingy...the silo..."

"What about it?"

"That's where our guys were," Peter said. "That's where they were holding them."

"Tell the extraction team to hold in place." Abby got out her tablet and opened the SentiMonitor page. She queried the overwatch drone to ping for life signs of the captives. The screen displayed the word *Updating* and three rippling dots.

Skelly seemed to wake up suddenly. "Tell the extraction team to move in and give us a sitrep."

"No," Abby replied. "We're not putting any more lives at risk."

"Peter," Skelly said. "Tell the extraction team to move in."

The tech's finger moved over his laptop.

"Peter," Abby said, "if you touch that fucking keyboard, you will never work in computers again."

"I think we need to take a beat," said Dylan.

Abby startled. She had completely forgotten Dylan was even in the room. Skelly seemed just as surprised as she was.

When she turned, Abby saw Landersmann standing in the doorway, and there were people behind him.

"You need me, boss?" Landersmann said to Skelly.

"Get out," Abby replied. She strode to the door and tried to slam it shut. Thanks to Dylan's boot kicking it in, the door no longer fit in the frame, so she dragged a chair in front of it.

The tablet in her hand pulsed. The SentiMonitor reported no life signs from either Zapasso or Stokes.

"Pull the extraction team out," she said to Peter. When he looked at Skelly, she felt a fresh surge of anger. "Do it!"

She threw the tablet to Skelly, who caught it. He winced when he saw the screen.

"Do it," he said. "Initiate exfil procedures."

"Peter," Dylan said in a calm voice. "I think you should leave now. Monitor the extraction team progress from the bullpen. Let us know if there are any issues."

Peter stood and departed without a word.

Silence descended over the small room like a killing frost. Skelly collapsed into the chair behind the desk.

"What were you thinking, Manson?" Abby did her best to keep her voice calm and in control, but even she could hear the tremble of anger in her tone. "You ran an unauthorized operation, without Mama's oversight and analysis. You got two men killed by friendly fire."

Manson leaned over and pulled a bottle of Wild Turkey bourbon whiskey from his bottom drawer.

"Are you listening to me?" Abby said.

From the same drawer, he produced three glasses. He poured a generous shot into all three and pushed two across the desk. Skelly stood with the third glass in hand.

Abby moved forward, her thighs touching the edge of the desk. "I'm talking to you, Manson."

Skelly looked her in the eye, lifted his drink. "To absent friends."

Abby slapped the glass out of his hand. Liquid splashed across the desk surface. The glass spun, hit the wall, shattered. The sharp-sweet smell of bourbon hit Abby's senses, and the rage that she'd been barely holding back broke free.

"You just murdered two of our men," she shouted. "That's a court-martial offense."

"Court-martial." Skelly's tone dripped with disdain. "Listen to yourself, Abby. We left the military a long time ago —or did you forget that part?"

"We're supposed to be the good guys," Abby shouted back.

"The good guys?" Skelly laughed. He caught one of the still full glasses by the rim and drank it off in one shot. He pointed at the closed door. "Those people out there? Me? You? We work for a paycheck, lady. You want to fight for God and country, go enlist in the army."

"We're better than this, Manson," Abby said. "We're not just a bunch of mercenaries. We have a mission."

Skelly rolled his eyes. "Do you ever stop and listen to your-self? Wagner and Sentinel, we're the same. We kill people for money. That's our job."

"No."

"Yes." Skelly slammed the empty glass on the desk. His cheeks were flushed red, his chin set. "Those guys who died? Zap and Shipwreck? They knew the risks when they signed their contracts. Shit happens. You know it, I know it, and if Joe were standing here right now, he'd agree with me."

Abby felt something go *snap* inside her head. Her mind flashed red, all thoughts froze in place. Her face flamed with anger as she fought to put words together. When the words happened, they poured out like a break in a dam.

"How dare you." Abby didn't even recognize her own

voice. "You use my husband's name to justify murder?" She picked up the remaining glass and hurled it against the wall. Bourbon and glass blasted apart. "You are finished, Manson. Done. Get on the next plane home."

Someone grabbed her arm.

"Abby," Dylan said.

"What?" she shouted.

For the second time, she'd forgotten Dylan was even in the room. Her heart hammered. She felt her arm shaking in his firm grip. She turned, focused on his face. He looked calm, centered. Her anger peaked and ebbed.

"Let's not be hasty," Dylan said.

Abby blinked at him, unable to process the words she'd just heard.

"What?"

He took her free hand. "You're upset," he said. "We all are, but—"

"But what, Dylan? Two men *died*." She shook free of his grasp.

"What happened was unfortunate," Dylan said, "but Skelly is not wrong here. We cannot let our people become Russian propaganda pawns."

He sounds so reasonable, Abby thought, like he's talking about something he heard on NPR.

Behind her, on the other side of the desk, Skelly stirred.

"Look, Abby, I could've handled this better. I shoulda called you first. But you know what it's like in the field, right? Long hours, no sleep. We're outgunned, and I was trying to—"

"You shut up," Abby snapped at Skelly. To Dylan, she said, "Are you serious? You just saw two men murdered, and you're saying we should overlook that detail?"

"I'm not condoning what happened, but think of the big picture here," Dylan said. "Our mission is to keep the Russians bottled up and keep Ukraine out of the news. We're accomplishing that mission. Yes, this is a setback, but—"

"But?" Abby interrupted. "But we killed two of our own guys, so let's have a toast and call it a day? Is that what you were going to say, Dylan? Is that how the CIA operates?"

Dylan's expression tightened. "In my role as CIA liaison officer, I need to insist that you do not preemptively remove Skelly from the field operation."

Abby's fists were clenched so tightly, she could feel her fingernails cutting into her palms. It took everything she had to keep her voice under control.

"I'm taking over the Ukraine operation," she said.

"Abby," Dylan said, his tone so very reasonable. "You have a company to run, and don't forget about the phone call you got when we landed."

She breathed out, still feeling the emotion in her breath. Serrano wanted to see her first thing tomorrow with a personal update about the situation in Ukraine.

"How about two weeks?" Dylan said. "That will give Manson time to turn over the operation."

"That...should be fine," Skelly said.

Abby faced him, and they locked eyes. "I want you out of here in two weeks. No exceptions. I have your word on that, Manson?"

Skelly smiled. "You're the boss."

24

Warsaw, Poland

Although he'd left the Nezyvna refugee camp days ago, in some ways the camp hadn't left him.

The smell of the place still clung to his clothes. Fresh mud, old sweat, and human desperation were all scents that did not wash away easily.

Don rubbed his eyes, feeling the grit like sand on his eyeballs. He and Harrison worked late and got up early, but every time he tried to sleep, he dreamed about the camp.

If his time as an analyst had taught him anything about life, it was that as an American, he'd won the geographical lottery. The refugees he'd met in the camp were college professors, doctors, taxi drivers, farmers, and housewives. Normal people, no different than him, whose only misfortune was being born at the wrong geographical coordinates.

"Don? You still with us?" The voice from the speakers of the laptop echoed around the high-ceilinged office in the Agencja Wywiadu. Jakub had set him and Harrison up with a secure conference room to work in.

Harrison, seated next to Don, answered for the both of them. "Sorry, guys, we're beat. Let's go through this one more time and call it a night...er, morning."

Don squinted at the clock in the lower right-hand corner of the laptop screen. Two a.m., Warsaw time. His mind wrestled with time zone math. That made it eight p.m. back at the Emerging Threats Group in Virginia.

Don smiled for the benefit of Michael Goodwin and Dre Ramirez on the other end of the secure videoconference. "I'm fine, Dre. Thanks for asking. It's been an eventful couple of days."

"Well, you look like crap," she replied in her normal brusque manner. "Harrison's right: let's recap. Michael and I will take the night shift here."

Since he wasn't supposed to be working the Ukraine problem, Don deliberately kept the analyst team small. He trusted the people on this call with his life—on a few occasions, that had been actually true—and he respected their analytical talents. If there was something more to the Ukraine situation than another Russian power grab, this team would ferret it out.

"Put up the regional map again, please," Don said.

The laptop screen filled with an image of eastern Europe with Ukraine at the center. The map populated red dots with data tags, indicating Russian military units.

"I've never seen anything like this," Harrison said, a note of concern in his tone. "It looks like the whole Russian military is on the move."

It was true. In addition to the ongoing conflict in Ukraine, the map showed heightened Russian military activity on the borders of Kazakhstan, Georgia, and Chechnya in the south. Russian naval patrols in the Black Sea had instituted a de facto blockade against Ukrainian ports. There were reports of civil unrest in Moldova and Romania, suspected to be the result of Russian disinformation campaigns.

The Rosgvardiya, the Russian National Guard, was on alert as well. They'd been deployed to the rear guard of the Russian Army for "enhanced security," which was Luchnik's way of quelling dissent in the military ranks.

Ironically, the only bright spot was in eastern Ukraine. The Ukrainian military, reinforced by NATO-provided weaponry, had slowed Russian advances for the moment. In fact, observed Don, they were giving the Russians a downright pasting.

"If Ukraine is the goal," Dre said, "why aren't they throwing everything they have into that fight? Instead, they're moving forces into Belarus."

"Luchnik is using Belarus to change the narrative," Harrison replied. "In Ukraine, he's the aggressor, but in Belarus, he's a savior."

The past forty-eight hours had generated a torrent of social media posts showing Russian soldiers rescuing orphans, feeding refugees, and bringing order to the capital of Belarus. The Russians were masters of sharp power, the manipulation of public opinion via news media and other information outlets. The Russian "patriotic hackers" had proven once again that they had the ability to shape the narrative. Public outrage over the Russian takeover attempts in Ukraine had lessened, replaced by public approval of their assistance to Belarus.

"What's the latest intel from NATO?" Don asked.

"It's a mixed bag," Michael said. "Like the rest of us, NATO is trying to figure out Luchnik's next move. They're in a holding pattern."

"That doesn't apply to Poland," Harrison said. "Jakub tells me they think the Belarus situation is a distraction. The Polish military is preparing for a Russian breakout into western Ukraine. If the Russians cross the Dnieper River, the Poles are convinced they won't stop until they take the whole country. Once Ukraine falls, Poland is next on the menu for Luchnik. This is what they've been fearing since the Soviet Union fell in 1991."

Don studied the map. Blue dots representing Polish Army units clustered at the five-hundred-kilometer border with Ukraine. A few more units were posted farther north, along the border with Belarus, but Don knew those units were swamped with responding to the refugee crisis.

Jakub had briefed them earlier. Following the assassination of the Belarusian heads of government, panicked rumors seized the refugee camps. Fearing they would be sent back to their places of origin, thousands of refugees flooded across the Polish border. Rounding them up was a full-time job for the military.

Far to the north, where the country of Poland touched the borders of NATO ally Lithuania and the Russian oblast of Kaliningrad, was a single Polish Army unit, the 1st Warsaw Armoured Brigade.

"The Poles have made up their own mind about what's going on," Harrison said, "and they're taking action."

"Won't that be an issue with NATO leadership?" Dre asked.

"I don't think the Poles care," Harrison replied. "This is not a game of strategy for them. This is survival. The way they see it, once the Russian genie is out of the bottle, it's not going back in. They are not going to let that happen."

Michael spoke up. "I've done an analysis on Russian maneuvers over the last thirty years. Every time Luchnik has violated a border, there was an incident of civil unrest which prompted the invasion. Crimea, Georgia, Chechnya, Kazakhstan. Usually, that incident was manufactured by Russian intelligence. Is it possible the Russians are behind the bombing in Minsk?"

Harrison threw up his hands. "I've asked myself the same question, Michael, but I don't see it." His tone showed his exasperation. "Belarus was already a puppet state. The Russians could do whatever they wanted under the old regime. There were Russian officials in that room. Luchnik's a cold bastard, but would he blow up his own people?"

Don could feel his attention slipping away. He needed sleep.

"Okay," he said, "Dre and Michael, take what we have so far and draft a report. We're gonna sign off for the night." He ended the video call and sat back in his chair.

"I think I'm too old for fieldwork, Harrison," he said.

"You and me both," the other man replied. "I haven't felt this tired since...I don't think I've ever felt this tired." Harrison sat up in his chair. "Maybe we're looking at this the wrong way. Maybe the Russians have bitten off more than they can chew this time."

"Meaning?" Don asked.

"Meaning, what if the freedom movement in Belarus saw an opportunity and took it?" Harrison said. "What if Luchnik's the victim this time, not the perpetrator?"

"I think that's called irony," Don replied. "But suppose you're right. Why all the activity in the Black Sea? Why look like you're trying to start something in Chechnya or Georgia?"

"He's chumming the water. Trying to confuse the situation."

"It's working," Don said.

"The US has to get involved, Don," Harrison said. "Without the United States, NATO won't act."

Don nodded.

"You just told Dre and Michael to draft a report," Harrison said. "What do you plan to do with it?"

"I don't know yet," Don said.

"Well, you can't send it up the chain," Harrison continued. "Otherwise, you'll have Dylan Mattias dancing on your undershorts. You're not supposed to be here, remember?"

Don almost wished he hadn't come on the trip in the first place. Between the haunting visit to the refugee camp and the lack of progress, the trip was a bust.

"We need more analytical horsepower on this," Harrison continued. "We're missing something, I can feel it."

"What if," Don said in a thoughtful tone, "I had a way to get more analytical resources and convince the President to engage with NATO?"

"If you're granting wishes, I'll take a unicorn," Harrison said with a yawn.

"I have an idea," Don said.

"If it involves a good night's sleep, I'm in."

"I think I know somebody who can help us solve both problems," Don said.

"Who?"

"A friend," Don said. "At least, I think she's still a friend."

25

25,000 feet above the Atlantic Ocean
250 miles east of Washington, DC

Abby made sure there was a flight attendant for the flight back to Washington, DC. She and Dylan had not spoken since they'd left the Sentinel command post, and the young woman seemed to sense the iciness between her customers.

"Mr. Mattias would like to join you for dinner, ma'am," she said to Abby an hour after they'd left Ukraine airspace.

"I'll be dining alone," Abby replied.

Although her filet mignon was melt-in-the-mouth tender and paired spectacularly with her favorite Malbec blend, the meal was wasted on her. She might as well have eaten a protein bar and a bottle of water for all the enjoyment she received from the food.

She ordered coffee with dessert. Cherries jubilee, another of her favorites. She had to admit the contractor who ran their private flights understood customer service.

Dylan approached from the back of the plane, coffee in

hand. He gestured at the empty seat across from Abby. "May I?"

Inside, Abby sighed. Might as well have this out now, she thought.

Dylan sat, smiled, drank coffee, looked out the window. There was a full moon riding over a silver sea. Abby stared at the moon and waited him out.

"I thought I'd give you time to cool off," he said finally.

Abby said nothing.

"Look," Dylan tried again, "I know you're disappointed I didn't support you with Skelly—"

"Don't pretend to know me, Dylan." Her reply came out louder and with more heat than she'd expected. Abby cut a quick glance to the flight attendant, who was sitting in the galley. The young woman did not look up. She either hadn't heard or was smart enough not to acknowledge it.

Abby leaned forward, lowered her voice. "You think because we slept together that I'm expecting special treatment from you? Don't flatter yourself."

"What happened was unfortunate, but—"

"Two of my men were killed by friendly fire!" Abby shot back. "I'd call that more than unfortunate."

"Grow up, Abby," Dylan replied, his face flushed. "Your company was hired to conduct covert operations in a foreign country. Did you really think that people wouldn't get killed?"

"Don't patronize me," Abby said. "I've done my time in the field. I've lost good men and women in combat. But they were killed by the enemy, not their own people."

Dylan paused. The conversation was going nowhere, and they both knew it. He motioned to the flight attendant for more coffee.

As she refilled their cups, she said, "Ms. Cromwell, your dessert's melted. Can I bring you a fresh serving?"

Abby looked at her cherries jubilee. The vanilla ice cream had turned to soup.

"You can take it away," Abby said. "I've lost my appetite."

She saw Dylan's jaw muscle twitch, the first crack she'd detected in his composure.

Score one for humanity, she thought. The robot has feelings.

Dylan let the silence drag on. Abby waited him out. She wasn't about to fall for the oldest trick in the interrogator's handbook. If he wanted to engage her, then he'd have to make the first move.

"Skelly's tactics are unconventional," Dylan said, "but he's getting the job done."

Abby leaned forward. She kept her voice low and calm. "Manson Skelly murdered two of my men. An accident? Maybe. I hope so, I really do. But let's get one thing clear: if you say one more word to minimize what he's done, I swear to God, I will take this public and burn down the house around us. Are we clear?"

Dylan's eyes narrowed. His jaw rippled with tension. "I don't respond well to threats, Ms. Cromwell. I am still your liaison officer, so we can do this the easy way or—"

"I'll take the hard way, Mr. Mattias." Abby sat back in her chair, looked out the window. "Now find another place to sit on my airplane."

The moon shone in the night sky, the mottled gray of the surface features clearly visible. Once for a middle school science project, she had memorized all of them. The names came back to her now: Sea of Tranquility, Sea of Serenity, Sea of Crises, Ocean of Storms...

She looked away, her eyes searching for the lights of the east coast of the United States, and her memory wandered.

Her mind wrestled with how much of her conflict with

Dylan was based in fact and how much in pride. In his own way, Skelly was executing Sentinel's mission in Ukraine. He was getting results, and their client, who also happened to be the most powerful man in the free world, was pleased.

But Abby was unhappy. This was not how she had envisioned her company. Sentinel was supposed to be a force for good—with the emphasis on *good* instead of *force*. Once upon a time, she and her husband had believed that was possible... but was it?

Has the world changed, Abby wondered, or is it just me? If you want to play the game of war, there are costs that must be paid. Costs of blood and treasure. In the heat of battle, mistakes happen. People die. The application of technology only made that problem worse. In World War One, the machine gun turned the battlefield into a killing field. In Taiwan, her company had used assassin drones to the same effect.

She drank cold coffee, less for the caffeine and more to feel the acidic bite on her tongue. Any sensation to tear her brain away from these spiraling thoughts.

Abby opened her phone and scrolled through a news feed. Most of the stories were about President Serrano's barnstorming campaign across the country. He had a stated goal of at least one event per day campaigning for other members of his party in advance of what was shaping up to be a very competitive midterm election. At each visit, he talked about his human infrastructure plan to put millions of young people into high-paying trades, and polling in support of the new initiative was strong. One news site even posted a Serrano Streak, which counted how many days in a row the President held an event for one of his party members. He was up to fifteen.

She searched for news about Ukraine. Routine updates

and political condemnations, but nothing substantive. The *New York Times* story about the two operatives had not been updated.

Abby knew she should be happy about that, but instead she felt sick inside.

Are we better than Wagner, she wondered, or just another mercenary organization that kills for money?

The Washington skyline came into view. The lighted city was beautiful. She picked out the Capitol, the white spike of the Washington Monument in front of the Reflecting Pool, and the White House.

When she was a girl, her father sometimes brought her downtown. Just the two of them. They might visit the Smithsonian or walk along the Mall. Even at that age, Abby realized her life was different than other kids her age. There was the family money, of course, but it was more than that. Her father had expectations for her. It was strange to her that she could never remember him actually giving voice to his expectations, but they were always there.

She joined the military as much for her father as for herself. She met Joe there, and her father had approved of that decision, too. He didn't live to see her and Joe—and Manson— found Sentinel Holdings, but she suspected he would have agreed with their mission. He would have been proud of her. That was all she wanted. All she'd ever wanted.

And now? she wondered. Bitterness crept into her thoughts. Now, I'm sleeping with CIA agents and getting my own people killed.

Her phone buzzed with an incoming call. She flipped it over. The caller ID read: Don Riley.

"Hello?" she said.

"Abby, it's Don." He sounded dead tired. "Can you talk?"

She sneaked a look around the edge of her seat. Dylan sat

a few meters away, his eyes closed.

She faced forward again. "I can. How have you been?"

"I've been..." Don's voice trailed off. "Well, I'm sick about the whole situation, if I'm being honest. If I share something with you, will you promise not to pass it on to Dylan Mattias?"

Abby stopped herself from giving a wry chuckle. "I can assure you that anything we talk about will stay between us."

"I'm in Poland now," Don said. "Warsaw, to be exact. Any intel coming out of Sentinel has been designated close hold, so I'm trying to develop some insight into the Ukraine situation."

"You've been cut out of the loop and yet, you persist."

Don laughed. "I'm sorta wired that way, I guess. I'm a do-gooder."

Abby closed her eyes. "I used to think that way."

"That's why I called, Abby," Don said. "I think you still do, and I'm calling to ask for a favor."

"Anything, Don."

"You should hear me out first. It's a big one."

"Hit me," Abby said.

"I want you to talk to the President."

Abby didn't answer.

"Are you still there?"

"Why would I do that, Don?"

"You have a personal relationship with him," Don said. "Maybe you can convince him that keeping NATO at arm's length is a mistake. There's a lot of moving parts and a ton of disinformation, but I know in my gut that this is about more than just Ukraine. If we move quickly, we might cause Luchnik to rethink his plans."

"And those plans are what?" Abby asked.

Don blew out an exasperated sigh. "I wish I knew, which brings me to my second favor."

"Two in one day," Abby said. "Now you're asking a lot."

"I want you to give me access to intel coming out of Sentinel," Don asked. "I know that puts you in an awkward position, but—"

"I'll give you access to Mama," Abby interrupted him. "No restrictions."

Silence on the other end of the line.

"Don, are you there?"

"You realize what I'm asking, right? You're going against your own liaison officer."

"Are you trying to convince me not to do the favor you just asked for?"

"No, I'm grateful," Don said quickly. "I'm just wondering what's changed."

"Everything," Abby said.

She resisted the urge to look back at Dylan. Sentinel was her company. It was time she made decisions that were in the best interests of her company.

"Coordinate with Josh," she said. "I trust you to be discreet."

"Thank you, Abby," Don said. "I really mean that. If I'm right, and I hope I'm not, this could save a lot of people."

"I'm sorry," Abby replied. "I should've fought to keep you as liaison officer. Instead, I let others make decisions for me. I didn't use the power I had. I'm sorry for that."

"Take care, Abby," Don said and hung up.

"Who was that?" Dylan's voice was right behind her chair. Abby flipped the face of her phone flat against her thigh so he couldn't see the screen. He moved into her line of sight.

"Who were you talking to?" he repeated.

Abby looked out the window. The lighted shape of the Capitol dome slid beneath the wing of the aircraft.

"A friend," Abby said.

26

Rapid City, South Dakota

Tomas Horst arrived in Rapid City, South Dakota, at four o'clock on a Sunday afternoon.

He was in an excellent mood, well rested. Herr Mueller had provided him with a first-class ticket for his trip from Vienna to the United States, and Tomas had taken full advantage of all the perks of elite travel.

Following his return from Dubai, Herr Mueller paid him half of the agreed-upon fee for his services. With the money, Tomas paid off his secret loan and made reservations for the trip to Paris with his wife for their anniversary. Maybe, after Herr Mueller paid him the rest of the money, he would even upgrade them to first class.

Whatever qualms Tomas may have harbored about Herr Mueller and his work in the Basement were gone. Money like this was too good to pass up.

He'd never been to the American Midwest, so after he secured his rental car, instead of going straight to his hotel, Tomas drove east on Route 90. The interstate highway was arrow-straight, flanked on both sides by gently rolling hills cloaked in green.

Accustomed to driving on the autobahn, Tomas pushed the rental car, a Hyundai Elantra, to 150 kilometers per hour. That was as fast as he dared to go in the compact vehicle, but even at that speed, other cars easily passed him. It seemed the German autobahn and the American interstate highways operated under the same rules after all.

I wish Liesl could see this, Tomas thought. But Herr Mueller would not have allowed it. In fact, he was breaking Herr Mueller's rules right now. His instructions were to go straight to his hotel and order room service. Tomorrow morning, he had three stops to make, then a three p.m. flight to catch.

But how could he stay indoors with this glorious weather?

The sun was starting to set, bathing the landscape in golden light. He topped a shallow rise, and on the right side of the highway, Tomas saw a grouping of brown lumps in a fenced field.

Buffalo, he thought as he slowed the rental car and pulled into a small parking area.

The light was failing, and the small lot was deserted. Gravel crunched under his shoes as Tomas crossed to the fence line.

A herd of some thirty animals grazed fifty meters away. The last of the daylight touched their wooly brown backs with gold, and Tomas spotted some babies suckling their mothers. Between the herd and the fence, a massive old bull grazed. He was so close that Tomas could hear him tearing grass with his teeth.

The animal was breathtaking. It stood at least a meter and a half tall at the humped shoulders, and two curved horns crowned the head of the beast. Patches of wooly winter fur had sloughed off the animal's flanks, revealing ripples of muscle.

Tomas pulled out his phone and tried to take a selfie with the buffalo in the background.

"Would you like me to take your picture?" a voice asked.

Tomas had not heard any other cars enter the parking lot, but when he turned around, he saw a large pickup truck parked next to his rental car. The man who'd spoken was medium height and slight of build, dressed in blue jeans, a denim shirt, and a cowboy hat.

"Yes, please," Tomas said, passing the man his phone.

The man pointed the camera at Tomas. "Say cheese."

Tomas did as he was told and accepted his phone back. He would send these pictures to Liesl tonight.

"It's a fine-looking animal," the man said. "Where you from?"

"Germany," Tomas replied.

"There used to be millions of buffalo across the Great Plains," the man continued. "Then the world changed."

"I've seen *Dances with Wolves*," Tomas said. "The movie. It has lots of buffalo."

The man's face was lost in the gloom of twilight. "You staying around here tonight?" he asked.

"I have a hotel room in Rapid City," Tomas said. "I was hoping to get a picture of the baby buffaloes to send to my wife, but the light is gone."

"Another time, maybe," the man said. "You should get going. It gets pretty dark out here after the sun goes down."

Tomas walked back to his car. The tiny rental was dwarfed by the pickup truck parked next to it. The truck was dark blue or black, with heavy chrome wheels and the word RAM in silver block letters across the grill.

"Thank you," Tomas said.

"Don't mention it." The man hoisted himself into the driver's seat of the truck and rolled down the window. "Have a good trip," he called over the rumble of the powerful engine.

Tomas navigated to the edge of the highway and turned back toward Rapid City. There were few cars on the road at this hour. In his rearview mirror, he saw the truck reach the highway and turn to follow him.

———

At eight o'clock the next morning, Tomas parked his rental car in front of The UPS Store on Haines Avenue. The business occupied an end unit in a new-looking strip mall. Inside, a middle-aged man, whose name tag identified him as Tony, greeted Tomas.

"Can I help you?"

"Yes, please, I wish to rent a mailbox," Tomas replied.

Tony gestured to the wall of brass-colored boxes. "That's what we do here. Did you need a big one or a little one?"

"A small one is fine."

Tomas filled out the rental agreement while Tony helped another customer.

"I'll need two forms of ID," he said as he looked over the completed agreement, "and a method of payment."

Tomas used his passport and his Austrian driver's license.

"You moving to South Dakota, Mr. Horst?" Tony asked, peering at the driver's license through reading glasses.

"I need the address for a business venture," Tomas replied. "I'll pay one year in advance. Is cash acceptable?"

"Man after my own heart," Tony replied, passing him the key to his new mailbox. "Number one-three-six is all yours. Good luck with your business, Mr. Horst."

As Tony moved away to help another customer, Tomas

extracted an envelope from his inner pocket and used a pen from the counter to write a name across the front. Herr Mueller had been very clear in his directions: Tomas was to write the man's name on the envelope just before he placed it in the new mailbox.

Tomas pocketed the new mailbox key and moved on to his next appointment.

The law office of Samuel T. Jefferson, Esq., was a tiny store-front on Main Street sandwiched between a bar called the Brass Rail Lounge and a record store, Black Hills Vinyl. There was an open parking spot right in front of the bar.

A bell over the door jingled when Tomas entered. Behind a reception desk sat a young woman dressed in blue jeans and a white tank top. A blue fingernail moved along the surface of her mobile phone. She did not look up as she asked, "Can I help you?"

"I have an appointment with Mr. Jefferson at ten o'clock," Tomas said. "I'm early."

"No worries." The young woman raised her voice. "Daddy, your ten o'clock is here." She looked up at Tomas and smiled. "Go right on back." She turned her attention back to her phone.

Samuel T. Jefferson, Esq., was a tall, lean man with skin the color of red clay and an impressive handlebar mustache. He wore blue jeans, cowboy boots, and a tight black T-shirt that read Sturgis Motorcycle Rally.

He showed Tomas to a seat and returned to his place behind the desk.

"What can I do for you today, Mr. Horst?"

"I need to set up a holding company," Tomas said.

"Well, you have come to the right place, then." Jefferson plucked a pair of reading glasses from his desk and positioned himself in front of his computer. "You have a name picked out for this endeavor?"

"I wish the company to be called Pandora Corporation," Tomas said.

Jefferson spelled out the name as he typed. He peered over his glasses at Tomas. "Address? We can use this address for a small extra fee."

Tomas passed the lawyer a business card from The UPS Store. "Please use mailbox number one-three-six."

"Righty-o." Jefferson typed the information in. "And does your company have any assets?"

Tomas withdrew from his breast pocket a sheet of paper with the registration information from Paris Corporation, the shell company he had established in Dubai. "I wish the Pandora Corporation to be the sole owner of this company."

"Can do," Jefferson said. "I see you are the nominal director of Paris Corporation. Do you want the same arrangement here?"

"Yes." Tomas held out his passport, but the lawyer waved it away. "That won't be necessary, Mr. Horst. No need for the government to be sticking their nose into your business." The printer across the room sprang to life, and Jefferson got up to retrieve the pages. "I just need your John Hancock right here."

Tomas had no idea what a John Hancock was, but he assumed it meant his signature, so he signed both copies.

Jefferson handed him one sheet. "I keep a copy, and this one's yours."

Tomas hesitated. Herr Mueller's instructions were very clear. "I do not need a copy," he said.

Jefferson shrugged. "Suit yourself." He dropped both copies onto his desk. "Anything else I can do for you, Mr. Horst?"

"Yes," Tomas answered. He held up the sheet of paper

containing the details of the Paris Corporation. "Do you have a shredder?"

Of course Jefferson had a shredder, and Tomas was welcome to it. The single sheet disappeared with a noisy *bzzzt*.

"Will that be cash or charge, sir?" Jefferson asked.

Tomas paid in cash and was on the sidewalk a few minutes later.

He checked his watch and blew out a breath of frustration. His next appointment was over an hour from now.

He thought about the adorable baby buffalo calves. If only there was some way to move the appointment up, he would have time to drive back out to the buffalo herd before his flight.

But he didn't know who he was meeting with. All he knew was the person was supposed to meet him at the Brass Rail Lounge, next to the lawyer's office. Not knowing what else to do, Tomas entered the bar.

After the bright sunlight, Tomas paused to let his eyes adjust to the dark interior. It was only midmorning, before the lunch crowd, and the room looked empty.

"Well, lookee here. My friend from the buffalo herd." The same man Tomas had met the evening before was seated alone in a booth next to the door. A pint of beer stood on the table before him.

"Hello," Tomas said awkwardly.

"Join me," the man said, smiling.

Tomas froze. He was supposed to meet someone. What if this man scared the person away?

"I—I can't," Tomas said. "I have to..."

To what? he thought. Think, you idiot. He cursed himself for not following Herr Mueller's directions exactly.

"Have you seen the sunflower fields yet?" the man called.

Tomas's head snapped around. That was the phrase his

contact was supposed to use to identify himself. Was it possible the man he had met the prior evening was his contact?

Tomas blinked. What was his response? Herr Mueller made him memorize the words exactly...something about flowers. The words came to him in a flash of memory.

"I thought they didn't bloom until July," Tomas said, approaching the booth.

"The sunflowers will bloom early this year," the man replied, watching Tomas with cold eyes. "Sit," he commanded.

Tomas did as he was told.

"You're early," the man said in a low tone.

"I—I thought—" Tomas stammered.

"Never mind," the man said. "Do you have it?"

Tomas dug the mailbox key from his pocket and slid it across the table. With a swipe of the man's hand, the key disappeared. He stood up. "You need to learn to follow directions, Tomas." The man waved his hand at the bar. "Gotta run, Sally. Take 'er easy."

A waitress approached Tomas. "What can I getcha, hon?" she asked.

Tomas blinked. The entire encounter had lasted less than five minutes. He was done. The last thing Herr Mueller had instructed him to complete was over, and he was—Tomas checked his watch—more than two hours early!

"Sorry." Tomas got up. "I just remembered I need to be somewhere."

He walked briskly out of the bar and got into his rental car.

Plenty of time to go back to the buffalo herd and get a few photos of the babies before his flight left at three o'clock. He nodded to himself. Plenty of time.

27

Hotel Bel-Air
Los Angeles, California

Abby sat back as the waitress set a plate of glazed chicken breast, roasted potatoes, and green beans in front of her.

I guess that's what $135,000 buys you in politics these days, she thought. Although she'd grown up in a wealthy family, this was too much, even for someone with her background. She chewed a bite of chicken that probably equaled a week's wages for the young woman who'd just served her. The meat was cooked to perfection, and the citrus glaze paired perfectly with the chilled Sauvignon Blanc.

To her left, Dylan seemed to be having similar thoughts. He inspected a roasted potato speared on his fork, then put it in his mouth and chewed thoughtfully.

Abby had been to political fundraising dinners before, although never one this expensive, but Dylan was probably a first-timer. She doubted the CIA officer had a spare $135,000 lying around to throw at his favorite candidate.

The Garden Ballroom of the Hotel Bel-Air felt a million

miles from reality. The twelve-acre estate, nestled in the canyons above the exclusive community of the same name, wore its Hollywood history like royal robes. Pictures of Grace Kelly, Cary Grant, and Marilyn Monroe tastefully adorned the hallways of the main hotel.

Around two dozen tables, under the handmade starburst chandeliers, sat the California uber-rich. Abby picked out movie stars, tech billionaires, politicians, and old money. An heiress to a fortune built on salad dressings gave a shrill laugh that rose above the hum of conversation. Dressed in Prada, she wore enough gold and diamonds to jumpstart the economy of a small Caribbean country.

President Rick Serrano was working the tables. He was a master of his craft. A fist bump for the tech bros, a kiss for the monied madams, a well-placed joke for the businessmen, somehow Serrano made every gesture seem both genuine and intimate.

Abby allowed herself a wry smile. It didn't feel so special when Serrano turned his charms on her.

The President had doffed his jacket and removed his tie. His white dress shirt was unbuttoned at the collar and he'd rolled his sleeves up. He looked every bit the confident leader, a regular guy who'd just taken a break from kicking ass and taking names to stop in and say hello to his peeps.

Over coffee and dessert, in a carefully choreographed casual setting, Serrano sat on a stool in the center of the room and spoke with his audience like he was Dean Martin on a Las Vegas stage.

In a tone alternating between urgency and hope, he made his case. The midterms were in eighty-six days—but who's counting, he joked. He needed every person in the room to open up their wallets tonight to help his party to stay in power. Heads nodded in agreement.

Serrano took a softball question about the upcoming infrastructure bill. He nodded gravely. "Yes, it's a start on my agenda," he agreed as he name-dropped a few California projects, "but there's much more work to do, and I need allies in Congress to help me."

It's like a game to them, Abby thought. She'd contributed handsomely to Serrano's run for president, even hosted a dinner like this one back in Sterling. Like the people in this room, she'd convinced herself that by writing a big check she was making the world a better place.

Abby looked down at the table, laden with glasses, plates, crumpled napkins, half-drunk bottles of wine. Not a single dollar of the money raised tonight was going to feed a hungry child or build a road or buy a new airplane for the military. Every single penny would be spent on TV ads, political consultants, internet targeting.

What a waste.

Her mouth was dry, her stomach sour. Abby took a sip of water.

"Are you okay?" Dylan asked.

"Fine," she hissed. What the hell is wrong with me? she wondered.

"Mr. President," said a man from one of the front tables. "Tell us what's going on in Ukraine."

Serrano frowned and laced his fingers together as he considered the question. "This country has been at war for almost two years," he said in a solemn voice. "We didn't go looking for a fight, but once it was in front of us, we did what America has always done. We took the fight to the enemy, and we defeated them. We stood on the right side of history. Taiwan is free today because of America."

"Because of you, Mr. President," someone called out. Abby

saw some heads nodding in agreement, but she also sensed a change in the air.

Apparently, Serrano felt it too. He stood up, shaking his head.

"I want to make it clear that Ukraine is not Taiwan. Ukraine is in Europe's front yard. Ukraine's not a member of NATO, and NATO should not be directly involved in defending Ukraine. We can and will provide the Ukrainians with all the aid they need, but it's their fight to win."

He paced the tables. "I feel bad for these people, I really do, but this is not our fight. My granddaddy used to say: go to bed with dogs and you wake up with fleas. That's what President Luchnik is, a dog with a bad case of fleas. But I think Luchnik has gone too far this time. The uprising in Belarus is payback for his sins. He is losing in Ukraine because the Ukrainian people are fighting like hell to protect their democracy, and now he needs to send his troops to Belarus to keep the peace. I am confident this Ukraine situation will resolve itself without American involvement."

It was all Abby could do not to keep her mouth from gaping open at the torrent of bullshit her ears had just taken in. America was already involved—using covert action to strike at Russian interests inside Ukraine. Next to her, Dylan shifted in his seat.

But his words had the desired effect. All the heads in the room were nodding now. Serrano had threaded the rhetorical needle with the skill of a master. In her mind, she imagined the cash register ringing.

A young woman appeared at Abby's elbow. "Ms. Cromwell," she whispered. "I've been asked to conduct you and Mr. Mattias to the Presidential Suite for a private meeting."

As Abby followed the young woman out of the ballroom,

the audience clapped for the President. Serrano said something, and the room rippled with laughter.

Describing the Presidential Suite at the Bel-Air as a "suite"
was like calling a Ferrari a compact car. The sitting room of
the suite looked out onto a full-sized private swimming pool
ringed with mature palm trees swaying in the breeze.

Abby and Dylan faced each other in matching armchairs,
the silence as solid as the marble coffee table that separated
them. Abby hadn't held a full conversation with Dylan since
their flight back from Ukraine, and to her relief, he'd simply
given up trying. If he still had feelings for her, he hid them
well. For Abby, her anger had ebbed to the point where she
was able to separate which parts of the encounter in Ukraine
were personal and which were professional.

Talking to Don Riley helped. He'd managed to visit
Sentinel headquarters twice in the past few days, and he'd
briefed her after each session with Mama.

Despite President Serrano's assurances to his donors,
things were not going to resolve themselves in Ukraine. At
least, not in the way that Serrano had indicated to his audience of donors. A combination of unfavorable weather and a
recalcitrant Ukrainian military had slowed down the invasion,
but Don assured her that would not last long. The Russian
military machine would eventually grind up what was left of
the Ukrainian resistance.

Abby heard voices in the foyer, and both of them rose to
their feet. A door slammed shut and Serrano's voice carried
into the room, sharp and angry.

"I told you I didn't want any questions on Ukraine,"
Serrano said. "Do I have to draw you a fucking picture?"

"Mr. President, I can't control the donors. These dinners
are supposed to be an open forum, sir."

Serrano appeared in the doorway, trailed by his campaign manager.

"Give me a minute, Abby," he called with a wave, "I want to get this makeup off."

When he appeared a few minutes later, he wore a fresh T-shirt. Without makeup and the politician's smile, his features looked sharp and haggard. Like most presidents, he had gained considerable gray in his hair, even though his first term was not even half gone.

"We're in here." He led the way into a room with a ten-seat, marble dining room table where a secure videoconference setup occupied one end of the table. The President faced the screen and gestured for Abby and Dylan to sit. They took chairs across from each other. At a nod from the President, a technician turned on the screen and left the room.

"How're we doing, Irv?" the President asked Chief of Staff Irving Wilkerson.

"Fine, sir," Wilkerson replied.

"Good evening, Mr. President," said National Security Advisor Valentina Flores, looking particularly ominous in a coal-black blouse buttoned at the neck and blood-red lipstick.

Serrano cracked open a water bottle. "Valentina."

A third image popped into view, a man in the uniform of a US Army four-star general.

"General Kranik," Serrano said, "thank you for joining us. I know this is an inconvenient hour for you."

"Not a problem, sir," Kranik replied.

Any dim hope that Abby may have harbored that this meeting was not going to be about Ukraine vanished. General Roger Kranik was the Supreme Allied Commander Europe, or SACEUR. He was also dual-hatted as Commander, US European Command. Put simply, he was the most powerful military officer in Europe, with responsibility for all US military operations in Europe and with NATO.

"General," Wilkerson said, "I wonder if you can fill us in on the situation on the Eastern front."

Kranik was a man of economy. He spoke precisely, making each word count. "The situation is escalating, Mr. President," the general said. "The European Union is extremely concerned about the stability of both Ukraine and Belarus. The allied military commanders are requesting an immediate, coordinated military response to bolster the Eastern front.

"In the absence of American leadership," he continued, "the situation is becoming chaotic, with every country acting in their own interests. The Poles have massed forces along the border with Ukraine. They are convinced that President Luchnik's next move is a strike across Ukraine and into Poland."

"And how would the Polish Army fare against the Russians?" Serrano asked. "If it came to that, I mean."

The question seemed to fracture the general's stolid composure, but he recovered quickly.

"The Polish Army is a modern fighting force, equipped with state-of-the-art US armaments. M1A2 Abrams tanks, Bradley fighting vehicles, Stryker APCs, they've invested in the best and they're well trained. Lieutenant General Farley over at US Army Europe routinely rotates his forces into Poland to train with their ground forces. I'm sure they'd put up a fight, but the numbers are on the side of the Russians."

"Of course," Serrano said, "all this assumes that the Russians even get to the Polish border, right? I hear the Ukrainians are giving them hell."

"Mr. President," Flores said, "there's been a development on that topic."

Serrano took a sip of water. "Is this good news?"

Flores shook her head. "We have new intel that indicates two Russian airborne divisions will be added to the fight within the next few days. The Ukrainian units will be no match for hardened infantry forces. Our analysts predict that the Russians could take Kyiv by the weekend."

"What then?" Serrano started to chew his lip. "Will Luchnik be happy with half a loaf? Will he stop in Kyiv, or is he going to continue to make my life bloody miserable?"

"It's unclear, Mr. President," Flores answered. "The intel community is divided as to Russia's ultimate goals. This could go any number of ways."

"They all have one thing in common, though," Serrano said. "They're all bad for my administration."

There was a moment of tense silence, then Wilkerson spoke. "It would be bad for the country, sir, and NATO."

"That's what I meant," Serrano replied. The President looked out the window, chewing his lip. It was dark now, and the underwater lights in the swimming pool cast shimmering reflections across the thick trunks of the palm trees.

When he looked back at the screen, his expression was hard, resolute.

"The United States' position on this matter has not changed: This is an internal matter for the European Union. It's time the countries of Europe took care of the problems that are going on in their own damn backyard. General, offer all the intelligence and logistics support they need, but we need to steer clear of this mess."

"Understood, sir," Kranik said.

"Thank you, General." SACEUR's image disappeared from the screen.

"That settles our official position," Serrano said. "Let's move on to the unofficial efforts." He looked at Abby. "I think Sentinel has done an outstanding job in Ukraine, Abby. If your people weren't there, there would be Russian tanks in Independence Square right now."

"Thank you, sir." Abby felt the words stick in her throat.

Serrano smiled. "Don't thank me yet, Abby. I'm about to make you even richer than you already are. I'm expanding your contract to include operations in Belarus."

"Sir, I—" Abby began, but Serrano steamrolled over her.

"That jackal Luchnik is up to his eyeballs in shit in Belarus. I want your people to go in and put the screws to him. Mess with his supply chain. See if you can find these resistance fighters and get them some help—"

"Mr. President," Abby interrupted.

Serrano stopped talking suddenly, and Abby realized she'd almost shouted. She felt Dylan's eyes on her. She could almost feel him telling her, *Be careful, Abby.*

But careful was the attitude that had gotten her here in the first place. Maybe it was time to be the opposite of careful. She took a deep breath and continued in a more controlled tone.

"Mr. President, I'm here to notify you that I plan to cease operations in Ukraine," she said.

Serrano looked like he'd been slapped. "You can't do that."

"I can, and I will, sir," Abby said. "I've made up my mind."

The President's face lost the surprised look. His jaw snapped shut, his brow clenched together.

"Do you have any idea what's at risk here, Abby?" His words came fast and hot. "The midterm elections are in eighty-six days. If we get involved in Ukraine in the next eighty-six days, my party will get slaughtered in the elections. My presidency will be over."

Abby nodded calmly. "I understand, sir, but I'm not finished speaking."

Serrano threw his hands in the air. "Well, by all means, then, please continue."

"I think you're making a mistake by not involving NATO. The intel my team has gathered indicates that Russia will not be satisfied with eastern Ukraine. The US should be doing everything possible to deter Luchnik right now, not to placate him."

Abby leaned forward. "Sir, I think the lack of US involvement is making NATO look weak. The EU countries will put up a resistance, but the only organization that can truly match the Russian military head on is NATO, led by the United States."

"You're out of line, Ms. Cromwell," Wilkerson replied. "When we want your analysis on foreign policy matters, we'll ask for it."

"With all due respect," Abby shot back. "Right now, my company is this country's foreign policy. I have more people on the ground inside Ukraine and better intel than the whole of the United States' intelligence community."

"You're also under contract, Abby," the President said, his tone acid, "and you will fulfill that contract to the letter. As for drawdowns, we can have that discussion in November. For now, you will continue operations in Ukraine."

Abby said nothing but held his gaze, willing herself not to look away. Twice this man had railroaded her into doing something she'd known was wrong at the start. There would not be a third time.

"I want to be crystal clear about my instructions," Serrano said. "I expect you to fulfill the letter and the spirit of our contract. If you try to slow-walk me, or make anything other than your very best effort, I will bury you. This little company you founded with your husband that means so much to you, I will end it."

Still, Abby held his gaze. The air between them boiled

with anger. The silence was so complete that Abby could hear the steady sound of her own breathing.

In...out...in...out...

Serrano looked away, and the spell broke.

She stood, her chair a scraping whine across the tile floor.

"Thank you for your time, Mr. President."

---

28

50 kilometers north of Bialystok, Poland

At 0920, Lieutenant Colonel Donat Wozniak gave the order for the tank battalion of the 1st Warsaw Armoured Brigade to pull off onto the shoulder of Route E67 and shut down their engines.

As his driver maneuvered the tank to the side of the road, Wozniak stood tall in the tank commander's cupola. He turned, shading his eyes from the morning sun, and peered down the line of fifty-eight M1A2 Abrams tanks behind him.

Truly, a magnificent sight, he thought, but they were headed in the wrong direction. The Russians were in Ukraine to the south. His unit was headed north to the border with Lithuania.

All down the line, the 1,500-horsepower gas turbine engines that powered the state-of-the-art tanks shut off, blanketing the forest in silence. In the stillness, he heard the calls of tank crews to one another.

A two-tone siren wailed in the distance, and Wozniak saw flashing lights racing alongside the column. An ambulance.

As it approached, the siren ramped up in frequency and intensity, then it passed by in a blare of noise and light.

"Civilian traffic accident, sir?" asked his gunner, looking up from his position inside the turret at Wozniak's feet.

"Looks like it," the tank commander replied. He ground his teeth in frustration.

The brigade movement from Bialystok to Suwalki was only 110 kilometers, but it was along civilian roads, most of them two-lane highways like this one. A four-meter-wide tank like the M1A2 took up the entire roadway, and the battalion stretched over two kilometers in length.

Wozniak was glad he was not in charge of coordinating the brigade movement. Even with the Russian threat all over the news, there were local municipalities who objected to the damage the treads of a seventy-ton tank could do to the surface of a macadam highway.

And then there were civilian drivers who seemed to believe that somehow the laws of gross tonnage did not apply to them as they raced past the column in their little cars or tried to dart through crossings.

That's the price of peace, his father used to say. People forget. They get soft.

Wozniak's father always seemed ambivalent about the price of peace. As a career military man, he had served as a young conscript in the Soviet Army inside Poland. He'd seen the fall of the Soviet Union in 1991 and the disbandment of the Warsaw Pact. Dark years for the military of the newly independent Republic of Poland followed, but he persevered. Polish armed forces were accepted into NATO in 1999, leading to a massive internal reorganization.

Wozniak earned a commission in the post-NATO era. It was a good time to be in the military. Spending was high, and the Polish leadership worked hard to bring their military personnel and equipment up to exacting Western standards. The Armed Forces of the Republic of Poland went to an all-volunteer force during that period and were part of the NATO-led Coalition Forces in Afghanistan and Iraq.

Still, Wozniak knew that he could count on one hand the soldiers in his unit that had seen shots fired in anger. Wozniak himself was not among those few.

The wail of another ambulance penetrated his thoughts. As the vehicle raced by in a din of sound and light, he realized the accident up ahead must be serious. He passed word over the radio to his company commanders to join him at his tank for an ops brief.

"Request permission to dismount, sir," the gunner asked over the intercom.

"Granted," Wozniak said, "but stay close." He passed the same order on to his company commanders, reminding them to have crews pull their short-halt preventive maintenance checks.

To his left, the loader, Private Bendek Kaminski, boosted himself out of his own hatch. He stood on the turret and stretched, then slid down the side of the tank. The gunner, Sergeant Filip Nowak, followed him out the same hatch. On the main body of the tank, in front of the turret, his driver, Sergeant Kasper Zielinski, poked his head out of his own open hatch. The tank driver maneuvered the vehicle from a reclined bucket seat using a handlebar-and-grip throttle arrangement like a motorcycle. With the hatch closed, he drove using three vision blocks, or periscopes, that afforded him a 120-degree arc of forward viewing. In low light, the center vision block also had night vision capability.

Wozniak watched his tank crew head to the edge of the woods to relieve themselves. One of them pulled out a mobile phone and opened a music app. The sound of a hip-hop beat drifted up to Wozniak's position. Zielinski flashed his dance moves in the tall grass.

All his crew were in their early twenties. At forty-seven, Wozniak was old enough to be their father. Yet, in the unlikely event his tank saw action against the Russian Army, they would rely on each other to fight their tank as a team.

Wozniak grabbed his map case, boosted himself out of the TC hatch, and climbed down to the ground. The main body of the tank rose nearly to his shoulder. An armored skirt hung down partially protecting the treads. He moved to the front of the vehicle and spread a large-scale topographical map across the woodland-green painted surface. The long barrel of the 120mm main gun cast a shadow across the map.

Wozniak studied the map while he waited for his team to join him. He and all of his officers had tablets with electronic versions of the same map, but he preferred to work with the paper version, especially when he was trying to get the "big picture," as his American trainers liked to say.

Captain Szymon Kowalski, Bravo company commander, his most junior captain, arrived first and saluted Wozniak.

"No saluting in the field, Szymon," Wozniak growled. "We're in wartime conditions, remember?"

"Yes, sir," the young officer said. "Sorry, sir."

Captain Kowalski was the same age as Wozniak's gunner, and he possessed a nervous streak that worried Wozniak. How would he hold up in combat conditions?

Don't worry yourself about that, Wozniak thought with a trace of bitterness about their assignment away from the action. The only Russians you're going to see are on the side of a vodka bottle.

He scanned the map, his eyes picking out the topographical details of one of the most studied pieces of real estate in all of Europe.

The northeast corner of Poland abutted three countries: Belarus, Lithuania, and the Russian oblast of Kaliningrad, which was the entire reason why Wozniak's tank battalion was being sent north.

Kaliningrad was a 220-square-kilometer triangle of territory placed under Soviet control as part of the Potsdam Agreement in 1945. Unfortunately, following the dissolution of the Soviet Union in 1991, the land was separated from Mother Russia by the newly independent states of Lithuania and Poland. A sixty-five-kilometer border between Poland and Lithuania separated Belarus and Kaliningrad, a piece of land known as the Suwalki Corridor.

Poland, Lithuania, and their NATO partners fully recognized the danger that Kaliningrad posed to the alliance, which is why this section of Europe had been studied so intently by military planners for decades. It was also why 1st Warsaw Armoured Brigade was being sent north, far away from the expected Russian attack along the Ukraine border.

It was obvious to anyone with common sense that the Russians had no interest in Kaliningrad at this moment. The government collapse in Belarus could not have come at a worse time for the Russian Federation. Just as they were intensifying their push in Ukraine, the Russian military now had to bring order to the Belarusian mess. Luchnik had clearly set his sights on taking Ukraine. Just this morning, Wozniak had seen the NATO-provided intel about two Russian airborne divisions being added to the Ukraine front.

Although Wozniak was determined not to let his disappointment in their assignment show to his staff, it was difficult. This was the moment that his entire generation of military leaders had trained for: a Russian attack on their homeland. There was so much historical weight in this moment. He, of all people, a man from a long, proud line of

Polish military heroes, deserved to be on the front lines of this war. His family name alone had earned him that right.

And yet here he was, his tank parked on the side of the highway hundreds of kilometers from the action.

His battalion XO, who had been bringing up the rear of the tank column, jogged up to the gathering, out of breath. The company commanders shared a secret smile at their portly XO's physical conditioning.

Wait until you get old, you pups, Wozniak thought. He signaled the battalion S3 to start the briefing.

The S3 ops officer, known as "The Stick" by the battalion for his upright posture and his spare physique, delivered a succinct briefing.

"The combat engineers are preparing positions for us here." He pointed to a spot on the map outside the town of Suwalki, about five kilometers from the Lithuanian border. "Alpha and Bravo companies are along this ridge, facing north. Charlie company will be in reserve to the south."

Wozniak noted with approval that the battalion was in an elevated position, inside a tree line with excellent sightlines across a broad valley. To the west, a series of lakes and rivers formed a natural barrier for an enemy advance. To their east was Lithuania.

The S4 covered the logistical details of their deployment: meals, fuel, maintenance issues and the like. There were no questions.

The S2 intel officer took over the briefing. "We see no indication of troop activity along the Kaliningrad border," he said. "In Belarus, the Russians have deployed the 12th and 13th Guards Tank regiments of the 4th Guards Tank Division around Minsk to secure the capital city. They're reinforced with a number of Guards Motor Rifle regiments as well." The intel and ops officers continued with details the company commanders had heard many times before. Target reference points for the expected axis of attack, artillery support plans, all things they had wargamed out a hundred times in training.

Wozniak sensed a restlessness in his staff. The intel brief was hardly changed from the day before, yet all of them had mobile phones and access to social media and numerous news outlets.

"What's going on with NATO, sir?" The XO asked what everyone wanted to know the answer to. "Any change in posture?"

Wozniak considered his response. The real answer was that because the United States was taking a hands-off approach to Ukraine, NATO leadership was missing in action. The NATO member countries received standard intel briefings, but even there it seemed like they were phoning it in, as his American friends would say.

For Wozniak, who had grown up inside the NATO infrastructure, the effort to combat Russian aggression in Ukraine felt rudderless. Left to the European Union alliance, most of the member countries did whatever they considered to be in their own national interests. For Poland, that meant massing troops along the Ukrainian border and cracking down hard on the refugee flow coming across the Belarus border.

And, of course, sending Wozniak's element to guard against Russian aggression from their western outpost on the Baltic Sea.

"We're still receiving regular intel updates from our NATO allies," Wozniak said. "That's all we should expect for the time being."

He heard the tank commander's radio squawk. He climbed the front of the tank and crawled up the turret until he could lean down the TC hatch. The interior smelled faintly of hydraulic oil and gunpowder from their recent live-fire exercise.

The traffic accident blocking their way had been cleared. The battalion should be moving again in another ten minutes.

Wozniak acknowledged the order and stood on the turret, looking down at his staff. He saw the questions on their faces. Questions he had no answers for.

"Mount up," he said. "We roll in ten."

29

Washington, DC

The text from Director Blank reached Don's phone at 0619:

Meet at WH 0745.

Don put down his coffee cup, his first of the morning. He hadn't been to the White House since his disastrous briefing at Camp David. A thrill of elation coursed through him.

Abby got through to the President, he thought. I'm back in the game!

Hurriedly, he packed his laptop into a computer bag, grabbed a light jacket, and headed for the door. He did not want to be late to his meeting with the Director. He checked his watch. An hour and twenty minutes to get downtown and find a parking spot during rush hour was cutting it way too close. Don decided to take the Metro.

He cleared the White House security checkpoint at 0737. As he gathered up his computer bag and jacket, a young woman approached.

"Mr. Riley," she said, "Director Blank asked me to escort you to the meeting."

It quickly became apparent to Don that they weren't headed for the Situation Room. As she led him into the warren of White House staff offices, he lost his sense of direction. She stopped at the door of a small conference room.

"The Director's expecting you." She hurried away.

The Director was not alone. Seated at the small round table in the center of the conference room was Dylan Mattias.

Director Blank offered a humorless smile. "Sit down, Don."

The room was the size of a closet and the table small enough that if all three of them put their elbows on the table and leaned forward, they might bump heads.

An intimate setting for an ass-chewing, Don thought bitterly as he took the other seat at the table.

Dylan wasn't exactly gloating, but he wasn't wearing his usual poker face either. In fact, based on the tinge of red in his cheeks and the narrowing of his eyes, he seemed mighty pissed.

"Good morning, Dylan," Don said.

The other man's glare took on laser intensity.

"I assume you know what this is about?" the Director asked.

"I wouldn't want to hazard a guess, sir," Don replied.

"C'mon, Riley," Dylan said, "you were told to stay away from Sentinel, and you went right around the operational security measures."

Don breathed a small sigh of relief. At least Dylan hadn't found out about his visit to Poland.

"I'm not sure what you mean," he said.

"You got Abby Cromwell to give you access to intel coming out of Ukraine," Dylan said.

"She told you that?" Don countered. He could tell from Dylan's reaction that the answer was no.

"Gentlemen," the Director said, "let's try to take this down a notch."

"Sir," Dylan began, "I put a close hold on the Sentinel intel for a reason. This is a highly sensitive operation, and Riley is not cleared for it."

"I'm well aware of Don's clearance level, Dylan," Blank replied. "I'm also aware that we have a nasty habit of overclassifying information. We're on the same team, and I don't see a great harm in letting Don have a crack at the intel. Emerging Threats only works when that team can see all the intel sources, all at once. Creating silos is a bad idea—something we should have learned a couple decades ago."

"I think the President's Chief of Staff would have a different view on the matter, sir," Dylan said quietly. He shot Don a sharp look.

During his career at the CIA, Don had often made Dylan Mattias angry. The two were not exactly contemporaries. Dylan had more seniority and technically outranked him, but Don's involvement at the center of some of the highest-profile national security challenges in the last decade had elevated his status inside the Agency. He knew that Dylan saw him as competition in their career advancement, but Don had never seen it in quite the same light. He and Dylan came at the problem from different angles, with different experiences.

Not that he didn't envy Dylan, at least a bit. Whereas Don was awkward, Dylan was smooth, athletic, and sure of himself. While Don often developed a feeling about a piece of intel and doggedly ran down every scrap of evidence to vet his theory, Dylan built his analyses using only the intel at hand.

"Director," Dylan said, "the fact remains that I put a close hold on the information coming out of Sentinel for operational reasons. Don violated that security protocol."

"And what harm did we cause by having another qualified

team take a look at Sentinel's operations in Ukraine and Belarus?" the Director asked. "Surely there's value in getting a different opinion, Dylan."

"Sentinel's in Belarus?" Don asked. He hadn't spoken to Abby in several days and had not been able to visit The Ranch. Based on the over-the-top reaction from Dylan, something had changed. "Since when?"

"That's none of your concern, Riley," Dylan snapped. He looked back at the Director. "Sir, this is exactly what I'm talking about. He's like a dog with a bone. You have to put a stop to this."

"Why don't you head to the briefing, Dylan?" the Director said. "I'll be along shortly."

With a final glare at Don, Dylan departed. The Director slumped in his chair.

"Riley, you have a way of...pissing people off."

"Dylan and I have different styles, sir—"

"I'm not talking about Dylan." The Director leaned forward, his voice angry. "I had a meeting with Wilkerson this morning. He seems to think you've been coaching Ms. Cromwell on the best foreign policy options in Ukraine, and she passed them along to the President, who was not pleased with her unsolicited opinion."

There was nothing to say, so Don said nothing.

"I'm sure Dylan was happy to throw you under the bus," the Director continued, "but he's also not wrong. Why can't you leave it alone, Don?"

"Sir, this is going to blow up in our faces."

Blank slammed his fist on the tiny table. "Did you determine that during your side trip to Poland?"

Don swallowed.

"Did you think that no one would figure it out, Don? We're

an intelligence agency, we know how to track down plane tickets."

"Director," Don said, "I have as much recent experience with Luchnik as anyone in the Agency. I think we're not considering all the possibilities."

"I think *you're* not considering all the possibilities, Don," the Director said. "One of which is that the people at the top, the people we take orders from, don't want to consider all the possibilities. Have you thought of that?"

Don decided to try one more time.

"Sir, politics is not something we're supposed to concern ourselves with."

The Director groaned. "Grow up, Don. Politics is what drives the country. We elect people to make decisions, and guys like you and me do our best to serve those elected decision-makers. We don't interfere in policy decisions—that's not our job."

"I'm trying to do the right thing, sir."

"I believe that, Don, but actions have consequences, and unfortunately, Chief of Staff Wilkerson wants you to feel the consequences of your actions. My hands are tied."

"What does that mean?" Don asked.

"I'm placing a letter of reprimand in your permanent file," the Director said.

Don felt a numbness seep into his brain. "A letter...?"

"Consider yourself lucky. Wilkerson wanted me to fire you." The Director stood. "Look, I need to go. I'm sorry, Don. I had no choice."

He held out his hand, and Don took it without getting up, an automatic action for his overwhelmed mind.

"Take a minute and gather yourself, Don," the Director said in a kind voice. "It's not so bad."

That's a lie, Don thought as the door closed behind his

boss. A letter in his permanent file would cripple his career. Not only would it limit his ability to advance, but any new assignments would go to others with clean service jackets.

He cursed at himself. The Director was right. Dylan was right. He should have minded his own business.

Don got to his feet, pulled on his jacket. He rammed his fists into the pockets and was surprised to feel the crunch of paper in his left jacket pocket. He pulled out a crumpled plain white envelope, the small size one might use to send a personal note. He flipped the sealed envelope over and froze when he saw the word printed on the front:

Pandora.

Don dropped the envelope onto the small table and backed away. Pandora was the name of the bioweapon he and his team had found in a secret lab buried under the desert in Sudan.

Where had that come from? He pulled out the chair and sat down again, staring at the sealed envelope.

He retraced his movements from the morning. He'd put the jacket on when he left the office. Had he put his hand in the pocket? Yes, he was sure of it. The pocket had been empty when he left his office, and he'd worn the jacket the entire time on the Metro.

Don's head snapped up as he recalled getting off the train at the Farragut West Metro Station. Someone had bumped into him. A man or a woman? Don couldn't remember.

He got down to tabletop level and squinted at the envelope. There was something inside the cheap paper. He'd heard a *clink* when he'd dropped it.

Glass? he thought. No, a metal sound.

Don rubbed his neck. All the Pandora samples had been destroyed and the bioweapon required aerosol dispersal, but the memories of that operation still haunted him. A little caution was warranted.

He extracted a pen from his pocket and poked at the envelope. It made a faint scraping sound as it slid across the Formica tabletop. Don knelt on the floor and lifted the envelope with his pen. He angled his head to put the envelope between his eyeline and the bright recessed light overhead.

There was something inside. He carefully picked up the envelope by holding the edges between his thumb and forefinger and held it closer to the light.

He saw the outline of a key.

He gently put the envelope back on the tabletop, pulled out his phone, and snapped a picture of the front side. He thumbed through his contacts, selected one, and sent the image.

It took five seconds for his phone to ring.

"Liz," he said. "I need a favor."

30

Pavel Kozlov ordered his driver to pull off the road at the edge of the woods. The small town in the valley before them was bathed in silver moonlight. It wasn't much of a town. A few houses clustered alongside a single-lane secondary road, a garage, a church, and a bakery. There wasn't even a stop sign or a streetlamp.

In fact, the town of Maraziskes had only two reasons for Pavel's interest: it was a few kilometers off the A16 highway that ran east-west from Vilnius to the border of Kaliningrad, and it was occupied entirely by a group of Russian-speaking families.

Tiny ethnic enclaves like this one were common all over the world. A group of people, usually extended families, who shared a common language and culture lived close to one another. There were hundreds of similar Russian groups all over Lithuania.

Maraziskes was just singularly unlucky.

Pavel got out of the car and lit a Prima. He waited until his crew of eight was gathered around him before he spoke in a low tone.

"You were all selected for this operation because you are all assholes," he began. He let the laughter ripple around the circle before he stopped it.

"But you're all my hired assholes, so you will follow directions. First, keep your masks on at all times. This will be livestreamed, and you do not want your ugly faces on the internet.

"Second, if you speak, you speak in Lithuanian. No exceptions." This presented a problem for Pavel because his grasp of the Lithuanian language was limited to ordering a beer and buying cigarettes. Still, The Chef had insisted he direct this operation personally.

For a man who liked to lecture Pavel on the benefits of strategic thinking, his boss seemed to do an awful lot of micro-managing.

"Third, this is Alexei's show. If he tells you to do something, you do it."

Alexei, always the practical joker, did a pirouette and finished with an exaggerated bow. "For my first order, I want you to all line up and kiss the famous royal ass of Leonardas Petraukas."

"Get it out of your system now, Alexei," Pavel growled. "When we get back in the car, I want you all business."

"I'm getting into character, boss," Alexei insisted.

He wasn't wrong, Pavel thought. Although one of the Wagner Group's computer hackers had created the internet character of Leonardas Petraukas over six months ago, Alexei had brought the character to life.

The hackers resurrected on social media a group known as the Lithuanian Activist Front. The original LAF, a far-right underground resistance organization founded in 1940, was short-lived. The group, dedicated to Lithuanian independence, executed an uprising and established a provisional government of Lithuania which was dismantled by the Nazis after only a few months.

On the internet, nothing ever goes away, and so the LAF was resurrected. The original group had the added historical patina of being both anti-Semitic and anti-Russian.

Perfect for The Chef's purposes.

Over a six-month period, Leonardas Petraukas, a.k.a. Alexei, made regular posts, videos, and the occasional livestream from prominent Lithuanian landmarks and from an undisclosed location. For security reasons, he always wore a black mask emblazoned with LAF in gold letters. The Russian bots, both real and the human variety, amplified his message until the LAF had thousands of followers.

Tonight was going to be Leonardas Petraukas's crowning performance as leader of the LAF.

"Any questions?" Pavel asked the group.

There were none. He snagged Alexei's arm as the man made his way to the car. "Don't fuck this up, Alexei."

The man grinned, his teeth white in the dim light. "You mean Leonardas, right?"

They rolled into the tiny hamlet of Maraziskes with their headlights off. The town, bookended by a tiny Russian orthodox church at one end and a garage at the other, was still, silent, and dark. As the darkened vehicles crawled along the single-lane road, his men bailed out and positioned themselves in front of the houses. Pavel placed the cars a hundred meters past either end of the town, with orders to halt any incoming traffic.

He walked down the center of the main street, his Heckler & Koch G36 assault rifle hanging from its sling. He'd ensured all his men were using the standard-issue weapon for the

Lithuanian armed forces. Details mattered. The last thing he wanted was some internet jockey questioning the validity of their video.

He pulled down his black watch cap and snugged the black bandanna over the bridge of his nose until only his eyes were visible.

The houses were sad, mostly single-story stone and brick dwellings. The people who lived here didn't have much, and they were about to have a lot less. He passed the bakery where the writing on the plate glass window was all in Russian and scanned the line of cars parked along the street. The nicest one was a white BMW M4 with a dent on the front fender.

Pavel smashed in the driver's side window with the butt of his rifle, plucked the pin from an incendiary grenade, and tossed it inside the car. He loped to the other side of the road and took cover behind a van. He heard a *whoosh* as the grenade ignited.

It took about five seconds for the thermite to burn through to the gas tank of the BMW. The explosion shattered the stillness of the peaceful night. The BMW lifted off the ground and settled down with a crash. Pavel grinned as he felt the van protecting him rock from the blast.

His team moved in unison. Spraying the fronts of the houses with gunfire, they burst inside, ripped people out of their beds, and drove them into the street where Leonardas Petraukas waited.

"Good evening, enemies of the state," Leonardas crowed as he marched in front of the gathering. "I am Leonardas Petraukas, the leader of the Lithuanian Activist Front—and your worst nightmare."

The glare of the camera lights cast shadows across the dazed audience. Pavel counted eighteen townspeople. They were dressed in an assortment of nightwear, from oversized T-shirts to gym shorts to a few traditional white nightdresses. There were two families with small children.

A man from one of the families stood up and advanced on Leonardas. "What do you want?" he shouted.

One of Pavel's men stepped in and decked the man with rifle butt. The man dropped to the road and did not move.

"Stay down, you Russian spy!" Leonardas shouted. He pointed an accusing finger at the rest of them. "You are all guilty of treason against the state of Lithuania. Tonight, you will confess to the LAF."

Pavel noticed a young woman, the wife of the beaten man, was not looking at Leonardas. She clutched a small girl, maybe six years old, to her body, and her head was down. She wore glasses, and he saw a gleam of light in the lenses.

She had a mobile phone, he realized.

Pavel moved past Leonardas, seized the girl, and tore her away from her mother, exposing the phone.

"No," the woman screamed as he tossed the girl behind him. The woman tried to move back into the crowd, but he waded in after her. When he finally grabbed her arm, she went for his eyes with her fingernails. Pavel slapped her hard, ripped the phone from her grasp.

She had dialed 112. Lithuanian emergency services. The police had been notified.

"Gun!" one of his men cried.

That's when the shooting started. The woman's arm was still in his grasp. Her body danced as blossoms of red appeared on her chest. She stopped struggling, crumpled, and he let her go.

Over the heavy *thwack* sounds of suppressed gunfire, he heard the scream of a little girl. Then it stopped as if someone had closed a door.

"Cease fire!" Pavel roared.

He turned to see Leonardas giving the cut sign on the recording. In the silence, he heard the thin wail of a siren. Where the black strip of road traveled up the side of the valley, headlights emerged from the woods. Red and blue flashing lights sparked in the darkness.

The police car reached the valley floor and sped up. He saw the lights outline the Land Rover blocking the road into town. When the police car slowed down, his driver opened fire from a concealed location on the side of the road.

Pavel cursed to himself.

Around him, bodies lay in heaps, some moving, most not. The little girl lay on her side, blond hair covering her face, a pool of blood forming around her head. When he turned her over, Pavel saw that the other half of her face was missing.

The Land Rover that had been posted on the far side of town raced toward them, screeched to a halt. His men moved to pile into the vehicle. Pavel took the front passenger's seat.

The driver pulled away from the site of the massacre and accelerated the two hundred meters to the second vehicle, where half the team got out. He steered around the bullet-riddled police car. The siren was dead, but the lights still flashed. The lone policeman was slumped behind the wheel.

"That footage was epic," Alexei crowed from the back seat. "Leonardas Petraukas already has hundreds of views, and people are sharing it like crazy."

Pavel grunted a noncommittal reply. Somewhere along the road of life he had gone from a soldier who killed other soldiers, to a mercenary who killed other soldiers, to a guy who killed people for money. Didn't matter who, he even killed little girls.

The car left the woods. Pavel could see the lights of the A16 in the distance. In thirty minutes, they'd be safely across the border in Kaliningrad.

A drop of rain hit the windshield, then a second. Thick clouds covered the moon.

He settled into his seat, feeling empty as the adrenaline left his body.

Well, he thought, at least The Chef will be happy.

31

FBI Laboratory
Quantico, Virginia

Don met Liz Soroush in the lobby of the FBI Laboratory complex located on the Marine Corps Base in Quantico, Virginia.

"We have to stop meeting like this, Don," Liz said as she hugged him. She attempted a laugh, but the effort fell short. Neither of them wanted anything to do with anything associated with the term *Pandora*.

Years before, the Emerging Threats Group uncovered a secret laboratory used to build a bioweapon known as Pandora. Unfortunately, a single dose of the deadly agent escaped before Don's team was able to secure the lab. In the hands of a young terrorist, the Pandora bioweapon ended up in Iran. Liz and Dre Ramirez entered Iran as covert operatives to recover or destroy both the terrorist and the weapon.

They succeeded in their mission, but they paid a price: months in an Iranian jail.

Liz's dark hair had threads of silver. When she kissed him

on the cheek, she smelled of jasmine. "I hear you're making friends and influencing people in all the right places," she said.

"News travels fast," Don said.

"No, bad news travels fast," Liz said. "You doing okay?"

"I deliberately disobeyed an order and got caught," Don said. "I kinda feel like I gave up my right to complain when I made the choice."

Liz shook her head. "Always the martyr."

They signed in at the desk, and Don clipped a visitor's badge to his lapel. Liz led him to an elevator. "Does this mysterious envelope have anything to do with your being in the doghouse with the Director?" she asked.

"I don't see how," Don replied. "Then again, these days I feel like I'm missing more than I'm getting."

The elevator door opened. "I gave the package to Linda Tressler. She's a supervisor here and one of the best I've ever worked with. She handled it personally as a favor to me."

Linda Tressler's office reminded Don of his own workspace, a shrine to paper. Judging by the towers of reports stacked beneath the window, she had made an effort to clean up before their arrival. Her desktop was clear except for two plastic evidence bags lined up precisely parallel to the edge of the blotter. One bag held the envelope with the word *Pandora* on it, and the other held a small brass key.

Liz made introductions, and they took seats across from Tressler's desk. She was late thirties with brown hair pulled back into a neat ponytail and large, dark-rimmed glasses that slid down her nose.

"You gave me a tough one," Tressler began. "I'm afraid I don't have much to offer you in the way of answers."

She picked up the bag with the envelope in it. "This is a number 6 ¾ plain white envelope, made with twenty-pound bond paper, manufactured by Mead Corporation. If you go into any Walmart or Target, you'll find this brand. I have some in my own home."

"Fingerprints?" Don asked hopefully.

"Only yours, I'm afraid," Tressler said.

"What about the lettering?" Liz asked.

Tressler blew out a breath. "Same deal. Bic ballpoint pen, medium point, black ink. Sold by the thousands every day all over the world." As if to illustrate her point, she plucked a pen from her top drawer. "I've probably got ten of them in this office alone."

She laid the plastic bag flat and slid it across the desk. "It is hand lettered, as you can see. Our handwriting experts believe it was written by someone who is right-handed but used their left hand to write the single word."

"What significance does that have?" Don asked.

"It's possible that we might have their handwriting on file and they wanted to make sure we couldn't get a match," she said. "It also might just be one more layer of subterfuge from someone who was going out of their way to give you a key without letting you know who it was from."

"What about the key?" Liz asked.

"That's where this gets really intriguing." Tressler held up the second plastic envelope to show them a short brass key. "This is a copy of a key, so any identifying information on the original is gone. It's for a small lock, possibly a lockbox, safety deposit box, or even a mailbox. As far as we can tell, it's never been used. It was cleaned in solvent after it was milled, so we can't even learn anything from the duplication process."

"Do you have a database of key duplicators?" Don asked, feeling like he already knew the answer.

"There's thousands of them," Tressler said. "You could get a copy of this key made at any mall, hardware store, or Home

Depot in the country." She leaned back in her chair and pushed up her glasses. "In summary, whoever gave this to you went to extreme lengths to keep the origin of this key anonymous. The only unique thing about this entire situation is the name on the envelope. Who is Pandora?"

Don and Liz exchanged a glance. "It's not a person," Liz said, "at least we don't think so. We believe it references an operation we were both involved in."

"It's something you recognized immediately, then?" Tressler asked Don.

Don nodded. "It's not a name I'm likely to forget. Ever."

"Is the operation and the name common knowledge?" she asked.

"That's what bothers me," Don replied. "Very few people would know that word and my association with it."

Tressler pushed both clear plastic bags across the desk. "I'm finished with these. You can take them."

Don felt deflated. He was sure that the FBI lab would be able to offer some clue that he could follow up on. "That's it? We're at a dead end."

Tressler looked up in surprise. "Dead end? I should think your next move is obvious, Mr. Riley."

Don looked at Liz. "I don't see it."

"Whoever did this went to a lot of trouble to give you the answer but not the question," Tressler said. "I think they'll be in touch. All you have to do is wait."

32

Moscow, Russia

The plan is working.

The thought raced through President Luchnik's mind. It made him want to pound his desk, pump a fist in the air, and shout with triumph.

Instead, he glared at the four men seated on the other side of the desk in his private study. Their individual reactions to his look ranged from sober to comical.

Yakov's cheeks were flushed, his eyes bloodshot, and his rumpled uniform looked like he'd slept in it. It was just past three in the morning, and Luchnik wondered what brothel they'd rousted him from.

Foreign Minister Irimov's heavy eyelids shielded him from Luchnik's gaze, but there were other signs of the aging statesman's frame of mind. His fingers plucked at the sleeve of his jacket, and the forward hitch of his shoulders indicated a man who was assessing the situation.

Unflappable Federov met Luchnik's eyes without hesitation—without even blinking. The head of the FSB had worked out Luchnik's plan already, and he was ready to serve, as always.

And then there was Nikolay. His nephew spent less time looking at his uncle and more time taking the measure of the other men in the room. Luchnik wondered if the younger man found his older colleagues wanting. Federov's suggestion to bring Nikolay back to Moscow had been the right call. Luchnik feared that his nephew was not ready for the next step, but the last few weeks had proven the President wrong. Nikolay took to the politics of Moscow like a graceful swan to the waters of the Volga River.

Someday, Luchnik thought, he will be ready to take my place as the leader of an expanded, more secure, and much more powerful Russian Federation.

Luchnik cut a fresh glance at Yakov. In the meantime, Nikolay's position as Deputy Defense Minister was a useful backstop in case Yakov drank himself to death.

He turned to the monitor where a video was frozen in mid-action on the screen. He touched a button on his laptop and the video sprang to life.

A nighttime scene, harsh with the glare of spotlights and the scufflings and scrapings of background noise. An enormous man, dressed head to toe in black, strutted for the camera. He wore a black balaclava with the letters LAF emblazoned in gold across his mouth.

The famous Leonardas Petraukas, leader of the far-right Lithuanian Activist Front, performed for his internet followers in a livestreamed video.

It was all Luchnik could do not to laugh out loud. The Chef had outdone himself this time. The construction of the fake LAF and the character of leader Leonardas Petraukas was nothing short of genius.

"You are all guilty of treason against the state of

Lithuania," Leonardas shouted, beating his chest. "Tonight, you will confess to the LAF."

The "treasoners," a terrified group of men and women ranging from grade schoolers to pensioners, shrank back from the larger-than-life figure. Even their clothing was perfect, Luchnik thought. T-shirts and old workout gear. One old woman wore only one fuzzy pink slipper and a ratty housecoat.

What happened next occurred so quickly that Luchnik had needed to rewind the recording and watch it in slow motion to fully appreciate the action. A woman used her child, a blond girl, to shield her mobile phone. A man, dressed in black, rushed in and tore the child from her arms. Luchnik saw the gleam of the mobile phone screen.

A single gunshot, dulled by the recording device, sounded. Then all hell broke loose.

Screams, the *pop-pop-pop* of multiple weapons firing. All around the man in black, people dressed in white underclothes stood and were cut down by gunfire. Red blotches appeared on their clothes as if by magic, and they fell like rag dolls until the man in black, still standing, was surrounded by fallen bodies.

Darkness hemmed the scene, making it appear as if the bodies were trapped in a pool of light. The camera zoomed in on the head and torso of the little blond girl, then the video ended.

Luchnik felt giddy with exhilaration. He wanted to laugh out loud at the magic of the video. It took his breath away. If he had tried to personally direct a movie designed to outrage Russians everywhere, he could not have done a better job.

Careful, he thought. This is not the time and place.

Instead of the joy he felt at this magnificent piece of political art, he worked up an expression of rage and sprang to his feet. His desk chair crashed back against the wall. Yakov startled as if he'd drifted off to sleep.

"We cannot allow this to go unanswered," Luchnik roared. "This requires an immediate military response."

Irimov stirred. "Mr. President, I agree this is compelling, but this video has not even been authenticated. If we wait a few more hours—"

Luchnik cut him off. He stabbed a finger at the bottom of the screen.

"It has half a million views already!" Luchnik shouted. "It's only been online for a few hours. People all over the world are demanding justice for these innocent Russian lives lost."

The Chef ran a full-service operation. Not only did he create the internet persona of Leonardas Petraukas and execute the livestream event, but he was boosting the video to viral status using his army of hackers. Even if the original video was taken down, people had already uploaded copies all over social media.

Luchnik watched with something like wonder as comments spilled down the screen. The Chef was still hard at work.

"This is an outrage!" Luchnik shouted. "We must act." He wheeled on Defense Minister Yakov. "What units do you have outside of Minsk?"

Yakov blinked as if his brain had slipped out of gear.

"The 12th and 13th Guards Tank regiments from the 4th Guards Tank Division, along with a number of Guards Motor Rifle regiments," he said. "But they are equipped for a security mission, Mr. President."

Luchnik slapped his hand against the monitor with the frozen image of the dead girl. "*This* is a security mission. Security for the Russian-speaking people of Lithuania who are cut off from the Rodina. I am ordering you to march on Kaliningrad. Secure the Suwalki Corridor between Belarus and Kaliningrad."

"Now?" Yakov asked.

"Immediately," Luchnik shot back. "Tonight."

"But, sir, those units don't have artillery attached to them. We'll need to plan air support. If we enter Lithuania, we'll be exposing those units to a NATO response."

"You have tanks, don't you?" Luchnik stood over Yakov. For God's sake, the man even smelled like a whorehouse.

"Of course, Mr. President. The 12th and 13th Guards Tank regiments are equipped with our newest tanks—the T-14 Armata."

"Then you don't need artillery support, Yakov! It's less than a hundred kilometers, man. You could drive there in a tank before breakfast tomorrow."

"That's true, sir, but the Lithuanians—"

"The Lithuanian Army has not mobilized, Yakov. You get the same intel reports that I do. What are you worried about?"

"Sir," Irimov said quietly, "this action would be a direct provocation of NATO."

"We don't have a choice, Sergey," Luchnik said. "You saw that video. Those were Russians, and they were slaughtered like sheep. We have an obligation to provide safety to the Russian-speaking people of this world."

Foreign Minister Irimov had been with Luchnik for longer than any member of the cabinet. If there was anyone on the planet who could spin this issue in Russia's favor, it was Sergey Irimov—and both men knew it.

Their eyes met. Irimov nodded to show he understood.

"I'll make sure that our internal news sources amplify the message, Mr. President," Federov added. "We'll give the video heavy play. I don't foresee any significant domestic resistance. The evidence is compelling."

"Thank you, Vladimir," Luchnik said. He held back a smile.

And just like that, he thought, the final piece of my plan falls into place.

He'd had his doubts. The plan carried significant risk, mostly around the United States' response to his aggressive moves in the Ukraine and Belarus. But, as they liked to say in America, that ship had sailed. Anything Serrano tried to do now would be too little, too late.

Now, with success in his grasp, Luchnik realized he'd been right all along. The world was his for the taking. At this juncture of history, he was invincible.

He clapped his hands together, a sharp sound in the quiet office.

"Come, gentlemen, we all have much work to do. Off with you. I'll call a cabinet meeting in the morning."

Luchnik motioned with his eyes for Nikolay to stay. When the door closed behind the three older men, Luchnik went to the bar and poured two glasses of vodka. He handed one to Nikolay and threw an arm around his nephew. Together, they walked to the hand-painted map that adorned the wall of his office.

He held out his glass. "*Na zdorovie.*"

"*Na zdorovie,*" his nephew replied. Their glasses clinked. Both men drank.

"Did you stage the incident in Lithuania, Uncle?" Nikolay asked.

Luchnik allowed a smile to tease his lips. "Are you accusing me of something, Nikolay?"

"I just want to know the truth, Uncle," he said. "The whole truth."

Luchnik touched the map. He ran his fingers along the western border of the Russian Federation. Starting in the

Black Sea, he cut through eastern Ukraine, up through Belarus, across the tiny gap of land between the corner of Belarus and the oblast of Kaliningrad to the Baltic Sea.

"The truth," Luchnik said. "The truth is that this is a new day for Mother Russia. For most of the last century, we have been living under the heel of the United States. We shed Russian blood for them in World War Two and they turned on us. They scorned our way of life. They drove us into financial ruin, and then when the Soviet Union collapsed, they picked over our bones."

Luchnik felt the unevenness of the brush strokes of the map under his fingertips.

"The truth, Nikolay, is that our leaders were weak. They played the Americans' game, and they lost it all. Our great nation, once an empire, was reduced to ruin by weak leaders."

He gripped his nephew's shoulder, looked him in the eye. "But I am not weak. I will not play the Americans' game. They will play *my* game. The United States is no longer the great country it once was. The world is a different place."

Luchnik slapped the flat of his palm against the map. "In a day, maybe two, you will see the dawn of a new Russian Empire. From the Arctic Ocean to the Black Sea, we will build a wall against our enemies. I started this journey by annexing Crimea in 2014." He chopped his hand across the gap between Belarus and Kaliningrad. "I finish it here, today. Once we cut off the Baltic States, we will pick them apart piece by piece, just like they did to us."

Luchnik took his nephew's glass and refilled it.

"You ask me if I planned the incident in Lithuania?" Luchnik shrugged. "Guilty."

Their eyes studying the map, both men drank.

"There will be a NATO response, Uncle," Nikolay said.

"There will. But it will be too little, too late."

Nikolay touched the map at the Suwalki Gap. "And the Poles? They have an armored brigade here."

"If they get in our way, we will crush them."

Luchnik let the silence lengthen. The vodka warmed his belly, relaxed his frame.

"Nikolay?"

"Yes, Uncle."

"Are you with me?" Luchnik asked.

His nephew faced him, and Luchnik saw his late sister in the younger man's eyes. He felt her looking down on the two of them now.

"Always, Uncle."

33

5 kilometers south of Simnas, Lithuania

Dawn was still an hour away when Lieutenant Colonel Donat Wozniak stood in the cupola of his M1A2 Abrams tank and squinted into the darkness of the Lithuanian countryside.

He sucked in a deep breath. The air smelled of summer rain.

The tank bucked as it ran over a stone wall that had probably been there for five hundred years. He heard the fieldstones crack under the weight of his massive vehicle. The front of the tank sloped down as they entered a cow pasture. Behind him, he heard the next tank in line cross what was left of the stone wall.

Thank God for GPS, he thought, casting a glance down at the newly installed MAPS system. The Mounted Assured Precision Navigation system was supposedly unjammable. He picked out the dots that represented the column of fifty-plus tanks behind him and said a little prayer that this technology did everything the American manufacturer claimed.

Even before the brigade issued the order to move out, Wozniak had sent a scout platoon racing for the Lithuanian border. Their job was to pick out the fastest route for his tanks to get to their first objective, which they transmitted back to Wozniak in the form of a trail of blue dots across his MAPS screen like breadcrumbs. The last thing he needed was for his tanks to get mired in mud, or worse, lost.

If all went as planned, the route he followed would slice from the south into the Russian flanking force traveling on Route 131 as they passed through the tiny town of Simnas, Lithuania. The highway ran through a wetlands area, and if he could get there ahead of the Russians, he knew he could wreak havoc on their advance guard.

The column ran dark and in radio silence. His company commanders had their orders. They knew their mission, a mission they had trained for since they'd entered the tank corps. What none of them expected, including Wozniak, was that they would be the front line. Right now, the 1st Warsaw Armoured Brigade was the only thing standing in the way of the Russians ripping open a corridor between Belarus and Kaliningrad.

And Wozniak's tanks were the tip of the spear.

The news of the Maraziskes Massacre tore through social media with bot-fueled intensity. The Russian response took less than two hours—another sure indicator that the "massacre" had been staged. NATO-provided intel showed troop movement by elements of the 12th and 13th Guards Tank regiments of the 4th Guards Tank Division. By five a.m., columns of Russian tanks moving in Battalion Tactical Groups arrived at the Lithuanian border. Infantry fighting vehicles were mobilizing behind them.

The Russians did not stop at the border crossing.

By this time, Foreign Minister Sergey Irimov was conferencing with leaders of the European Union member countries, explaining that because Russian blood had been spilled, the Russian Federation had no choice but to defend their brothers and sisters.

This was a humanitarian mission, he insisted, necessary only because of the virulent anti-Russian prejudice of the people of Lithuania. The forces in Minsk were the closest source of aid to the Russian victims. He scoffed at the idea that the tank regiments entering Lithuania had anything to do with opening a land bridge between Belarus and Kaliningrad. The very idea, Irimov insisted, was ludicrous.

As NATO and the Lithuanian military mobilized, the weather turned against them. Thick, low cloud cover blanketed the region, hindering aerial observation of the unfolding situation on the ground. A cold rain began to fall.

At 0530, the Russian charade fell apart. When the column reached Vilnius, it broke into two. The main column bypassed the capital and proceeded on the A16, toward the tiny village of Maraziskes. A second element, consisting of two Battalion Tactical Groups, took the southerly Route 131.

The Russians claimed they had taken a wrong turn as they navigated the roads around Vilnius. To help sort out the problem, they left a company of mechanized infantry outside Vilnius.

Wozniak, who'd been summoned to Brigade HQ at the first hint of Russian movement, saw the unfolding situation with clarity. This was not a war of days, he realized, this was a war of hours. Given half a day, even less, the Russians could secure a foothold in the Suwalki Corridor from which it would be difficult, if not impossible, to dislodge them without a major combat operation. The Russians, once they held the corridor, would dig in and call for diplomatic discussions. It was the Crimea playbook, except this time it was taking place in a NATO-allied country.

At 0547, Wozniak received his orders:

Movement to contact. Find and destroy the Russian columns advancing along Route 131. When the primary objective was accomplished, continue north to highway A16 and engage the main Russian column.

The hasty mission brief took all of five minutes. Wozniak selected the area near the town of Simnas for the assault. A series of large lakes bracketed the highway. If he could trap the column there, the Russians would be hemmed in by water on either side and restricted to front and back movement. They would be unable to maneuver off the road because of the marshes.

A perfect place to kill the enemy.

At least that was the plan, Wozniak thought as the rain ran down his face.

On the MAPS display, Charlie company broke off from the column, turning right. While the rest of the battalion stopped the Russian armored advance, Charlie company would assault from the Russians' left rear flank.

He cast an eye skyward, thankful for the cloud cover. If he didn't know exactly where they were, Wozniak prayed the opposite was also true. His last report was a column of Russian tanks were forty kilometers to the west, making an average speed of advance along the highway of between forty and fifty kilometers per hour.

The math said his unit would be in position to intercept the Russians, but it would be a close call.

His face twisted into a rueful smile. Only yesterday he had been cursing his bad luck at being sent so far away from the action. His grandfather had a saying that seemed appropriate now: Don't call a wolf out of the woods.

The Russian plan had fooled them all. NATO, the EU, even the Polish military command. By keeping all eyes focused on the escalating conflict in Ukraine, Luchnik was able to make his play to reunite Kaliningrad with the Russian Federation.

And my tanks are the only thing that stand in his way, Wozniak thought.

The MAPS display told him they were less than three kilometers from Route 131. He broke radio silence to order his trailing tanks to form a right echelon on him. On the MAPS screen, the dots representing the following tanks drifted apart and to the right until the formation on the screen was a diagonal with each tank spaced at least fifty meters from his closest neighbor.

Wozniak found he was gripping the edge of the hatch so tightly that his fingers were cramping. Relax, he told himself, forcing his fingers to unclench.

Inside the turret, the gunner, Nowak, searched for targets, switching between low and high magnification, looking for thermal signatures in the darkness ahead. Under Nowak's control, the long muzzle of the tank's 120mm gun scanned back and forth from straight ahead to sixty degrees to the right, the expected threat axis.

Wozniak dropped back inside the turret to his seat but left his hatch open. In the red light of the turret interior, Kaminski was seated to his left at the loading station. The young man looked like he might throw up at any minute.

On the thermal imaging display, Wozniak saw the flash of light at the same time as he heard the gunner call out.

"Target! Tank!" Nowak shouted over the open circuit. "Two o'clock!"

Wozniak made out the low-profile shape of a Russian T-90 tank moving along the highway. Then he saw another, and another, with some T-72s mixed in for good measure.

He felt a flash of hope. The Russian tanks were traveling close together, too close together. And these were not the T-14 Armatas they'd come to respect as they studied the Russian armor over the years. These were older tanks.

Where the headphones of his CVC helmet pressed against his skull, he felt the hammering of his own pulse. He tried to control his breathing.

"Sir!" the gunner screamed again. "Tank!"

"Gunner, sabot, tank," Wozniak replied in a steady voice.

"Up!" the loader announced. There was already a sabot round in the firing chamber. Kaminski stood back from the breech of the main gun in expectation of the recoil.

"Identified," the gunner announced as he lased the target for range.

Twenty-one hundred meters. Too far, Wozniak thought. His tank was the closest to the highway, which meant everyone behind him was farther still.

Let them get closer. The Russians hadn't seen them yet. The closer he could get, the more likely he could kill them.

"Identified, sir," Nowak said.

"We'll let them get a little closer, Sergeant," Wozniak said. "Keep your pants on."

Seventeen hundred meters.

Wozniak switched to the battalion circuit. "All units, this is Romeo Six-six, close to fifteen hundred meters. Fire at will." He pulled the TC hatch closed with a clang.

The right echelon formation swung forward as the tanks ranged across his right flank sped up.

Fifteen hundred meters.

"Fire," Wozniak said.

"On the way," Sergeant Nowak replied.

There was a *WHUMP*, more a feeling than a sound, and the forward motion of the tank hitched.

On the thermal display, the first tank in the Russian column erupted in white flames.

"Target, cease fire," Wozniak shouted. The second tank in line clipped the one in front, then slewed off the highway. It exploded in a ball of fire as one of the other Polish tanks scored a hit.

To his left, the loader sprang into action. As the expended aft cap left the breech, he bumped a lever with his knee and an automatic door slid open, revealing a row of shells. He hoisted a fresh round from the ammo rack, a pointed sabot round, pivoted his body, and inserted it into the open breech. The breech door closed. The whole operation took five seconds.

"Target, tank," Nowak said as he brought his gun to bear on a fresh target.

"Gunner, sabot, tank," Wozniak replied.

"Up!" the loader shouted.

"Identified."

"Fire!" Wozniak said.

Another target turned into a flaming wreck.

Seeing a sabot shell hit an enemy target was almost a religious experience for Wozniak. The round was essentially a giant dart of depleted uranium. When it hit an armored surface at 1,500 meters per second, it penetrated and exploded into a spray of metal fragments. At tanker school, the vivid training description claimed that it "liquified everything inside."

From his viewport in the tank commander's cupola, Wozniak could see their attack had not been perfect. At least a dozen Russian tanks had already passed the edge of the lakes that were supposed to constrain their movement. The initial attack had stopped the column but had not bottled them up as he'd planned.

A Russian T-90 ran off the highway and drove straight at the Polish line. He fired, and Wozniak saw a flare of an explosion out of the corner of his eye. The Russian managed to get off a second shot before he was taken out.

Wozniak cursed as more T-72s and T-90s poured out of the gap.

"Zielinski!" he shouted. "Forward, now."

The tank lurched forward as the driver accelerated.

The turret tracked right as Nowak targeted one of the fleeing tanks. Wozniak used the TC override to slew the turret and the gunsight onto the gap where another T-72 was moving.

"Gunner, sabot, tank!" Wozniak roared.

"Up," said Kaminski as he slammed back against the steel wall of the turret.

"Identified," Nowak replied as he laser-ranged the target.

"Fire!"

"On the way." The tank hitched, the breech slammed back, and the smoking aft cap dropped into the bin on the floor of the turret.

Wozniak stared at the screen. The Russian was still moving. His turret pointed directly at them.

"Lost!" Wozniak shouted. "Reengage."

"Up."

"Identified." Nowak re-lased the target for range. The display read five hundred meters.

"Fire!"

Both tanks fired at the same time. Wozniak heard the Russian shell glance off the sloped armor of the turret. In the gunsight, the Russian tank erupted in flame.

"Cease fire!" Wozniak shouted. He scanned for fresh targets, but the road and the surrounding field around them was full of burning tanks.

"Nowak, what do you see?" he asked.

"No targets, Colonel." Nowak's voice sounded shaky.

"Driver, halt," Wozniak ordered.

As the tank ground to a stop, Wozniak opened the TC hatch and stood up.

It was like a scene from hell. The air was heavy with the smell of burning diesel and cooked flesh. Flames hissed in the rain, dancing yellow light illuminating the scatter of tanks strewn across the field. In the distance, he could hear Charlie company firing on the Russian tanks trapped between the lakes.

Wozniak switched to the battalion frequency and called for a sitrep. Alpha company had lost four tanks, Bravo company two. Six tanks meant twenty-four of his people had died in the space of—he checked his watch—nine minutes.

In exchange for his six tanks, they had killed eighteen Russian T-90s and T-72s. A three-to-one kill ratio.

This was a war of minutes, he reminded himself, and he had none to waste.

Wozniak passed a sitrep to brigade, then ordered Alpha and Bravo companies to form a new column on him for the movement north. Charlie company, under the XO's command, would follow as soon as possible.

Brigade came back with an update that 3rd and 1st Mechanized Battalions were on the move, ETA to Simnas one hour. The 3rd had orders to secure the battlefield at Simnas while the 1st would follow Wozniak north.

Wozniak acknowledged the update, but his attention was already focused on the MAPS display. His scouts had left him a trail of blue dots, showing him the fastest route for them to intersect the A16 highway.

There were more Russians to deal with, a lot more Russians, and these would not be the older models. The next engagement would be against the state-of-the-art T-14 Armata tanks.

Wozniak ordered his tank north, leaving the burning wreckage behind them.

What's more, he thought, now the Russians know we're coming.

34

10 kilometers south of Sventragis, Lithuania

If anything, the weather had gotten worse, which suited Lieutenant Colonel Wozniak just fine. He stood in the cupola of his tank and let the rain stream down his face.

He was soaked—and that was just fine with him, too.

The adrenaline rush from the battle had faded, leaving Wozniak empty inside. His stomach felt sour, but he took a bite of the soggy candy bar in his hand anyway and chewed automatically.

Over the intercom, his young crew relived the battle.

"How many'd we get, Nowak?" Kaminski asked. "How many kills?"

"Five," the gunner said with a note of pride. "Maybe six. That'll be up to the colonel to call it."

Wozniak chose not to engage. They're kids, he thought. Let them deal with their stress in their own way.

He sank his teeth into the candy bar and chewed. Twenty-four men and women of the 1st Armoured had already died today. And it wasn't even dawn yet.

Zielinski, the driver, also stayed out of the conversation. He knew his TC wanted him to concentrate on driving.

The scouts had the battalion take Route 181 for the transit north to highway A16. It was about twenty kilometers from Simnas to the tiny village of Sventragis, along a single-lane paved road that wound through the Lithuanian countryside. The MAPS display identified the wooded area to his left as the Zuvinto nature reserve. Wozniak made a mental note of the terrain. You never knew when you might need a place to hide.

They were making good time. On the straight sections of road, Zielinski was able to get up to seventy kilometers per hour, and Wozniak ordered his column to keep close formation.

It was a risk, he knew, but he was more worried about the clock than about an attack from the air. Although the poor weather offered him safety, it also reduced his intel about the advancing Russian column. If he didn't get into position before the enemy arrived, this would be a very short engagement.

The battalion net sounded in his headphones. "Romeo Six-six, this is Rabbit One. At Point Banana. No sign of enemy passage."

Wozniak dropped back into the turret and pulled up his area map. The scouts had set up outside of a small town along the A16, ten kilometers east of their destination. He breathed a sigh of relief. They were in time. The Russians had not arrived yet.

Had the Russian column pulled back? Wozniak wondered. Not likely, but he had to assume the enemy was forewarned of danger on the road ahead. For his last attack, he'd had the element of surprise against a smaller force. This time, he needed a strategy to deal with superior numbers of a wary enemy.

"Rabbit One, Romeo Six-six, copy. Advise on contact, out."

His early warning trigger was in place. Now to set the trap. Wozniak unfolded the topographical map. "Kaminski, help me out here." The loader held the edge of the map as his commander studied the terrain.

Thirty kilometers to the east, the A16 made a ninety-degree turn where it crossed the Neman River at the town of Prienai. Immediately after that, the highway passed through a five-kilometer stretch of thick woods.

If he were the Russian commander, Wozniak would be wary of the woods. A properly dug-in enemy, screened by the forest, could decimate a column of tanks. But would he be worried enough to divide his column at Prienai?

Wozniak was betting no. The Russian operation had clearly been planned as a blitz across the Suwalki Gap. The Russian commander would follow his orders.

But if he expected an enemy ambush, he'd also be relieved when he emerged unscathed from the thick woods. The countryside opened up to pastures and plowed fields, hedgerows, and stone fences. Tank country. The Russian commander would breathe easier, maybe even drop his guard just a bit.

Wozniak shook his head. He still had to deal with the Russians' superior numbers. Even with a three-to-one kill ratio, in a head-to-head battle, Wozniak would lose.

The plan that he'd been turning over in his mind came into focus. He knew his terrain, he knew his forces, and he knew the threat axis. Wozniak switched to the battalion net.

"All units, this is Romeo Six-six actual, stand by for orders."

He waited for acknowledgments from his company commanders, then continued: "Bravo company proceed to"— he read off the coordinates for a tree line north of the highway three kilometers to the east of Sventragis—"then take cover and turn off your engines."

"Romeo Six-six, Bravo Six-six, roger."

Charlie company and the XO would be the last to arrive on scene, Wozniak ordered them to deploy around the small town, south of the A16. The XO acknowledged his orders.

"Alpha company," Wozniak continued, "deploy in echelon formation along the threat axis, north to south. Take cover and turn off your engines."

"Romeo Six-six, this is Alpha Six-six, roger," the Alpha company commander responded.

Wozniak took a deep breath. In a normal situation, an attack of this importance would be analyzed and considered from all angles, looking for weaknesses. But time was as much his enemy as the Russian tanks. The fate of his entire battalion rested on his judgment.

He pictured the battlefield in his mind's eye. The A16 formed a straight east-west line. Bravo company was positioned to the north and east, on the right flank of the Russian column. Further down the highway, on the Russians' left flank, was Charlie company. And in front of the Russians, in a line perpendicular to the threat axis, Wozniak would be waiting with Alpha company.

"The following is the order of battle," Wozniak said. "Alpha company will begin the attack. Frontal assault, close range. The goal is to get the Russians to commit to destroying the targets in front of them. When the end of the enemy column passes Bravo company's position, Charlie company will engage from the southern flank. When the Russians have fully committed, Alpha will disengage and I will give the order for Bravo to attack from the rear. This three-sided attack depends on precise timing." Wozniak lifted his finger off the press-to-talk button and counted to three.

"Any questions?" he asked.

There were none. Wozniak looked up to see the town of Sventragis appear on their right. It was a small town of a few dozen closely packed houses, a commuter town, he realized. There were lights on in some of the houses.

"Very well," Wozniak said into the microphone. "Deploy at will. Establish good cover and shut down your engines." He desperately hoped the rain would cool their thermal signatures. "If the Russians break through here, it's open country all the way to Kaliningrad. Good hunting."

Wozniak switched to the tank circuit. "Sergeant Zielinski, get on the A16 and head west. Let's find a place to hide."

"Yes, sir," the driver replied.

"Is this a hammer and anvil, sir?" Kaminski asked, still studying the map.

Wozniak smiled in spite of himself. "You've been studying military tactics, Private Kaminski?"

The loader shrugged. He was the most junior of the crew and a tough kid, but Wozniak had seen promise in the young man. He started to ask his loader if he wanted to be considered for an officer program, then stopped himself.

Maybe we should just focus on living to see lunchtime, he thought.

"Yeah, Kaminski," he said, "this is a hammer and anvil."

"I hope we smash the shit out of the Russians, sir," Kaminski said.

"That's the plan, Private." Wozniak hoisted himself up into the cupola.

Less than a kilometer west of the 181-16 junction was a tree line running north-south, anchored by a large stone barn and smaller house made of the same material. Wozniak gave the order for Alpha company to deploy in the tree line.

For their hiding place, he ordered Zielinski to drive past

the barn to a copse of trees fifty meters off the A16. The driver navigated the tank into the trees, behind a stone wall. The position gave the gunner an excellent sightline down the highway.

"Shut down the engine," Wozniak ordered, "and let's get some camouflage in place."

The ever-present whine of the gas turbine engine faded. Wozniak kept an eye on the MAPS display to see how his company commanders deployed their units. Alpha company settled in around his position with a tank every seventy-five meters or so, depending on camouflage opportunities and taking into account natural obstacles like ponds and groups of trees. Bravo and Charlie reported that they were in position.

Satisfied, Wozniak climbed down from the tank. The crew had already disguised the tank profile using tree branches and some scrap lumber scavenged from the nearby farm's trash heap.

"Good job, gentlemen," he said. "Get something to eat, but stay close."

The rain stopped, and the air was still. The last gas turbine within earshot shut down, and Wozniak heard a rooster crow from the other side of the barn. The heavy gray clouds seemed lighter. He breathed in the earthy smells of the farm and tried to make himself relax.

It was the dawn of a new day.

Zielinski got out his phone and played some music, a heavy hip-hop beat. He nodded his head as he ripped open an MRE packet. Wozniak thought about telling him to turn the music down but let it pass. He wasn't hurting anything.

"*Labas rytas*," said a voice behind him.

The music stopped, and Wozniak whirled to find an old man standing beside his tank. He was dressed in torn coveralls, mud-caked work boots, and a misshapen sweater.

The man repeated the greeting—at least Wozniak supposed it was a greeting. He responded in Polish, but the man shook his head.

"English?" he asked.

The old man showed a gap-toothed smile and held his thumb and forefinger a centimeter apart. "Little bit," he replied.

"The Russians are coming." Wozniak pointed east, down the A16. "You need to leave."

"This is home," the old man said. "We not leaving."

"We?"

A woman appeared from the tree line. She had a loaf of bread under one arm and a pail of milk in her hand.

"My wife," the old man said. "Regina. I am Kostas."

The woman handed Wozniak the loaf of bread. "Eat."

He tore off a piece and handed it to Zielinski. The bread was a dark rye and still warm from the oven. It had a sweet, nutty flavor. Wozniak closed his eyes for second to chew the bread. He hadn't even realized he was so hungry.

The woman produced a tin cup from her pocket and dipped it into the pail of milk. That too was still warm and heavy with cream, probably fresh from the cow. Wozniak finished the cup and handed it to Zielinski. The tank crew set to work devouring the food.

"Thank you," Wozniak said. "But I need you to leave. It's not safe here."

"This is home," the old man said again.

Wozniak blew out a frustrated breath. "Do you have a basement?" he asked. "A root cellar?"

Regina nodded, watching the tank crew eat. "I get more bread."

"Thank you, but—"

The radio in the TC hatch came to life. "Romeo Six-six,

this is Rabbit One. Contact east! Twenty-five T-14 and twenty-five APC moving west along the A16. Speed fifty."

Wozniak hauled himself up the side of the tank and seized the handset. "Rabbit One, copy all. Out."

The contact report populated on his tactical display. The same report would be appearing inside the turret of every tank in his battalion right now. Every tank commander would understand what it meant.

An enemy battalion of modern tanks and armored personnel carriers would be here in ten minutes. This would be the Russians' lead column—the advance force—and their orders would be to move fast and destroy any Lithuanian forces that were in the way of the main body.

Wozniak gripped the side of the hatch so hard he felt the metal edge cut into his palm.

Get it together, he told himself. Then he turned and jumped down to the ground. His tank crew looked at him, and in the pale morning light, they all seemed so young. Too young for what they were about to do.

"Thank you for the food," Wozniak said to the farmer and his wife. "I need you to go to your root cellar now and stay there until this is over."

Regina took her husband's hand and picked up her empty milk pail. "Good boys," she said to the tank crew.

Without another word, Wozniak and his crew climbed into their tank to wait.

---

35

1 kilometer east of Sventragis, Lithuania

Ten minutes felt like an eternity.

Wozniak glared at the targeting display with fierce intensity. Although they knew the exact line of approach the enemy would take, Nowak scanned the gunsight across an arc in search of targets. The image flickered back and forth between high and low magnification.

The battalion circuit invaded his thoughts. "Romeo Six-six, Rabbit One, second armor battalion is passing now. Same mix of tanks and APCs."

"Copy that, Rabbit One."

The display populated with another fifty enemy contacts. His stomach clenched.

"Tank, dead ahead." Nowak's shout over the intercom snapped Wozniak back to the moment.

He watched the boxy white shape on the high-mag thermal display. "I see him, gunner," he said. "I want you to know that we're going to let him get really, really close before we fire."

"How close, sir?"

As close as I can stand it, Wozniak thought. "Five hundred meters, maybe less. We need to fit these two Russian battalions inside our kill box."

Wozniak switched to the battalion circuit. "Alpha company, engage on my command. Charlie and Bravo, stand by, all engines off."

He paused, then said on the tank circuit, "Gunner, sabot, tank."

"Up!" responded Kaminski almost before Wozniak finished speaking. The expected sabot round was already loaded.

"Identified," Nowak said. "Range, one-five hundred meters."

The battalion circuit cut in. "Romeo Six-six, Rabbit One. Second enemy battalion is stopping. Repeat, they are stopping short of Bravo's flank position." Wozniak could hear the strain in the scout's voice.

He cursed to himself. Why were they stopping? He looked up at the leaden sky. Did they have aerial intel about the trap? Despite the chill of the morning, he felt sweat break out under his arms.

"One thousand meters," Nowak said.

Wozniak switched his own gunsight to high magnification. The lead tank showed white-hot on the thermal display. The turret of the oncoming tank was unmanned. The T-14 Armata's three-man crew operated their tank from an armored capsule contained in the front of the hull. They used an automatic loader instead of a fourth crew member. Wozniak had read the automation led to longer reload times, possibly twice the time required for a human loader. He was about to test that theory in real life.

"Range eight hundred meters," Nowak reported.

"Rabbit One," Wozniak said on the radio, "Romeo Six-six, status of second battalion."

"Not moving, sir." The scout sounded like he was whispering. "Two officers are on the road, talking on cell phones."

Wozniak gritted his teeth. "Six-six, out."

"Six hundred meters, sir," Nowak said. On high mag, the image of the incoming tank filled the screen. Behind the lead tank, vehicles followed at a spacing of only about twenty meters. That would be a costly decision for the Russian battalion commander.

"Five hundred meters!" Nowak said.

"Understood, gunner. Stand by."

He could hear the breathing of his crew over the intercom. Slow and steady was Zielinski, Kaminski short and shallow, gunner Nowak puffing like an injured bull. The scent of expended gunpowder from their previous battle was sharp in Wozniak's nostrils.

"Three hundred fifty meters," Nowak reported.

The turret of the lead Russian tank scanned the road ahead, looking for threats. How well hidden was his battalion? How long could he wait?

Wozniak heard Nowak take in another noisy breath in preparation for another range report, when the battalion circuit came to life.

"Romeo Six-six, they're moving!"

"Two hundred meters!" Nowak said.

"Fire!" Wozniak said.

"On the way." Nowak's response was lost in the *WHUMP* of the round leaving the barrel of the main gun.

"Alpha company, engage!" Wozniak shouted over the battalion circuit.

The thermal display saturated white as the lead tank exploded.

"Charlie company, engage!" Wozniak ordered.

Next to him, the breech opened and the aft cap of the spent round dropped, still smoking, into a bin on the floor. Kaminski was already reaching for another shell to reload.

"No new targets!" Nowak said.

The front of the enemy column was destroyed, burning, obscuring the targets behind them. He must not give the Russians time to regroup.

"Driver, move out!" Wozniak shouted. The gas turbine whined to life, the tank surged over the low stone wall in front of them, and they were racing across a pasture toward the highway.

"Tank!" Nowak shouted.

"Up!" bawled out Kaminski.

"Identified!" The display showed a range of seven hundred meters.

"Gunner, fire and adjust," Wozniak ordered, releasing the gunner and loader to fire without his command.

"On the way—" *WHUMP*, the forward motion of the tank pulsed as another shot left the barrel of the main gun.

Wozniak divided his attention between the targeting display showing Nowak's engagements and the MAPS display showing the location of his own tanks.

WHUMP! Another round left the tank. The acrid smell of fresh gunpowder filled the turret as the breech opened and the aft cap dropped out. Kaminski slammed a fresh shell into the breech.

On the targeting display, Russian tanks and APCs fanned out from their column formation into a line facing Wozniak's Alpha company. On the MAPS display, he counted eight blue dots as Alpha company advanced on the Russian line.

Eight? Had he already lost two tanks?

From the bottom of the screen, Charlie company, still at full strength, directed fire on the Russian flank.

WHUMP!

The scene from Wozniak's viewport showed only clouds of smoke outside. The thermal display was cluttered with burning hulks, making it harder for Nowak to find targets. The gunner scanned the turret across a sixty-degree arc.

"Driver, slow," Wozniak ordered. The speed of the tank slowed to a crawl.

"Romeo Six-six, Romeo Six-five." The XO's voice came over the battalion circuit. "They're retreating. The Russians are falling back!"

"Bravo company, engage!" Wozniak ordered. On the MAPS display, the blue dots that represented Bravo company wheeled to close off the Russian avenue of escape.

WHUMP! Nowak fired another round at a Russian APC.

They passed between two raging fires throwing off clouds of oily smoke. A few minutes ago, these lumps of burning metal had been the lead tanks of the Russian column. Ammunition from one of the burning tanks exploded, and a blossom of fire and smoke lit up the rectangular viewports above his head.

Nowak carefully assessed each object in his gunsight for any enemy tanks that might be disabled but not dead yet. Wozniak joined the search using his own independent targeting screen, checking sectors opposite Nowak.

He thought he spotted movement on a Russian tank burning white on the screen, but it was hard to tell. Just as he was about to move on, the tank turret moved.

"Gunner, battlesight, tank!" Wozniak said, slewing the turret using the TC override.

"Identified!"

"Fire," Wozniak ordered.

WHUMP. The burning tank exploded.

Wozniak stared at the screen as a new tank, hiding behind the burning hulk, slid into view. The gun barrel was aimed right at Wozniak.

Nowak reported the new target just as Wozniak yelled, "Driver, move out!"

To his left, Kaminski was just loading the next round into the breech. The Russian tank fired, and Wozniak felt the round impact somewhere on the turret. Wozniak's gunsight display went black.

"Fire!" He switched to view Nowak's display. The round hit the oncoming Russian tank. There was an explosion, but the tank emerged from the smoke and fire.

"Reengage!" Wozniak called out.

"Identified!" Nowak said.

It felt like Kaminski was moving in slow motion. Wozniak watched the armored door separating the ammo locker from the turret creep open. The loader seized a new round, withdrawing it from the rack with two hands, then he spun and tipped it into the open breech. The breech door slowly closed.

"Up."

"Fire."

"On the way."

WHUMP.

The Russian tank burst into flames.

"That was close, sir," Nowak said.

"Kaminski," Wozniak replied, "you will never be replaced by a robot in my tank."

___

With the remnants of the 1st Armoured tank battalion, Wozniak combed through the battlefield. Fifty-caliber fire echoed as his tanks hunted down any Russian infantry that had disembarked from their armored personnel carriers.

The brigade circuit let him know that the Polish 1st and 3rd Mech Battalions were approaching from the south and three battalions from the Lithuanian Iron Wolf Mechanized Brigade were approaching from the north. The remaining tanks of the 1st Armoured were to withdraw to a rally point and await orders.

Wozniak gave the order for his battalion to regroup a short distance from the farmhouse where the battle had begun.

Wozniak opened the TC hatch and stood in the cupola. His fifty-caliber machine gun and remote sighting assembly were both gone, no doubt sheared off by the last engagement with the Russian T-14.

The air was foul with smoke, churned earth, and spilled fuel. Somewhere off to his left, ammunition in one of the burning hulks cooked off in a booming fireworks display. Russian or Polish? He couldn't tell, didn't care.

They'd held off the Russians. That was what mattered.

But the cost made his heart ache. Of the fifty-eight tanks he'd started the night with, only twenty remained. Thirty-eight tanks lost, four personnel to a tank crew...he tried to do the math, and his brain failed him.

When Wozniak made the preliminary casualty report to brigade, his tank crew was stunned into silence.

"Jesus Christ," said Nowak finally.

"I don't think he had anything to do with it," Zielinski replied.

Wozniak stood in his cupola and breathed in the filthy air.

When he thought about how close to death they'd come, Wozniak felt his stomach seize. Their survival had come down to how fast a twenty-year-old kid could load a shell into a hole. If Kaminski had been half a second slower, his tank might be among the flaming carcasses that littered this killing field and the Russian tank commander would be the one living to fight another day.

"Driver, halt," Wozniak ordered.

He looked through the smoke to see if the barn was still standing. He wondered if Regina and Kostas had lived through the morning.

Wozniak tipped his head back and looked straight up at the sky. There was a tear in the gray clouds, a slash of blue appeared. The weather had been his friend last night, but that was about to end.

Brigade was trying to raise him on the radio. Wozniak took one last breath of the foul morning air and dropped back into his tank.

36

Tysons Corner, Virginia

Don slouched in his desk chair. He skimmed the daily intel brief on his computer screen, keeping one eye on the muted TV. This was one of those instances when current events moved so quickly that civilian news reporters often had more up-to-date intelligence than any classified sources.

The commercial playing on the TV ended. A woman with long brown hair stood on a rooftop, clutching a heavy microphone. In the background, thick columns of smoke clouded the horizon.

The chyron underneath her picture read VILNIUS, LITHUANIA. Don unmuted the TV.

"I'm speaking to you this afternoon from Vilnius, the capital of Lithuania. In the predawn hours, Russian tanks crossed the border from Belarus in what appears to be a bid to open a corridor between Belarus and the Russian state of Kaliningrad, two hundred kilometers to the west. The Russian advance was preceded by a cyberattack that temporarily disabled communications inside the Lithuanian military."

Back in Washington, the anchor, whose conservative dark blue suit matched his serious expression, nodded gravely. "That sounds serious, Andrea. Be safe out there."

He allowed the field correspondent to sign off, then shifted to a new camera. "And how is the Serrano administration handling this new crisis? For that, we go to our White House correspondent, Randy Albertson."

Randy, with the White House in the background, picked up the handoff. "I think the answer is: not very well. With the midterm elections looming, the last thing President Serrano wanted was another international conflict. But it seems that's exactly what he's getting. A statement issued from the White House condemns the Russian invasion of Lithuania and says they are in consultation with our NATO allies—"

Don muted the TV and threw the remote on his desk in disgust.

If the President had just let his intelligence community dig into the Russian problem the way it deserved, all of this might have been prevented. Instead of analyzing the problem holistically, he used a private military contractor to "manage" the Ukraine situation.

While we tried to protect a tree, Don thought, Luchnik was lighting the forest on fire.

The politically expedient solution had turned into a time bomb, and there was not a damn thing anybody could do about it now.

Don turned back to his computer. With a sigh, he opened his unclassified email and reached for his coffee cup.

The mug paused midway to his lips as Don stared at the screen. The subject line of the message at the top of the queue was a single word:

PANDORA.

He clicked to open the email. Inside was a ten-digit number. A phone number?

Don picked up his mobile phone and typed in the numbers. The call was answered on the first ring.

"UPS Store." The voice had a slight drawl.

Don cleared his throat. "Can you tell me where your store is located, please?"

"Rapid City, South Dakota, sir. Haines Avenue."

Don thought for a moment. "Do you rent mailboxes?"

"Absolutely."

Six hours later, Don entered The UPS Store on Haines Avenue, Rapid City, South Dakota, with FBI Special Agent Liz Soroush in tow. He hung back, allowing Liz to do the talking.

A genial middle-aged man in a company polo and a name tag that read Tony greeted them. "How can I help you this afternoon, ma'am?"

Liz showed him her FBI identification. "We'd like to look at your customer list for mailbox rentals."

Tony frowned. "Ma'am, unless you have a warrant, I can't do that."

"What if I have a key?" Don said.

Tony crossed his arms. "If you have a key, there's nothing I can do to stop you."

Don held up the duplicate key. "I don't know which box it opens."

Or if it even opens any box in this store, he added silently.

Tony took the key. "People are not supposed to duplicate these," he said. "It's against the contract they signed when they rented the box." He looked at Liz. "Is this like national security or something?"

Liz raised her eyebrows but said nothing.

Tony bit his lip in concentration. "I suppose there's no reason why you couldn't try the key in any mailbox. If it doesn't open anything, nobody's harmed."

"That sounds like a good compromise," Liz replied.

It took thirty minutes for Don to insert the key into 135 mailboxes and find out it did not work. On number 136, the key moved one quarter-turn to the right. Don put the key back to the twelve o'clock position and turned it again.

"Liz?" he called. "I think I found it."

Tony took Liz behind the bank of mailboxes. She shined a penlight into the mailbox slot. "There's an envelope inside," she called to Don. "Go ahead and open it."

Don turned the key again and opened the square brass door. Using gloves, he carefully extracted the sealed envelope. Holding it by the edges, he turned it over.

DON RILEY was written on the front of the envelope in block letters.

He held it up to the light. Inside was a thumb drive.

"I just rented that box a couple a weeks ago," Tony said. "German fella, I think. He had an accent, anyway."

"I need to see his paperwork, Tony," Liz said. "Right away."

Fifteen minutes later, she ended a phone call. "Tomas Horst, Austrian national, was killed in a single-car traffic accident on the same day he rented that mailbox."

Tony had closed the store, and Liz had forensics people en route from the local FBI office. The unopened envelope lay on the counter.

"I need that thumb drive, Liz," Don said. "Whoever put it there went to an extraordinary amount of effort to make sure it got to me. I need to have a look at it right now."

Liz blew out a breath. "It has your name on it, and you had the key, so I guess it's yours."

While Don got out his laptop, Liz put on gloves and slit the end of the envelope open. She inserted the thumb drive into the USB port on his laptop.

Don scanned for viruses and found nothing. He opened the thumb drive.

Twenty-five folder icons showed on the screen. He ran his gaze down the list of names. *Paris, Romeo, ABC, Kensington, Ocean Blue...* Nothing labeled *Pandora.*

He clicked on a folder. A list of documents scrolled down the screen. He opened one at random. A property deed for a condominium in Miami Beach. Another was a bank statement for a Cayman Islands numbered account.

"I don't think 'Pandora' refers to the virus, Don," Liz said, looking over his shoulder. "I think maybe it's 'Pandora' like the Pandora Papers." She pulled out her phone. "I'll call Reg Bowerman over at Treasury."

Don continued clicking on random files to see who owned all these assets. Most of them were random names or other companies, but there had to be a reason why someone had given these files to him.

He opened a bank statement and saw a name that he recognized.

"Wait," he said. "I have a better idea." He got out his own phone and dialed a number from memory.

"It's me," Don said when Abby Cromwell answered. "I need another favor."

37

White House
Washington, DC

The headline of the *Washington Post* spanned the full width of the front page: *CARNAGE IN LITHUANIA*. Immediately below the bold type was a panel of three grainy pictures.

A man dressed in black with the gold letters LAF on his balaclava. Contorted bodies dressed in nightclothes and workout gear, pale limbs against a dark rainy night.

And the blond girl. The internet had even given her a name: Sasha. Twenty-four hours ago, little Sasha was an unknown kid in a tiny village in Lithuania. Today, she was an international headline. The girl's unseeing eyes stared out of the picture at Abby.

The worst part, Abby thought, is that it's all a lie.

Mama's analysis of the facts produced an 87 percent probability that the Maraziskes Massacre, as the incident was now being called, was a hoax. A brutal killing designed to provide the Russian Federation with an excuse to invade Lithuania and open up a land corridor to Kaliningrad.

Of course, she didn't need an artificial intelligence to tell her what she already knew in her heart, but somehow assigning a probability to the reason for Sasha's death gave her odd comfort.

Abby clenched her eyes shut against the morning sun. She gritted her teeth until she felt her jaw muscles pop.

All of this could have been prevented, she thought. Don Riley was right again, but because he told the truth, no one believed him. No, that wasn't right either. No one wanted to believe him, because it was inconvenient. Because a poll said people didn't care. Because there was an election...because, because, because.

She opened her eyes as she felt the car turn onto Pennsylvania Avenue.

And I'm just as guilty, she thought. I helped cover it up by helping the President keep up appearances in Ukraine.

Her rational mind told her there was more than enough blame to go around, but her heart knew the truth. She had Sasha's blood on her hands.

The road outside the White House gate was flanked by protestors. One woman with a red face held up a sign: *Hell, no, we won't go*. On the other side of the street, a man held up a competing placard: *Russians are baby killers*.

Perfect. Abby sighed. Luchnik wins again. As he'd done before, the Russian dictator managed to inject his venom into the bloodstream of American politics and achieved the desired immune response.

Sound. Fury. Division. Chaos. To her, the saddest part was that the Americans who bought into the Kremlin's lies didn't even realize they'd been duped.

Hybrid warfare, she thought. It's a wicked problem.

She flipped the newspaper over. Another headline: *NATO struggles to respond to Russian invasion*.

The car slowed at the gate, and Abby disembarked. As she processed through security, she spied Dylan Mattias waiting on the other side. He smiled as she approached.

"What an unpleasant surprise," Abby said.

"Where you go, I go," Dylan said. "That's the job description. Unless you manage to get me fired today."

Abby stopped, faced him. "I want to be up front with you," she said. "Even though you don't deserve it. I'm getting Sentinel out of Ukraine, and I'm telling Serrano today."

"You can't do that, Abby," Dylan said.

She started walking again. "Just try and stop me."

Dylan grabbed her arm. "Don't, please. Go along with it—for now. Starting a brawl in the middle of a National Security Council meeting does not help your cause."

Abby jerked her arm back and crossed her arms.

"Look," Dylan said. "I'll handle it. If we work together, we can get Sentinel out of Ukraine without making an enemy of the most powerful man in the world. I'm asking you to trust me."

The image of Sasha's face floated in Abby's mind.

"Trust you?" she said, not even bothering to hide the sarcasm. "Have you forgotten about our last trip to Ukraine? Remember the one where we slept together and then you stabbed me in the back with Manson?"

"Grow up, Abby. One has nothing to do with the other. I can have feelings for you—and I do—and still make the tough calls in the field."

"The tough calls?" Abby snapped. "Like the ones where my people die because Manson got an itchy trigger finger?" She clenched and unclenched her fists. Her anger hovered right under the surface, just waiting to break through.

Then clarity struck. "Why am I here?" she asked. "The

Ukraine operation is covert. Only a few people in the NSC even know about it."

Dylan smiled. "You're here because of me. I recommended to the Director that you be in the meeting so you can see how critical it is for us to maintain the pressure in Ukraine."

"Oh," she said, feeling her anger drain away. "So, you're trusting me not to pee in the national security pool."

"I'm trusting you to do the right thing."

Abby looked away. Did this change anything? she wondered.

Dylan looked at his watch. "Is that a yes?" he asked.

"I haven't made up my mind yet," Abby said. "That'll have to be good enough for now."

"If that's your way of saying I have to trust you," Dylan said. "Then, I'll take it."

They marched into the White House side by side and took the stairs down to the Situation Room. Inside the room, controlled chaos was the order of the day. All the principals were already seated at the main table with staffers crowded close as they briefed last-minute details. The air snapped with tension, buzzed with the drone of too many words in too short a time.

The main viewscreen at the front of the room was split. The right side showed the green-and-gold coat of arms for the Supreme Allied Commander Europe. The left side showed a map of the Suwalki Gap. Although the name was on the lips of every newsperson this morning, until today, Abby hadn't even known that tiny corner of Europe had a special name. Abby would have liked to study the red and blue dots populating the map, but Dylan urged her on.

National Security Advisor Valentina Flores looked up, and they locked eyes for a moment. Flores's expression could not have been more transparent.

Don't rock the boat.

Abby glared back at her and followed Dylan to her seat behind the Director of the CIA. Next to the Director, Secretary of Defense Kathleen Howard huddled with the new Chairman of the Joint Chiefs.

Abby had clashed with the prior Chairman, but she found herself now wishing that General Nikolaides was still in his old job. Yes, they had their differences, but with the blinding clarity of 20/20 hindsight, she believed that if Nikolaides had been in charge, there would have been a much different response to Ukraine.

I helped get him fired, she thought. *Him, and Don Riley.*

Serrano entered the room at a fast walk, shoulders thrust forward, fists clenched. Chief of Staff Wilkerson shut the door with a solid thump, and the room rose to their feet as one. In the silence that followed, the President jerked out his chair and sat down. As a politician known for his genial personality, Serrano always went out of his way to greet his audience.

Not today. His jawline was a ridge of muscle, and his eyes darted about the room with fevered intensity.

"Seats," he snapped. "We've got a lot to cover."

The video screen at the end of the table showed the head and shoulders of General Kranik.

Serrano nodded curtly. "General, good morning. What's the status over there?"

"Good morning, sir. Our intel is still pretty sketchy, Mr. President. The weather is a major issue for our aerial assets. I can report this: the Russian armored advance through Lithuania was stopped in its tracks early this morning."

"The Lithuanians were able to respond?" Serrano asked.

"No, sir. The bulk of the fighting was done by the Polish Army. A single tank battalion raced up from the south and took on the Russians head-to-head. Damn fine bit of work, sir."

"And what are the Russians doing now?" Serrano said.

"Regrouping for another bite at the apple," Kranik replied. "But that also gives us time to reinforce our position. The Lithuanians are in the fight, and the Poles have moved reinforcements into position. We can provide air support as soon as the weather cooperates. That'll make a big difference, but the allies really want to see some action on the part of the United States, Mr. President."

"Sir?" Secretary of State Hahn interrupted. "I can speak to that."

Serrano nodded. The sour expression on his face told Abby that the President both knew what Hahn was about to say and did not want to hear it.

"Lithuania has formally invoked Article 5 and requests full, unequivocal support from all NATO members. Separately, they're asking for a public statement of support and a concrete and immediate American military movement to demonstrate our resolve to the Russian Federation.

"Additionally, both Estonia and Latvia are expected to request NATO troop deployments in their countries to reinforce their borders with Russia."

"I guess that's what it's come to?" Serrano said, his voice tight with anger. "Everybody wants Daddy to be in charge."

Abby felt the sting of the words, and they were not even directed at her. A quick scan around the room told her she was not alone.

Serrano's gaze locked on the Secretary of Defense. "Kathleen, I'm sure you have a recommendation as to what our—" He looked back at Hahn. "What were the exact words, Henry?"

"A concrete and immediate American military movement

to demonstrate our resolve to the Russian Federation," Hahn said crisply.

"That," Serrano said to Howard. "What he said."

Kathleen Howard cleared her throat. "Mr. President, the Chairman and I have come up with a plan that we can implement in stages. Supplementing NATO airpower should be our immediate priority. We have to prevent the Russians from breaching the Suwalki Gap.

"Next, mobilize US ground forces in Germany and deploy them to Poland. The 82nd Airborne and the 101st are both back from deployment in Taiwan. We recommend they be positioned in Latvia and Estonia to stabilize the Baltic States."

She paused, looking for a reaction from Serrano. She got nothing. He stared at her dead-eyed.

"Finally," Howard concluded, "get the Second Marine Expeditionary Force underway from the East Coast immediately."

"The Second MEF?" Serrano asked. "Is that really necessary?"

The new Chairman spoke up. General William McCleave was a US Army armor officer with a round face and wavy gray hair. He spoke in a clear baritone with a slight Southern twang.

"Sir, I think it's fair to say, we've been one step behind the Russians for this entire campaign. But for a single battalion of Polish tanks—they're US-made tanks, by the way—we'd have a major crisis on our hands. I think it's more than prudent that we get the Marines underway ASAP."

Serrano studied the new Chairman with narrowed eyes.

Maybe, Abby wondered, he was wishing he had Nikolaides back.

"Henry," Serrano turned back to State, "why aren't the Russians attacking out of Kaliningrad? If our position in the

Suwalki Gap is so precarious, why isn't Luchnik attacking from the other side?"

"I can hazard a guess, Mr. President," Hahn said. "If his bid to establish a land corridor between Belarus and Kaliningrad fails, he can always withdraw back into Belarus. In his mind, he just resets the game back to the beginning. If he involves Kaliningrad directly, he puts that territory in play. That's just a guess, sir."

Serrano shook his head. "That's not like Luchnik. If he has a way to win, why hold back?"

"There's another possibility, sir," Hahn said, "but it's out there."

Serrano barked out a bitter laugh. "We're about to commit the United States military to a possible World War Three scenario for the third time in less than two years," he said. "I don't think anything is too 'out there' to consider."

"The oblast of Kaliningrad under the post-Soviet Russian Federation has always been a little independent of Moscow," Hahn said. "They live surrounded by enemies on all sides. The people are anti-elitist. Maybe that sentiment has bled into the military."

"I don't follow."

"Maybe they were ordered to attack and they said no," Hahn replied.

"A mutiny?" Serrano said. "Next thing you're going to tell me is that there's another coup against Luchnik."

Hahn shook his head. "I'm saying this entire attack went down in the space of hours. That's lightning speed for any military, especially Russia. We didn't hear a peep about it, so that tells me it was probably a closely held plan. Maybe they didn't have time to get Kaliningrad onboard."

Serrano rubbed his chin. He suddenly looked older, Abby

thought. As if the full impact of the decision he was about to make weighed on him in this moment.

There was no good move for the President. The country was divided. Any move he made was going to hurt him with half of the voting public. In a word, he was screwed.

"Secretary of Defense," Serrano said.

"Sir."

"I am ordering you to put the military movements we just discussed into effect. If the Russians want a fight, then we'll give it to them." He looked at the video screen. "General Kranik, please let our allies know that we have their backs one hundred percent. I will be making an address to the nation this evening to that effect."

"Yes, sir." Abby thought Kranik sounded relieved.

"General," Serrano said, "when this is all over, I'd consider it a personal favor if you'd look up the Polish tank battalion commander and buy him a beer for me."

"I'll do that, sir."

Serrano rapped his knuckles on the table and stood. The room rose to their feet.

"Ladies and gentlemen, let's get to work."

38

The Kremlin
Moscow, Russia

Vitaly Luchnik placed his palms flat on the mahogany table of the Security Council Meeting Room. White skin on dark wood.

He focused on his hand placement, positioning each hand the same distance from the edge of the table. Each finger held exactly the same way, thumbs tucked against the knuckle of the index finger.

It was a trick he had learned as a child, a way to distract himself when anger threatened to overtake his actions.

He stared at the table as if his gaze might burn through the wood.

This is not happening, he told himself. The plan was perfect. Flawless. Every trick, every deception he'd garnered from four decades of dealing with the West had come together into the perfect plan.

The Ukraine, Belarus, the incident in Lithuania. Each one

a shining example of his masterful ambition. Each one a step closer to his glorious dream of a New Russian Empire.

Luchnik began to count in a whisper. *Odin...dva...tri...*

Only one thing remained to complete his plan. The keystone of the New Russian Empire was capturing the Suwalki Corridor. Opening a land bridge between Kaliningrad and Belarus. He had cleared the field of enemies, diverted their attention hundreds of kilometers away. The land was there for the taking...

And yet...and yet...

His right hand, still pressed flat against the table, began to tremble. Luchnik balled both hands into fists. His head snapped up.

The eyes of every cabinet member were locked on the Russian President. No one shifted in their seat, no one blinked, no one even dared to breathe heavily.

Luchnik's gaze rifled down the line of faces until he found the Defense Minister.

"What happened?" Luchnik's voice barely rose above a whisper, but in the stillness of the room, he might as well have shouted.

Yakov's upright shock of thick gray hair was greasy and dented by his uniform cap. His face seemed to have succumbed to gravity. The bags under his eyes dragged down his lower eyelids, his jowls swung loosely when he turned his head to meet his president's gaze.

"Sir, I—"

"Stand when you address me!" Luchnik shouted. His fingers clenched in a spasm of rage. He wanted to leap over the table and beat Yakov's face in with his bare hands. This fucking moron might have ruined everything.

Yakov recoiled, then shot upright into a posture of rigid

attention. His chair scraped back, a wailing noise that echoed in the cavernous room.

"Tell. Me. What. Happened," Luchnik said.

"The armored advance in the Suwalki Gap was stopped," Yakov said.

Luchnik felt the rage creeping up his spine like a parasite, each vertebra tingling with heat as he fought for control.

"How?" he said.

"The Poles sent—"

"The Poles?" Luchnik interrupted. He had half expected resistance from the Lithuanians, but the Poles?

Even the weather was in their favor, Luchnik thought. NATO airpower was all but grounded by the thick clouds over the Suwalki Gap last night.

Yakov looked at him expectantly, and Luchnik realized his mind had drifted. He hadn't slept in over twenty-four hours.

"Continue," he barked at the Defense Minister.

"The 1st Warsaw Armoured Brigade was encamped outside Suwalki, Mr. President," Yakov said. "When our forces crossed into Lithuania, so did the Poles. They attacked the lead Battalion Tactical Group from the 12th Guards Tank Regiment along the southern axis of advance." He swallowed, looked as if he might be sick. "Many units were lost, sir."

"And?" Luchnik pressed.

Yakov cleared his throat. "Polish forces intercepted the lead columns from the 13th Guards Tank Regiment along the A16 highway. We suffered losses, sir. The advance was halted. At that point, the Lithuanian Army joined forces with the Poles, and our forces withdrew to defensive positions. We will make a breakthrough, Mr. President. I am confident of that."

Luchnik fell back in his chair, feeling winded, as if he'd just been punched in the gut. His mind whirled. Nothing made sense.

"What was the size of the Polish force?" he asked.

"A tank battalion, sir." Yakov answered tentatively, like he didn't understand the question.

"Yes, I understand the Polish tank battalion attacked the southern advance," Luchnik snapped. "But who attacked the northern advance?"

Yakov blinked. "It was the same tank battalion, Mr. President."

Luchnik felt like the floor had opened up beneath him. "The same unit?"

"Yes, sir. What remained of the Polish tank battalion after the first engagement continued north and set up an ambush along the A16 highway."

"Defense Minister Yakov, how many tanks were in the southern flanking force?"

"A regiment's worth, Mr. President. Mostly T-90 and T-72s, with supporting infantry fighting vehicles and armored personnel carriers. It was the 12th Guards Tank Regiment."

"And they were all destroyed by the Poles?" Luchnik asked.

Yakov shifted on his feet. "Yes, Mr. President, the Poles used terrain features to box in our forces. And then they attacked."

"What were the Polish losses?"

Yakov licked his lips. "Unknown, sir."

Luchnik leaned forward. "You're telling me that what remained of the Polish tank battalion continued north to meet the 13th Guards' advance?"

Even a plodding thinker like Yakov could see the endpoint of this line of questioning. "Yes, Mr. President."

"And the remainder of the Polish tank battalion met and stopped the advance of our forces on the A16 highway?"

Yakov swallowed. "Yes, sir. With reinforcements from the Lithuanian Army."

"How many tanks are in a Polish tank battalion, Defense Minister Yakov?"

"Fifty-eight, sir."

"And how many Russian tanks did this Polish tank battalion destroy, Yakov?" Despite his best efforts, Luchnik heard his voice sliding up the register.

"Total losses were fifty-two destroyed and another fifteen damaged to the point they were abandoned."

Luchnik's collar suddenly felt too tight. A single battalion of Polish tanks had stopped his army cold.

"It's worse than that, Mr. President," Federov said.

Luchnik startled, then turned to focus on the man sitting to his left. With his intense focus on Yakov, he'd almost forgotten the rest of the cabinet was still in the room. The President barked out a laugh.

"Enlighten me, Vladimir," he said. "How could this utter shitpile of incompetence be worse?"

"During the night, we lost secure communications with the military command in Kaliningrad. If we had been able to attack the Poles from the rear, we might have been successful in our bid to secure the Suwalki Corridor."

"How could that happen?" Luchnik asked.

Yakov started to answer, but Federov cut him off. "We're still investigating. When Defense Minister Yakov tried to bring Kaliningrad assets to bear, there was no way for the Kaliningrad command to authenticate his orders. General Vasilenko refused to accept the orders."

The feeling of being punched returned. "Is this true, Yakov?"

"Yes, Mr. President." The Defense Minister's voice trembled with emotion.

"Where is General Vasilenko?" Luchnik demanded.

Federov cast a sidelong glance at Yakov. "He's gone into hiding, Mr. President."

"Hiding...?" Luchnik's mind snapped into focus. Someone was working against his plan, against him. This was a plot against *him*. By *his* military.

"Defense Minister Yakov," Luchnik said.

"Sir!" Yakov's posture was ramrod straight, eyes forward.

"You are relieved of your duties," Luchnik said, his tone acid. He turned his attention down the row of faces. "Admiral Sokolov."

Nikolay stood at attention. "Yes, Mr. President."

"Congratulations, Admiral." Luchnik found it hard to keep the pride out of his voice. "You are the new Minister of Defense for the Russian Federation."

Nikolay looked down the long table at his uncle. His eyes were so much like his mother's...

This is sooner than I'd planned, Luchnik thought, but he's ready. Thanks to Federov. It's better this way. If there was a plot against him in the military, Nikolay would put a swift end to it.

There was still hope for his grand dream of a New Russian Empire.

"Your first order of business is to take Viktor Yakov into custody. He will be tried by a military court." Luchnik rose from his chair. His body tingled with anger, like insects crawling across his skin. He needed to move, so he paced.

"Your second order is to find General Vasilenko and kill him. Then kill his wife and his children. If he has a dog, kill the dog. If the child has a fucking hamster for a pet, then kill that, too. I want everyone to know what happens if you disobey a direct order from the President of the Russian Federation."

Luchnik stopped behind Yakov's quivering form. Sweat

slickened the back of the man's neck, and he breathed in short, hard gasps.

"Yes, sir," Nikolay replied. He nodded toward Director Kulukov, who immediately motioned to the Rosgvardiya security man at the door. The Russian national guardsman took Yakov into custody. The rest of the cabinet looked away as their colleague left in disgrace.

Luchnik watched the other men at the table. Were there others against him?

No, he decided. Either by incompetence or by action, Yakov had blown their opportunity to effect a lightning strike into the Suwalki Gap, but he was gone now. It was up to the rest of them to get the plan—*his* plan—back on track.

He caught Nikolay's eye and motioned for him to take Yakov's vacant chair. Eyes followed the young admiral as he moved to the seat next to Federov. Nearer to the seat of power. Closer to his uncle. Luchnik felt a surge of fatherly pride in his young protégé.

No one spoke, no one looked at their president. Luchnik smiled to himself. They were all afraid.

"Now," he said into the silence. "How do we unfuck this situation?"

"Mr. President," Irimov said, his tone grave. "We have made great territorial gains in the Ukraine, but in Lithuania, the element of surprise is lost. NATO will fight back."

Luchnik watched his Foreign Minister with slitted eyes. This man was his oldest adviser, a friend of sorts. He was always the voice of reason, but also first to defend his country to a hostile world. Besides, it took guts to speak up after seeing Yakov led off to certain death.

"Continue, Sergey."

Irimov cleared his throat. "Mr. President, let us take advantage of NATO's confusion and consolidate our gains in the Ukraine."

"Wise counsel, Mr. Foreign Minister. What about the Suwalki Gap?"

"Mr. President." Irimov's voice took on a note of pleading. "The plan was sound, but we failed to execute. To stay in Lithuania is to invite a war with NATO. We've been to that place before, sir, and only narrowly survived."

"So, what is your recommendation, Foreign Minister?"

"I recommend we withdraw, sir."

Luchnik ran his eyes down the table. "What about the rest of you? You want to give up when we are so close to victory?"

They said nothing, but their eyes gave them away.

Cowards, he thought. Small men with small minds who failed to see the brilliance of his plan. The New Russian Empire was within his grasp. Luchnik could feel it.

He caught Nikolay staring at him. The younger man had a different look in his eye than the others. They were afraid, but he was...Luchnik tried to identify the emotion his nephew's eyes conveyed.

Hope? Ambition? Pride? Yes, Luchnik thought. Pride. He was proud of his surrogate father for having the guts and the vision to change the world.

"No," Luchnik said out loud. "We will not withdraw from the Suwalki Gap. I took an oath to protect my country, and only I can do that now. We will not back down. NATO will yield."

"Mr. President," Nikolay said, "I recommend we put the forces on the borders of Latvia and Estonia on high alert."

Luchnik nodded at his nephew, pride forming a lump in his throat. Between the two of them, they would resurrect the Russian Empire.

"Make it so, Defense Minister."

39

Sterling, Virginia

"Truce." Abby raised her crystal tumbler.

"Truce," Dylan echoed. He extended his own glass across the desk, and they touched rims. Their eyes met.

Can I trust you? Abby thought. She sipped her drink, a Bowman single-barrel bourbon, studying Dylan over the rim of her glass.

Do I have another option? she wondered. It was going to take friends in high places to keep her company safe from the most powerful man in the world. If anything, the Russian move in Lithuania had only increased Serrano's desire to expand operations in Ukraine.

Abby rolled the liquid across her palate, enjoying the complex flavors. Toffee, dried fruit, nuts. She felt the tension in her shoulders melting.

"I never pegged you for a bourbon gal," Dylan said.

"Always and forever." Abby took another sip, knowing she was just putting off the hard conversation. Had he lied to her again to keep her quiet during the meeting at the White

House, or did he actually have a plan to get her company out of Ukraine?

Dylan held up his empty glass. "I saw some really fine scotch over there. Do you mind?"

"Help yourself."

She watched him rise from the chair and head to the bar. Seeing him move reminded her why she'd been attracted to him in the first place. It was his confidence, she decided. Even now, while she fretted about their upcoming confrontation, he was able to act as if this was just a drink between friends.

Dylan returned to his chair and crossed his legs. He sipped the scotch and leaned his head back, eyes closed. "Now, *that* is a drink. I didn't know you could buy Benromach 35 in the US."

"You can't," Abby said. "We bought it in Scotland."

"We...?" Dylan frowned. He looked at the glass. "This is your husband's whisky. Oh, I'm so sorry."

Abby waved. "Don't be. I think scotch tastes like it was aged in a leather boot. I only keep it for sentimental reasons."

Her eyes drifted to the framed picture on her desk. Abby, Joe, and Manson crowded into the frame. Wool hats and flannel shirts. Younger, smiling. Happier times.

Where was that picture taken? she thought, then recalled the hunting trip in Montana, when Manson's girlfriend went to stay in a hotel because the three of them spent all day in the woods.

"Tell me about him," Dylan said. "I see you smiling. You must have been happy together."

"We were." Abby sat up in her chair and set her drink aside. "But that's not why we're here, is it? This afternoon, you told me you had a plan to get my company out of Ukraine. You asked me to trust you."

"I did." Dylan placed his drink on the edge of her desktop. "Thank you for that."

"Well?" Abby spread her hands.

"We need to do this in stages," he said. "Put someone you can trust in charge of the operations in Ukraine, and we'll slowly walk back the missions in the region."

"Okay," Abby said. "I hope there's more to your plan than a slow retreat."

"There is." Dylan leaned forward, elbows on knees. "While the Lithuanian situation has everyone's attention, I'm going to push through a change in the rules of engagement for Ukraine. By the time we get Skelly out of the field, the new ROE for Sentinel Holdings will limit operations to west of the Dnieper River."

"You think the Russians are going to stop their advance at the river," Abby said.

Dylan nodded. "The Russians have been messing around in eastern Ukraine for fifteen years. I think this big push was all a deception to draw in Poland and NATO. The real prize was always the Suwalki Gap."

"You can get the ROE changed?"

"The Director will support me," Dylan said. "The intel shows a change in the status quo. Unless NATO is willing to cross the Dnieper River and remove them, eastern Ukraine is now part of Russia. Nobody has that kind of appetite."

Abby picked up her glass again. That could work. In fact, it was the perfect insider move. Sentinel Holdings was contracted by the CIA. If the CIA gave them a different mission, there was nothing to do but follow orders.

"I like it," she said.

Dylan picked up his own glass. "I thought you might." He met her gaze across the desk. "How about I buy you dinner? Let's start over, Aberdeen Cromwell."

Not a good idea, Abby, she thought.

Her phone pinged with an incoming alert from Mama.

Abby frowned at the screen, then sat up and pulled her laptop from her purse.

"Problem?" Dylan asked.

"Not sure," Abby replied. "I had Josh set up an alert so I'd be notified every time Manson ran operational scenarios through Mama. I just got a ping." She glanced at her watch. "It's two a.m. in Ukraine."

Abby pinched her lip as she scanned the operational details. She stopped as soon as she saw the weaponry selected. "We have a problem."

Dylan put down his drink and came around to her side of the desk. When he leaned over her shoulder to see the small laptop screen, she felt his breath paint her cheek.

"What's a K-10?" Dylan asked.

"It's a prototype weapon. Not field tested, and what he's targeting goes against everything we just talked about."

"We have to stop him," Dylan said.

Abby logged in to the Sentinel secure VTC program and dialed the Ukraine operations center. Peter, the same tech they had met on their last trip, answered.

"Ops," he answered automatically, his attention directed away from the screen. He turned his head and saw Abby. "Uh, hello, Abby. Did you know that you dialed in on the main line?"

"Yes, Peter," Abby replied, not even trying to hide the sarcasm in her tone. "I wanted to make sure my call was answered promptly. Let me speak to Manson. Now."

Peter looked off screen, nodded. "Um, sure."

The screen changed stations, but instead of Manson Skelly, it showed the face of David Landersmann. He had a broad smile plastered across his face. "Abby, hi. I understand you're looking for the boss. He's not here—"

"Cut the shit, Landersmann," Abby snapped. "I know he's

there because he just logged in to Mama's ops planning program. The only secure line in the whole country with enough bandwidth is in that building."

"Abby—"

"If I'm not speaking to Manson in the next three seconds, I will stop your paycheck. You may think Manson can prevent me from firing you, but unless you like working for free, you'd better start pushing buttons."

Landersmann's lip curled in disgust, but he tapped the keyboard.

Manson Skelly had gone full mountain man. His dark hair was long and swept back from his forehead. She saw his full beard was shot with silver.

We're all getting older, she thought, but not necessarily wiser.

"Abby," Manson said, "I was just about to call you."

"Really."

"Absolutely. No secrets, remember?"

"Enough, Manson." She could feel her blood pressure rising, and she fought for control. Why did she let this idiot push her buttons like this? "I've seen the mission you were running through Mama, and there's no way that's happening."

"Abby," Skelly said in mock surprise, "are you spying on me?"

"Manson, I saw what you were planning. It's outside the scope of the ROE. It's illegal."

Skelly cocked his head, then put his hand on his chin like he was thinking. "Is it?"

"K-10 is not field tested," Abby said. "We have no idea how the units will operate in combat conditions."

"No better way to find out." Skelly sounded like he was enjoying this back-and-forth.

"This operation is not authorized," Abby said. "It violates the rules of engagement."

"The operation has already gotten the green light, Abby. I had the authorization in hand before I ran it through Mama."

Abby cut a look at Dylan. He looked just as puzzled.

"Authorization from who?" she demanded.

"Above both of our paygrades, Abby. I have a verbal order to throw out the ROE. I'm supposed to take the hurt factor up to eleven as fast as possible." He grinned smugly. "Somebody wants to make an impact, and they've decided that I'm the man for the job."

"As CEO of Sentinel, I am telling you right now: this mission is not authorized. Do I make myself clear?"

"I hear your words, I understand your words, and I don't give a shit, Abby. I'm literally a man on a mission."

Abby wanted to put her fist through the laptop screen, but instead she gripped the edge of the desk, her knuckles white from the strain.

"I mean it, Manson," she said. "Don't do this."

"I's just following orders," Manson said, his voice dripping with sarcasm.

Abby felt Dylan's body close behind her as he leaned toward the screen.

"Ah, CIA man," Manson said. "I thought you might be lurking in the shadows. I suppose you want to speak your piece, too?"

"As the authorized representative of the US government, I am ordering you to stand down, Mr. Skelly," Dylan said.

Skelly shook his head. "No can do, G-man. You have been superseded, my friend."

"That's not possible," Dylan said.

Skelly adopted his thinking pose again, hand on chin. "Well, let me review my chain of command. You work for the

CIA, and the CIA works for the White House, so if the big man in the White House calls me with new orders...I think you done got outranked, boy."

"The President called you?" Abby said. Would Serrano do that? she wondered. He just might.

Skelly shrugged. "Close enough."

"Manson," Abby said. "You are ordered to stand down and discontinue all operations. I'll be in Ukraine in the morning, and I'm taking command of the operation. Is that clear?"

Skelly's smug façade dropped. He glared at the camera, his lips peeled back from his teeth in a snarl.

"You have your orders, Abby," he said. "I have mine."

Skelly ended the call.

Abby snatched up her phone and called Josh. He answered on the first ring.

"I need the plane ready to go in an hour." Abby realized she was talking way too fast, and her heart was racing. She took a deep breath. "I'm going to Ukraine."

Dylan's hand touched her shoulder. Warm, heavy, reassuring.

"Mr. Mattias is going with me," she added without looking up.

"I'll see to it, Abby," Josh replied. "Anything else?"

"Is there any way to lock Manson out of access to Mama?" Abby asked the question though she was pretty sure she knew the answer.

"Not quickly, no," Josh said. "His access is hardcoded, just like yours."

Abby cursed. They'd made that decision together, she and Joe and Manson. Equal partners, no one ever gets locked out.

Except by death, she thought. Joe's access was revoked upon his death, leaving her and Manson as the sole superusers on the system. Even today, only she and Manson could grant direct access to Mama.

"Keep monitoring Manson's activity on Mama," she ordered. "I don't trust him."

"Of course." Josh hesitated. "There's one more thing. Are you alone?"

Abby did not look up at Dylan. "Go ahead."

"Don Riley called. He wants to access Mama tonight. He said you authorized his visit."

Dylan's hand still touched her shoulder. It felt good. She could sense her anger draining away. Abby looked up and smiled at him.

Can I trust you? she wondered.

"That's fine, Josh," she said into the phone. "We're leaving for the airport now."

40

Oleksandriya, Ukraine

"You have your orders, Abby," Skelly said. "I have mine."

On the video screen, Abby opened her mouth, but Skelly ended the call before she could respond.

He laughed in the empty room. Man, that felt good, he thought. I am so tired of listening to that woman yap.

There was a time when they'd been colleagues, even friends. But that was because of Joe. He brought people together. Without that emotional glue, their diversion of interests was inevitable. They'd made it work for a long time, much longer than Skelly expected, but the last year of unrelenting, explosive growth just brought them into conflict more and more.

The break was inevitable. It was time to part ways.

Time, thought Skelly. Time was not on his side if he wanted to complete this operation before Queen B arrived in the Ukraine to seize his throne.

He raised his voice. "Landie!"

The office door opened so fast that Skelly wondered if Landersmann had been listening to his call. "You rang, boss?"

"The mission we were planning?"

"Yeah?"

"It's on."

"Okay." Landersmann came into the room and shut the door. "When do you want to go?"

"Tonight."

"Manse," Landersmann said. "Tonight is too soon. We need time to prep the K-10s, and we don't even have an insertion plan yet."

"It needs to happen tonight, Landie. End of story. You have questions, I have answers. Let's make whatever decisions we need right now."

Landersmann extracted a tablet from the pocket of his cargo pants. "Okay, fine. How many K-10s do you want for the op?"

"How many are in the depot?"

Landersmann tapped the tablet. "Eighteen. Fourteen are fitted with fifties, the rest have Gustafs."

Skelly tugged at his beard. The choices were a Barrett M82 .50-caliber sniper rifle and a Carl Gustav M3 reloadable weapon that fired a variety of 84mm ammunitions ranging from anti-tank to anti-personnel round.

"I'll make this easy for you," Landersmann said. "It takes minimum two hours to reconfigure a K-10."

"Fine," Skelly said. "Go with what we've got on hand."

"Roger that. How many K-10s do you want for the mission?"

"All of them," Skelly said.

"All? Boss, are you sure that's a good idea? This is every K-10 we have in the entire company. If there's a problem, we'll be shit out of luck."

"The point of this mission is to make some noise, Landie. Use all of them."

Landersmann lowered his tablet. "Are you sure about this, Manse?"

Skelly leaned across his desk. "If you ask me that question one more time, you won't have to wait for Abby to show up to fire your ass. Copy that?"

"Got it." Landersmann picked up his tablet. "How do you want to deploy the K-10s?"

Skelly considered the question. The safest deployment method would be to drive the weapons systems to within ten kilometers of the target and set them loose, but the depot was a two-hour drive to the west, safely out of the conflict zone. Two hours there, load time, plus two hours back, then another two to four hours to get the K-10s to the drop-off point, assuming no issues.

Too much time, he thought.

"How about a HALO drop from a C-130?" Landersmann asked. "Once they wake up, you can rally them."

The K-10s were capable of traveling at up to thirty-five kilometers per hour for their five-hour battery life, but there was no way to control where they landed with any certainty.

Skelly shook his head. "They could land anywhere. Somebody's living room, for God's sake. The middle of a highway. We'll see them on some internet video."

"We can't do a low-altitude drop from a C-130 over a conflict zone," Landersmann said. "We'll get shot out of the sky."

"What about the gliders?" Skelly asked. "How many K-10s could we fit in one of those?"

The Silent Arrow cargo delivery drone was an autonomous glider designed to provide aerial resupply into situations where manned aircraft were unable to fly. Deployed from the cargo bay of a C-130 flying at twenty-five thousand feet, the glider was equipped with an autopilot system, GPS navigation, and LIDAR for remote landing capability.

"We've never used them before," Landersmann said.

"How many K-10s can we fit in an Arrow?" Skelly repeated.

Landersmann consulted his tablet. "According to the specs, we could handle six K-10s in each Arrow, and we could fit three Arrows inside a C-130." He sighed. "Are you sure you want to put all of our K-10s inside a couple of flying shoeboxes?"

"It's perfect," Skelly replied. "We drop the Arrows on this side of the Dnieper River, and they glide across to the landing zone. Even if somebody picks them up on radar, they'll have the signature of a civilian plane, not a military jet."

"Boss, I'm just gonna say it one last time," Landersmann said with a pleading quality in his voice. "This is a terrible idea. The target, the timing, the whole thing is gonna blow up in our faces."

"You let me worry about that," Skelly replied.

"But what about—"

Skelly stopped him with a look that could cut glass. Landersmann got the message. He came to sloppy attention and gave a mock salute.

"Yessir, yessir, three bags full," he said.

"Fuck you, Landie."

"Fuck you back, boss." Landersmann executed an about-face and goose-stepped to the door.

"I want those bastards in the air in three hours," Skelly called after him. "I'll upload the mission parameters now."

As the door closed behind his second-in-command, Skelly considered the topographical map on his laptop screen.

The fact that he was even allowed to consider a mission like this blew his mind. But according to the man on the phone, the White House wanted to shake the Etch A Sketch on the Siege of Kyiv. That's what the news whores were calling the Russians' last push to dominate the whole of eastern Ukraine.

The capital city of Kyiv straddled the Dnieper River, which snaked its way from the Belarusian border to Crimea, an area of Ukraine that had been pieced off by the Russian Federation in 2014.

Crimea was an appetizer, Skelly thought. Now Luchnik was back for the main course.

The Russian front had advanced to the Dnieper River in several places, but in Kyiv, the Ukrainians were putting up a serious resistance. Everyone involved in the conflict knew that capturing—or losing—the capital city of Kyiv was a key element in their road to victory.

Kyiv was only about thirty miles south of the Belarus border. The Ukrainian military had long seen the strategic value of the capital as a military target, and they had set up a defensive arc that began at the Belarusian border and extended eastward. Since Kyiv was situated on the Dnieper River, the Ukrainians wisely used geography to their advantage, forming an eastward-facing defensive line anchored in the south at the city of Pereiaslav on the Dnieper and curving all the way to the north.

Inside this Ukrainian defensive arc was a warren of prepared positions, armor, artillery, air defenses, and at least fifty thousand regular Ukrainian Army and civilian militia. Although NATO was not officially in the fight, the allied countries provided all manner of armaments, logistics, and intelligence support to Ukraine. A number of nongovernmental organizations were also on the ground providing humanitarian aid to those fleeing the renewed fighting. In fact, the city of Pereiaslav was home to a large contingent of British medical personnel working for Doctors Without Borders. They'd told the international press they'd remain in Kyiv even if the city fell.

The British made a big deal about their location, calling their position the "anchor" for the evacuation of eastern Ukraine and the humanitarian center supporting Kyiv.

But Skelly was more interested in the Russian military positioning. He zoomed into the area around the city of Lubny. Located seventy-five kilometers due east of Pereiaslav, the countryside to the north of Lubny was home to the Russian command post for the whole Ukraine operation.

Skelly switched to video surveillance of the area.

According to Mama's assessment of the intel, this Russian CP was home to two division commanders overseeing the attack on Kyiv. The main building was an inflatable tent the size of a department store and surrounded by a host of smaller tents and vehicles. Two kilometers to the west was a fuel depot and an ammunitions dump. On the live feed, Skelly could see hundreds of Russian soldiers hurrying around the camp.

A target-rich environment, to be sure, but not something Skelly would have considered attacking even in his wildest dreams. That is, until he got the phone call.

The man on the other end of the secure line had identified himself and got right to the point.

"Mr. Skelly, I'm calling you with a change in mission," he said.

Skelly had recognized the voice. "Yes, sir. If this is a contract issue, I suggest you take it up with my CEO."

"I'll deal with Ms. Cromwell in my own time. For now, I need a major distraction against those Russian bastards, and I think you're the man to deliver it."

"I'm listening," Skelly said.

"Find a target—I don't care what it is—and get the attention of the Russian military. Make their lives a living hell."

Skelly started to ask a question, but the man cut him off.

"I'm not interested in details, Mr. Skelly," he said. "We each fight battles in our own way. I have politics, you have bullets. Throw out the rules of engagement. Just get the job done, by whatever means necessary and as quickly as possible."

"Yes, sir," Skelly said, still wondering if this guy really knew what he was asking for.

"Whatever you do, make it big enough for them to drag Luchnik's ass out of bed. I want him to realize that the gloves are off. Am I making myself clear?"

"Whatever means necessary?" Skelly asked.

"Whatever means necessary."

Then the line went dead.

Skelly cycled back and forth between the video imagery and the topographical map until he settled on a primary and secondary landing zone for the K-10 insertion about five kilometers west of the Russian CP. A few more minutes of searching was all that was necessary to select an extraction point ten kilometers south of the target.

Skelly grinned as he punched a button to upload the mission details to the ops center computer.

Whatever means necessary, Skelly thought. *Be careful what you wish for.*

Despite his misgivings, Landersmann managed to get the mission prepped and the C-130 in the air by four a.m. Skelly joined him in the ops center to watch the Silent Arrow glider deployment using the overwatch drone.

"I'm calling this Operation Russian Nesting Doll," Landersmann announced to a round of appreciative chuckles.

"Just get the K-10s on the ground in one piece, funny guy," Skelly growled.

"Approaching the drop point," one of techs announced. "Big Bird is at twenty-five thousand feet and ready to execute."

Skelly checked the map. The C-130, designated Big Bird, was thirty kilometers west of Pereiaslav, headed due east. He shifted his gaze to the video feed in time to see the C-130's rear ramp lower to the open position. He nodded at Landersmann.

"To Big Bird," Landersmann said. "Drop the first doll."

The order went out. A few seconds later, a dark box shape popped out of the cargo plane.

"Package is launched," a tech announced. "Stand by for deployment."

The Silent Arrow cargo drone had folded wings that were supposed to deploy as soon as the unit was free of the mother ship.

Nothing happened. The box fell through the sky.

"Twenty thousand feet. No deployment."

Skelly cursed.

"Do an override!" Landersmann said. "Deploy the goddamned wings."

"There is no override, sir," the tech replied. "It's all automatic. Fifteen thousand feet and falling."

"Fuck," Landersmann said and repeated the oath several more times before turning to Skelly. "I recommend we abort."

Skelly looked at his watch and shook his head. "Tell the pilot to turn around and line up for another run. Have the air crew double-check the setup."

"Manson," Landersmann said under his breath. "We just turned thirty million dollars' worth of autonomous weaponry into a fucking meteor. Are you sure you want to try again?"

Skelly's look was enough for Landersmann to turn back to the waiting ops team. "Set up the bowling pins, people. We're going again."

Ten more minutes slipped away as the C-130 ran a race-track turn and verified the glider setup.

Landersmann approached Skelly. "Look, I don't want to be that guy, but this is crazy, Manson."

Skelly put a meaty hand on his friend's shoulder. "Do you trust me, Landie?"

"Sure."

"Then trust me when I say that if you don't get the remaining twelve K-10s on the ground safe and sound, I will fire your ass. Capeesh?"

"We're ready, sir," the lead tech announced.

Landersmann sighed and turned around. "Russian Nesting Dolls, take two. Tell Big Bird they are clear for deployment."

For all his bravado with Landersmann, Skelly was rattled. He looked at the clock in the corner of the computer screen. Abby would be on the ground by noon. If he had executed the mission successfully, he'd have the White House on his side. If not, she'd fire him—or worse.

"Package is launched," came the announcement. "Stand by for deployment."

Skelly watched the box fall from the back of the C-130. It dropped toward the ground.

C'mon, he thought, you piece of shit. *Open.*

Two wings sprouted from either side of the falling box. The glider hung in midair.

"It worked!" Landersmann crowed. "It fucking worked. Drop the next one. Now!"

"Package three is launched," the tech said. "Deployment is successful."

The two gliders—they really did look like shoeboxes, Skelly thought—drifted eastward. In the predawn hours,

Skelly could see lights poking through the mist that cloaked the landscape. He caught a gleam of water, the Dnieper River.

"Both gliders are on base course to primary LZ," the tech called out. "Running steady at twelve thousand feet."

Another thirty-eight minutes passed before the gliders made a final approach to a field about five kilometers west of the Russian CP.

"Shifting to LIDAR mode for landing," the tech announced.

The light detection and ranging radar scanned the ground ahead using laser to form a 3D representation of the upcoming terrain.

"Landing trajectory selected."

Skelly held his breath as the first glider touched down. It bounced once, then rolled to a stop. The second glider halted ten meters away.

"Yes!" Landersmann pumped his fist in the air and did an awkward dance. "I knew we could do it!"

Skelly let the celebrations go on for exactly fifteen seconds, then he let out a shrill whistle.

"Wake up the pack," he ordered.

41

5 kilometers west of Lubny

When K-10 unit 789 came to life in the back of a Silent Arrow cargo delivery drone, its first action was to run a self-diagnostic.

Structural integrity, optical, laser-ranging, and audio sensors all passed system checks. Battery level at 100 percent. The .50-caliber Barrett sniper rifle, semi-automatic with suppressor attachment, had a full ammunition loadout. The ten-kilogram self-destruct charge in the belly of the beast was intact and unarmed.

With onboard checks complete, the K-10 unit queried for a GPS location. It received an immediate ping from the Sentinel Condor overwatch drone flying at seventy-five thousand feet over eastern Europe. In addition to the positional fix, the Condor downloaded a mission update, priority override.

Mission complement reduced to twelve K-10 units. Unit 789 designated as mission Alpha, the pack leader.

It took another 0.76 seconds for the unit's gyroscope to

accept the new GPS fix and correlate its physical location to the onboard topographical map program.

Twelve seconds after the Silent Arrow cargo drone landed in a Ukrainian field, K-10 unit 789, now known as Alpha, rose from its stowed position on four limbs. It released the claws which had kept it locked in place on the cargo drone's floor.

Alpha initiated the secure battle circuit and queried its pack. Eleven responses, laden with system updates, flooded back. One K-10 unit had not received the new mission, so Alpha conducted a field override. The eleven members of the pack appeared on the internal map program as blue vectors. Alpha ordered the pack to assemble at a GPS location, which the video overlay showed to be a wooded area.

The silence of the predawn darkness filled with the whirr of gears, the scritch of claws on steel, and the rhythmic thud of steel feet on damp earth. The pack used laser ranging to move among the trees. A grazing deer, shown on the IR sensors as a white outline, startled at the sight of twelve mechanical creatures advancing toward him. The image was captured, profiled, and rejected as a non-hostile. The deer bounded away, unharmed.

With the pack assembled at the rally point, Alpha transmitted an update to the Condor. Three seconds passed in the still forest before Alpha received a reply.

Relocate to target. Avoid detection. Aggression level: defensive force only.

No sooner had the reply landed in Alpha's communications buffer than the orders were distributed to its team. The still of the summer morning crackled with the sound of weapons being extended from armored bodies and lethal rounds being racked into firing chambers. The pack consisted of ten Barretts and two Gustaf recoilless rifles.

Following the mission profile, Alpha organized the pack

into two six-unit squads with one Carl Gustaf in each squad. Alpha led the first squad, and it designated a Bravo to lead the second.

The squads set off in different directions at a pace of fifteen kilometers per hour, using preplanned, terrain-following routes to provide them maximum screening and protection from Russian surveillance systems. Alpha and Bravo took point on each squad, with the rest of their members ranging behind them at twenty-meter intervals.

The squad leaders modified the route as needed based on local conditions. A fallen tree posed no issue for Alpha. It leaped over the meter-high obstacle with ease.

Alpha paused when the squad came to a paved road. Audio sensors detected the approach of a motor vehicle, and Alpha immediately ordered the pack into a down position. From the edge of the road, optical sensors tracked the incoming truck headlights. The onboard database classified the vehicle as a Ural-5323, heavy-duty, high-mobility, military cargo vehicle, capable of a twelve-thousand-kilogram payload. IR sensors showed only two potentially hostile thermal signatures, both in the cab of the oncoming truck. Alpha aligned the sights of the Barrett sniper rifle on the driver and tracked the target.

The roar of the diesel engine filled Alpha's audio sensors, but there was no indication that their position had been compromised. A trail of diesel exhaust hung over the road as Alpha ordered the squad to resume travel across the road.

The squad arrived at the target site twenty-six minutes before sunrise. Alpha ordered the pack to down positions and crept forward at half height for visual reconnaissance. On the other side of the target, Bravo was performing the same maneuver.

The Russian command post was stirring in the dim light.

The thermal signatures of twenty-eight potentially hostile targets registered on Alpha's IR sensor. The K-10 unit correlated the visual features on the optical sensor to the video information provided by the Condor drone, identifying ingress-egress points and ranking targets by priority. From the other side of the camp, Bravo performed the same function. Their combined data inputs knitted together an assessment of Russian troop positions, building configurations, lines of approach, fields of fire, and concentration areas for both the Barretts and the Carl Gustafs. The two K-10s iterated until the final mission details locked into place.

Alpha transmitted the mission plan to the Condor and released attack parameters to the pack. These parameters were merely guidelines for the individual K-10 units. Once the battle began, the pack employed cooperative threat engagement algorithms to execute an attack in a rapidly changing environment.

Alpha detected the sound of a snapping branch. A new thermal signature, potentially hostile, emerged from behind a tree. Alpha laser-ranged the target at fifty-three meters. From a down position, it estimated to a greater than 99 percent probability that the camouflage armor hide would be invisible to the Russian guard. The target reticle centered the man as he zipped up his fly. The muzzle of the Barrett sniper rifle locked on the target.

Alpha queried the Condor for mission release authority. Three seconds—an eternity for Alpha's digital brain—passed before it received the next message.

Execute mission. Aggression level: extreme prejudice.

Alpha's first shot took down the Russian guard. The .50-caliber bullet penetrated the guard's body armor in the exact center of his back. His body was thrown forward three meters by the force of the blast.

Had he lived for three more seconds, he might have seen Alpha pass by him in the early morning light. A log-shaped creature with a camouflaged hide, balanced on four mechanical legs, moving as fast as a car over uneven terrain. A weapon protruded from the back of the beast. He might have seen the weapon spit fire and heard the suppressed rimshot of a heavy-caliber bullet dispatching the guard posted another fifty meters downrange.

But the Russian soldier didn't see, hear, or think any of those things. He was dead before he hit the ground.

Alpha advanced at maximum speed toward the target. The designation of extreme prejudice simplified the decision-making process for the attacking pack. All targets with a thermal signature of human within a one-kilometer radius were targeted for termination.

Alpha emerged from the tree line at maximum speed of thirty-five kilometers per hour, dispatching three hostiles on its path to the command tent. Sensors detected a massive explosion to the east, which it identified as one of the Bravo fire teams taking out the fuel depot using an 84mm rocket-assisted projectile fired from the mounted Carl Gustaf, as per the mission plan.

Even though it was only sixty-eight seconds since the commencement of the attack, Alpha and the pack began to receive incoming enemy fire. The heavy-caliber rounds sprayed the pack member on Alpha's right flank, disabling the unit's sensor package and cutting down two of the unit's limbs.

Alpha skidded in the mud as it conducted evasive maneuvers against the incoming fire. The heavy-caliber rounds tore through the soft ground in its path, throwing up fountains of dirty water. Taking cover behind a heavy truck, it ordered a packmate to flank the enemy position and destroy it.

Updates flowed over the battle circuit in an unending

stream. Two more packmates were down. Alpha ordered the three disabled units to initiate a simultaneous self-destruct sequence with a fifteen-minute delay.

Rather than utilize the entrance points for the command tent, Alpha and two members of its squad ran at the side of the inflatable tent at maximum speed. They tore through the canvas material, bursting into a high-ceilinged room packed with computer equipment. Thirteen hostiles were dispatched in the space of three seconds. Alpha charged forward. Its priority task was to find and destroy the communications center.

Alpha barreled into a computer workstation, its legs automatically righting its frame as it took a corner at high speed. The wall of a glass conference room lay dead ahead, and it plowed into it. Showers of glass rained down like ice. Its sensors detected a thermal signature under a desk, and it dropped to a down position to dispatch the threat.

Using audio sensors, it screened out the blasts from the heavy-caliber weapons fire, searching for sounds between 100 and 200 hertz.

It detected a signal, a human male voice, speaking in Russian.

"I say again," the voice said, "this command post is under attack—"

Alpha locked onto the signal and sprang back to all fours. It careened through the opposite glass wall toward the sound. The door to the secure radio room was reinforced steel, but Alpha did not slow down. Two rounds from its Barrett destroyed the lock, and what was left of the door gave way to its 110-kilogram mass.

The secure space measured four meters by six meters, but at least 60 percent of the space was taken up by banks of cryptographic machines and computer racks. Its entrance was met with gunfire. Bullets pummeled its armor hide, one of which hit the barrel of its Barrett, disabling the targeting feature. Alpha dropped to the down position to recalibrate its sights.

While the recalibration progressed, sensors registered eighteen rounds had impacted its body. The onboard database classified the enemy weapon as an MP-443 Grach, a 9mm Russian standard military-issue sidearm.

Alpha's audio sensors registered two voices, both Russian.

"What's it doing?" one said, a higher-pitched voice, probable female.

"I don't know." Male, the same voice Alpha had heard making the distress call. "Let's see if we can go around it."

Recalibration complete.

Alpha rose to full height, targeted the hostiles, and fired two shots.

The mission clock, which had started as soon as the execution order had been issued, read 13:12. Its portion of the mission complete, Alpha queried the pack for status.

Kill reports flowed in. Two more packmates were damaged. It issued self-destruct orders to the disabled units and synchronized the detonation window for all disabled units. Through the walls of the command tent, Alpha detected multiple secondary explosions from the ammunitions dump.

It issued the order for the pack to withdraw to the exfil point, where they would shut down to conserve battery power before extraction.

Awkwardly, Alpha backed out of the narrow radio room door. Its metal claws left bloody tracks on the linoleum floor.

42

Sterling, Virginia

"What we have here, Don," Treasury Agent Reggie Bowerman said, "is the keys to the kingdom."

Don Riley, Harrison Kohl, FBI Special Agent Liz Soroush, and Bowerman were gathered at the interactive data screen in the AI lab at the Sentinel headquarters. The clock on the wall above the door read four a.m., and Don had promised Abby they'd be out before five.

His hope was that Mama would be able to make sense of the information contained on the mysterious thumb drive he'd recovered from the South Dakota UPS Store. On Liz's advice, he'd brought Bowerman into the project.

"He's an expert on terrorist financing and financial crimes, Don," Liz had said. "He's spent the last five years tracking the dirty money of Russian oligarchs. You need him on the team."

Bowerman was a tall, rangy figure with graying hair and a trace of a Canadian accent. They'd been at it since midnight, but unlike everyone else in the room, the Treasury agent appeared fresh and enthusiastic, as if he drew energy from his work.

"Which kingdom are we talking about?" Don replied.

"Mama, put up the rogues' gallery, please," Bowerman said. He gestured dramatically as a row of twelve faces appeared on the interactive screen. Beneath each mug shot was a series of bracketed data tags.

"We've been able to catalog about sixty percent of the information on the thumb drive," Bowerman continued. "What you have here is the Panama Papers, the Russia edition."

Don and Harrison both moved closer to the screen.

"That's Prime Minister Mishinov," Harrison said.

Bowerman nodded. The grin on his face told Don how much he was enjoying his time in the spotlight. "That's correct. In addition to six numbered bank accounts in the Caymans, Bermuda, Switzerland, and other exotic locales, Mr. Mishinov owns a number of properties in Monte Carlo, New York, and Miami Beach. Based on what we've uncovered so far, he's worth about 1.6 billion dollars."

Don listened as Bowerman talked through the illicit holdings of several other members of Luchnik's inner circle with Harrison.

How is this possible? Don wondered. *Who could possibly have access to this level of information? And why would they just give it to him?* As good as this looked, years of analytical experience told Don to tread carefully. In the world of intelligence, there was no free lunch. It was just too easy.

"I hate to look a gift horse in the mouth," Don said, interrupting Bowerman, "but how much do we know about the provenance of this information?"

"Not as much as I'd like," Liz replied. "Mama, put up the South Dakota file, please."

The headshot of a young man appeared in the center of the screen, a passport photo of a man in his late twenties with short brown hair.

"This is Tomas Horst," Liz said. "Twenty-seven years old, married, lived in Vienna, and worked as a legal apprentice at the firm of Badertscher, Holenstein, Vischer, and Partners. According to his wife, he traveled to Rapid City, South Dakota, last month. She says it was a business trip, but the law firm where he worked said that Tomas was in the United States for personal reasons."

"Who bought his ticket?" Don asked.

"Horst bought the ticket using his personal credit card," Liz replied, "but I have a friend at Interpol looking at his finances on the downlow. His wife said he got a major bonus at work, but the law firm says no. There's something there, but it's going to take some time to figure it out."

Don grunted his understanding.

"Horst arrived in Rapid City on a Sunday evening," Liz continued, "rented a car, and stayed at the Rushmore Hotel and Suites. On Monday morning, he rented a mailbox at The UPS Store, then traveled to the law office of Samuel T. Jefferson, Esq., where he set up a holding company"—she nodded at the screen—"Pandora Corporation. He concluded his business by late morning and was booked on a three p.m. flight back to Vienna. A few hours later, Horst was killed in a single-car accident on Route 90 about twenty miles east of Rapid City. His Hyundai Elantra was totaled after he rolled it off the highway. The police estimate he was doing at least ninety miles per hour."

"You think he was making a run for it?" Don asked.

Liz shrugged. "There were no witnesses to the accident. Horst was not wearing a seat belt, and his neck was broken. His wife believes that he was going to photograph a buffalo—

at least that's what he told her the night before. We never found his phone, by the way."

Bowerman picked up the narrative. "The Pandora Corporation has one asset: it is the sole owner of the Paris Corporation. Paris is another shell company, based in Dubai, which was set up by Horst six weeks before he traveled to South Dakota."

"Why South Dakota?" Harrison asked.

"That's the billion dollar question, Harrison," said Liz. "South Dakota has some of the strictest privacy laws and most lax oversight in the country. This attracts all kinds of customers who want to keep their identity hidden and their assets secret. If we hadn't been tipped off about the existence of the Pandora Corporation, there's no way we would have found it. Even if we did know about it, without the thumb drive, it would take us months of legal wrangling to get access to this level of information."

"But why?" Don said. "Why me?"

"Don," Bowerman countered, "I don't think you appreciate what you have here. The Paris Corporation has subsidiary status at shell companies all over the world." He pointed at the wall screen. "This list was carefully groomed. Each shell company leads to the hard assets of Luchnik's inner circle. Bank accounts, real estate, yachts, art—billions of dollars directly linked to an individual. I've run a team of analysts for five years, and we don't have a tenth of this information. Like I said, this is the key to the kingdom, my friend. The question is: What do you want to do with it?"

"No," Don replied, "the question is who gave it to me? If I can't trust the source, I can't use the information."

"Here's a place to start." Liz put up a headshot of a dour-looking, jowly man with thinning hair and glasses. "Herman Mueller, sixty-three years old, German citizen, works at the same legal firm as Horst. He is listed on the company website as an account consultant in the Vienna office."

"We know Herr Mueller very well," Bowerman added. "He is suspected to be the brains behind a money-laundering operation in Zurich known as the Basement. His biggest client is the Russian oligarchy."

"You think Mueller is the one who's feeding us this information?" Don said.

"No," Liz replied. "No one is feeding *us* information, Don. They're giving it to *you*, specifically."

"Who?" Don said.

"I don't know who, but I can appreciate their methods. They began this months ago, and they've compartmentalized the information all along the way. They slipped a key into your pocket on the Metro, right? Why not just slip the thumb drive into your pocket?"

Don rubbed his face. He was bone-tired, and his brain was not up to the task of following Liz's logic. "I don't know."

"They wanted a way to pre-position the information inside the US where you could access it, but only if and only when they wanted you to do so."

"And," Bowerman added, "by forming the holding company in the United States, they made sure that you could legally access all of this information. Because of the way the laws work in South Dakota, you would never even know about the Pandora Corporation unless they told you."

"*Pandora* is something that only you would recognize, Don," Liz said. "A name that you would take seriously from the start. This entire scheme is designed around you."

"I assumed the name referred to the Pandora Papers," Bowerman said, referring to the 2021 leak of millions of sensitive documents revealing the secret offshore accounts of hundreds of world leaders and public officials.

"That's one possibility," Liz said, with a meaningful look at Don.

"It makes no sense," Don said.

"Sure, it does," Harrison replied. "There's only one logical conclusion. You have an informant inside Luchnik's inner circle. This is a coup."

"Don't you start with me," Don snapped. "The last time we said there was a coup against Luchnik, we almost started World War Three. This has to be a setup."

"Maybe you're asking the wrong question, Don," Harrison said.

"I'm too tired to play games, Harrison. Just tell me what you're thinking."

"Maybe the question we should be asking is: Why now?" he said. "As Liz already said, whoever is behind this set it up months ago, but they waited until now to give you the goods. What's happening now?"

"Lithuania," Don said. "Whoever is behind this is telling us that Luchnik crossed the line."

"Like I said," Harrison replied. "A coup."

Don stared at the line of twelve Russian oligarchs on the screen. He ran through the names in his mind: Irimov, Yakov, Mishinov, Sokolov, Federov... The who's who of Luchnik's inner circle, men who had been loyal to the Russian leader for decades. These men were like family to Luchnik, bound to him by blood and money. They owed him everything.

Was it possible one of them was willing to betray their leader? he thought. What was in it for them?

Don looked at Liz and Bowerman. "I have an idea."

43

Minsk, Belarus

In the dim light of the hotel room, the woman's white skin had a luminescent quality. The ends of her long dark hair brushed against Pavel's face, snagged in his beard. He tried to catch the flesh of a heavy breast in his teeth and snapped at air.

She laughed, a throaty chuckle in the dark, and arched her back. Pleasure racked his body as he matched her thrust for thrust. He tried to brush the hair away from her face, but she eluded his grasping fingers.

Bam-bam-bam.

Christ, someone was at the door.

Go away, he thought, thrusting harder. I'm almost there.

The sound of her panting filled the room around Pavel. Her thighs tightened around him—

Bam-bam-bam.

"Go away!" Pavel roared.

His eyes snapped open.

A dark room, alone. Through a gap in the drapes, he made

out a desk, a sofa, the bed he was lying in, and the pup tent his erection made in the bedsheets.

Bam-bam-bam.

"I'm coming," Pavel shouted. He rolled out of bed and pulled on his trousers sans underwear. He was halfway to the door before he realized his own joke.

I'm coming, he chuckled to himself. That's a good one.

Through the peephole, he saw Alexei standing in the hallway. The man wore only trousers, and his face was heavy with sleep. Pavel jerked open the door.

"What?" he said. The air of the hallway was cool against the sweat on Pavel's chest.

"Answer your fucking phone," Alexei snarled and stalked away. "The Chef's trying to call you."

"Meet downstairs in fifteen," Pavel called after him. "Tell the others."

Without turning around, Alexei raised his arm and extended a middle finger. "Tell them yourself."

Pavel slammed the door shut and turned back into his room. The interior of the Minsk Hotel had been updated for the modern era, but the bones of the original Soviet architecture were still there.

He sniffed the stifling atmosphere, heavy with the meaty smells from the steak and fries he'd eaten last night before falling into bed. Pavel crossed to the window and threw open the drapes. He blinked into the midmorning sunshine.

What day was it? He'd lost track of time, each day running into the next. Pavel and his crew were supposed to be back in Ukraine by now. On paper, the trip had seemed simple. A quick flight from Kaliningrad back to Ukraine. First, weather shut down the airport, then NATO shut down the airport.

Plan B, drive back to Ukraine via Belarus, had turned into a clusterfuck of epic proportions. The drive should have taken them an hour, two at the most. Instead, it took them eighteen hours to make their way from Kaliningrad to Minsk. Pavel probably could have walked there faster.

To lower their profile, he ditched most of their weapons in Kaliningrad and split up the two Land Rovers. Still, everywhere they turned, it seemed like they ran into Lithuanian military columns headed south to the Suwalki Gap. Pavel had not seen that many tanks since his time in Syria.

They drove hundreds of kilometers out of their way, nearly crossing into Estonia at one point. Even though they stayed to secondary roads, Pavel's car had been stopped eight times by local authorities. Each time they were turned around, forcing them to spend hours doubling back, trying to find a path through to the Belarusian border.

By the time Pavel's car reached Minsk, it was past midnight. He and his crew were irritable, hungry, and dead tired, so he booked them into the Minsk Hotel for the night.

During the long drive, they listened to the radio and Alexei kept them up to date on social media. The Russian advance through the Suwalki Gap had been stopped.

How was that possible? Pavel wondered. He had handed them the perfect setup. How could the Russian military manage to screw up so badly? All they had to do was drive sixty-five kilometers, for God's sake. No wonder The Chef was pissed off.

He picked up his mobile. While he'd been dreaming of the mysterious dark-haired woman, he'd missed six calls. Three from The Chef and three from Kirill, the man he'd left in charge of the Ukraine operation.

With a sigh, he dialed The Chef's number. He didn't even hear it ring before a voice came on the phone. "Where the fuck are you?" his boss demanded.

"Minsk," Pavel said. "The army screwed up the whole operation. Our setup was perfect, and they blew it."

The Chef hissed in frustration. "That's not why I'm calling, you idiot," he said. "What's going on in the Ukraine?"

Now Pavel regretted not calling Kirill first. "I don't know," he said.

The Chef cursed. "I pay you to manage the big picture, Pavel. The strategic picture, you know? Get your ass back to the Ukraine and sort it out." He hung up.

Pavel clutched the phone, wanting to throw it against the wall. He hated it when The Chef hung up on him. It was disrespectful to the good work he did. The good *strategic* work he did. While Pavel was out in the field with his ass on the line, The Chef was back in Moscow getting blow jobs for breakfast.

Without me, that asshole is nothing, Pavel thought as he dialed Kirill.

"Where the fuck are you?" Kirill answered.

"Unless you want a beatdown the next time I see you, I suggest you change your attitude."

"Did you hear what happened down here?" Kirill replied in a slightly less angry tone.

"I left you in charge," Pavel said. "Apparently, that was a bad call on my part. Why don't you do your job and give me a report I can use?"

"There was an attack on a Russian CP outside Lubny," Kirill said.

"How is that our problem?" Pavel replied. "I think the Russian military is capable of dealing with their own shit. What happened? Artillery strike?"

"That's the problem, boss," Kirill said. "Nobody knows what happened. Somebody came through and wrecked that place in, like, ten minutes. Three hundred armed soldiers and there are only three survivors—two of which are in a coma."

"Aerial assault?" Pavel asked.

"No, ground assault. The military says it was British commandos, but it's all bullshit."

"Why?" Pavel said. "British commandos are badass. I've seen them in action."

"Trust me, these are not British commandos," Kirill said.

"What are you talking about?" Leaving Kirill in charge was a mistake. Pavel saw that now. His mobile phone buzzed with an incoming text, and he held it away from his ear to see the screen. Kirill had texted him a file.

"Watch that clip," Kirill said. "I'll wait."

Pavel clicked on the MP4 file. The picture was grainy, dark. The sound kept cutting out because nearby gunfire over-whelmed the microphone. In the flash of an explosion, Pavel saw the outline of a soldier in profile raise an AK-74M assault rifle. Pips of light sprouted from the muzzle. The soldier staggered, a blast of black jetting out of his back. He fell backward.

A new shape moved across the field of view. It looked like a log, horizontal on four metallic legs. He thought he saw a flash of light on top of the log, but the thing moved really fast, and then it was gone. Pavel thought maybe he'd imagined it.

"What the fuck is that?" Pavel said.

"Slow it down to quarter speed," Kirill said. "Watch it again."

At the slower speed, the soldier died dramatically. Pavel realized the man was wearing body armor, so the bullet that took him down had to be a heavy-caliber round since it went completely through the man's body.

The log-shaped thing appeared, and Pavel froze the video. He zoomed in. There was a protrusion on the top of the log, and he could see a muzzle flash.

"It's a robot," Pavel said.

"That's what I think, too," Kirill said. "The military says it was the Brits—that's their story. But I called a guy I know in intel, and he sent me this clip. Those are not British commandos."

Pavel grunted. There was only one company with that kind of advanced technology and a willingness to use it.

Sentinel Holdings.

He found himself grinning. That Manson Skelly guy had one enormous set of balls.

"Pull our teams out of the field," Pavel said. "I'll be there by lunchtime. We'll figure it out."

"What about the military?" Kirill asked.

"If the Russian military command wants to blame the Brits, what do we care? Just get our guys out of the way."

"Copy that, boss."

Five minutes later, he met the other three members of his team in the underground car park. They all looked as tired as he felt, and they piled into the car in silence. From the front passenger seat, Pavel concentrated on drafting a text to The Chef. He probably should call him, but he really didn't want to talk to his boss again, and he didn't want the rest of his team to know about the killer robots.

The driver made his way through the car park and up the ramp. He jerked to an abrupt stop and swore.

Pavel looked up. The street before them was filled with people. Old, young, parents with children, couples holding hands, all headed toward Independence Square. Most were laughing and some were singing. The driver laid on the horn, and three girls, their faces painted in the red and green of the Belarusian flag, waved at him.

"What the hell?" Pavel said, craning his head so he could see around the corner.

"Don't you ever look at social media?" Alexei said from the

back seat. His head was thrown back, and his eyes were closed. "It's Sunday. It's the freedom march."

"I thought the city was under martial law," Pavel said.

"Not since the Russian military moved into Lithuania," Alexei replied. "The opposition declared Sunday a day of peaceful protest. They're marching to the Government House to demand freedom from whoever is in charge now." Alexei peeled open one eye. "The post didn't say who was in charge now."

The Chef might want to know about this, Pavel thought. He called up a map on his phone and pointed to a spot a few blocks east of their current location. "I'm gonna check it out. Meet me here in twenty minutes."

Pavel shouldered his way through the crowd, which grew even denser as he entered Ulitsa Sovetskaya, the long pedestrian mall that ran in front of the Government House. Staying on the edge of the crowd, he tried to see what was going on but to no avail. Finally, he hoisted himself up onto the stone foundation of a lamppost and stood up. From this vantage point, he could see the whole area.

The half-kilometer mall was a mass of people all dressed in white, with more pouring in from every direction. The crowd spilled out onto the four-lane road that ran parallel to the Ulitsa Sovetskaya, stopping traffic in both directions.

Pavel could not even hazard a guess at how many people were there, but it had the feel of a festival, or maybe a rock concert. He even saw some people bodysurfing across the crowd. Belarusian flags were everywhere.

At the very end of the mall, in front of the Government House, was Independence Square. Half of the square was barricaded off, and on the steps of the Government House, the Russian Army had parked three BTR-80 armored personnel carriers. The 14.5mm machine guns on the APCs were trained on the crowd, and Pavel picked out Russian infantry stationed along the perimeter. A Russian captain, bullhorn in hand, stood on the center APC trying to speak to the crowd of people at the barricade.

Pavel heard a chant start somewhere behind him. It turned into a call-and-response.

"*Sva—*" shouted one end of the mall.

"*—body,*" came the response.

Svabody, the Belarusian word for *freedom*.

The chants increased in intensity. People swayed in rhythm.

Sva...body...sva...body...

The swaying became a wave, rippling from one end of the mall to the other.

The Government House rose above the crowd, a ten-story structure of tan stone and tall windows. The seat of the National Assembly was one of the few buildings to survive the Great Patriotic War. In front of the structure stood a statue of Lenin. The black figure rose above the seething sea of white.

As Pavel watched, a young couple scaled the statue. The man boosted the young woman up until she was sitting on Lenin's shoulders, her legs wrapped around the neck of the statue. She waved a Belarusian flag as the Russian captain shouted into his bullhorn.

Svaaaa...bodyyyy...svaaaa...bodyyyy...

The crowd looked like a foaming riptide as it surged back and forth down the length of the mall. The amplitude of the tide increased.

Svaaaa...bodyyyy...

The barricade in front of the Government House collapsed, and white-clad bodies spilled into the open space. The Russian captain froze in place as the crowd surged through the breach. Pavel saw people running up the broad stone steps.

"Don't do it," Pavel said.

The sound of one shot reached his ears, barely perceptible over the roar of the crowd. Then another, then three, then a wall of staccato gunfire like a thousand snare drums.

Dozens of white-clad bodies, now peppered with red, fell on the steps. Men and women surged around the armored personnel carriers, began to climb up the sides. The Russian captain used the bullhorn to clock a young man in the head. He turned to his soldiers, shouting something.

Pavel ducked behind the stone foundation of the lamppost just as the Russian soldiers fired their machine guns into the crowd.

44

Oleksandriya, Ukraine

As a kid, Abby Cromwell used to chew her fingernails, a habit which her father detested. The pair of them battled about her habit for years, until one day, when Abby turned eleven, she just stopped. She decided that she was going to change the way she presented herself to the world, and that was the end of fingernail chewing for her. Over the years, Abby built up that story in her mind as proof that she was master of her environment.

Except she wasn't. In times of real stress in her life, Abby still reverted to the childhood habit she'd kicked at the age of eleven.

When the fasten seat belts sign came on in the cabin of the Sentinel private jet, Abby was noshing on the tip of her right index finger. She looked out the window. Ragged clouds partially obscured the agricultural patchwork that was the western Ukrainian countryside.

In the plush leather seat across from her, Dylan Mattias

held a mobile phone to his ear. He closed his eyes as he listened, nodding.

"Yes, sir...I understand, sir...We'll be available, of course."

Dylan hung up, dropped the phone into his lap.

"The Director's headed to the White House," he said. "He said we can expect a call about next steps."

Next steps, thought Abby. What a perfectly quaint way to say *murder*. Her eyes dropped to the tablet in her lap, then lifted back up to Dylan with a questioning look.

He shook his head. "I didn't tell them everything. I figured you'd want to understand the extent of the damage before I offered any details."

Abby let the silence grow. On the table between them, two mugs of coffee sat untouched, growing cold.

"We should turn around," Dylan said. "I think our time is better spent in DC right now. There's going to be a lot of damage control."

Damage control, Abby thought. Another nice euphemism.

She clicked open the tablet again and queued up the video. The point-of-view cameras on the K-10 units were excellent. War crimes in high-def, perfect for the congressional hearing.

The technologists at Sentinel had started calling the units K-10s as a joke. If actual war dogs were called K-9s, then their creation must be the next generation of K-9...ergo, the K-10.

Like wolves, the K-10s operated in a pack formation. Through distributed computing and cooperative threat engagement, the autonomous platforms executed the mission as a team. If contact was lost with the CP, the alpha was authorized to make battlefield decisions.

This was her third viewing of Alpha's video feed, but even now she was picking up new details. Horrible details. She used her ragged fingertip to advance the video to the last few minutes.

Alpha advanced down a narrow corridor toward a door. The audio on the K-10 automatically blanked out when the unit fired its Barrett rifle. Two holes the size of quarters appeared in the door lock, and Alpha ran full-tilt into the closed door like a battering ram. It crashed into a computer rack on the opposite side of the door. Alpha shuddered as shots impacted the unit. It seemed to have trouble navigating its long body in the confined space. As it backed out of the shattered door and reentered at an angle, an alert flashed on the data stream alongside the video.

TARGETING SENSOR OUT OF ALIGNMENT.

The Russian command post radio room was long and narrow, crammed with equipment. At the end of the aisle, two people faced Alpha. The man was a Russian captain, mid-twenties, holding an empty handgun. Behind him, her face peeking around the man's shoulder, were the features of a young woman, her eyes wide with terror.

If it wasn't so horrifying, it would be hilarious. Their expressions were exaggerated, like something from a silent movie. The whites of their eyes, the gaping mouths, the way they tried to press back against the racks of computer equipment.

Except it wasn't a silent movie. The man shouted at Alpha and threw the empty handgun. Dylan had translated the final radio transmission that Alpha had detected from the man and translated his cursing at Alpha.

The perspective changed as Alpha went to a down position.

"Why did it do that?" Dylan asked, taking the empty seat beside her.

"It's recalibrating the targeting optics. The process takes a few seconds, and it's best to do it from a stable position, so the unit drops to the floor."

On the screen, the man and woman look at each other in surprise. The woman pushes him, and the man takes a tentative step forward.

Recalibration complete.

Alpha rose, the camera perspective shifted. The man backpedaled, slipped, the woman tried to catch him and failed. A hole appeared in the woman's chest. Her body stiffened, she fell sideways. The man died a split second later.

"Jesus," Dylan whispered. He'd also seen it multiple times, but the images had staying power.

Abby shifted tabs to the BBC website. *Russian attack on British medical camp kills 53.*

She scanned the article for updates.

...An unprovoked Russian artillery attack on a British-led Doctors Without Borders post outside of Kyiv has killed an estimated 53 medical personnel and support staff. The Prime Minister is expected to call for NATO to open a second front against the Russian Federation forces in eastern Ukraine...

"Are the Russians saying anything yet?" Dylan asked.

Abby shook her head and clicked the tablet closed.

What were they waiting for? she wondered. Or was the attack by the K-10s so complete that they really didn't know what had happened? Between the ruthless killing efficiency of the K-10 pack and the explosions in the fuel depot and ammo dump, was it possible there were no survivors?

No, she decided, there were always survivors. They would find a few and maybe some video from a mobile phone. It would take time, but the truth would come out.

And when it did, she'd be ruined.

"What the hell was he thinking?" Abby said.

Dylan reached for her hand. "What's done is done," he

said. "You ordered him to stand down, and he did it anyway. This is not your fault, but that's not how this will play out. You're the face of Sentinel. That's why I think we should go back to DC, right now. If we act quickly, you can get ahead of the story. Skelly's made his own bed, let him lie in it. You need to protect yourself." He squeezed her hand.

Abby shook her head. "I can't. Not now. I'll shut down the operation. Then I'll go back."

She eyed him. How much of this was because he cared for her, and how much was Dylan trying to protect himself? She chewed her thumbnail, hating herself for thinking it and yet unable to stop the thoughts.

Abby looked out the window. It looked like it was going to be a nice day. The green fields adjacent to the runway flashed by. In the distance, she saw grazing cows. It all looked so normal and peaceful, yet no more than sixty miles away some three hundred Russian soldiers had been slaughtered by robot assassin dogs.

Sentinel had always been more than a business to her. It was a dream, a dream shared by three friends. They said they would be a force for good in the world...

You're a fool, Aberdeen Cromwell, she thought. A goddamned fool.

She cursed under her breath in a steady beat, feeling the rage at Manson Skelly soak into her tired body like water into dry sand.

The plane touched the runway, bounced, then rolled toward the terminal.

By the time the taxi dropped them outside the warehouse that housed Sentinel's Ukraine operations, Abby's rage had reached supernova levels.

There had been no Sentinel car waiting for them at the airport, so Dylan found them local transportation, a battered Lada taxi. While Dylan made small talk in Russian with the cab driver, Abby stared at the horizon and tried to remember to breathe.

She was out of the car almost before it stopped, leaving Dylan to deal with the taxi driver. Abby strode to the steel door and seized the handle.

It was locked. She glared at the camera.

"Open. The fucking. Door," she ordered. She felt the handle shift as the magnetic lock clunked open.

The operations center was manned with a full complement of six techs behind computer workstations. Landersmann, serving as watch officer, was speaking when she entered. He paused, and everyone turned around to look at her. She heard Dylan come in behind her.

Landersmann wore a stupid smile on his face, half leer, half feigned innocence. "Welcome, Abby," he said.

Abby unlocked her jaw long enough to say: "Where is he?"

"In his office. I think he's expecting you—"

Abby walked away while he was still talking.

The lock on Skelly's door that she had broken last time she was here had been patched with duct tape. She pushed the door open so hard it bounced off the wall and sprang back.

Manson Skelly sat behind his desk. He shut the lid of his laptop and looked up at her. "I expected you an hour ago, Abby. I was just cleaning out my desk. I'm ready for our turnover." He smiled at her and laced his fingers behind his head.

Abby's arms twitched. She tried to speak, but no words came out.

Dylan closed the door behind him and advanced to stand beside her. Skelly's eyes alighted on Dylan.

"You brought your CIA boyfriend," he said with mock seriousness. "That'll make this go quicker."

Abby's brain unfroze. "Do you realize what you've done?"

It must have been the tone of her voice, but she got a reaction from Skelly. The muscles corded in his forearms as he leaned onto the desk.

"My job."

Abby moved to the desk, leaned forward until they were face to face. "You're a killer, Manson."

"You don't get it, do you?" Skelly said. "You never made the mental leap."

"What are you talking about?"

"He gets it." Skelly aimed a finger at Dylan. "If you kill a guy as a civilian, you're a murderer. If you kill a guy as a soldier, you're a hero. If you kill a guy as a contractor, it never happened."

"You crossed a line, Manson."

"There is no line, Abby!" Skelly threw his hands in the air. "This is the part that you don't understand. You want to change the world. I've decided to accept the world as it is. I get an order, I follow the order." He made an imaginary gun out of his thumb and forefinger. "Simple, point and shoot. Not point and consider the geopolitical ramifications of my actions."

He blew on the forefinger muzzle of the imaginary weapon. "I get things done."

"The Russian counterattack killed doctors," Abby said. "Nurses, wounded soldiers. Your attack caused that—that's on you. I'm not going down for this."

"Going down for what?" Skelly looked at Dylan. "The

Russians killed those doctors, not us. Besides, we work for the CIA. The Company, you know? This is all covert. What you say happened never happened."

Abby started to respond, but the buzzing of her mobile phone stopped her. The caller ID said: The White House. She cursed to herself.

Still holding the phone, she leveled a finger at Skelly. "I suggest you find a good lawyer, Manson. You're going to need it. Now, get out. I've got work to do."

Skelly's face was a mix of emotions. She tried to work it out, but the phone buzzed again.

"I'm gone, Abby," he said. "Good luck to you."

Good luck, she thought. Was he fucking serious? He was going to jail! She started to answer him, but the phone buzzed again, distracting her.

Skelly disappeared out the door. Dylan followed him out, and she was alone.

Abby took a deep breath and answered the phone.

45

The Kremlin
Moscow, Russia

The fluttering in his vision was back. Luchnik squinted at the report in front of him, trying to block out the annoying tremor that jiggled in the far right of his field of view. He suddenly wondered if his eyelid was moving, too. That would mean others could see what was happening—

"Shall I continue, Mr. President?"

Nikolay's voice intruded on his runaway thoughts, soft but firm. He was glad that he had promoted his nephew to the role of Defense Minister. Federov's advice had proven useful yet again.

Luchnik looked up, met his nephew's gaze. The tremor wavered like a flag fluttering in his peripheral vision. He bent his lips into a smile.

"Continue, Defense Minister."

Without consulting his notes, Nikolay turned to the row of ministers.

"Elements of the United States' 82nd and 101st Airborne Divisions are arriving in Estonia and Latvia. We expect them to set up defensive positions along our border. In addition, the Swedes and the Finns are on high alert. Their naval forces are repositioning to escort the US Navy amphibious force into the Baltic."

"How long do we have?" asked Irimov.

"The United States Second Marine Expeditionary Force will enter the Baltic Sea within the next forty-eight hours, Foreign Minister," Nikolay replied crisply.

Luchnik looked down at the papers in front of him.

Two days, he thought. If he allowed the United States to enter the Baltic Sea, then his plan was over. His plan had always depended on speed. A blitz across the Suwalki Gap to capture the tiny land bridge before anyone could react.

But that traitor Yakov had fucked that up for him. Now he had to rely on backup plans. Plans that exposed him to much more risk.

But it was worth it, he reminded himself. And he was so close. Just one more push—

"What is the status in the Ukraine?" a new voice broke in. Prime Minister Mishinov did not often speak up in Luchnik's cabinet meetings. He cleared his throat, cast a side glance at Luchnik. "What can you tell us about the attack on the command post at Lubny?"

He knows, thought Luchnik. That bastard knows the truth.

Luchnik paused, but Nikolay had the matter well in hand.

"British commandos raided at dawn," the Defense Minister lied. "Our forces were caught by surprise, and they paid the price." Nikolay grimaced as if the thought caused him real pain. "I am finding many instances of poor leadership and sloppy security practices in my review of the force readiness. I am pleased to say that our retaliation against the British was both swift and decisive."

"Mr. President, the counterattack destroyed a Doctors Without Borders medical camp," Mishinov challenged. "Our reprisal has drawn NATO forces into the conflict on yet another front."

"Enough," Luchnik said. He needed to keep these men away from the topic of the Ukraine and the attack on the Russian command post. They were nervous enough about the invasion into Lithuania. How would they react if they knew that an entire Russian command post had been wiped out by killer robots?

"The incident is under investigation, Prime Minister," Nikolay said. "I promise you, I will get to the bottom of this matter and take appropriate corrective actions."

Little Mishi offered a humorless smile in return.

"The situation right now demands that we focus our attention on Kaliningrad," Luchnik said.

Blank faces stared back at him. He saw the doubt in their eyes, the fear. He wanted to scream at them.

How could these idiots not understand? he thought. A land bridge to Kaliningrad meant everything to Mother Russia: a seaport on the Baltic, an unbroken border that stretched from the Arctic Ocean to the Black Sea. Most importantly, they would split off the Balkans from NATO.

These morons at the table would laugh at that idea, saying that a narrow strip of land between Poland and Lithuania was not worth the effort. But the NATO leaders saw the significance of his move, and they were running scared. That was all the reassurance Luchnik needed.

He was doing the right thing.

"Mr. President?" Mishinov interrupted for the second time in one cabinet meeting. Luchnik could not remember when that had last happened. Little Mishi wore his normal supercilious look, but he waited for an acknowledgment before proceeding.

Luchnik sensed the tremor in his vision returning. He nodded.

"I think we should discuss the situation in Minsk, sir," Mishinov said.

Luchnik stared at him until Little Mishi shifted uncomfortably in his chair.

What is your angle? Luchnik thought. Out loud, he said, "What is there to discuss, Prime Minister?"

"Sir, despite our media blackout, videos are showing up all over the internet. This blunts our influence campaign. We're now seeing increased support for NATO in areas where we had gained—"

"What do you suggest, Prime Minister?" Luchnik interrupted.

"Well, sir, we could acknowledge the situation, but say the officer in charge panicked. Bring him back to Moscow and put him on trial—"

"Put him on trial?" Luchnik leaned forward out of his chair and planted both fists on the dark wood. He felt his right eye spasm. His rational brain knew that he was overreacting, but he could not seem to stop himself.

"In Lubny, hundreds of Russian soldiers were slaughtered in cold blood. Where is NATO's accountability for that? Do you see them putting anyone on trial? Yet, when a fine young Russian officer puts down an insurrection that was incited by the West, you think he should be put on trial?"

Luchnik glared at Mishinov, his look daring the other man to challenge the President's version of the truth.

I own you, Little Mishi, Luchnik thought. I can end you just as quickly.

"We are not aggressors, Prime Minister," Luchnik concluded. "We were protecting our government."

Mishinov dropped his eyes, nodded. "Yes, Mr. President," he said. "It was merely a suggestion."

Luchnik took his seat in the awkward silence that followed the confrontation. He had two days to solve this problem before the Americans arrived. NATO would not launch a full-scale attack without the American Marines, but they had ample forces to continue their holding action. The only option left was to break the status quo.

"I believe the right course of action is to attack from Kaliningrad into Lithuania," Luchnik said.

It was as if he'd set loose an army of fire ants in the room. Everyone shifted in their seats. They shuffled papers and drank water, anything to pretend they had not heard what their leader had just said.

"Mr. President," Irimov intoned. "I believe that would be a very risky maneuver."

Luchnik leveled his gaze at Federov. "Have communications been restored with Kaliningrad military command?"

The head of internal security nodded. "Restored and tested. There will be no more issues."

"And have you found General Vasilenko yet?" Luchnik asked.

Federov looked back at him with his unblinking eyes, displaying neither fear nor emotion. "Kaliningrad is a small place. It's only a matter of time."

Time, thought Luchnik. The one commodity I am lacking.

"Mr. President." Irimov's voice held an edge of concern. "I believe we should discuss alternative plans."

"Sergey," Luchnik said, "how long have we worked together?"

Irimov offered a faint smile. "Too many years to count, sir."

"And how many times have you seen me back down from a fight?" Luchnik said.

"I have never seen you back down from a fight that you know you can win, Mr. President." He hesitated, looked down the table just as Mishinov looked up. The two men exchanged glances. "I do not think that this fight is winnable, Mr. President."

There it was, thought Luchnik. The challenge to his authority. Members of his own cabinet, men he had groomed for years at great expense, were willing to cut and run in his hour of greatest need.

"Every fight is winnable, Sergey," Luchnik replied. "As long as you are willing to accept the costs."

"The cost is too high, Mr. President," Irimov said, his eyes shifting down the table again.

Luchnik's mind latched onto the move. Was Irimov moving against him?

"Is that what you all think?" Luchnik asked the room. "That we should withdraw?"

As if confirming his suspicions, Prime Minister Mishinov spoke up again.

"We are spread too thin, Mr. President," he said. "We should pull back into Belarus and secure our gains in the Ukraine. The land corridor to Kaliningrad is lost."

"It is not lost until I say it is lost!" Luchnik declared. "This is not some game of chance, gentlemen. Statecraft is a game of skill. It requires patience. Daring. Sacrifice."

The room was utterly still. It seemed that no one even dared to breathe.

This is the moment, Luchnik realized. The traitors will reveal themselves.

"We will launch an all-out assault in the Suwalki Gap," Luchnik said. "A simultaneous attack from the east and the west, from Belarus and from Kaliningrad. We will break through. No matter the cost."

He ran his gaze down the table. The faces showed fear, doubt, uncertainty. He felt the flutter in his eye again. He was so close...

"Mr. President," Irimov began in a shaky voice. "I don't—"

Out of the wavering edge of his vision, Luchnik saw a man stand up.

It was Nikolay, and his features were twisted into a mask of disgust.

"What is wrong with all of you?" he shouted. "How long has my uncle led this country?" The veins stood out on his neck, and his face was flushed red. "Thirty years! And you've all benefited from it. Your bank accounts are fat, your women are gorgeous, and your dachas are beautiful. But when your leader needs your support, you act like a bunch of old women. You disgust me." He spat on the table.

Nikolay turned to Luchnik and came to attention.

"Mr. President, give the order. I will see it done."

Federov got to his feet, faced Luchnik. "You have my support, sir."

One by one around the table, the cabinet members stood and pledged their support to their leader. Irimov was the last to rise. He hung his head.

"I apologize, Mr. President."

For the first time in days, Luchnik felt the tremor in his vision fade away.

46

Oleksandriya, Ukraine

Abby had no choice but to leave Landersmann in charge of the Ukraine operation. She wasn't comfortable with the decision, but Chief of Staff Wilkerson had been crystal clear about the President's wishes.

The headlights of the Sentinel Land Rover illuminated the gate of the private airport. The security guard, also a Sentinel employee, checked IDs and let them pass. The Sentinel jet was the only plane on the tarmac.

Be back in Washington, DC, for a nine a.m. meeting at the White House, Wilkerson ordered. The President expected a full brief on the Ukraine situation.

Situation, she thought. Another one of those words designed for pleasant company. A way to take something ugly and make it presentable.

Of course, the meeting demand only took place after he finished chewing her out about how she'd mismanaged the entire campaign. Wilkerson hinted that there would likely be a congressional hearing on the matter, and he made it clear that he expected her full support with the Serrano administration.

This, Abby thought darkly, is a meeting to get our stories straight.

In the seat next to her, Dylan spoke into his mobile phone, his voice a soft murmur. She couldn't make out what he was saying. She allowed a wry smile. Maybe they taught you that at spy school.

The driver held her door, and she stepped outside. The summer evening was warm, a gentle breeze blew across the runway. The jet hadn't started yet, so the flight line was quiet. Behind her, the car door slammed, and Dylan joined her.

"Look at that," he said, looking up.

Abby surveyed the sky. "What?"

"The stars," Dylan said.

"Oh." The night was so clear that she could see not just individual stars but what looked like clouds of interstellar bodies. She tried to remember the constellations her father had taught her as a kid, but none came to mind.

"I wanted to be an astronomer when I was a kid," Dylan said. "I was going to find the next Earth and help colonize it." His voice was distant, like he was lost in a memory.

"You never told me that before," Abby said.

Dylan let out a short laugh. "There's a lot I haven't told you —and some things you haven't told me."

If they were having a moment, the moment was over. "What's that supposed to mean?" Abby asked in a sharp voice.

You're tired, she reminded herself, and this guy is not your enemy.

"The phone call was from the Director. Don Riley asked to see him in the morning. He says he has new intelligence on the Russia situation. The Director is under the impression he had help from Sentinel. Do you know anything about that, Abby?"

"No," Abby lied. She mounted the steps of the jet.

"Can I get you anything, ma'am?" the flight attendant asked.

"Bourbon. Neat." Abby walked back to a leather captain's chair and collapsed into the soft cushions. She closed her eyes as the jet's engine started, the whine slowly building in intensity.

Sleep, she thought. You need to sleep on this flight if you want to be fresh in the morning.

But her brain would not cooperate. She reviewed the day in her mind. Landersmann had been helpful, she had to admit, and he kept good records of all the operations.

Manson had been a busy boy. As always, his ops pushed the envelope, but that was his style. Take it right up to the line. That was Manson's way.

But using the K-10 pack as assassins on a Russian military command post blew past every possible guardrail. There was no record of any prior authorization from the White House as he claimed, which made her believe he was lying. That was the only explanation that made sense.

She'd asked Wilkerson about any change in the rules of engagement, which he denied. Still, she thought, the White House was getting what they wanted. The attack on the Russian CP and the subsequent counterattack on the British-led medical camp had changed the balance of power in the region.

Any countries that were inclined to give Russia the benefit of the doubt in eastern Europe had deserted their ally. After the attack on the Doctors Without Borders camp, the Russian Federation was a pariah in the international community. Hell, even Iran dropped their support for Russia at the United Nations.

Manson Skelly was going to pay the price, but the White House reaped the rewards. For his part, Skelly was in the wind. No one had seen him since he'd walked out of the Sentinel command post earlier that day.

The door to the jet closed, blocking out the whine of the engine. In the sudden quiet, she heard a glass hitting the table in front of her. When Abby opened her eyes, Dylan stood before her, his own glass in hand. He indicated the seat across from her.

"May I?"

Abby nodded, took her drink. The first sip of bourbon was always the best. The rich aromas of caramel and honey, the warmth on her tongue, the burn of the alcohol. She let out a sigh.

"First time I've seen you smile all day," Dylan said.

"Bourbon'll do that."

The jet started to move.

"I'm sorry," Dylan said. "I accused you of helping Riley. That was wrong of me."

"I lied to you," Abby replied. "Not even sure why—just a reflex, I guess. I let Don use Mama for some sort of analysis he was running."

Dylan's face went tight. "I knew it."

The jet reached the end of the runway and made a wide turn.

"It's my company," Abby snapped. "I'll do what I want."

Dylan started to respond, then stopped. "You're right. I get a little competitive when it comes to Riley." He gave a tight smile. "It's an automatic reaction with me."

Dylan paused, then asked, "Did he tell you what he was working on?"

Abby shrugged. "Financial analysis was all he said. He needed Mama's computing power to get it done faster."

The jet started to roll forward.

"Huh." Dylan sipped his drink. "More power to him. Who knows what'll happen to us when all this comes out."

"Well, if the spy thing falls apart, you can always be an astronomer."

As Dylan laughed, the jet left the runway, gaining altitude at a steep angle. He extended his glass.

"To new beginnings," he said.

Still laughing, Abby leaned forward, pushing against the gravity that held her in her seat. Just as the rim of her glass touched Dylan's, the plane heeled violently to starboard.

Her glass flew from her grip, careened off the ceiling, amber drops of bourbon spraying in an arc. The plane jinked and dove. Abby's head bounced off the wall, then her body was smashed flat into the cushions.

Across from her, Dylan gripped the arm of his chair. He was looking out the window. His mouth moved, but she couldn't make out what he was saying.

Fighting against the gravity, Abby craned her neck to follow his gaze out the window.

She saw a pip of light, like a match in the darkness. It grew rapidly, coming straight at them. The jet made another evasive maneuver, and she lost visual contact with the object. But she knew what Dylan was trying to tell her.

Missile.

Light flared across Dylan's face as the missile exploded next to the jet. The fiery shrapnel ripped into the skin of the Bombardier Global 7000, shredding aluminum, carbon fiber, insulation, leather, and human flesh.

The blast did not kill Abby Cromwell.

The shell of the plane around her evaporated, and she

looked up into a dark sky. Stars, the sky was filled with millions of stars.

The press of gravity holding her in her seat disappeared. The rush of air and the whine of the jet engine faded. She could hear her own breathing, feel her own thundering heartbeat.

Abby hung in space.

Then she fell.

47

___

There were moments when Don felt like the whole world was working against him. President Serrano was having one of those days—and he looked it.

Sitting behind the Resolute desk in the Oval Office, the President was finishing a phone call. He had his eyes closed, and he pinched the bridge of his nose as he listened. A five o'clock shadow bruised the sallow skin of his cheek. His suit jacket was off and he'd loosened his tie, exposing the sagging skin of his neck. To Don, the most powerful man in the world seemed vulnerable.

"Senator, I understand your point, but have you..." The President's words trailed off when he spun in his chair to face the darkened windows.

President Serrano's day started off as a catastrophe and went rapidly downhill from there. The headline in the *Washington Post* told the story:

Serrano's Secret War, it read. The front-page exposé was a tell-all of Sentinel's activities in Ukraine. As Don scanned the article, he wondered about the source. Could it be Abby? He'd sensed she was unhappy about her deepening involvement in the Ukraine crisis, but the article was as brutal on her as on the President. If she'd leaked the story as a mea culpa for her actions, she was paying for it now.

There were immediate calls for congressional hearings and for new regulations on private military contractors. A group of House firebrands held a press conference demanding that the United Nations reopen an investigation into Serrano's use of autonomous weaponry in the Battle of Taiwan. Hasty polls showed the President hemorrhaging support from both sides of the aisle, and political talk shows floated the idea of impeachment.

During his frequent campaign stops over the last few months, a picture of a triumphant Serrano at a Rose Garden press conference was splashed everywhere. Don, who had been at that event, recalled Serrano's jubilant mood as he claimed victory over the Chinese in the Battle of Taiwan. Abby Cromwell had been there, too, but she was normally cropped out of the picture.

The *New York Post* found an uncropped version with Abby Cromwell standing at the President's side. They ran it on the front page under the headline: *Soldier of Mis-Fortune.*

Don followed the breaking news alerts during the day, and the hits kept coming for the President. His infrastructure package, which had enjoyed rare bipartisan support only a few days ago, was now dead in the water. Even his own party didn't want to be associated with a Serrano-supported resolution.

And then there was the actual conflict itself. The thing that Serrano had wanted so desperately to stay away from was now staring him in the face. He'd now committed US troops—the ready brigades from the 82nd and 101st Airborne Divisions

—to Estonia and Latvia, billions of dollars in aid to Ukraine, and was leading the NATO effort against Russian aggression in eastern Europe.

The problem was that Luchnik was not backing down. Despite having lost all support in the international community, the Russian President was like a dog with a bone. European leaders made diplomatic approaches to the Russian Federation and were rebuffed. The Russian Foreign Minister insisted the NATO aggression into Russian-speaking territories was a violation of human rights and an infringement on the security of the Russian Federation. Foreign Minister Irimov claimed that Russian forces outside of Kyiv had been attacked by British commandos and Russia's artillery response was both reasonable and justified.

We're going backward, Don thought, and the stakes are about to get higher.

The Second Marine Expeditionary Force was about to enter the Baltic Sea. If the Russians were upset now, how would they feel when a division of Marines embarked and the amphibious landing force showed up in their backyard?

Don feared this would not end well. Luchnik was playing a losing hand: a stalled military thrust in the Suwalki Gap was only made worse by the news of a civilian massacre in Minsk. Yet the Russian leader only doubled down. Again.

Into this mix, Don was about to propose to the President a new plan, something that might solve the crisis, or it might make it much, much worse.

Don had studied conflict his entire adult life. Luchnik was entering "death ground," the point of no return, the point in a conflict where his choices were either fight or be annihilated. The Russian President had ignored all of the diplomatic off-ramps offered to him. He showed no signs of backing down, which left the US and NATO with few options other than to engage and destroy the Russians.

The President's voice intruded on Don's musings, bringing him back to the moment. He sat on the couch in the Oval Office with a silent CIA Director Blank to his right. Chief of Staff Wilkerson and National Security Advisor Valentina Flores engaged in a whispered conversation on the opposite sofa.

Don wondered what strings the Director had pulled to get him into the Oval Office. It was clear that neither Flores nor Wilkerson wanted him here, no matter what he had to say. No one had offered refreshments, and Don's mouth was dry.

"Well, thank you, Senator," the President said. He slammed the phone back into the cradle.

They all stood as Serrano approached the sitting area. He gave a distracted wave and collapsed into the armchair between the two sofas.

"McClintock bailed," he announced.

"We'll get him back, sir," Wilkerson replied. "It'll cost us, but we can get him back."

Serrano slouched in his chair, crossed his legs. He pointed at the bold headline on the *Washington Post*. "What about Abby Cromwell? Is she the leak?"

"I thought you'd want to ask her that yourself," Wilkerson replied. "She's flying back from Ukraine tonight."

"I can't believe she would do that to me," Serrano said.

"Sir, we don't *know* that it's her," Wilkerson said carefully.

The President grunted, looked at Flores. "You were very confident, Valentina, that if we stood up to Luchnik, he'd back down. I don't see that happening."

Flores adjusted the lapel of her suit jacket. "Mr. President, the Russian position is untenable. If you give him a way to save face, I'm sure he'll take it."

"You know what?" Serrano's voice turned sharp. "I'm tired of playing Luchnik's game. Diplomacy means nothing to that man. He sees this as a dog-eat-dog world, and I'm feeling pretty damn hungry right now. Let the French make the call to Luchnik. If he wants to talk to me, then he has my number. In the meantime, let's get our Marines on the beach and see how he likes his chances then."

Flores shifted in her seat. Her voice took on an urgent quality. "Mr. President, if we allow the Second MEF to enter the Baltic Sea, we are going to significantly raise the stakes on this crisis. Perhaps we could slow down the amphibious task force to give the diplomatic endeavors more time?"

Serrano was already shaking his head. "It's too late for that, Valentina. I'm screwed either way, and I am tired of this dance. Luchnik started this, he needs to end it."

The Director spoke before Flores could respond. "There might be another way, sir."

Serrano followed the Director's gaze to Don. The President looked as if he'd just realized Don was in the meeting. "Riley," he said with a tired smile. "Tell me you have a way to make this all go away."

Don passed out single-page summaries of the financial data. He explained how his team had linked the listed shell companies to members of Luchnik's inner circle.

Serrano pursed his lips as he studied the sheet. He clocked a glance at Wilkerson.

"This seems too good to be true, Mr. Riley," Wilkerson said. "How did you get this information?"

"The provenance of the information is the issue," the Director said. "We don't know who gave it to us."

Flores's eyes bored into Don. "Explain that, please."

"A key was slipped into my pocket on the Metro," Don said. "A mailbox key. Later, I received an email that led me to a

UPS Store in South Dakota. The key fit one of the mailboxes, and there was a letter inside addressed to me. It held a thumb drive."

Wilkerson snorted. "You expect us to believe that someone just decided to drop this information in your lap? This has to be a setup. This has Russian deception written all over it."

"It could be an elaborate hoax, I agree," Don said. "Or it could be an off-ramp."

"I don't follow," Serrano said.

Don took a deep breath. "Someone could be trying to take down Luchnik."

"A coup!" Wilkerson stared at the ceiling. "Riley, you're like a broken record. This is a setup"—he slapped the paper down on the coffee table—"and you're in on it, Riley."

Don flushed. "Sir, I didn't ask for this—"

"Didn't you?" Wilkerson interrupted. "This feels really convenient to me. If the point of this is to destabilize Luchnik, why didn't this mysterious coup plotter give the information to the *Washington Post*?"

"Because they want to control the outcome," the Director said.

"What does that mean?" Wilkerson demanded.

"If you'd let Riley finish a sentence, he'll tell you."

"Irv." Serrano sat forward in his chair, giving Wilkerson a calm-down gesture. "Don, finish your brief."

"The obvious move with this information is to publicly expose the Russian oligarchy," Don said. "That would impact Luchnik's domestic power base inside the Russian Federation. It might cause Luchnik to back down, but it would also be destabilizing. It might start a revolution, or it might cement Luchnik's grip on power."

Don held up the sheet of paper. The graphic on the paper

was arranged like an org chart, a series of linked boxes. The box at the top read Pandora Corporation.

"Pandora Corporation is a holding company which owns this Dubai-based company, Paris Corporation, which in turn owns hundreds of other shell companies that are linked to members of Luchnik's inner circle. Whoever set this up knows what they're doing. They didn't just give us a list of assets, they gave us access—direct access—to those assets."

"Access to what?" Wilkerson said in a testy tone.

"The Pandora Corporation is registered in the United States," Don said. "We've consulted with Treasury, sir. We can legally seize these assets."

Serrano squinted at the paper. "Continue."

"I think the person that gave me this information did it for a reason." Don took a deep breath. "I think they want help from us to stage a coup against Luchnik."

The room was quiet.

"I think we can do it, Mr. President," Don said, the words coming faster now. "We know enough about his cabinet to be able to target specific members. If we play our cards right, Luchnik gets taken out."

"And then what?" Flores said. "Who takes over?"

"We don't know," Don said.

"Luchnik is the devil we know, Mr. President," Wilkerson said.

Serrano sat up in his chair. "The devil we know is a pain in my ass, Irv."

"It could be worse, sir," Wilkerson insisted. "It could always be worse. Whoever set this up is one devious son of a bitch. I smell a rat."

Serrano nodded. "He's right, Don. The only thing worse than a nuclear power with a crazy man in charge is a nuclear power with no one in charge. What's your plan to control the outcome?"

"We're working on that, sir," Don said.

"Well, the Marines are on their way, so you're on the clock." Serrano handed the sheet of paper back to Don. "Set up the operation, but until you can give me some assurance of success, it's all on hold."

"Yes, sir," Don replied. From the other side of the coffee table, Wilkerson started to speak.

"Don't bother, Irv," Serrano said. "It's there if we need it— providing Riley comes up with a plan that doesn't involve starting World War Three."

Wilkerson glared at Don. Serrano, who had seemed so fiery only moments before, sank back into his chair and sighed.

There was a soft knock at the door, and a messenger entered. She handed a folded piece of paper to Wilkerson. He read the note, refolded it, and passed it to the President. When Serrano read the note, a shadow clouded his features.

To Don's surprise, Serrano handed the note to him.

"Sir?" Don said.

"I know Abby was a friend of yours, Don," he said.

It wasn't until Don opened the note that he realized the President had used past tense in his description.

Aberdeen Cromwell's plane was shot down over Ukraine. All passengers presumed dead.

48

Puzonys, Lithuania

In the days following the Battle of Sventragis, the NATO military support operation turned the killing fields into a supply depot.

Sometimes in the late afternoon, Lieutenant Colonel Donat Wozniak took a break from the never-ending work of rebuilding his shattered tank battalion to walk the half-kilometer north of the A16 highway to where the combat engineers had towed the battle wreckage. The Polish tanks had been taken to a maintenance collection point and salvaged, so it was only Russian equipment here. Dozens of T-14 Armata tanks and T-15 APCs, blackened and twisted like some macabre art exhibit.

His emotions were always close to the surface during his afternoon walks. There was a wonder at the sheer level of destructive force that was laid out before him. There was deep sadness at the men and women under his command who had been killed.

But mostly, he felt pride. At first, Wozniak was ashamed of this feeling, as if he was some kind of warmonger. But over time, he slowly came to terms with the emotion.

He was trained for war. He led men and women who were trained for war. What had happened here—the killing, the destruction—was not his fault. His country had called, and he had performed his duty to the best of his ability.

Among the NATO forces stationed in the Suwalki Gap, Wozniak and his unit achieved a sort of celebrity. Alone, the tank battalion of the 1st Warsaw Armoured Brigade had destroyed three Russian Army Battalion Tactical Groups in a single night.

Within a day of the battle, Wozniak's battalion was reinforced to his full complement of fifty-eight American-made M1A2 Abrams tanks, including repairs to his own unit. The XO had survived the Battle of Sventragis, but two of his original company officers were among the KIA. Between the two of them, he and the XO tried to spend as much time as possible working with the new tanks and their crews to prepare them for whatever lay ahead.

For seven long days, NATO and Russian forces each reinforced their positions along highway A16 in the Suwalki Gap. The Neman River, which ran north-south through the Lithuanian countryside, made a series of oxbow turns near the city of Prienai. This area of woods and waterways was the dividing line for the two armies. Wozniak had studied the area. It would be good cover for the NATO forces when they eventually had to deal with the Russian invaders.

But the order to attack did not come.

While NATO and Russian airpower held the hostilities in check, diplomats talked, troops moved, and Wozniak attended meeting after meeting to plan for the coming battle.

Modern surveillance gave both sides ample information about their enemies. The Russian war machine was fearsome. He had engaged Russian armored battalions, but that force had been only the tip of a very long and heavy spear, and he'd had the advantage of surprise.

Now, there were multiple Russian divisions—this time with artillery—and more Russian forces were on the way. The NATO forces—Polish, Lithuanian, and American—were outnumbered already, and the math was not going in the right direction.

To Wozniak's way of thinking, the Russian problem did not diminish with time. The longer they waited, the worse the coming battle would be for NATO.

And there would be a battle, he was sure of that as well. Despite frantic diplomatic efforts by European nations, the Russians were sticking to their story about "saving" Russian-speaking peoples in Lithuania, and President Luchnik showed no signs of backing down.

The other puzzling aspect of the Russian problem was Kaliningrad. The Russian exclave had not participated in the attack in the Suwalki Gap and even now showed no signs of mobilizing. The diplomats took this as a good sign, but Wozniak thought that interpretation seemed optimistic. Russians could not be trusted, everyone knew that.

Wozniak expected the arrival of the United States Second Marine Expeditionary Force would break the deadlock, and he was right. When the Marine amphibious forces approached the Kattegat, Wozniak's battalion was given orders to a front-line position in the wooded area south of Prienai.

With Wozniak perched in the cupola, his tank crossed across the Neman River at Puzonys. Sunlight poked through the tree canopy, the dappled light hiding the battle scars on his tank. The whine of the gas turbine engine shattered the silence of the forest, but all in all it was a pleasant afternoon for a drive through the woods in his seventy-ton tank.

Next to him, Kaminski stood in his own open hatch. He pulled a CVC headphone off one ear.

"Sir, can I ask you something?" he said.

The radio circuit was silent, and they were under cover for the moment. "Sure, Private."

"What are *husaria*?"

Wozniak knew the rest of the crew was listening to the answer. Following the Battle of Sventragis, there had been a social media push to rename the 1st Warsaw Armoured Brigade.

"The Polish Hussars were heavy cavalry units in the 1600s," Wozniak said.

"You mean, like, horses and knights?" the young man asked.

"Exactly, they got their name from huge vertical wings they flew behind their saddles when they rode into battle. They were known as the Angels of Death."

"That sounds cool, sir."

"I have no intention of becoming an angel anytime soon, Kaminski."

"I hadn't thought of it that way, sir."

Wozniak grunted and turned his attention back to his topographical map.

It took another hour to get his battalion in place. They occupied the edge of a forest, his tanks in a line. The Russian front line was about twenty kilometers directly in front of them. Beyond the trees was a vast expanse of open country-side, cultivated fields, and pastures separated by fences and hedgerows. He'd be able to see the Russians coming from two or three kilometers away. The only real cover for the enemy was a copse of trees about a half-kilometer directly in front of his position.

As the battalion positioned their tanks, shut down their engines, and rigged camouflage, he walked from tank to tank, chatting with the tank commanders and their crews. It was easy to tell which tanks had been part of the original battalion, the battle veterans. They were all nervous about the coming engagement, but the veterans carried themselves with an extra measure of steady confidence. He inspected camouflage netting, inquired after maintenance status, and tried to display self-assurance that he did not feel.

At 1900, as the sun was starting to set, he held another briefing with his company commanders. He listened as his staff ran through the myriad of details that accompanied the running of a tank battalion: fuel, maintenance issues, a soldier had fallen and broken his arm, EMCON procedures, watch stations. Intel on the enemy was unchanged: Russian forces were unusually active, expect an attack at any moment.

Wozniak surveyed his officers in the dim light. More than half of the battalion was brand new, untested in battle. How would they perform? he wondered, then laughed at himself. How would *he* perform? Although he had survived the Battle of Sventragis, Wozniak felt no less nervous about the coming engagement than he had before his first actual battle.

"Sir?" the XO said, his face a blur in the darkness. "Anything to add?"

Wozniak hesitated. He needed to say something, but what?

"Trust your training, trust your crew," he said. "When it happens, it will happen fast, but your training will take over. Just focus on your job, and support each other." He chuckled. "The best thing you can do is get some sleep. Good luck and good hunting."

There was a chorus of yes, sirs. He made a point of shaking

each man's hand before they left. He might see them in the morning...or he might never see them again.

Back at his tank, Wozniak unrolled his sleeping bag on the back deck behind the bustle rack. He lay on his back, hands behind his head, and stared up into the darkness of the forest above him.

To his surprise, he fell asleep.

49

The Kremlin
Moscow, Russia

"You wanted to see me, Uncle?" Nikolay's voice was soft.

Luchnik's shoulders ached from hunching over the monitor, studying the faces of his cabinet members from hidden cameras. He straightened at the sound of his nephew's voice and spun in his chair.

"Nikolay," he said. The tremor in his eye had gotten worse. The right side of the younger man's face seemed to quiver in and out of focus. He could feel a migraine building at the base of his skull.

He searched his nephew's face. A frown of concern clouded the younger man's features.

"You remind me of your mother," Luchnik said. He remembered when he'd taken his sister in, her and her young son. Even then, at her lowest point, she'd been a proud woman, strong. He saw the same strength in her son. The trembling in his vision eased.

"You wanted to see me, Uncle?" Nikolay repeated. "It's almost time for the meeting."

"Let the bastards wait!" Luchnik said. He could tell by the way his nephew reacted that he'd spoken too harshly. "I wanted to talk to you first. Alone."

"Of course, sir." Nikolay dragged a chair close and sat down. "How can I help?"

Luchnik was distracted by movement on the security monitor. Prime Minister Mishinov hurried across the room and took the Foreign Minister's arm. The two huddled close in a conversation away from the rest of the pack. Those treasonous bastards, thought Luchnik.

"Uncle?" Nikolay repeated.

Luchnik dragged his attention back to his nephew. "I'm going to order a full-scale assault into the Suwalki Gap today. I want you to follow my orders to the letter. No matter what happens in that room." He pointed at the security monitor.

Nikolay sat up. For a second, it looked like he was going to protest, but he nodded his head. "Our men are ready, sir. But NATO has significant defenses in place. The losses will be..." He seemed to search for the right word. "There will be losses, Mr. President."

"There are always losses, Nikolay," Luchnik said. "If we can secure the land bridge into Kaliningrad, we will call for a ceasefire. We will negotiate from a position of strength."

"Yes, Mr. President." Nikolay hesitated.

"What is it?"

"The civilian unrest in Minsk has increased," Nikolay said. "Our supply lines are at risk, sir. I recommend we withdraw some forces to secure the capital."

"No!" Luchnik snapped. Nikolay drew back as if he'd been slapped.

Too much, Luchnik thought. The migraine was making him irritable.

"Ignore Minsk," he said. "We must regain the initiative on the ground in Lithuania. We can reinforce Minsk later with additional troops from other military districts."

"I understand, Uncle," Nikolay said. But Luchnik detected a look on the younger man's face. Was it doubt? He needed Nikolay for this last push. He trusted Nikolay.

He reached out, gripped the younger man's hand. Luchnik's fingers were numb with cold, Nikolay's palm was warm. "Are you with me, nephew?"

Nikolay looked down at the clasped hands. He raised his eyes, met his president's gaze.

"Always, Uncle."

Luchnik drank a cup of tea after his nephew left. He watched on the monitor as Nikolay joined his fellow cabinet members in the conference room. The younger man did not converse with his colleagues, just stood behind his place at the table next to Federov. The FSB chief looked up from his mobile phone, nodded once, and dropped his gaze back to the tiny screen.

Luchnik massaged the back of his neck. The migraine hammered through his skull like a piston with every beat of his heart.

Just a few more hours, he told himself. It will all be over in a few more hours. He imagined the hand-painted map on the wall of his private office. First thing tomorrow, he would order the new Russian territories be painted red. The thought brought a smile to his lips.

Luchnik marched into the conference room and took his seat without preamble. After a few seconds of waiting, the cabinet ministers settled into their own seats.

They're sheep, Luchnik thought, unable to act unless I tell them what to do.

To his right, the image of Foreign Minister Irimov fluttered in his vision. When Luchnik faced him, the older man looked down, avoiding his eyes. Irimov looked even graver than usual, his long face mournful, loose jowls sagging.

"You disgust me," Luchnik murmured.

"Sir?" Irimov reared his head back.

Did I say that out loud? Luchnik thought in a moment of panic. He turned to Nikolay. "Defense Minister, report, please."

Nikolay repeated the update he had given to his uncle only a few minutes prior. The mood in the room was somber when he finished.

"What about the American Marines?" Irimov asked.

"The amphibious landing force will enter the Kattegat within the hour," Nikolay said, referring to the strait between Denmark and Sweden that led into the Baltic. "Intel reports suggest that the Americans will land in Lithuania, at Klaipeda, to reinforce their NATO ally."

Perfect, Luchnik thought. The timing was perfect.

"Mr. President," Foreign Minister Irimov said. "I think it is time we consider our options."

"There is only one option, Sergey," Luchnik replied. "The Americans have forced my hand."

"Mr. President—"

Ignoring him, Luchnik faced Nikolay. Irimov disappeared in a flutter of disrupted vision. "Defense Minister."

"Sir." Nikolay rose to his feet as if he sensed the importance of the moment.

Luchnik took comfort in the steadying bulk of Federov on his left, his unblinking eyes following the President's every move. With Nikolay and Federov, he could run this country.

Those two were strong, not like the rest of the men in the room.

"What action do you recommend?" Luchnik asked. The migraine returned with throbbing vigor, like a bass drum in the background.

"Mr. President, I recommend we launch a full-scale attack into the Suwalki Gap. The time is now, sir."

Irimov stirred. "Sir, I—"

Luchnik held up a hand to silence him.

"Defense Minister Sokolov, launch the attack in the Suwalki Gap immediately."

"Mr. President," Irimov said.

Luchnik ignored him. "Defense Minister, carry out your orders."

"Yes, sir." Nikolay saluted and marched out of the room.

Luchnik sat back in his chair, staring at the row of blank faces all turned to him. They were afraid. They would protest, but they would fall in line. He owned them.

"What do we do now, sir?" Irimov asked. His face had taken on an ashen hue.

"Now, Sergey, we wait."

50

Zurich, Switzerland

The toe of Liz Soroush's shoe made a rapid *tick-tick-tick* on the floor of the monitoring room.

"Liz," said Treasury Agent Reggie Bowerman from the seat to her right. "Please."

Liz stilled her nervous energy. "Sorry." She turned her attention to the video screen, where a man in his early sixties sat behind a table in an interrogation room. He had thinning dark hair combed straight back and plastered against his skull and wore wire-rimmed glasses.

Despite the early hour—it was not even six a.m. local time—Herman Mueller's jowly cheeks were ruddy from a fresh shave, and he was dressed in an iron-gray Armani suit, crisp white shirt, and bright pink tie with matching pocket square. He looked around the empty interrogation room with a bemused smile, like an elementary school student on a field trip.

Liz leaned close to Bowerman. "Does this feel wrong to you?" she asked.

The Treasury agent grimaced at the screen. "I'm not seeing a consciousness of guilt, if that's what you mean."

"No," Liz replied in a whisper. "I mean the whole thing. We know this guy's schedule. He never even gets out of bed before seven, and yet today, when we move to take him down, he greets us like freaking Prince Charles on holiday."

"You think there's a leak?" Bowerman whispered back.

Liz scanned the room. The Kantonspolizei station in downtown Zurich was state of the art. Although the Swiss police had been nothing but cooperative with Liz and her investigation, it was likely they were being monitored right now.

"Let me think a minute," she said.

The last time she'd met with Don had been at Sentinel HQ in Sterling, Virginia. While Don coordinated the operation to strip Russian oligarchs of their wealth, Liz's job was to find out who was behind the goldmine of information contained in the mysterious thumb drive.

She had only one lead: Herr Mueller of Badertscher, Holenstein, Vischer, and Partners, money launderer to Luchnik's empire.

Ironically, the Russian invasion of Ukraine and Lithuania made her job easy. Her European partners almost tripped over themselves in their effort to assist in her investigation. It took her only a single email to get round-the-clock surveillance placed on Mueller and only two meetings to work out how and when to pick him up for questioning.

Mueller was a man of rigid habit. He rose at ten minutes after seven every morning. At quarter to eight, he left his apartment, rain or shine, and walked two blocks to a café for breakfast, where he ordered two soft-boiled eggs, rye toast, and coffee in a French press. He read his email on a tablet while he ate and departed the café at quarter to nine, carrying a chocolate croissant in a small box. He arrived at his place of work at three minutes to nine, took the elevator down to the basement, and disappeared behind an EM-shielded wall, where he remained for the next twelve hours.

Herr Mueller received no visitors and had no known romantic relationships. On Saturdays, a housekeeper visited his flat to clean and prepare meals for his weeknight dinners, which she stored in the freezer along with detailed instructions on how to reheat the food.

A team broke into Mueller's flat but found no evidence of his secret business relationship with the Russian oligarchy. Mueller didn't even own a safe. The American operative who led the break-in team wrote in his report that the subject's life was as exciting as watching grass grow—in slow motion.

And yet, despite all of their preparations, Mueller had managed to surprise them. Their plan had been to roust him out of bed before dawn and transport the disoriented subject to the police station for questioning.

There was no benefit to letting Mueller realize that the Americans were behind his capture, so the takedown was conducted by the Swiss. The team of six entered Mueller's apartment to find the man fully dressed and waiting for them. Liz watched the video feed in disbelief as he greeted the police team in a cheerful voice and held out his wrists to be cuffed. He nodded as they read him his rights and escorted him to a waiting transport.

What did we miss? Liz wondered. Mueller had obviously been warned about the pending raid, so why hadn't he run?

"Liz." Bowerman nudged her with his elbow. He jerked his chin at the video screen, where two Swiss police officers were entering the room.

Mueller smiled amiably and got to his feet. He shook hands with both men as if they were at a business meeting. Liz didn't speak German, but she recognized police procedure. As one officer started to speak, Mueller waved his hands and said in English: "You're wasting time, officer."

"Excuse me?" the officer replied.

"These preliminary interviews are a waste of time," Mueller said. He looked directly at the camera on the ceiling. "I wish to speak to Special Agent Elizabeth Soroush."

"Holy shit," Bowerman muttered. "Who is this guy?"

Liz felt her shoulders lock up with tension. She forced herself to breathe. Her instincts were right; this was a setup.

"I don't know who that person is," the officer said to Mueller.

Mueller smiled. He unfurled his pocket square into a pink silk handkerchief and polished the lenses of his glasses. "Yes, you do," he replied in a calm voice, "and she wants to talk to me."

Liz bolted to her feet, sending the chair rolling behind her.

"Let's go," she said.

"Liz, we need to let the process play out—" Bowerman protested.

"There isn't time, Reg," Liz snapped. "Either he's useful or he's not, and right now, it seems like he knows a lot more than we do."

The interior of the interrogation room was dingier than it looked on the video screen. The floor was vinyl, and the walls were covered with some sort of cheap plastic. The atmosphere was warm enough that Liz started to sweat as soon as she closed the door behind her.

Herman Mueller had not aged well. Up close, she could see that his skin was flaccid and age-spotted. His too-wide grin showed yellowed teeth. He got to his feet when she entered and extended his hand. Liz ignored it. Mueller shrugged and indicated the seat across from him at the interrogation table.

"Please," he said, as if they were at dinner.

He laced his fingers together and leaned forward across the table. "Can I see some identification, Ms. Soroush?" He grimaced slightly. "I'm sorry to ask, but I need to verify who I'm speaking with."

Liz felt an odd flush of embarrassment as she removed her ID and tossed it onto the table. Mueller picked it up and studied it, then slid it back across the table to her.

"Again, I apologize for the rudeness of my request, but we are nearly out of time."

"So you said," Liz replied. "Time for what, Herr Mueller?"

He evaded the question. "I believe it is in both our interests to turn off recording devices, Ms. Soroush."

"You are under arrest for money laundering, sir," Liz said, trying to reestablish some level of control of the interview. "The law requires this interview be recorded as evidence."

Mueller's placid face clouded with anger. "We don't have time for this." He leaned across the table and hissed at her. "It's about Pandora."

It took everything in Liz not to react, but she succeeded. Holding Mueller's gaze, she mentally counted to ten. The older man squirmed in his chair, looked away. He had one card to play, Liz realized, and that was it.

"Reg," Liz called out, "stop all recordings for the next five minutes."

There was a long pause. "Done, Liz." The microphone clicked off.

Mueller's confident façade melted. "I want immunity," he said.

Liz crossed her arms. "Tell me about Pandora."

"He told me to say that to convince you that I was authentic. I don't know what it means."

"Who told you to say it?" Liz demanded.

Mueller shook his head. "That's not how this is going to work."

"Really."

"I get immunity, you get a phone number. What you do with it is up to you."

"Who is Pandora?" Liz asked.

"I don't know," Mueller replied. "These people don't talk to me directly. They use cutouts to protect their identity. I can say this: whoever it is, they know everything about my operation. From the way you reacted when I said Pandora, they know about you, too."

"Is it Luchnik?" Liz pressed.

"I don't know." Mueller sounded exasperated. He drew in a sharp breath. "I don't think so."

"Why not?"

Mueller hesitated. "They use cutouts, but there's a style to how these things happen. I don't think it's him."

"Then who?"

"I. Don't. Know."

"Guess," Liz ordered.

Mueller shook his head, pressed his lips together. He folded his arms. "I have a phone number. You have the power to ensure my freedom. That's the deal."

Liz let the silence settle over the room. There was a clock over the door behind her, and she heard the *tick-tick-tick* of the second hand like hammer blows in the stillness.

"Tell me the number," she said.

"You'll make sure I go free?"

Liz nodded.

"I have your word?"

Liz nodded again.

Mueller rattled off a series of digits. Liz pulled a notebook from her pocket and wrote them down.

Somewhere over her head, Liz heard a microphone click on.

"Liz." Bowerman's voice. "That's five minutes."

"We're done here." Liz got to her feet. Mueller's eyes followed her.

"Please arrange for Herr Mueller to get a ride home."

51

Puzonys, Lithuania

"Incoming!"

The scream that interrupted Wozniak's dream was primal, sharp with adrenaline and laced with fear. He snapped awake, sitting up just in time to see a ball of intense white light streak down from the sky and impact the woods behind him.

His world erupted in a massive explosion.

The force of the blast knocked him off the back of the tank. He hit the ground hard, tasted dirt. His ears rang. His head throbbed.

Wozniak forced himself to his hands and knees and scrambled back up the tank. He heaved himself over the bustle rack onto the top of the turret. He slithered down the tank commander's hatch, then twisted his body and pulled the hatch closed behind him.

To his left, Kaminski hugged his arms tight across his chest, his eyes white with fear. Wozniak pulled the CPC over his head, feeling the padding of the headphones nest around his ears.

"Report," he said on the open circuit.

"We're all in, sir," Nowak, the gunner, replied. "All buttoned up. Engine's on."

The viewports in the tank commander's cupola blazed orange with another nearby explosion, and the tank rocked in response.

Wozniak switched to the battalion circuit. "Company commanders, report in." His ears still rang from the first blast, and he knew he was shouting into the circuit.

Calm down, he told himself. Speak slowly. They're all watching you.

Bravo and Charlie came back immediately with sitreps. Alpha did not respond.

Another explosion. Wozniak looked out the viewports again. The tank fifty meters to his right was burning.

He switched to the brigade circuit and listened in. NATO forces were responding with their own multiple launch rocket systems and artillery. Wozniak craned his head so he could see the sky out of the viewports. In the predawn darkness, he could see shafts of light like shooting stars arc across the sky, some going east, some west.

"What is that, sir?" Kaminski asked.

"Rockets," Wozniak said.

The newest Russian MLR systems were fearsome weapons. Three-hundred-millimeter rockets with a range of a hundred kilometers that could blanket an area the size of twenty hectares.

The men in his tank did not speak, as if their silence would somehow protect them. Wozniak heard their breathing over the open circuit, and he sensed what they were feeling.

They'd risked their lives in battle against Russian tanks, but this was different. Here, there was nothing they could do except wait. Short of a direct hit, they were safe inside their tank.

But a direct hit was not impossible. Whether they lived through this moment depended on luck.

Just as quickly as it began, the barrage stopped. Wozniak waited a ten count.

Nothing.

He counted to ten one more time, then opened the tank commander's hatch and stood up in the cupola.

Devastation. The towering oak trees of the forest were gone. Shattered stumps remained, like white fangs in the dim light. Fresh craters were gouged out of the forest floor, and a layer of fine dirt covered everything. The tank fifty meters to his right was still burning.

Wozniak switched to the battalion circuit and called for damage assessments. He had Nowak receive the reports while he listened into the brigade circuit.

The Russian attack was on. A full assault, three lines abreast moving cross-country at top speed. Tanks in the front line, followed by APCs and infantry fighting vehicles. There were no Russian reserves. This was the attack they'd both feared and expected.

Their orders: all units engage.

The damage report was grim. His newly reinforced fifty-eight tank battalion was now forty-three tanks, a combination of kills and disabled units. He'd lost a quarter of his fighting strength in less than fifteen minutes.

Wozniak felt a slow burn of anger at the utter stupidity of this unprovoked war.

"All units," he ordered, "move out, line abreast."

The gas turbine whined as the tank rolled forward, Zielinski navigating carefully through the shattered ground. The last thing they needed now was a damaged track.

"Helos inbound!" Nowak called.

Wozniak pressed his binoculars to his eyes. On the horizon, he picked out a row of dots. They were too far away to identify, but there was only one reason to lead an assault with helos: to hunt enemy tanks.

He called for air support from brigade and switched to the battalion circuit. "All units, this is Romeo Six-six actual," he said. "Incoming helos. Target with machine guns."

The closing speed of the Russian helos was hundreds of kilometers an hour, and by the time Wozniak looked up again, he could see them with his naked eye. They dropped down to race close to the ground. The air reverberated with the deep-throated *chug-chug* of fifty-caliber machine guns engaging the incoming targets. He dropped back into the hatch, slammed the lid shut.

"Driver, move!" Wozniak ordered. Whatever cover they'd had from the forest was gone. Mobility was their best defense.

The first helo fired a salvo of anti-tank missiles. Wozniak saw the blaze of an explosion at ground level. A second helo tried hovering to take a shot, and it came under fire from machine guns.

Where were their anti-air defenses? Wozniak thought.

"Brigade, this is Romeo Six-six actual," Wozniak said on the brigade circuit. "We are under attack. Request immediate air support."

Two more Russian helos hovered and released rocket fire.

One of the enemy birds burst into flames and dove into the ground. Two NATO F-35s passed so close over Wozniak's tank that he felt the thunder of the jet engines above them.

"Yes!" Nowak shouted.

The Russian helos scattered just as his tank reached the edge of the debris field.

Wozniak popped the TC hatch and stood again. The

terrain ahead was a sea of waving green grass. The sun rose behind him, lighting the morning dew so that it looked like water all the way to the horizon. He looked to his right and left. The rest of his battalion was emerging from the rough ground of the artillery attack.

He switched to the battalion circuit. "Husaria," he said. "All units form a line on me. Max speed. Forward!"

Beneath him, the tank lurched ahead, cutting a trail through the waist-high grass. Dew released by the passing of the tanks sprayed into the air, painted his face with moisture. The sun caught the spray, and miniature rainbows formed in the mist.

It might have been the most beautiful thing he'd ever seen.

Wozniak dropped back inside and slammed his hatch shut.

The ride of an M1A2 Abrams tank at speed was luxurious. Wozniak swayed with the gentle motion as he studied the intel display. With both lines of Polish and Russian armor at max speed, they were closing at something like a hundred kilometers an hour. The enemy would be in range any minute now.

While Wozniak focused on tightening up his line of advance to account for lost units, Nowak scanned across the sixty-degree arc in front of them, flicking between magnifications as he searched the horizon for enemy tanks.

Wozniak felt his crew lock into the moment, their sharpened focus almost audible to him. He did not need to direct this crew anymore. They were veterans. They knew what to do.

Nowak's scanning stopped. Wozniak saw him focus on a point on the horizon, cycle through low to high magnifications.

"Target, tank." The gunner's voice was measured.

"Gunner, sabot, tank," Wozniak replied.

"Up!" Kaminski flattened himself against the far wall.

"Identified, range twenty-five hundred meters."

"Gunner," Wozniak said. "Fire at will."

52

White House Situation Room
Washington, DC

The National Security Council meeting was limited to the President's closest advisers—and Don. He occupied a seat at the main table next to CIA Director Blank, four places down from the President and directly across from Secretary of State Henry Hahn.

The new Chairman of the Joint Chiefs stood at the lectern at the front of the room. A graphic of the ongoing battle in the Suwalki Gap filled the screen behind him. The running clock in the upper right-hand corner of the screen showed the battle had been running for over three hours.

Don tried to imagine what it was like in the battle space. Armor, airpower, infantry, all grinding away at each other over a forty-kilometer front. His imagination failed him.

The room felt strangely empty without all the staffers lining the walls two deep, and when Chairman McCleave spoke, there was a hint of an echo.

"Mr. President, we're holding our own, but the Russians show no sign of backing down."

"That's not good enough, General," Serrano said. "I need to know we can stop them in the Gap. Otherwise, we need to make contingency plans."

"Sir," McCleave said, "the situation is fluid. If things deteriorate on the ground, we make adjustments. That's the best we can do, sir."

"Are there any signs of this conflict escalating beyond conventional weapons?" the Secretary of State asked. "Can we keep it contained?"

McCleave shot a look at the Secretary of Defense. "There's been a development in that area—not a good one. Before this meeting, I attempted to reach out to Russian Defense Minister General Yakov. My call did not go through."

"What does that mean?" National Security Advisor Flores asked.

Secretary of Defense Howard answered. "It's...possible he's been replaced."

"We have unconfirmed reports that Yakov is under arrest in Lefortovo Prison," Director Blank added. "That information is less than an hour old. We're trying to confirm, but given the poor performance of the Russian military in Ukraine and now in Lithuania, it's probable."

"Who's the deputy?" Serrano asked.

"Admiral Nikolay Sokolov," the Chairman said.

Serrano gaped. "Luchnik's nephew?" The President leaned back in his chair. "He's consolidating power."

"It's possible, sir," the Director said. "We know that the nephew also has strong personal ties to the leader of the Rosgvardiya. It certainly looks like a power move."

"Shit, he's not going to stop." The President turned his attention back to the Chairman. "Where are the Marines?"

McCleave changed screens to show a graphic of the Baltic Sea. "They're coming through the Kattegat, sir," he said, referring to the strait between Denmark and Sweden. "Once they make the turn east—"

"I don't need a navigation lesson, General," Serrano snapped. "How long until we can put Marines on the beach? Best possible speed."

"Eight hours to land Marines on Point Cocoa," the Chairman replied, circling the city of Klaipeda, Lithuania. "They head south from there to engage—"

"Not Cocoa," the President said. "I want to land them at Point Vodka."

"Sir?"

"You heard me, General. How long to put Marines on the beach at Kaliningrad?"

"Six hours, sir, but that would be—"

"Mr. President," the Secretary of State interrupted, "an amphibious landing by US forces in Kaliningrad would represent a significant escalation in this conflict. We would be invading sovereign Russian territory with US Marines."

"As a response to Russians invading sovereign Lithuanian soil," Serrano replied, acid in his tone. "Is there a difference, Henry?"

"The difference is that we're Americans, sir. Our actions matter. If we do this, we're no better than Luchnik." The Secretary of State and the President glared at each other across the expanse of mahogany between them.

Don wished he knew what Serrano was thinking. In the last day, the President's political world had collapsed like a house of cards. Although US public support for action against the Russians was high, support for Serrano as the leader behind those actions had cratered. His plan to keep Ukraine out of the news and to focus on domestic issues had failed spectacularly. Serrano was now shouldering the blame for having made the situation worse, and his enemies were feasting on his political corpse.

"You're right, Henry," he said. "We are better than this." Serrano suddenly smiled, but it was not a grin. It was more like a cornered dog baring its teeth. "I have no intention of putting Marines on the beach in Kaliningrad, but I want Luchnik to think I will."

"Why?" Hahn and the Chairman asked together.

The President turned to Don. "Mr. Riley? I think it's time you briefed the room on Operation Robin Hood."

All eyes in the room followed Don to the lectern. As succinctly as he could, Don described the financial information uncovered in South Dakota and implications to Luchnik's inner circle.

"What's the provenance of this information?" the Secretary of Defense asked.

"It's tricky," Don admitted. He explained the operation to take down the man in charge of the Russian money-laundering operation in Zurich.

"This contact just gave up the phone number," the Secretary of Defense said. "That's too easy, right? Do we know who the phone number belongs to?"

"No," Don said. "It's a valid Moscow number, two months old. The NSA has been able to track the usage history. Although the phone has never been used to make a call or send a text, it's been deliberately turned on over the past month. We have verified location data for that phone in the Security Council Meeting Room inside the Kremlin."

"So, all we really know is that someone in Luchnik's inner circle has a burner phone and we have their number," National Security Advisor Flores said. "But we don't know who it is."

"Yes, ma'am," Don replied. "That is correct."

"And you propose that we act on this financial information?"

"Seizing the assets of the people around Luchnik could be significantly destabilizing," Don said, choosing his words carefully. "It might be a catalyst for a change in leadership."

"Or it might make a desperate man push the button," Flores snapped. "Mr. President, don't you think that we should have more eyes on this problem than just Mr. Riley and his select team?"

"Why not just call the number and see who answers?" Hahn asked. "What have we got to lose?"

The Director answered the question. "This source, whoever he is, has gone to great lengths to hide his identity. Any outreach by us could blow his cover."

"I think it's risky, sir," Flores said. "Hold off. Give this more time."

"There is no more time, Valentina," Serrano said. "We need to flip the script on this problem. Luchnik is about to feel the full burden of his actions." The President looked at Don.

"Proceed with the operation, Mr. Riley."

The sun was over the horizon as Don exited the South Entrance of the White House and jogged toward the waiting UH-60 Black Hawk helicopter. Morning dew covered his shoes, and the summer air was already hot.

Don boarded, strapped in, and slipped on a pair of headphones from the crew chief. His stomach lurched as the helicopter lifted off.

"Welcome aboard, Mr. Riley," the pilot said. "We're looking at a fifteen-minute trip out to Sterling, sir."

His mind told him to savor the moment. A private helo transport from the White House would be something he'd tell his grandkids about...if he ever had any.

Instead, Don stared out the window as they rose above the White House and looped around to the east. Below him passed the Washington Monument, the morning sun coloring the Reflecting Pool leading to the Lincoln Memorial. The Capitol loomed in the distance.

Although the images registered, Don's mind remained engrossed in the problem at hand.

Was he doing the right thing? He tried not to think of what Luchnik's next move might be. Chemical weapons? Biological? Tactical nukes? Any of those would be devastating to the men and women on the front lines.

The only thing more dangerous than Luchnik was a cornered Luchnik.

That's not your problem, Don, he told himself. Stay focused. The President of the United States heard your proposal, validated it, and gave you a direct order. It's out of your hands.

When the Black Hawk touched down on the helo pad outside Sentinel headquarters, Josh was waiting for him. He quickly brought Don up to speed as they walked rapidly to the elevators.

"Skelly's in the Planetarium," he said, "and Mama's online."

"What's the probability of success she gives for the operation?" Don asked.

"The models show we can take down sixty-eight percent of the assets before the targets can react," Josh answered as they entered the elevator.

That wasn't the answer Don was looking for. "What about displacing Luchnik as a response to the operation?"

The doors opened onto the dome-shaped underground room of the Sentinel ops center, known as the Planetarium. Don held the door, waiting for the answer.

"Insufficient data," Josh said.

Don stepped out of the elevator. The room hummed with nervous energy. There were over a hundred people on the ops floor, a combination of CIA and Sentinel personnel broken into teams. Each team was assigned one oligarch and had been working round the clock on preparations to seize physical assets and drain bank accounts all over the world.

Convincing the Director to use a civilian facility to run the most sophisticated financial takedown in the history of the world had been no small task, but given the time constraints, Don insisted. He mounted the command cockpit steps, where Manson Skelly waited for him.

"Our fearless leader returns," Skelly crowed.

Don gritted his teeth. Somehow Skelly made every comment sound like a put-down. Don ignored him. "I have a go for the operation," he said. "Let's get our teams ready."

Skelly spun in his chair and flipped down the microphone on his headset. "All teams, this is the man in the big chair. We have a green light on this operation. Get your ground teams in place and report in as soon as they are ready for action."

He looked over his shoulder at Don and winked. "This is so fucking awesome, man. I love my job."

Don stared at the back of Skelly's head. He missed Abby. The preliminary investigation into her and Dylan's deaths had determined that their jet had been shot down by a Russian radar-guided surface-to-air missile fired from a Buk mobile system. There would be a more complete investigation, but that might be months away. The accident had happened in a war zone. Don wasn't holding his breath that anyone would ever get to the truth behind Abby Cromwell's death.

Don watched Skelly lace his fingers behind his head and flex his biceps. Was it possible he'd had something to do with it?

Don dismissed the idea. Abby and Skelly were partners, friends. Sure, there were disagreements, but...no, he decided.

Don paced. He knew it would take time to coordinate ground teams across a dozen time zones and legal jurisdictions. There were seizure teams in financial capitals, in tony marinas where mega-yachts were docked, near airport warehouses where valuable art pieces were stored in tax exclusion zones.

"How much longer, Skelly?" Don asked.

The bushy black-and-gray beard almost hid Skelly's pursed lips. "I'd say another forty-five minutes to an hour. You need a potty break before the fun begins?"

"I'm going topside to get some air," Don said.

When he stepped outside of the headquarters building, the humid heat of northern Virginia in full summer wrapped around Don like a wet blanket. Cicadas screamed at him as he crunched through the crowded gravel parking lot.

He pulled out his phone and scrolled to the unknown Russian phone number.

If he was about to upend the Russian power structure, wouldn't it be nice to know who was on the other end of this play?

Without thinking, Don tapped out a text and hit send.

Who is this? he wrote.

Immediately, Don regretted his action. He was sending a text in English to a Russian. What the hell was he thinking?

Three dots appeared. The person on the other end of the text was typing a message back.

The three dots pulsed. Don stared as if he could will an answer from the phone.

The three dots disappeared.

Don realized he was holding his breath, and he let out an explosive exhale.

His lonely text hung at the top of the screen, waiting for a reply.

"Don."

He jumped. It was Josh, standing a few feet away.

"Skelly's looking for you," he said. "They're ready."

Josh walked him to the elevator and pushed the button. "Destroy them, Don," he said. "Do it for Abby."

The doors opened, and Don got in. "For Abby."

Don marched right across the Planetarium floor and entered the command cockpit.

"Bossman," Skelly said with a wide grin. "We are ready to get rich."

"Mr. Skelly," Don replied, "you can address me as Don, Mr. Riley, or sir. Anything else is inappropriate. Clear?"

Skelly's smile evaporated. He shrugged. "Anything you say...*sir*."

"I'm glad we cleared that up, Manson," Don said. "Now, let's go make some Russian assholes really unhappy."

"Yes, sir."

53

The Kremlin
Moscow, Russia

"Defense Minister, report," Luchnik said.

Over the course of the last few hours, the battle in Suwalki Gap had raged on. Nikolay had been in and out of the room multiple times, receiving updates from the battlefield commanders and giving them additional orders.

The video surveillance on the large screen monitor was all but useless. The coverage was spotty, and when they had visual imagery, all Luchnik could see was smoke.

This is taking too long, Luchnik thought. Even accounting for the superior NATO airpower, the numbers clearly favored the Russian forces on the ground. His troops should have cleared a path to Kaliningrad an hour ago.

All eyes in the meeting room turned toward Nikolay. In the light from the two crystal chandeliers that graced the grand room, Luchnik could see his nephew's face was drawn, his complexion pale. He caught Nikolay's eye, and Luchnik did not like what he saw.

"Defense Minister," he repeated. "Report."

Nikolay swallowed, an indication of bad news to come, Luchnik realized. He seemed to be trying to tell his uncle something with his eyes, but what?

"No change, Mr. President," Nikolay said finally. "The southern end of the NATO line was softening, but they've reinforced it now."

"Send in the reserves," Luchnik said.

Nikolay swallowed again. "The reserves are already in, sir. Our advance is stalled. Our losses are significant, sir. I recommend that we—"

"No!" Luchnik's fist hammered the table.

It's all falling apart, he thought. Unless I can change the momentum of the battle right now, all is lost.

He could feel the eyes of the men in the room—men he owned body and soul—scrutinizing him with something like disdain or pity. Their gazes felt like ants on his skin. Their unspoken thoughts screamed at him: Vitaly Luchnik made the biggest gamble of his life...and lost. His right eye trembled with the indignation of the moment.

"Kaliningrad." Luchnik blurted out the word like an order.

Silence.

"Mr. President?" Nikolay finally said.

His nephew had that look again. What was that look?

"Launch an attack on the NATO forces from Kaliningrad," Luchnik said.

"Mr. President," Irimov said. "If you do that, then the United States Marines will—"

"I'm not finished yet, Sergey!" Luchnik shouted.

He heard a ringing in the silence that followed his outburst. Too loud, Luchnik thought. Too forceful. He clenched his eyes closed to stop the damn fluttering in his right eye. He drew in a deep breath and counted to four. He opened his eyes.

"I'm sorry, Sergey," he said to Irimov in a calm tone. "I don't like to be interrupted."

"It was rude of me, Mr. President." The Foreign Minister's tone was distant. "Please forgive me."

Luchnik smiled. "Of course, my friend."

He felt a calm wash over him. He knew what he had to do now. What the NATO commanders would never expect. This game was not over. He still had cards to play.

"Where is the US amphibious force?" he asked Nikolay.

"They've exited the Kattegat, sir," Nikolay replied. "They're in open water."

"Excellent," Luchnik said. "I want you to launch a missile strike on the American ships."

"Sir?" Nikolay locked eyes with him. The look was there again. What did it mean?

"I want you to use the battery of Zircon missiles in Kaliningrad," Luchnik continued. "The Americans will not be able to stop a full complement of hypersonic missiles. Obliterate the American amphibious task force."

It was as if he'd sucked the oxygen out of the room. Luchnik smiled, his migraine gone, the tremor in his vision disappeared. The air around him boiled with energy.

This is my moment, Luchnik thought. The event that will define me for all of history. I will be the man who restored the Russian Empire to greatness. A modern-day tsar.

"Mr. President," Irimov said, "this is inviting a NATO response that we may not be able to contain." He lowered his voice. "Sir, please don't do this."

Irimov's objection released the tension in the room, and it seemed as if every minister was speaking at once. Luchnik leaned back in his chair, at peace with his decision. Let them whine and carp at him. He knew what he was doing.

Mishinov, seated far down the table, pulled out his mobile phone and focused on the screen. He looked up, an expression of shock on his face. He leaned close to the man seated next to him, whispered in his ear. The man pulled out his own phone.

Nikolay, still standing, nodded to his uncle. He turned and left the room.

Luchnik watched him go with something like fatherly pride. This victory was as much Nikolay's as his. None of this would have been possible without his nephew's help. He closed his eyes.

"Mr. President." Irimov's voice interrupted his reverie. "Vitaly."

At the mention of his given name, Luchnik focused on the Foreign Minister. "What is it, Sergey?"

Irimov was holding his mobile phone. They were all holding their mobile phones. "It's..." Irimov's voice trailed off. He handed the phone to Luchnik.

The screen was on the homepage of the *Novaya Gazeta*, one of the few independent newspapers he'd allowed to survive to give the veneer of journalistic independence in his Russia.

The headline was a single word: *CORRUPTION*.

Luchnik sneered. He'd seen this headline a thousand times. He started to hand the phone back.

"Read it," Irimov said. His voice was hard.

Luchnik used the tip of his finger to scroll down the screen. The first two paragraphs were words he had seen before. Then he saw the list. A detailed breakdown of the assets of every man in the room with him.

Luchnik's head snapped up. Every eye was on him, every

gaze a glare. He swiveled his head to look at Federov. The head of the FSB was responsible for managing news content.

"How...?" he began.

Federov got to his feet slowly, as if shouldering a great weight. He looked his president directly in the eye, then he swept his gaze down the table.

"Mr. President, Ministers, you are under arrest for treasonous acts against your country."

Luchnik shattered the shocked silence with a laugh. He turned to the Rosgvardiya guards at the door.

"Arrest this man," he ordered.

The two guards did not move.

Luchnik's heavy chair made a screeching sound against the marble floor as he got to his feet.

"Bring me Kulukov," he roared. "Now!"

The double doors to the room opened, and Nikolay appeared. Behind him were at least a dozen heavily armed Rosgvardiya troops—and Kulukov.

Relief flooded through Luchnik as the armed men entered the room. Nikolay approached. His face was tight, his eyes hard.

"Uncle," he said. "It's over."

54

3 kilometers east of Puzonys, Lithuania

For Wozniak, time had no meaning. Thirty minutes might have passed since first contact with the enemy, or it could have been three hours; he did not know—or care.

The morning sun was lost behind clouds of thick black smoke. The air in the turret of his tank was sharp with the smell of gunpowder. So intent was his focus that Wozniak found himself forgetting to breathe.

Three things consumed his attention: the MAPS display told him the number and location of the remaining tanks in his battalion, the targeting display cycled as Nowak searched for their next target, and the folded topographical map that he held in his left hand told Wozniak what the terrain around them looked like.

WHUMP. The main gun fired again.

They had learned a lot about their enemy. Things that were not in tech manuals.

For one, the Russian T-14 Armata tanks were hard to kill. It was taking an average of two shots to take down one tank. A fact made real by their rapidly dwindling store of ammunition.

Kaminski pushed a fresh round into the open breech of the 120mm main gun. As the breech door closed, the young man stepped back against the wall in preparation for another firing evolution.

"How many rounds left, Kaminski?" Wozniak asked.

The young man held up eight fingers. They'd started the day with thirty-eight rounds.

The other thing Wozniak had learned this morning was that a human loader was much faster than the automatic reload function on the Russian tanks. Twice, when they needed a second shot to kill the enemy, the young man to his left had been the difference between living and dying.

Their tank had taken two hits during the morning. One was a glancing blow off the turret. The second hit impacted the right rear quarter. They felt that one, but the ERA fixed along the side of the tank did its job.

Explosive reactive armor were expendable blocks of explosive material sandwiched between two plates of metal. Used as an extra layer of protection over the fixed armor on their M1A2 Abrams tank, the ERA disrupted and deflected the incoming shaped charge of the Russian projectile.

If Wozniak ever met the engineer who designed the ERA on their tank, he owed that engineer a hug and as much beer as they could drink.

Assuming you live to the end of the day, Wozniak thought.

"Colonel," Nowak said over the intercom.

"What is it, gunner?" Wozniak answered.

"The field is clear up ahead, sir," Nowak said. "No targets."

"Forward, driver," Wozniak said. The tank picked up speed.

They ran for half a kilometer with Nowak continually

scanning the terrain ahead of them. Wozniak consulted his topographical map. The countryside did not offer much protection. The field really was clear.

"Nothing, sir," Nowak said, still scanning. "They're gone."

We broke through the Russian line, Wozniak thought. He'd been monitoring the brigade circuit. The battle raged on to their north and south, but his battalion had broken the enemy line.

With a growing sense of excitement, Wozniak reported his progress to brigade and advised he was going to use the gap to flank the Russian position.

"All units, this is Romeo Six-six," he announced on the battalion circuit. "We have a break in the Russian line. Surge forward. I repeat, surge forward now."

The tank picked up speed, settling into the gentle feeling of floating. He checked the MAPS display. The thirty-two remaining tanks in the battalion formed a flying wedge behind him, each tank trailing the one in front by fifty meters and offset. Their main guns would be searching a ninety-degree arc from straight ahead to their exposed side.

They rolled across once-green fields and cow pastures, over flattened fences, and past leveled barns.

One kilometer passed, then two kilometers, with no enemy contact.

"Where are they?" Nowak asked.

"Stay sharp," Wozniak replied.

"Coming up on three klicks, sir," Zielinski said. Wozniak could hear the strain in his voice.

"Contact! Left side!"

From the TC viewport, Wozniak saw one of his trailing tanks take a hit. Contact reports flowed in over the battalion circuit.

"Target, tank!" Nowak announced.

"Sabot," Wozniak replied.

"Identified. Nine-fifty meters."

On the targeting display, Wozniak made out a structure up ahead. An old stone barn. The familiar angular shape of a Russian T-14 emerged from behind the building.

"Fire!" Wozniak said.

WHUMP. Nowak scored a direct hit on the enemy tank.

Then a second tank emerged from behind the barn. Wozniak cursed to himself. They'd driven straight into a Russian ambush.

"Fire at will, gunner!" Wozniak turned his attention to the map. He had no idea how many more tanks were hidden behind that structure, and he needed to find cover.

His finger found a small stream in a shallow gully a hundred meters ahead.

"Driver, forward," Wozniak ordered. "Look for a stream. Get us out of the line of fire."

Seconds later, he felt the tank slope downward. From the TC viewports, he could see they were sheltered for the moment.

"There's at least one more still out there, sir," Nowak reported. "Maybe more."

Think, he told himself. To stay still was to get killed. But if they rolled up out of the gully, they'd expose their underside to the enemy tank—that was a sure way to die.

"Sir," Nowak said.

"I'm gonna launch smoke," Wozniak said. "Driver, go right. Follow the stream. When I give the order, I want you to bring us into the open. Nowak, that's when you take your shot."

"Yes, sir," they both said in unison.

Wozniak armed the smoke grenade launcher. "Go, Zielinski!" He punched the button. Outside, the M250 launcher punched out a dozen smoke grenades. They arced away from the moving tank like a spiderweb, blanketing a hundred square meters with a thick cloud of chemical smoke.

The tank pivoted and raced down the stream. From the viewports, Wozniak watched the level of the bank above them until it no longer concealed the top of the tank.

"Now, driver!" Wozniak shouted. The tank angled up, crested the steep side of the gully. The main gun slewed as Nowak searched for his target.

The enemy tank was close, too close. The image filled the entire targeting screen.

"Fire!" Wozniak shouted.

WHUMP. The round left the main gun...and glanced off the turret of the Russian tank.

"Reengage!" Nowak cried. "Re—"

Their tank slewed violently to the right. Wozniak's helmet slammed against the steel wall of the turret. A new smell filled the tank, the slick odor of hydraulic oil, the sharpness of ozone.

"We're hit!" Zielinski said. "The left track is gone."

"Target, tank!" Nowak cried.

Next to Wozniak, Kaminski staggered to his feet. Blood poured down the side of his face. The ammo door, run by hydraulics, opened a few centimeters, then stopped.

Kaminski put his fingers in the door and pulled. Wozniak leaned across and pushed the heavy steel plate.

"Kaminski!" Nowak said.

The door yielded enough to allow the loader to access a sabot round. He drew out the heavy shell. He tried to pivot to load the shell into the open breech and fell to his knees. Wozniak took the round from his arms and slammed it into the breech.

"Fire!" he yelled, pushing Kaminski out of the way.

"On the way!" Nowak replied.

Nothing happened.

"Misfire," Nowak said. "On the way," he repeated as he tried the manual firing device.

Nothing.

"Again," Wozniak said.

"Nothing, sir." Nowak's voice was calm. "Checking the breaker...breaker reset."

Wozniak's gaze swept to the targeting display. The Russian tank had stopped, its main gun leveled at their tank. Any second now, they'd be dead.

"Rearming the gun," Nowak said. "Negative response."

We're dead, Wozniak thought.

But the enemy tank did not fire.

The Russian tank began to back away, its main gun still aimed at Romeo 66. Then the main gun lifted, the tank slewed to the right and sped away.

"What the hell?" Nowak said.

"The Russians are retreating," came the call over the brigade circuit.

Wozniak slammed open the TC hatch. Although the air that flooded into the turret was thick with chemical smoke, to Wozniak it smelled sweet.

He climbed out of the TC cupola and stood on the turret. In the thinning smoke, he saw a group of four Russian tanks racing west, their main guns pointed away from the NATO lines.

The smoke gnawed at the back of his throat, made his eyes water.

"Everybody, out," he called down into the tank. "It's over."

55

From Don's position standing at the rear of the main auditorium of Finlandia Hall, the larger-than-life image of United States President Ricardo Serrano filled the big screen on the stage.

He was dressed in a dark blue suit, red power tie, and white shirt. Although it was nearly nine in the evening, Serrano was freshly shaved and his hair was ready for prime time. He looked and acted like a man who had been resurrected from political death, which was exactly what he was.

He cocked an eyebrow and stared into the distance, then he flashed a smile that lit up the screen. Although he knew it was ridiculous, Don felt that somehow Serrano was talking directly to him, and he was sure every other person in the room with a pulse felt the same way.

"You know," Serrano said in his heavy baritone, "for decades my country has talked about a 'Russian Reset,' but it's always been empty talk." He let a dramatic pause lengthen in the silent room. "Until now."

Applause, cheering, another just-for-you grin.

"Leadership matters," Serrano intoned. "Relationships matter, and that is why I am proud to call President Sokolov my new friend. Thanks to him, the world is about to become a very different place."

A roving cameraman captured Sokolov in the moment and beamed the image up to the big screen. Serrano turned toward the screen and clapped along with the audience.

Nikolay Sokolov stood, waved. With his swept-back blond hair and ready smile, he was old enough to be taken seriously and young enough to be attractive. The perfect antidote to his deposed uncle Vitaly Luchnik.

Don rubbed his eyes. He'd been brought on the trip to consult on the terms of the Helsinki Peace Accord, and the hours had been brutal. He looked forward to a good night's sleep before the formal signing ceremony at noon the following day.

On stage, Serrano was wrapping up his speech. He threw in a comment about "bipartisan peace"—whatever that meant —which Don presumed was for the American audience watching during their Friday lunch hour.

Don shook his head. The President had earned this moment, and he was making the most of it. Don had heard Serrano's political advisers whispering gleefully about his rise in the polls. A few bold pundits claimed he'd saved his party's fortunes for the upcoming midterms, now only weeks away.

But the cost was high, Don thought. Too high.

He eased the rear doors of the auditorium open and walked down to the Piazza, a wide mezzanine which was set up for a post-speech reception. Don snagged a glass of champagne from a passing waiter and walked to one of the tall windows set between ivy-covered pillars. The Piazza looked out onto an open park filled with people celebrating the peace agreement between the United States, the NATO allies, and Russia. Mobile phone screens winked like stars in a sea of humanity.

Don had to hand it to his president: the man knew how to seize a political moment. Serrano and Sokolov both knew the other needed a political win, and the scope of the Helsinki Peace Accord spoke to those needs.

Russian forces had withdrawn immediately from Lithuania following the battle in the Suwalki Gap. Russia promised reparations in the form of reduced oil and natural gas prices to both Lithuania and NATO for damages done during the hostilities. Sokolov further promised that the Russian presence in Belarus would last only until that country was able to hold democratic elections.

But Sokolov was also a shrewd negotiator. Russia kept parts of eastern Ukraine and all of Crimea. To quiet the Ukrainian outcry against their territory being bargained away, the remainder of Ukraine was granted a path to both EU and NATO membership.

A traditional deal might have stopped there, but Serrano and his newfound Russian ally were looking to change the game. The two countries made an agreement in principle to cut their nuclear stockpiles and issued a challenge to the United Kingdom and France to do the same. Not to be outdone, the European Union proposed a free trade agreement with the new leadership of Russia.

To Don's surprise, he'd even overheard Serrano mention to President Sokolov that Russia might even be welcomed into NATO at some point in the future. The Russian President didn't say yes, but he didn't dismiss the idea either.

Everybody got something in the agreement, so no one wanted to rock the boat.

The expansive Helsinki Peace Accord was silent about the role of private military contractors, who had done so much of the fighting in the Ukraine conflict. It was a topic lost in the good news of peace and prosperity, but one never far from Don's mind. There were questions there that needed to be answered.

He studied his haggard reflection in the dark window and wondered if anyone would notice if he just sneaked back to his hotel right now.

He sipped his drink, savoring the bite on his tongue. Already, the calls for a congressional hearing into Sentinel's activities in Ukraine were fading, as was the investigation into the deaths of Abby Cromwell and Dylan Mattias. Don had been around Washington long enough to recognize the slow-walk of an issue no one wanted to touch.

"Excuse me, Mr. Riley?"

The voice was soft and pitched high enough that Don expected to find a woman when he turned around. He was surprised to see a huskily built, bald man with crystalline hazel eyes and alabaster skin.

"My name is Vladimir Federov," the man continued. "I am—"

"I know who you are," Don said. He looked around. Why was the head of the Russian FSB talking to him? He would have to report this contact.

Federov stepped closer, lowered his voice. "I wonder if I might have a word." He gestured farther down the row of windows.

They walked slowly away from the few other people in the room.

"I'm a great admirer of your work, Mr. Riley," Federov said

finally. "I especially appreciated how you handled the crisis surrounding the Pandora virus."

Don almost dropped his glass of champagne. "It was you."

Federov nodded.

"Why?" Don managed to say. "Why me?"

"I needed a man I could trust."

"We don't know each other, Mr. Federov."

"Vladimir, please."

"Okay, we don't know each other, Vladimir."

"You have a reputation, Donald," Federov said.

"A reputation for what?"

"For doing the right thing."

Don didn't know how to respond, so he sipped his champagne. "Thank you," he said finally.

Their conversation was interrupted by a commotion at the end of the Piazza. The doors of the main auditorium swung open. Presidents Serrano and Sokolov descended the steps together surrounded by a crowd of people. The din of excited voices and laughter echoed through the open space. The two presidents each took a glass of champagne and touched the rims in a toast.

"Why did you do it?" Don asked.

Federov looked away, and Don followed his eyes to where Serrano and Sokolov were now posing for pictures with their arms slung across each other's shoulders.

"Sometimes we believe our actions are our own," he said in a voice no higher than a whisper. "Later we realize that we are merely tools in the hands of a skilled manipulator."

Don considered that answer. Was he saying that the real mastermind behind the coup was Luchnik's nephew?

"What happened to Luchnik?" Don asked.

Federov's shoulders hitched. "Retirement."

Don raised an eyebrow. Did that mean he was dead? It was

a question that had been debated fiercely inside the CIA without resolution.

Federov gauged Don's reaction and shook his head. "Our new president is not a heartless bastard. The man is his uncle. The old man will live out his days in some comfort, but his fortune has been donated to our rebuilding effort."

"Your name was on the list," Don said to Federov. "You lost a fortune."

"Money is not my concern, Donald. What I did was necessary for the security of my country. Thanks to you, it worked." His lips bent in a humorless smile. "When President Luchnik lost his way, it was...unfortunate. I am hopeful President Sokolov will live up to his potential. We had the right players this time, Donald. Next time, we may not be so lucky."

"Next time?" Don said.

Federov held out his hand. "I fear I have overstayed my welcome, Donald."

The handshake was perfunctory, forgettable even. There was a shout from the other end of the hall and a roar from the crowd. Don turned to see Serrano and Sokolov posing for more pictures, champagne glasses in hand.

When he turned back, Vladimir Federov was gone.

Don set aside his champagne. He'd suddenly lost the taste for it.

56

Noonu Atoll, Maldives

Manson Skelly relaxed in a deck chair, watching the sun slip below the horizon of the Indian Ocean. The sky shifted from deep orange to blood red, then darkness slowly bruised the color out of the sky.

The melting ice shifted in the glass at his elbow, reminding him to take a sip. He had the perfect buzz going: relaxed muscles, heightened senses, an inner feeling that he was one with the world.

And why not? he thought. You are one of the richest bastards on the face of the earth, and you run a private army that equals most small countries. It's good to be the king...

He heard a creak of wood on the deck behind him, but Skelly did not turn around. The private island was 187 kilometers north of the Male International Airport, accessible only by seaplane. His security team had blanketed the airspace and the ground with the finest personal protection assets in the world.

Skelly smiled to himself. The only thing he had to worry about here was getting a sunburn.

"This is a long way to travel for a meeting." The voice was deep, with a thick Slavic accent. The man made no effort to move into Skelly's field of view.

Skelly sighed. Apparently, he was going to have to get up and greet his guest. He hoisted himself to his feet and turned.

Pavel Kozlov was an inch or so taller than Skelly. He was thick in the shoulders and pecs and had a cool scar along his jaw. The man was dressed in what Skelly could only describe as Russian beachwear. Board shorts, flip-flops, and a polo shirt that looked like it was cutting off circulation to his biceps.

Skelly stuck out his hand. The other man's grip was like a vise. Skelly squeezed back until they'd both had enough.

"Drink?" he said.

Kozlov shrugged.

"Get this." Skelly picked up a silver bell from the table next to his chair and shook it. A clear tone rang in the night. A few seconds later, there was a thrumming of footsteps on the wooden dock and a young man dressed in a linen uniform appeared.

"Yes, Mr. Skelly?" the waiter asked.

Skelly cocked an eyebrow at Kozlov. "Vodka? Or is that culturally insensitive?"

Kozlov chuckled. "Do you have Tsarskaya vodka?"

"Of course, sir."

"Bring the bottle, Jeeves," Skelly ordered, "and two glasses."

As the waiter rushed away, Kozlov asked, "Is his name really Jeeves?"

"No, it's Ramon, but I'm paying him enough that I could call him Shithead and he'd still smile."

"If you did that in Russia, he'd piss in your vodka," Kozlov said.

Skelly hadn't considered that possibility. He drained his glass. He had to keep this buzz going.

Ramon returned with the bottle and two small glasses.

"Tell the ladies we'll have dinner on the lanai in an hour," Skelly said. "Until then, no interruptions."

"Of course, Mr. Skelly."

Kozlov poured two glasses and handed one to Skelly.

"*Na zdorovie*," he said.

"Same," Skelly replied as he drank off the shot. The ice-cold alcohol landed in his belly and spread into a gentle warmth. Kozlov immediately refilled his glass.

The dock extended fifty feet into the Indian Ocean. Apart from the tastefully lighted villa behind them, they were a hundred kilometers from any light pollution. The density of the stars above them looked like glittering sand on black velvet.

They drank again.

"Why am I here?" Kozlov asked.

"You helped me in my time of need, Pavel. I like to repay my debts."

"I don't understand." A pause as he refilled their glasses. "Ah, you mean the jet."

"Yes," Skelly said. He could feel the influx of vodka dulling his edge, but he drank again anyway. "Shooting down the jet was very helpful to me."

Kozlov touched the rim of his glass to Skelly's. "It was a war zone. All targets are valid."

Now that, Skelly thought, is how rules of engagement should work all the time.

"It's the thought that counts," Skelly said, laughing at his own joke. "I'm a rich motherfucker now, and I'd like to share with my friends."

"You want to pay me?" Kozlov asked.

"I had something different in mind," Skelly replied. "I propose a partnership. A Sentinel-Wagner merger."

"The Chef would never go for that," Kozlov said.

"I know. That's why I think there should be a change in leadership for Wagner. They need to break out of their old corporate identity as an arm of the Russian security forces. They need new blood at the top. Wagner needs your strategic vision."

The speech seemed to strike a nerve with his guest. Kozlov sat up in his chair. "You think I have strategic vision?"

"Absolutely." Skelly poured the vodka this time. "I think Wagner is being held back by The Chef, but with you at the top, the sky's the limit."

Skelly was aware that his words were slightly slurring together, but the other man seemed not to notice.

Kozlov leaned forward. "How will you do this?"

Skelly held up his drink. "The plan is already in motion, my friend." He paused. "Or, should I say, partner?"

"To partners," Kozlov said, clinking his glass against Skelly's.

"To partners," Skelly repeated.

Both men leaned back in their deck chairs. A gentle breeze blew in from the water. The moon rose, turning the ocean into a pool of quicksilver.

When Kozlov spoke again, his voice was drowsy. "What will we do?" he asked.

"Whatever we want," Skelly said.

THREAT AXIS
Command and Control #4

In the midst of a global manhunt, the leader of the world's largest private army sees his opportunity to upset the international order.

Ian Thomas is supposed to be dead. An international terrorist responsible for the bombing of the US Naval War College, he's been deceased for three years. But Don Riley, head of the CIA's Emerging Threats Group, is staring at a social media post showing him to be very much alive and on the run in South America.

The video of Thomas sparks a global hunt. But the world's most powerful nations aren't the only ones pursuing the most wanted man on the planet. The manhunt attracts an uninvited player: Sentinel Holdings, the largest private military contractor in the world. Helmed by ruthless CEO Manson Skelly, Sentinel's lethal capabilities rival those of most countries.

Sensing an opportunity to secure his place as a player on the world stage, Skelly uses his superior tech and global assets to insert himself into the chase...with catastrophic results.

Now, Skelly has decided that the international order is up for grabs, and Don Riley will need help from all the wrong places to stop him—before it's too late.

Get your copy today at
severnriverbooks.com/series/command-and-control

JOIN THE READER LIST

ACKNOWLEDGMENTS

We'd like to thank armor officers Colonel Ryan Kranc, US Army, and E. M. "Ted" Dannemiller II, USMA '75, for helping a couple of Navy guys to understand what it's like to ride around inside seventy tons of metal traveling at thirty-plus miles per hour over rough terrain in the middle of a battle. Without their insights into armor combat tactics and their unique perspective on armor operations, the tank battle sequences in this novel would not exist. Any errors are ours alone.

ABOUT THE AUTHORS

David Bruns

David Bruns earned a Bachelor of Science in Honors English from the United States Naval Academy. (That's not a typo. He's probably the only English major you'll ever meet who took multiple semesters of calculus, physics, chemistry, electrical engineering, naval architecture, and weapons systems just so he could read some Shakespeare. It was totally worth it.) Following six years as a US Navy submarine officer, David spent twenty years in the high-tech private sector. A graduate of the prestigious Clarion West Writers Workshop, he is the author of over twenty novels and dozens of short stories. Today, he co-writes contemporary national security thrillers with retired naval intelligence officer, J.R. Olson.

J.R. Olson

J.R. Olson graduated from Annapolis in May of 1990 with a BS in History. He served as a naval intelligence officer, retiring in March of 2011 at the rank of commander. His assignments during his 21-year career included duty aboard aircraft carriers and large deck amphibious ships, participation in numerous operations around the world, to include Iraq, Somalia, Bosnia, and Afghanistan, and service in the U.S. Navy in strategic-level Human Intelligence (HUMINT) collection operations as a CIA-trained case officer. J.R. earned an

MA in National Security and Strategic Studies at the U.S. Naval War College in 2004, and in August of 2018 he completed a Master of Public Affairs degree at the Humphrey School at the University of Minnesota. Today, J.R. often serves as a visiting lecturer, teaching national security courses in Carleton College's Department of Political Science, and hosts his radio show, *National Security This Week*, on KYMN Radio in Northfield, Minnesota.

You can find David Bruns and J.R. Olson at severnriverbooks.com/series/command-and-control